Available in September 2009 from Mills & Boon® Intrigue

HER BEST FRIEND'S HUSBAND

Gabe put his arms around Cara and pulled her into a gentle hug.

"If the answer's here, we'll find it."

She had gone very still in his embrace, but when he spoke she relaxed, leaned against him, into him, taking the comfort he offered. The shared contact, the warmth, eased the old pain even more, and he wondered that he hadn't realised it would do that.

"Thank you," he said, lifting her chin up with a gentle finger. "For still caring so much after all this time."

He didn't even realise what he was doing until his lips brushed hers. It hadn't been a conscious decision. But she was there, so close, looking up at him with that unwavering steadiness.

And the next thing he knew, he'd done it. He'd kissed her.

He couldn't regret it. But the acknowledgement didn't tell him how to deal with the unwelcome fact that Cara Thorpe had somehow stirred his first real interest in a woman in longer than he cared to remember.

THE BEAST WITHIN

It was bad enough she'd haunted his dreams. Now she dared to taint the name of his only love.

As angry as he was, Jag managed to bite back his imminent explosion. He studied Karen, this woman who might be his enemy disguised as an innocent, exploring her features.

What he found was a look of concern and uncertainty so raw, so real, the power of his emotions shifted. Softened. This woman did things to him he had yet to understand.

In her eyes, he saw the same kind of honesty he sensed in the Knights' healer, Marisol. The same pureness.

But it was too late to retreat, to rethink his actions. The beast still roared inside. The beast he'd always controlled…until this woman. If she was so innocent, so honest, why did she bring it to the surface?

First published in Great Britain 2009
Harlequin Mills & Boon Limited,
Eton House, 18-24 Paradise Road, Richmond, Surrey TW9 1SR

Her Best Friend's Husband © Janice Davis Smith 2008
The Beast Within © Lisa Renee Jones 2007

ISBN: 978 0 263 87321 4

46-0909

Harlequin Mills & Boon policy is to use papers that are natural, renewable
and recyclable products and made from wood grown in sustainable
forests. The logging and manufacturing processes conform to the legal
environmental regulations of the country of origin.

Printed and bound in Spain
by Litografia Rosés S.A., Barcelona

HER BEST FRIEND'S HUSBAND

BY
JUSTINE DAVIS

THE BEAST WITHIN

BY
LISA RENEE JONES

HER BEST FRIEND'S HUSBAND

BY
JUSTINE DAVIS

Justine Davis lives on Puget Sound in Washington. Her interests outside of writing are sailing, doing needlework, horseback riding and driving her restored 1967 Corvette roadster – top down, of course.

Justine says that years ago, during her career in law enforcement, a young man she worked with encouraged her to try for a promotion to a position that was, at the time, occupied only by men. "I succeeded, became wrapped up in my new job, and that man moved away, never, I thought, to be heard from again. Ten years later he appeared out of the woods of Washington State, saying he'd never forgotten me and would I please marry him. With that history, how could I write anything but romance?"

Chapter 1

"It's time, Gabe."

Gabriel Taggert looked at his father-in-law and wanted to punch him out. Which was odd, because he admired, respected, and yes, loved the man. And he would never do it, since at his own six-foot-one he towered over the slighter man.

"He's right, dear," Gwen Waldron said quietly, agreeing with her husband. She usually did. Not that she wasn't more than capable of standing up for herself if she truly disagreed; it was just that the forty-years'-married couple rarely differed in opinion.

"Just like that?"

Gabe's voice came out low and harsh, which startled him. Shouldn't he be over it by now? They all—meaning every well-intentioned person who knew what had happened—told him it was a process that was individual, that everyone had to do it at their own pace and in their own way. But despite the platitude, he was fairly certain most of them would expect his world to have gone on by now.

"Do you think we like this any more than you do?"

For the first time the undertone of emotion broke through in Earl Waldron's voice. Somehow that made the tightness in Gabe's gut ease a little.

"But it's been eight years." Gwen put her hand on his arm then, a touch he treasured because of who she was and hated because of who she wasn't. "You know she'd have been in touch, no matter what happened, if she could."

He supposed the worst part of what he was feeling was the knowledge, somewhere buried deep, that they were right. He fought to keep it buried, but with both of them digging at it now, he wasn't sure he could. The simple fact was, his wife was gone, vanished so completely that not having found a body didn't make it any less likely she was dead.

"We're not asking for a decision here and now. Just promise you'll consider it," Earl said. "Really consider it, son. We need to move on. And so do you."

"All right." He owed them that much, and he couldn't help it if the words came out a little sharp.

He stood there on the deck of the hundred-and-forty-nine foot boat that was his world these days and watched them walk down the gangplank. They'd been a huge part of his life for so long—accepting him as the son they'd never had and still treating him that way, even though the link between them was gone—that he couldn't imagine going on without them.

But then, he'd gone on with an even bigger piece missing. Not well, or with any particular grace, but he had gone on.

"Everything all right?"

The soft inquiry came from behind him, and Gabe turned to look at his friend and boss, Joshua Redstone, who was also the designer and builder of this dream ship. Gabe had been in the depths of the darkest hole when Josh had offered him the job of heading up his boat-building enterprise. And when the desk-oriented job had begun to pall a couple of years ago, Josh had seemed to sense it. He'd given Gabe the chance to be at sea again, with the captaincy of this lovely vessel, the latest and biggest to bear the Redstone name.

It was to be, Josh had told him, the literal flagship of Redstone, not to be sold as others had been, but to be kept for the use of the Redstone family. From division managers to file clerks, anybody who worked for Redstone, Incorporated and had the need would have access to the boat.

And Gabe had been among the first to learn exactly what Josh meant; the first weeklong cruise he'd captained had been for the concierge of one of the Redstone Resorts, whose husband had died in a traffic accident. She was but one of thousands of employees, and at a relatively low level on the Redstone chain, but Josh, as he always did, had heard about the death and had offered the boat to the entire family.

"Gabe?"

He snapped out of the memory as Josh gently prodded. "I...I'm not sure."

"Were they your in-laws?" Josh's drawl was barely discernable, telling Gabe how carefully he was picking his words. "Hope's parents?"

"Yes."

"Tough," Josh said.

Gabe turned to look at his boss then. "Yes," he agreed.

"They made a special trip out here to see you?"

Gabe nodded. And then, because no one knew better exactly how he felt, he let it out.

"They want my wife declared dead."

Josh was silent for a long moment. If it had been anyone else, Gabe might have assumed he had nothing to say, but the head of Redstone, Inc., was never one to speak lightly or without thought. That characteristic delay—and the drawl—gave some, to their detriment, the idea he was slow or lazy. They inevitably spent time afterward musing on the cost of their assumptions.

"They want their daughter declared dead?" Josh finally said, quietly.

And there, with the insight typical of him, Josh reminded him gently that their loss was as great as his. Greater, perhaps; they'd had Hope Waldron for twenty-nine years, he for only six of those.

"I know, I know." Gabe shoved a hand through his dark hair, realizing only after he'd done it that he'd still, after all this time, raised both hands as if he were wearing his officer's combination cap, to be removed before the gesture and resettled after precisely an inch and a half above his eyebrows, according to navy regs.

"Old habits die hard," Josh observed mildly, and Gabe knew he'd caught the lapse. "Old thoughts sometimes die harder."

"How long did it take you?"

The question escaped him before he could block it. Not for anything, even to ease his own pain, would he intentionally call up bad memories for this man he admired, respected, even loved, as did most who worked for him. Josh Redstone had built an empire that spanned the globe, employed thousands, and Gabe would be willing to bet there wasn't one of them who wouldn't walk into hell for the man. In part because they knew he'd do it for them—and had.

"I'm sorry," Gabe began, but Josh waved him to silence.

"How long did it take me to accept that she was gone?" Josh asked. "In my head, I knew it right away. But then, she died in my arms. I felt her go."

Gabe's breath caught. He hadn't known that. He'd known Elizabeth Redstone had died of cancer several years ago, known that Josh had been alone ever since, knew the common wisdom at Redstone was that she'd been his soul mate and he would never even try to replace her. But Gabe had never really thought about the details of it. Hope, he thought, would likely have had the whole story within minutes of meeting the man; she had always been good at getting people to open up.

An odd smile curved Josh's mouth, lifting it at one corner in an expression of ironic sadness. "I never thought of that as a particular advantage before, other than being with her until the end. But from your view, it is, isn't it? At least I knew, without doubt."

Gabe couldn't deny that, and instead fastened on Josh's answer to his question. He repeated his boss's words back. "You said you knew it in your head."

Josh's mouth quirked, and the steady gray eyes closed for a moment. Then he opened them and looked at Gabe. "You always were detail oriented."

"Comes from years of dealing with politically oriented navy brass," Gabe answered. "Most of the time what they didn't say was more important than what they did."

"I'm sure," Josh agreed. And then, after a moment, answered what Gabe hadn't really asked. "I'm not sure my heart, my gut, have accepted it yet. I know, logically, that it's crazy after all these years, but I still catch myself expecting to hear her voice, or thinking that she's just in the next room…."

Gabe smothered a sigh. That was not what he'd wanted to hear. He'd wanted to hear that it was over, sealed away in some silent, impenetrable place in Josh's mind, never bothering him, never surfacing unless he wanted it to. If Joshua Redstone, one of the strongest—and strongest-minded—men he'd ever met, couldn't get past this, what hope did he have?

"What brought this on now, after all this time?" Josh asked.

"The U.S. Postal Service," Gabe said wryly.

Josh blinked. "The Postal Service?"

"They just delivered a postcard to Hope's best friend. From Hope, mailed right before she disappeared. It really upset them."

Josh let out a low whistle. "Ouch. Eight years?"

To his own surprise, Gabe had to stifle a chuckle. Josh, he knew, would never tolerate that kind of thing. Redstone wasn't consistently in the top five highest-rated places to work because it was easy. It was Josh himself, and his reputation, that made a Redstone job among the most coveted. He hired the best, let them do what they did best, paid them well, treated them all with fairness, and mostly stayed out of their way. But above all he let them know that if they needed it, the full power of the Redstone empire was behind them.

"Why don't you head for open water?" Josh said.

Gabe drew back slightly. "What?"

Josh shrugged. "Take her out. Clear your head."

Only Josh Redstone would make an offer like that, to take a hundred-and-forty-nine-foot luxury yacht, complete with a media room and helipad, out for a spin as if it were a new car rather than the latest, and as yet unnamed, design from his fertile and incredible mind.

"Thank you," Gabe said automatically, "but—"

"You saying you don't do your best thinking at sea?"

Gabe's mouth quirked. "You can take the boy out of the navy, but you can't take the navy out of the boy?"

Josh grinned. "Something like that."

Neither of them mentioned that in Gabe's case, he hadn't been taken out of the navy, he'd quit. Gabe knew he'd had no choice, and Josh, when he'd learned the full story of what had driven a man who'd once chosen the navy as his career to leave, had answered in the best possible way: he'd offered Gabe a way out that didn't require him to leave his love of ships and the water behind.

"I've got to head back to my office," Josh said, and Gabe knew the reluctance he heard in his boss's voice was real. Josh was not an office-bound executive, even at Redstone Headquarters, which was as much a paragon of comfort and thoughtful design as this boat was.

"Take her out," he said again. "Put all this on the back burner, focus on something else for a while. It'll help you work through it, where chewing on it up front won't."

Gabe smiled at the rustic simile, thinking again of those who made the mistake of assuming the drawl and the down-home manner were all there was to Josh. It amazed him how anyone could look at the size and scope of Redstone and think that anyone less than a genius could have built it, but people were often ruled by their own filters and perceptions, a fact Josh frequently used to his advantage. And since his naval career had come to a crashing end because of such people, Gabe couldn't help but appreciate Josh's talent in that area.

"And," Josh added as he went down the gangway steps, "if you need anything, if Redstone can help, call."

Gabe nodded, knowing that what would have been a casual offer, never really intended for acceptance from most people, was something quite different coming from Josh Redstone. When he offered help to one of his huge family—which meant anyone who worked for and with him—he meant it.

In the seven years he'd worked for Josh, overseeing the smallest but one of the most loved—by Josh, anyway—divisions of the empire, so small it didn't even have its own name but rather existed as a sideline of the aviation division, he'd both seen and heard of the kinds of things Redstone had done for its people. The cruise he'd captained for the bereaved family had only been the latest in a very long string of things done that Josh took for granted; if you were Redstone, Redstone helped when you needed it.

Later that morning, when Gabe stood out on deck, having let the eager young first mate take the wheel for a while—although the boat had the newer, joystick type of controls, Josh was enough of a traditionalist to have also included the wheel—he had to admit his boss was right. Being out here, on blue water with the smell of the salt air and the sounds of the sleek red-and-gray vessel cutting powerfully through the water, soothed his mind and soul in a way nothing else could.

By the time they were back at the dock and he was overseeing the cleanup and making his log entry, he was resigned. He would do as the Waldrons had asked; he wouldn't fight them. Gwen's pain had been too real, too palpable, and he couldn't stand in the way of anything that might ease it, no matter how ambivalent he might be about it.

Besides, he thought, it might be a relief to him as well, when people asked, to be able to say with some truth that she was dead. It was so much more finite than "She vanished," less painful than

"She walked out on me without a word," and certainly less un-comfortable than "I have no idea where my wife is."

Of course, even if Hope were declared legally dead, it wouldn't resolve anything for him. He knew too well that it would always be there, hovering, that her "death" would be of legal status only, that he would be forever no closer to knowing what had really happened. No closer to knowing if she'd had an accident, or if the worse-case scenario that haunted him was true, that she'd been murdered and dumped somewhere.

But after eight years, he'd gotten better at living with that. He'd learned—

"Captain?"

He looked up from the ship's log entry at Mark Spencer, the young first mate he'd given the wheel to earlier.

"I thought you'd gone for lunch."

"I was, but…there's someone here to see you, sir," Mark said, seeming oddly nervous.

"The Waldrons?" he asked, hoping they would understand why he'd disappeared out to sea after they'd left.

"No. A…woman."

The way he said it, as if he'd had to choose among many de-scriptions, alerted Gabe. Whoever it was, she'd made an impres-sion. Hiding the first real smile he'd felt coming on since his in-laws had arrived this morning, he stood up.

"She asked for you personally, by name," Mark added, unable to mask the curiosity in his eyes. Gabe read the speculation there, knew what the younger man was wondering; had their reclusive, loner captain been holding out on them?

Not likely, he muttered inwardly, and the smile that threatened this time was wryly self-knowing.

"She give you a name, Mark?"

"Cara. She said you'd know."

Any urge at all to smile vanished. It seemed his painful day wasn't over yet.

"Where did you put her?"

"The main salon."

"Go see if she needs anything, a drink, food," he ordered, wanting a moment alone to deal with this next surprise.

"Already done, sir." Mark's formal tone told him his voice had been a bit sharp.

"Good job," he said, careful to keep his own tone even this time.

"I'm Redstone," Mark said simply.

That got him the smile, and it was genuine. "Thanks, Mark. Please tell her I'll be there in a moment."

"Yes, sir."

The young man executed a turn snappy enough to earn him approval from any Naval officer, and left the bridge.

Cara.

Gabe sank back into the raised captain's chair for a moment. She'd have that postcard with her, he thought. She'd expect him to look at it, read it. And for a moment he wondered if he could do this, if he could rip open those old wounds once more. If he could survive it if he did.

And then he realized it didn't matter. The wounds had never healed; the constant dig of uncertainty had kept them open and bleeding beneath the surface. There might be scars over them, but it wouldn't take much to tear those scars away.

A postcard would do it.

Chapter 2

Cara Thorpe, Gabe thought as he quickly finished his short log entry on the day's cruise.

She'd not only been Hope's best friend since elementary school, they'd been like sisters, and all the time he and Hope had been together, she'd been on the periphery, somewhere. She'd been so quiet she seemed to fade into the background, so much so that Gabe hadn't minded much when Hope had insisted she go with them to some party, or attend a function with other people. He'd even tried to set her up with one of his buddies now and then, someone he thought might see past the quiet exterior, but something always seemed to get in the way of it actually happening.

Cara had always been bright, beneath the shyness, and she'd gone away to get her master's degree shortly before he and Hope had married. She'd been home for the wedding, but Gabe hadn't seen her again until after Hope had vanished. Gwen had called her then, of course, to see if she had any idea where Hope was, or if she'd heard from her. She had, in fact, had a phone message from Hope that last morning, but it wasn't much help, only an excited promise to call her back with big news, the biggest.

The call had never come.

Cara had immediately come home to help in the search. Gabe only vaguely remembered the quiet, withdrawn young woman's departure several weeks later; he'd been too sunk in his own misery to worry overmuch about hers.

As he rose once more and headed for the large main salon of the boat, he shouldn't have been surprised that she'd show up now, not after being the one to receive that much-belated postcard.

Cara had likely never given up on the possibility of finding Hope alive and well. Hope had always said Cara was the most staunchly loyal person she'd ever known. That she'd often said it while pointing out how in her view that accolade didn't apply to him was something he tried not to dwell on. Hope's interpretation of loyalty hadn't quite meshed with his, and certainly not with the navy's. Which was one of the reasons, although not the main one, that he was no longer in the uniform he'd once expected to wear for life.

He slid open the large, glass door to the salon. It moved with the well-balanced, smooth silence expected on any Redstone vessel, and the woman seated with her back to him on the deeply cushioned couch upholstered in a rich, slate-gray fabric that looked like suede, didn't turn. For a moment he stood there, staring at the back of her head as sunlight streamed in through the glass.

Had her hair always been that rich, autumn-leaves color? He remembered it as just sort of brown. Long and straight, and plain. Maybe it was the sunlight, although he'd certainly seen her in the sun before. If she'd done something more than just cut it so that it fell in soft waves just to her shoulders, it was subtle, yet made a world of difference.

And then, as if she'd sensed his presence, she stood up, turned.

And stunned him.

The quiet little mouse was gone. This was the woman who'd left Mark speechless. This was a tall, perfectly curved, vibrant, auburn-haired woman dressed in a cool, pale green that reminded him of mint ice cream. It was luscious on a hot, Southern California day.

This was a woman who looked back at him confidently with bright blue eyes that had so often avoided his before. A woman who walked toward him with an easy grace quite unlike the awkwardly tall, quiet mouse, who had always seemed to be hesitant or hasty, depending on the circumstances.

"Gabe," she said softly as she came to a halt before him.

Had her voice always been so low and husky? Did he even know, could he even remember? She had always been so quiet, at least around him; Hope had said she talked all the time when they were alone, so he'd assumed it was just him she wasn't comfortable around. He'd even asked her once, on one of those days so long ago, why she didn't like him. She'd blushed furiously, said she liked him fine.

"Cara," he said finally. "You've…changed."

"Well, I should hope so," she said with amusement. "In eight years. You, on the other hand, naval officer or not, are still tall, dark and ramrod-straight Gabriel Taggert, aren't you?"

He didn't smile; Hope had teased him far too much about the military carriage that had been drilled into him early on for him to take the echoed comment lightly. More than once he'd been driven beyond irritation by her insistence that he learn how to "unbend," as if the way he stood or carried himself meant he was rigid and inflexible in mind as well.

"I'm sorry," she said after a moment of silence. "I didn't mean that in a bad way."

He shrugged one shoulder. "You're just repeating what she always said."

"I know." Something came into her voice then, a sort of regret. "I shouldn't have said it. It took me a long time to realize she was really digging at you."

His mouth quirked then. "Me, too."

"I thought she was proud." Those blue eyes, that he somehow hadn't remembered as quite so vivid, lowered then, in a momentary reversion to the mouse of old. "I would have been," she added softly.

The simple admission startled him, and to his surprise, moved him. "Thank you," he said, not sure what else to say. This woman had been part of a life he'd lost long ago, yet she looked and seemed so different now that he wasn't sure what to think of her at all.

She moved then, reaching for the small shoulder bag that matched the light green of her silky shirt. A gold chain glinted at the neckline, vanishing behind the first button. He wondered idly where it ended up, and sucked in a shocked breath as an image shot through his mind of some personal locket or charm resting gently atop breasts that were all woman.

He quashed the image instantly, feeling a bit as if he'd had a lustful thought about the proverbial girl next door. But he couldn't deny the fact Cara Thorpe had filled out some. Nicely.

She removed something from a side pocket of the purse and held it out to him, thankfully unaware of the misfire of his imagination.

"Obviously, this is why I'm here."

It was the postcard, he realized. And caught himself looking at it much as if it were a venomous snake he'd stumbled onto.

He couldn't face it, not yet. So he looked at her hands instead. Long, slim fingers, neat, not-too-long nails finished with a subtle shine that spoke of care but not vanity. No ring, he noted, glancing at her left hand. Nor any sign of one that had been worn for any length of time.

She was exactly one month younger than Hope, he remembered; the two women had celebrated together at the halfway point between their birthdays every year. So she was thirty-seven now. He found it hard to believe, if she'd left mousehood behind very long ago, that she hadn't been snapped up by some man. He couldn't be the only one who'd noticed the curves. And the eyes. And the new, confident air.

"Maybe I shouldn't have come here, but I thought you'd want to…see it."

He realized at her quiet words that he'd left her standing there with that damned thing in her hand for too long. He shifted his gaze to the card. The sight of Hope's familiar scrawl, as unruly as she had sometimes been, sent a jab of the old ache through him.

With the sense that he was breaching a dam holding back a host of pain, a dam it had taken him years to build, he reached out and took it.

She'd managed it, Cara thought. He'd taken the card from her, and she'd managed to keep from touching him in the process. That was success, progress even, wasn't it?

And for the moment, he was staring at the postcard in his hand, focused on it with that quiet intensity she'd never forgotten. She could look at him now, couldn't she? He'd never realize, or if he did, he'd think she was just watching for his reaction.

As, indeed, she would be.

Among other things.

Because now that she was face-to-face with him again, even after all this time, there was no denying that watching Gabriel Taggert do anything was and had always been one of her favorite activities.

She wanted to laugh at herself, as she had for so many years. She'd put girlish memories away, shaking her head in wry amusement whenever she thought of him and her own silly fantasies. But what she'd been able to do before, when she'd thought she'd never see him again, seemed impossible now that he was standing in front of her, all the six-plus feet, lean muscles, near-black hair and light-hazel eyes of him.

But she had laughed, back then. What else could you do when you realized you were a walking, breathing cliché? The only thing she hadn't been sure of was which cliché was the worst, falling for a man in uniform…or falling for her best friend's husband.

Not that she'd ever done anything about it. It wasn't in her. For the most part she played by the rules, and always had. She'd gotten more adventurous as she'd gotten older—oddly, her daring streak had begun about the time Hope disappeared—but the basic code never faltered: there were just some things you didn't do.

She'd known instinctively that it wasn't in Gabe, either, to betray his wife or his vows. Not that he ever would have for her, anyway, even if he had been that kind of man. Not for the quiet, withdrawn little girl she'd been; no man would have cheated with the likes of her.

But even if she'd been some gorgeous, chic, supermodel type, Gabe just wasn't that kind of man. Which, she knew, had been a big part of the attraction for her in the first place.

The problem now was, all the things she'd consoled herself with for the last eight years had been blown to bits.

It was a stupid kid thing, she'd told herself repeatedly. *You just wanted what you didn't have. It wasn't Gabe, not really. You just wanted what Hope had, not the exact person Hope had.*

She'd told herself that again and again, until she'd almost sold herself on the idea.

Until now.

Uh-oh, she muttered inwardly. She hadn't seen Gabe Taggert in years, and yet within five minutes the old feelings were as strong as ever.

At least he doesn't know, she told herself. She was spared that humiliation. She'd done that, at least, kept her silly feelings hidden from the man she could never have.

And you'll keep it that way, she ordered herself sternly. *Hope is still here, between us, and she always will be.*

She made herself focus on the present, watching as Gabe's face, tanned and attractively weathered from years on the water, changed as he looked at the postcard. The shock she had expected; it mirrored her own reaction. The envelope it had come in hadn't given a clue to the jolt that awaited, and the letter of apology from the U.S. Postal Service had been wryly amusing. But then she'd turned over the colorful mountain scene, wondering who had taken some long-ago vacation she was only now learning about, to see the handwriting that had once been nearly as familiar as her own. The energetic and wild scrawl had made her heart leap before she even realized why, before she saw the postmark and her mind jumped in with the explanation.

"That looks like Hope's writing," she'd said aloud at the time.

And then, seeing the signature crammed tightly in on the side edge of the card full of bursts of words that read like Hope's chatter, realizing it *was* Hope's handwriting, had made the bottom drop out of her world.

Thanks to Hope's parents Gabe had known this was coming, had known what she was handing him, but his shock seemed no less great; she understood that seeing it was different than simply knowing it existed. It was the difference between knowing something in your head and in your heart.

"Two miracles in one week," he muttered, and Cara knew exactly what he was reading, the last lines of scribbling that wrapped around the rest in typical Hope fashion; planning her writing space ahead had never been her style. The excess of exclamation points had.

Two miracles in one week, Cara!! I can't wait to tell you! I will as soon as I can, I promise. I would now, if Gabe were only here instead of out on that damned boat.

She remembered those words as clearly as if she were reading them again now.

He lifted his gaze to her face then. Those gold-flecked hazel eyes focused on her and she fought down the instinctive leap of her pulse.

"Do you have any idea what she was talking about?"

Cara shook her head. "All I know is how excited she sounded in that phone message, the day before she…disappeared."

He looked at the card again. Read the words again, and then again. Cara tried to imagine what it must feel like for him, to see this message from the woman he'd loved, to hold something she'd touched, after all this time.

"I'm sorry about the jab," she said. "About you being gone, I mean."

Gabe looked up at her, gave a one-shouldered shrug. "It doesn't matter. I know how she felt. I got used to it."

"I never understood that," Cara said softly. "She knew what your career was, and yet…."

Gabe's mouth quirked. "She wouldn't be the first woman to fall for a uniform, and then find the reality of military life too much to handle."

"But she loved you, not the uniform," Cara exclaimed.

"Maybe," Gabe said.

There hadn't been a trace of self-pity or bitterness in his voice, only the lingering uncertainty of a man who had pondered the question for a very long time.

Cara couldn't imagine what that was like, either, to have to wonder if the person you loved really loved you back, or just an idea you represented. She wanted to hug him, but knew quite well he wouldn't welcome the gesture.

And knew even better that it would be the worst thing she could possibly do for her own equilibrium. Just standing here with him was taking a toll on her stability.

He looked back at the postcard once more. Turned it over, stared at the picture for a moment, then flipped back to the side with the address and message.

And then his expression changed again. Cara saw his eyes narrow. He moved the card slightly. And muttered something under his breath.

He'd seen it.

This time his gaze shot to her face. "The postmark," he said.

"I know," she answered. "That's the main reason I wanted you to see it."

"The date."

"Yes."

She let out a breath she hadn't realized she'd been holding. His reaction, that sudden, tense alertness, told her that her own response hadn't been out of line.

Hope had mailed this postcard from a small mountain village

that, as far as she knew, Hope had never been to or even mentioned.

And she'd mailed it on the day she disappeared.

Chapter 3

"So you don't think I'm crazy?"

Gabe looked at the woman seated across from him. She looked like she belonged here, he thought. The little mouse was definitely gone, and this woman exuded a quiet sort of class that befitted the subtle elegance and style of the Redstone flagship.

He gave himself a mental shake; he knew he was rattled when he spent so much time dwelling on the presence of a woman he'd known for years instead of the stunning bit of the past he held in his hand.

"Crazy?" he asked.

"For thinking this—" she gestured at the postcard "—means something. More than just the post office needs a little work."

He smiled at the quip, grateful to her for lightening the mood a bit. But the truth of what she said was undeniable, as was the weight of it. They now knew what they'd never been able to determine before, where Hope had gone that day. Or at least, the direction she'd gone.

"We never even got close to looking here," he said, tapping the card against his palm.

"There was no reason to," Cara said reasonably. "Hope wasn't a mountain wilderness, back-to-nature kind of person. She never even mentioned this place, at least not to me."

"Or me," Gabe said.

"I…" She stopped, and he shifted his gaze to her face. For the first time he saw a trace of the old, hesitant girl he'd remembered.

"What?"

"I wasn't sure you'd even want to know, after all this time."

"Want to know? Whether my wife was abducted, killed or just plain walked out on me?"

The words burst from him so fervently it startled him. It had always been there for the last eight years, this gnawing question, but he thought he'd managed to successfully blunt the edges of it by keeping it buried deep.

Apparently not, he thought wryly.

"Why on earth would she have walked out on you?"

"For someone else?" he suggested.

"Oh, please."

Cara seemed sincerely astonished at the idea, which mollified his fervor and soothed the tangled emotions he didn't like admitting to.

"You don't think so?" He hadn't really been convinced himself, if for no other reason than Hope had never contacted her parents. Even knowing they wouldn't have approved of an affair, he couldn't picture her leaving them worrying endlessly.

"Hardly. She was foolish sometimes, but not a fool."

That surprised him; he'd thought Cara considered Hope the feminine ideal, in the way somewhat plain girls sometimes idolized their more glamorous sisters. Not that Cara was plain, at least, certainly not anymore.

"We'd had our…moments," he said, somewhat hastily.

"I know that. But I also know she was happy, in those last days. Very."

"When I told her I was leaving the navy, she…seemed that way. She called it…a miracle," he said, only now realizing she'd used the word on that postcard as well. But what was the second miracle she'd written about?

Cara gave him a look then that he couldn't quite interpret. It seemed almost sad, although about what he couldn't guess.

"She *was* happy," she said. "I know that card seems like her same old griping about you being gone, but she really had lightened up about it, after you said you were leaving. I couldn't believe it."

His brow furrowed as he looked at her. "You couldn't believe what?"

"I was…shocked. I never thought you'd really do it. I thought you loved the navy."

Those quiet words jabbed at him. He looked down at the card, not to read it again—he already had the words committed to memory—but in order not to look at Cara and see the look he now recognized as pity, or something close enough to it that it rankled.

"I never thought you'd give in to her…whining."

Whining? An odd word for her to use to describe her best friend's discontent, he thought, and his gaze flicked back to her face.

"Is that what you think? That I quit because my wife nagged me into it?"

"It seemed that way." She had the grace to look uncomfortable. "On the surface," she added, in a conciliatory tone.

"Thanks for that much," he muttered.

"You're still in uniform, of a sort," she said.

He glanced down at the red polo shirt he wore, with the Redstone logo—a graphic of the *Hawk I*, the small jet that had begun an empire—on the left chest. Paired with crisp khakis, just as the rest of the crew wore, it was a uniform without looking like one.

"Josh doesn't go in much for formality."

"I've read about him," she said. "He seems almost too good to be true."

Grateful for the change of subject, Gabe nodded. "Anybody

else, I'd probably agree with you. Not Josh. He started with nothing and built Redstone the hard way, one brick at a time, with his own hands. One person at a time, with his own judgment."

She studied him for a moment. "You're happy here," she finally said.

"Yes," he agreed. "I've got a great boat under me, and better, I answer to a man I respect completely."

It was as close as he'd come to the real reason he'd left the navy, and he wasn't about to come any closer with this woman he hadn't seen in years.

He turned his attention back to the postcard. "It was mailed at eleven-twenty, according to the postage label meter. About the time it would take to get up there if she left where we lived then in San Diego at nine."

"And Hope rarely got herself moving to go anywhere before nine," Cara agreed.

This third dig was too much for Gabe to ignore. "I always had the idea Hope could do no wrong in your book."

Cara shrugged. "Time was," she said. "But a funny thing happened. I grew up."

Gabe's breath caught as she put her finger on the very thing that had always bothered him; Hope hadn't seemed inclined to do that at all. She'd wanted the carefree life she'd always had, and hadn't been happy with one reality had presented her. But she'd been so alive and vibrant that everyone had accepted it as just part of her unique charm.

"Don't get me wrong," Cara hastened to add, "I love her. She was the sister I never had, and I'll always feel that way about her."

Gabe noticed the confusion of present and past tense, but didn't comment; he'd felt that way too often himself to make an issue of it. And more than once, in the dark of night, he had faced his innermost thoughts, admitted to the silence that it would be easier to know she'd left him. That she'd met someone who could give her the full-time attention she wanted. At least then he could be angry, or hurt, or stir up some righteous indignation. Something. Anything.

Hell, it would even be easier to know she was dead than to live forever in this limbo.

"What about you, Gabe?"

The question startled him out of the grim reverie. "What?"

"I was surprised when I talked to Hope's parents. I'd assumed you'd have taken the legal steps by now. To have her declared dead, I mean. It's been long enough, hasn't it?"

"Death in absentia?" Gabe said, his mouth twisting into a humorless smile. "A very inconclusive ending."

"But necessary, for you to go on with your life."

"I'm here and alive, aren't I?"

There was pure curiosity in her look then. "But…haven't you ever wanted…I mean, hasn't there been someone, in all this time, that made you want to—"

"No."

There had been, in fact, women in his life. Briefly. But when the subject of his status arose, that usually brought things to a quick end. He wondered how many of those women suspected he'd had something to do with his wife's disappearance and had run for their lives. He couldn't blame them, not really; too often it was the truth, and none of them had gotten to know him well enough to trust in his innocence. The fact that he'd been half a world away aboard an amphibious assault ship had been a pretty unassailable personal alibi, but there were conspiracy theorists everywhere, too many of them writing the news, it seemed.

And in the end, he hadn't cared enough to pursue it. That part of him seemed numb, and he wasn't sure he didn't like it that way.

"Do you think it would be worth looking into?"

Again her question snapped him out of the unpleasant thoughts. He wasn't usually one to get lost in his head like this, and it bothered him that he was now. It had to be Cara, he thought. Just her presence, so familiar and yet so changed, that had his mind spinning into all these old, dark places.

"Do you even want to?" Cara asked after a moment when he didn't speak.

Her tone was even, non-judgmental, and he had the feeling that if he said no, she'd accept it. And if she thought less of him for it, she would never let it show. Not just because she'd always kept her thoughts to herself, although she had, but because he sensed the classy demeanor was real, not just a facade.

"Is it worth it?" He echoed her words, running them through his head.

"I don't know. My first thought was to call the police. But I couldn't drag it all up again, if it's going to come to nothing. Hope's parents…"

Her voice trailed off. He knew exactly what she meant, and slowly shook his head. The memory of the pain in those much-loved, worn faces made his chest tighten.

"They've been through enough," he said.

She nodded. "Calling them, telling them, was so hard. They took it so hard…I didn't know what to do. So instead of calling the police, I came to you."

Something in her voice made his chest tighten even more. "Why?"

It was out before he thought, and he wondered why he'd asked, when in fact it didn't really matter why she'd come here. She had, and it was in his lap now.

"Because no one has a bigger stake in this than you," she said simply.

"Yours is pretty big," he pointed out. "She was your best friend for most of your life."

"Yes," she agreed. "But she was your wife. It doesn't get any bigger than that."

Oddly, it was her assessment of the marriage relationship that he focused on, rather than the old ache of speaking of Hope in the past tense. Interesting, he thought. And wondered again if she'd married somewhere along the line. And then, suddenly, he was asking her.

"Did you marry someone, Cara?"

She looked startled at the sudden shift. But she answered, with the direct honesty he'd always remembered, the honesty he was glad hadn't been glossed over by the more sophisticated appearance.

"No. I was engaged. He was killed."

In seven short words she made him regret he'd ever asked, wish he'd smothered his curiosity.

"I'm sorry."

"Me, too. He was a nice guy."

He wondered if he should ask what had happened, now that he'd lifted the lid on that box of troubles.

"It's all right," she said, her voice still even. "It was six years ago. It's not…raw, anymore."

Six years. Fairly soon after Hope had vanished. Connection? he wondered. Had she gone looking for comfort and found it in some…nice guy's arms?

None of your business, he told himself. And gestured abruptly with the card.

"I'm not sure this is enough to go to the police with, not after all this time."

"I wasn't sure, either," she said. "But it seemed as if I should do…something."

He looked again at the postmark, at the date and time that would be a marker in his life for as long as he lived. Could he really pass up the chance to get answers? Perhaps too much time had passed, perhaps nothing would come of it, but could he really just walk away, hand this card to Cara and pretend he'd never seen it, that this message from the past had never arrived at all?

He knew he couldn't. His gaze flicked back to Cara's face, and he suddenly knew she couldn't, either. If he said no, she would accept it, but she wouldn't walk away from it herself. She wouldn't forget, wouldn't even try. He wasn't sure how or why he was so certain of it, but he was. Maybe he'd known the little mouse better than he'd realized; tenacity had always been one of her qualities, he thought now.

"I just don't know what I could do," she said. "The police, they have resources, ways of checking on things, that I don't have."

He wondered for the first time what she was doing these days. He vaguely remembered she'd been a business and marketing major in college, and wondered what that had translated into in a real-life career.

And then her words stirred up something in his head.

They have resources, ways of checking on things, Cara had said of the police.

...if you need anything, if Redstone can help, call.

Josh's words echoed, and Gabe suddenly realized that while he wasn't the police, he certainly had some sizable and impressive resources at his disposal. Maybe even Redstone Security, the much-vaunted and incredibly effective private security force that had grown along with Redstone to handle problems around the world. He'd heard stories he wouldn't have believed were he outside Redstone, of things they'd done, operations they'd pulled off, all without stepping on the toes of law enforcement. In fact, he'd heard they were the envy of cops wherever they went, for both their freedom and those resources.

And wouldn't it just figure, he thought, if the job he'd taken in near desperation while floundering in the aftermath of his wife's disappearance, turned out to be the instrument of his finally discovering what had happened to Hope?

"Let me make a call," he told Cara.

He took his cell phone out of his back pocket.

He was about to find out if all the stories were true.

Chapter 4

"**E**xpected you."

Gabe blinked. "You did?" he said into the phone.

"Josh said."

St. John's terseness was legendary at Redstone, and anyone who'd dealt with Josh's right-hand man had had to learn to translate. But he was so incredible at what he did, so efficient, and had sources Gabe figured even Josh didn't know—or want to know—about, that no one was about to quibble that they had to pay extra close attention to follow his extraordinary verbal leaps.

"Already?" Josh had only left here this morning.

St. John didn't answer. Gabe supposed his comment didn't require one; he should have known Josh wouldn't dally if he thought one of his own might need help.

"A list?" St. John asked.

Gabe shook his head, thinking dealing with St. John as liaison was going to be interesting. Technically, his title was vice-president of operations, but anyone who'd been around very long knew there were few aspects of Redstone St. John didn't know more about than seemed humanly possible.

"Not yet, not really. All I need right now is some info on Pine Lake, California. It's a little town up in the San Bernardino mountains. Near Lake Arrowhead."

"Target?"

This seemed oddly familiar, Gabe thought as he answered. "I'm trying to backtrack someone from a postcard that was mailed eight years ago."

If St. John thought he was crazy, he kept it to himself, as it was rumored he did most things.

"Going yourself?" was all he said.

"Yes. Shortly."

"This your cell?"

"Yes."

Gabe stifled a lopsided smile as he stopped himself from giving the number St. John no doubt already had from caller ID. The other part of his reputation was that he had little patience for people who belabored the obvious.

"Before you get there."

"Uh...thanks," Gabe said, his hesitation marking the time it took him to realize St. John had hung up without another word.

"Who was that?" Cara asked.

"St. John. Josh Redstone's right arm."

She lifted a brow. "You look...taken aback."

"I am," he admitted. "He's a little like listening to a machine gun."

And suddenly he had it, the source of that familiarity. It had been like the old days in the navy, on war games or training exercises; the more tense or dangerous things got, the fewer words were spoken. Commands, reports, decisions, they all got shorter, sharper and tenser.

"He talks," Gabe mused aloud, "like he's at war."

"Perhaps he is," Cara said.

Gabe focused on her then. "What?"

She lifted one shoulder in a half-shrug that echoed his own earlier one. "There's more than one kind of war, isn't there?"

Gabe thought of his own personal war, with the memories of Hope and the questions she'd left in her wake. "Yes," he said, acknowledging her insight with a nod. "Yes, there is."

"So, we're going to Pine Lake?"

He blinked. "We?" He'd thought he'd just head up there, ask some questions, poke around a little. He hadn't intended on having company.

"You did say I have a big stake in this. And the card came to me."

He couldn't argue with that, so didn't try. "All right," he said. "Let me go change clothes."

As he went to the spacious cabin allotted to the captain of this latest Redstone boat, a space that managed to be luxurious and utilitarian at the same time, he didn't wonder if he was going to regret this. He already knew he would.

He just wondered how much.

"Sorry for the delay. I had to leave some orders with the first mate."

Cara, who had been standing before a glass case, studying the intricately detailed, one-eighth scale model of the boat she was now standing on and marveling at the kind of mind that could take something like this from idea to reality, glanced at her watch before she turned. It was only a little after one.

"Not a problem, we have…plenty of time."

She thought she covered her quick intake of breath fairly well as she turned and saw him. Well enough, she hoped.

Gabriel Taggert in naval uniform had been stunning. In the more casual Redstone attire, he'd been extremely attractive.

In snug jeans and a long-sleeved dark gray T-shirt he was sexy as hell.

He frowned suddenly. Cara's next breath caught; had he seen her reaction after all, had he somehow guessed what simply looking at him had done to her pulse rate?

"Do you have a jacket or sweater or something?"

She knew she must be looking like an idiot, staring blankly at him, but she was having trouble making the shift from contemplating flat abs and the appeal of back pockets to the mundane question.

"What?"

"It's warm here, but it'll be cooler up in the mountains. It's only March, and it might be in the forties or so. Could even still be snow around."

"Oh. No, I don't."

She felt even more foolish now; she should have realized a man like Gabe wouldn't waste any time, but would want to do whatever could be done and do it now. She should have come prepared.

He turned and walked back down the hallway he'd apparently come out of. She had a moment to appreciate the view, but quickly made herself turn away, not wanting to get caught gaping at him.

But when he came back and tossed her a soft, fleecy sort of zipper jacket that had the Redstone logo embroidered on the front, it was something else that sent her reeling; it was his. She knew it was, because she could smell the faintest trace of the clean-scented aftershave she'd always associated with him.

God, you're hopeless!

She'd meant to chide herself out of her stupid meanderings, but instead it sounded, even in her head, pitiful.

"I meant to ask," she said hastily as she resisted lifting the jacket to her face for a deeper breath, "you were wearing the same thing as the rest of the crew. No special uniform for the captain?"

His mouth quirked. "Yeah. I get to wear a ball cap with the boat's silhouette stitched on it."

"Oh."

"Sorry, no scrambled eggs."

He remembers, Cara thought with a start. *He actually remembers.*

It was one of her most vivid memories, that day when he'd sailed out and she'd gone with Hope to see him off. It had been only the second or third time she'd met the new man in Hope's life. He'd been wearing one version—she hadn't known there were so many kinds—of a dress uniform and in her ignorance of things military, she'd asked him what all the gold on his visor was.

He'd grinned at her, and explained. And she'd promptly fallen for him.

And apparently she'd never gotten around to standing up again.

"Seat belt," Gabe said absently.

"Got it."

Cara shifted in the seat of the low-slung coupe; the Lexus was a nice change from her little compact, and it was pure luxury to be able to completely stretch out her legs. They had decided, since he knew how to get to where they were going, that he'd drive. Once she'd seen the sleek, dark blue car, she was glad she had agreed. She wondered if he had trouble with other cars, as tall as he was.

"Nice car," she said now. "Redstone pays well, obviously." She'd heard that anyway, but it was hard not to comment on it when she was sitting in the evidence.

"It does," Gabe said. "But it's not just that. There's another, financial benefit to working for Redstone."

"What's that?"

"Mac McClaren."

Cara's brows shot up. "The gazillionaire treasure hunter?"

"And the guy who gave Josh his start, when all he had was a pilot's license, a design in his head and a dream. That Spanish galleon he found helped build the foundation of Redstone." Gabe smiled. "Of course, he's pouring money into his wife's pet cause now. There are a lot of homeless animals eating better these days."

"I didn't realize he was connected to Redstone."

"Most people don't. But the man's a lot more than a treasure hunter. He did that mainly to prove his father had been right about where that ship had gone down. He's also a financial genius, and he's at the disposal of anybody who works for Redstone. Including—" he gestured at the interior of the car, the rich leather, the polished wood "—me."

"Nice perk," she said.

"One of the benefits of working for a guy who makes friends for life," Gabe said.

She looked at him curiously. "Is he? A friend, I mean? Is that how you ended up there?"

"He is now," Gabe said, "but I didn't even know him when he offered me my first job at Redstone."

"How'd that happen?" she asked, intrigued now. "It's not like you see advertisements for them."

He chuckled. "No, Josh doesn't have to advertise. People are lined up literally around the world wanting to work for him."

She noticed he hadn't actually answered her. "So, how?" she persisted.

When he hesitated, then let out a compressed breath, she knew she hadn't imagined that he had been dodging her question.

"He'd read about the…incident that made me quit the navy. He was angry. Asked some of those friends he has about it, friends in or with connections to the military. My name came up."

There was a flatness in his tone that made her remember their earlier conversation.

I never thought you'd give in to her…whining.

Is that what you think? That I quit because my wife nagged me into it?

"Why did you really quit, Gabe?"

"Hope, remember?" She'd irritated him now. Or he was still irritated by her earlier assumption.

"Hope was…a very social person," she began, needing to say something, anything.

"Yes," Gabe acknowledged. "And she needed someone who could be there for that kind of thing, social occasions. I couldn't give her that, not the way she wanted."

"But…she knew that, going in. She had to."

"She thought she could deal with it." He lifted a hand from the polished mahogany steering wheel to the back of his neck, rubbed as if it were aching. "She couldn't. Long deployments take a huge toll. It takes an incredibly strong person to be a military spouse, in the best of times."

"I can only imagine," she said softly.

And *strong* was not a word Cara would use to describe Hope. Beautiful, vivacious, energetic, impulsive, yes, but strong? No. Not when she remembered all the seemingly endless phone calls where Hope had whined—not a flattering word, but the only one that really fit—about her husband's absence. As if he had chosen to leave, as if he'd abandoned her intentionally.

He lapsed into silence, apparently focused on driving although traffic was light. She waited, and when they'd pulled to a halt at a stop light, quietly asked again.

"Why did you really quit?"

He turned his head. Her breath stopped in her chest. She'd never seen him look this way before. He'd always seemed intense to her, but there was something in his eyes now that made her almost afraid to move.

It took her a moment to realize what she was seeing; there was more of the military officer left in Gabriel Taggert than she'd thought. This was the kind of man who did what others were afraid to, who knew things, did things, went places the average person going about their comfortable life never had to think about, precisely because there were men like Gabe in the world, willing and able to do it for them.

It was only with great effort that she managed not to look away from that fierce gaze.

"I quit," he said in measured tones that hinted at a lingering anger, "after twenty-three good, honest, heroic people died because some *politicians*—" he snarled the word "—decided it would upset the balance of power in the entire world if they were warned about an attack on them in time to defend themselves."

Cara smothered a gasp. "They could have warned them? And didn't?"

He looked away then, back to the front as the light changed, as if even now he was completely aware of his surroundings.

When he went on, his voice was quieter, but she didn't mistake that for calm.

"They chose not to, knowing what would happen. They didn't just let them die, they sacrificed them on the altar of political expediency. They died, horribly, without ever knowing why." He sucked in an audible breath. "Which may have been better than knowing the truth."

Judging by the fact that he was still angry after all these years, she tended to agree with that.

"I didn't know, Gabe. I'm…I don't know what I am. Sick, maybe. That something like that could happen. Be allowed to happen." She hesitated, then made herself ask. "The ones who died…they were your people?"

He flicked her a sideways glance. "They were navy," he said.

The words were simple, but they spoke volumes about the man. And told her that everything she'd ever thought about him was true.

Chapter 5

"I'm sorry, Gabe. For ever thinking you'd quit your career for…anything less than something like that."

He glanced at her again. Her words had surprised him. Not as much as the fact that he'd told her what he just had, when he rarely spoke of it at all, but she'd still surprised him.

"I would have thought you'd expect me to quit, if Hope demanded it."

Her mouth quirked. "There was a time when I suppose I might have," she said. "I'm not particularly proud of that at the moment. Hope's demands seem rather petty stacked up against the real reason you left."

That surprised him, too. Perhaps he'd gotten used to thinking Hope's version of what a woman needed was the only one.

"So how did Redstone happen, then?" Cara asked.

He'd told her so much already, there didn't seem to be any reason not to give her the rest. He kept his eyes on the road now that they were on the freeway, but his peripheral vision was as good as it had been in the navy, and he could see her fairly clearly.

"Somebody he knew told Josh I'd quit, and why. He tracked me down. Offered me a job running his maritime division. I took it." She saw one corner of his mouth curve up slightly. "Saved my life, after Hope."

He said it lightly, in an effort to negate the intensity of the past few minutes.

"I should have been in touch more, then," she said, as if she suspected there was more truth in the words than his tone admitted to. "I was so caught up in my own grief at the time I was afraid I'd break down sobbing every time, and I didn't think you'd appreciate a weepy woman pestering you. Besides, I—"

She stopped suddenly and looked down at her hands in her lap. He risked a glance then, and he saw that her cheeks were pink. He let a moment pass while he turned his focus back to the roadway.

"You what?"

"At the time, I'd never been in love, not really, so I didn't really realize what it feels like to have the one person you love most ripped out of your life without warning."

"And now you do."

He said it softly, and it wasn't a question.

"Yes."

"Who was he, Cara?"

"His name was Robert. He was a police officer. Killed in the line of duty, during an armed robbery. He got between the robber and a little girl."

She recited it as if it were a speech she'd memorized. He imagined it probably was; it was easier to answer the inevitable questions if you had an answer packaged and ready, one that you didn't have to think about. He knew that from his own miserable experience.

"I'm sorry. We lose too many good guys."

He meant it, and tried to let it show in his voice. When she looked at him, and gave him a smile he realized she didn't think he could see, he knew she'd gotten it.

"Yes, we do. And he was definitely one of them."

He let a moment pass, in silent tribute to a man he would never know, before he said quietly, "I wouldn't have minded you calling, Cara. Even crying. Especially crying."

He glimpsed her sudden, startled look out of the corner of his eye, sensed her sudden stillness. And wondered what his wife had told her that had made her assume he would want nothing to do with someone because they were grief-stricken and expressing it in the most common way.

He felt a little jab of guilt at the thought; Hope was gone, and the arrival of this much-delayed postcard didn't change that. He shouldn't be having negative thoughts about her. Hope hadn't been perfect, he knew that, but he'd loved her, been captivated by her easy charm and vivacious beauty. And the fact that she had loved him had been flattering in a way, even if now he wasn't sure exactly what she'd loved.

"I wanted to," she admitted. "Except for Hope's parents, you were the only one I knew who was hurting as much as I was, but I didn't want to make it worse for you."

The thought that she'd worried about that, even then, touched him, more deeply than he ever would have expected. Disconcerted, he seized on the first thing that came to mind.

"We can't tell them what we're doing," he said. "Gwen and Earl, I mean. It may—likely will—come to nothing."

"Of course we can't. We have to do it, I couldn't rest if we didn't. But I wouldn't raise their hopes for anything, when it's all so…nebulous."

Her words stabbed at him, and his voice was tight when he spoke again. "It's new ground in the search," he admitted. "But you're not thinking we're going to find her up there, are you?"

Cara blinked. "Hope? You mean…alive? God, no."

He breathed again; he'd always suspected little, shy Cara lived a great deal in her mind, and for a moment he'd feared she might have built some kind of fantasy in her head about finding her dearest friend alive and well.

"In the beginning," she said, in the tone of an embarrassed admission, "I wondered. I used to lie awake at night, picturing Hope living a new life somewhere, maybe with a new name, like she'd seen something and ended up in witness protection, maybe with amnesia, silly things like that."

It was so close to what he'd been worried she was thinking he was disconcerted all over again. Perhaps he'd known her better than he'd realized.

"Not silly, under the circumstances," he said, all the while glad she knew now the thoughts had been seriously implausible.

"I know that, now. Grief does crazy things to you. Coupled with uncertainty, it's almost unbearable." She took in an audible breath. "That's why I know we can't say anything to Hope's parents. It's not that I'm expecting to find her, but if we could find out what happened to her, it might…not *help*, nothing can, but at least they'd know."

"Closure?"

He hated the word; it made him think of people expect you to pick up and go on as if nothing had happened once the funeral was over, because you had *closure*. But now he was beginning to wonder. Cara had lost someone, too, and she'd clearly managed to get past it. Was the difference just that, that she'd had closure, where he was left forever wondering?

She shrugged. "I'm not much for buzzwords like that, but there's something to the theory, I think. Especially when it's something like this, where you simply don't know what happened. It's too easy to slip over the edge and start clinging to thoughts like I had in the beginning, to slide into the madness of believing them."

Her words hung there between them for a moment while he negotiated a traffic slowdown for a stalled vehicle on the center divider of the freeway. When they were clear, he glanced over at her.

"You don't think the Waldrons are doing that, do you?"

"No. For all her sweet acquiescence, Gwen is a strong woman. She wouldn't, and wouldn't let Earl, either."

Gabe couldn't have agreed more with that assessment. And her easy statement of it reminded him once more of the quiet girl who would never have spoken of someone of her parents' generation in such a way. "You've really gone and grown up, haven't you?"

She smiled then, a flashing, bright expression that nearly stopped his heart in his chest.

"It happens," she said, her tone so teasing he couldn't help smiling back.

And just like that the mood in the car changed, from a rather edgy tension to an easy camaraderie he was thankful for; it was much easier to handle.

When they started up the mountain highway called the Rim of the World—for obvious reasons, given the curves and steep drop-offs that marked every mile—they were talking like the old, fairly close friends they'd been. He asked about her own parents, found out they were living in Oregon, where her father was headed toward a happy retirement of endless fishing and her mother was building yet another of the beautiful gardens she was known for. She asked about his father in turn, and smiled when he told her the admiral was still as gruff and feisty as ever at sixty-one, and running his staff ragged down in San Diego.

"He never remarried, after your mother died?"

"No. He says there's not another woman on the planet who would put up with him the way Mom did. Having lived with him myself, I tend to think he might be right."

She laughed, and an unexpected warmth flooded him again.

Strange, he thought. He never would have thought seeing quiet little Cara Thorpe again would stir up so much emotion in him. True, she'd been a big part of his life for a while, although always on the edges, and he'd accepted her at first because he loved Hope and she was her best friend. But later he'd come to like the quiet girl for herself, enjoyed trying to gently nudge her out of her shyness, to get her to open up and talk to him.

He'd seen flashes of a different Cara back then, times when she'd surprised him with a cogent, astute observation about something that had made him realize she was indeed the personification of still waters running deep. But he'd been wrapped up in first true love, and hadn't thought much beyond that about the girl who was the quiet shadow of the lively, vivid Hope Waldron.

Cara Thorpe now would stand in no one's shadow, he thought suddenly. Not in looks, demeanor, or personality. She—

The ring of his cell interrupted his thoughts. He hit the button on the hands-free system built into the controls of the Lexus.

"Taggert."

"Smallest village in the county. No sheriff's substation. Two restaurants, one twenty-room motel, some touristy stuff. Post Office in the back of the general store. Same person running it for thirty years. Anson Woodruff. Town gossip. He's there now."

Gabe stifled a grin at St. John's clipped, concise report, and at Cara's bemused expression as the man's brusque voice sounded in the car.

"Thank you," he said.

"More?"

"Not yet. I'll let you know."

The click was audible as the connection was severed.

"I gather that was…the machine gun?" Cara said.

"It was."

"I see what you mean. He's always like that?"

"I don't know for sure. This is the first time I've dealt with him at any length on the phone."

"Surely he's not like that in person?"

"No, he's mostly silent," Gabe said, still grinning. "At least, he has been the few times I've met him. He's got quite the reputation for being a man of no words. So when he does talk, you'd best listen."

"He seemed…efficient in the extreme."

"That's the other part of the reputation," Gabe said. "Josh says if you ever hear him talking normally, look out. That's when he's the most dangerous."

"Dangerous? Odd word for a business executive, isn't it?"

"Not when you meet him."

She seemed to ponder this for a moment. But when she spoke again, it was about their destination.

"We start with Anson Woodruff?" she asked.

"Seems the most logical. Let's hope he has a good memory."

Cara smiled. "In my admittedly limited small-town experience, it seems town gossips usually do."

He laughed, and even as he did he marveled a little that he could, given the mission they were on.

And it was a mission, he couldn't deny that. That he was on it with the most unlikely of people didn't change that.

No matter how much Cara Thorpe had changed.

Chapter 6

Mr. Woodruff, as it turned out, all seventy-two years of him, had an excellent memory.

And absolutely no problem with sharing everything in it, without even asking who they were or why they wanted to know. The problem, Gabe soon realized, was in keeping him on the track they wanted.

"That was the summer the old roadhouse burned down," he was saying now, rubbing a hand over his bald head as if it were a long-standing habit. "Never seen such a fuss, although if you ask me, it was no great loss. Place had turned into a dive, nothing but drunks and pool players every night. Firemen had to go in and pull those sorry drunks out. And we only have a volunteer fire department you know, they're not—"

"It must have been awful," Cara said, just as Gabe was about to impatiently yank the man back to their original question. "Was this before or after you saw Hope?"

"Your friend?" the man asked, as if it had been hours ago, not ten minutes, when they'd first come in to ask.

"Yes," Cara said patiently.

Gabe himself was ready to snap, *Yes, the only reason we came in here!* but realized Cara's approach was much more likely to be productive.

"Oh, before," Mr. Woodruff said. "She came in the very next day. Lovely young woman. I told her all about the fire, she was very interested."

I'll bet you did, Gabe thought. He let Cara continue; if the old gent preferred to talk to another lovely young woman, far be it for him to interfere.

"How did she seem to you?"

"Seem? Why, a pretty young girl. Charming, just charming. She bought that card, went over to the café to write it, then came back and mailed it."

"So she wasn't…upset, or distraught, anything like that?"

Mr. Woodruff drew back slightly, his thick, bushy gray brows lowered. "Upset? Why, no, she didn't seem to be. In fact, she seemed very happy, excited even. Bubbly," he added, smiling.

That was Hope, all right, Gabe thought. Except when she was upset at his long absences, she'd always been that way.

"You're sure?" he asked.

"My memory," Mr. Woodruff said primly, "is razor-sharp."

Yeah, he definitely preferred talking to Cara, Gabe thought. *Can't blame the old guy for that.*

Cara asked quickly, "She didn't seem like she was unhappy, or frightened or anything?"

Mr. Woodruff frowned at that. "No, not at all. And I would have remembered, I think. I don't like seeing pretty ladies in distress."

He gave Cara a smile Gabe was sure was supposed to be charming in turn. The man was a flirt, Gabe realized suddenly, and had to hide a smile as his irritation vanished.

Cara chatted on for a few more minutes while Gabe inwardly laughed at himself; after eight years, he was suddenly in a hurry?

So Hope had been happy. He hadn't been wrong about that.

But they were no closer to knowing why she'd been here in this little hamlet to begin with. Or what had happened after she'd come in here, bought that postcard, scrawled her hasty, excited message on it, and dropped it in the mail.

It was very Hope-like, that after calling and being unable to reach her friend, that she would write something. She was always scribbling things down, and had kept journals she'd made him swear on his honor never to snoop into. He'd kept his word, although he'd let the police look through them when she'd first vanished. They hadn't been much help, since they'd ended about the time she'd gotten her new laptop computer, and he assumed she'd begun to keep her journals electronically.

At last Cara bid the affable Mr. Woodruff goodbye, and they turned away from the postal counter in the back of the store. It was one of those small, old places that nevertheless seemed to have everything you could possibly need. A little expensive, although not exorbitant given what it probably cost to keep the place supplied; not a lot of variety, but all the essentials were there, from fresh produce to souvenir T-shirts to spark plugs. Gabe imagined the locals both avoided it and welcomed its presence, depending on how desperate they were to avoid a trip down the mountain road to other shopping options.

The old wooden floor creaked as they walked, and it was an oddly comforting sound. Cara paused to smile at a display of chain saw parts next to stacked bundles of kindling.

"The implication being if you buy the one you don't need the other, I suppose," Gabe said.

Cara grinned at that. "Good marketing."

Gabe glanced back at Mr. Woodruff's domain, where the man was gesturing widely as he told another story to yet another captive listener, a woman with a small child in her arms. No wonder he'd lasted thirty years there; it was the perfect venue for him to have a constant, rotating audience.

"I'm glad you thought to bring that photograph," Gabe said as they continued through the store.

"It's always in my wallet. I know it's of both of us, but it's clear enough of her."

"Yes. He recognized her right away. She hadn't changed much, since then."

He didn't point out that Cara herself was barely recognizable as the same woman.

"No, she hadn't. Even though it's almost eleven years old." She paused, then said in a voice that seemed quite different, "It's the one you took. In La Jolla that time."

It took him a moment, but he finally remembered. "Your joint birthday bash."

She smiled, seeming pleased he'd remembered. "Yes."

His ship had been in port in San Diego for some refitting work, and Hope had been deliriously happy that he was going to be around for several months. So happy that it infected everyone around her, even quiet Cara, who had joined in the fun wholeheartedly when, at Hope's insistence, they went out for dinner at Hope's favorite restaurant. Hope had always been good at that, loved planning things down to the last detail. And she'd always been generous with her friends, Cara most of all.

He even remembered the moment when he'd snapped the shot; the two had posed at the beach park, on the bluff above the rocky, sheltered cove that was one of the seaside community's major attractions.

It was also the day he'd asked Cara why she didn't like him.

"I always wondered if you were mad at me."

It was out before he thought. And Cara looked so astonished, he knew he'd been wrong about that before she even answered him.

"Mad? Why would I have been mad at you?"

"I married your best friend. She didn't have as much time with you after that, when I was around."

"But you included me so often," she said, a slight urgency in her voice that puzzled him. Her next words explained the tone to him. "And you never, ever made me feel like…like a fifth wheel. I never thanked you for that. Not many men would have put up with Hope wanting me along so much."

"I never thought of you like that, a fifth wheel," Gabe said. "I was glad she had a friend like you, to rely on when I couldn't be there for her."

"Well," Cara said wryly, "I could do that, since not much else was going on in my life, wallflower that I was."

"You were…quiet," he said, somewhat carefully.

She laughed, and it was a genuine one, light and pleasant. "That's an understatement."

"Obviously you outgrew it," he said, that laugh making him unable to stop himself from teasing her.

"I'll take that as a compliment."

"It was meant that way. You've really…blossomed," he finished a bit lamely; it sounded impossibly corny to his ears.

"That wouldn't have been hard. I was very…unsure of myself, back then."

"I thought you were just shy. Or like I said, didn't like me."

"I liked you." She looked away quickly, then back at him. He thought he heard her take a quick breath, and when she went on, her words came out quicker than usual. "Too much. I had a bit of a shy girl's crush on you."

Gabe stared at her. "You what?"

"I thought I did, anyway. It took me a while to realize it was mainly that I wanted what Hope had. The love, the feeling, not necessarily…the person."

It happened so fast Gabe could barely keep up, the astonishment at her admission, and the sudden refutation of it. To his amazement, he found himself feeling oddly disappointed when she explained she'd essentially been in love with the idea of what he and Hope had, not him.

This was a revelation he didn't quite know what to think about; he'd never thought of himself as the kind of man who needed women falling all over him. He'd wanted Hope, and he'd gotten her, and that had been more than enough, while the good part lasted. So why this sense of letdown because Cara Thorpe had decided she hadn't had a crush on him? Especially when he'd never known she even thought she had?

"So we know Hope was really here the day she disappeared, and she bought, wrote and mailed that card the same day."

Cara had obviously moved on, perhaps embarrassed by what she'd admitted. Since he wasn't at all sure how he felt about it, he welcomed the change of subject.

"Yes," he agreed. "But we still don't know why she was here."

"Or where to go from here," Cara said.

"Well, if she stopped here to get and mail that card, maybe she did something else, too. Let's ask around, maybe—"

"Hello?"

They both turned at the hesitant interruption. It was the woman who'd been after them at the postal counter. The child she held, a dark-haired little girl who looked about two, was dozing on her shoulder.

"I'm Laura Ginelli. Mr. Woodruff said you were asking about Hope Taggert."

Gabe and Cara exchanged a quick glance. He chose his words carefully, using present tense, for reasons he didn't stop to analyze. "You know her?"

"I haven't seen her in years, since she stopped coming up here."

Gabe went still. He knew Cara had picked up on the same thing he had, when she asked, "Stopped?"

"Yes. Without a word. I always thought that was strange, but she was kind of…flighty that way, my grandmother would say. No offense, if she's related to you or something."

"I'm Gabriel Taggert," Gabe said, watching the woman for a reaction.

"Oh! I should have guessed," Laura said with a flashing smile that lit up her dark eyes. "She said you were the personification of tall, dark and handsome."

Gabe blinked as Cara laughed. "Isn't he just?" she said to the woman.

Gabe was rarely at a complete loss for words, but he was now. Not that he didn't appreciate the compliments, but he was never sure how to deal with such open admiration. Was he supposed to say thank you, or what?

Fortunately, Cara saved him from the awkward moment. "I'm Cara Thorpe," she said to the woman. With a glance at Gabe, she added, "Hope…was my best friend."

He noted the change of tense, and agreed with her; this woman obviously had no idea anything unusual had happened. Cara quickly explained about the much-delayed postcard.

"Oh, you're the one she wrote to, then?" Laura said after marveling at the belated delivery. "I wondered who on earth she'd been sending a postcard of this little burg to, and she said she hadn't been able to reach you by phone."

"You seem to remember pretty well, for something so long ago," Gabe said, careful to keep his tone merely curious.

"I do," Laura said. "I'm good with that kind of thing, and besides, I remember because it was the last time I saw her, and I always wondered why she never came back."

"So you saw her that day?" Cara asked. "The day she mailed that card to me?"

Laura nodded, and gestured across the street to the small coffee shop they'd noticed when they arrived. "I used to work over there, until my older son was born. Hope would come in when she was in town, for a milkshake. She loved them, and they make them the old way, with a big blender, not out of a machine."

"Strawberry," Gabe said softly.

"Yes," Laura said with a smile. "Anyway, she came in for one, and was writing on a postcard. When she finished, we chatted a little, like always."

And then the smile faded as she looked at them. She seemed to realize finally that there was something not typical about their questions.

"Something's happened, hasn't it?"

"That day," Gabe said, his voice tight despite his efforts, "was the last day my wife was seen anywhere."

Chapter 7

Laura Ginelli gasped. "What?"

"She disappeared," Cara said, knowing there was no way to tactfully break such news. "No one's seen or heard from her since."

"But…that was years ago!"

"Yes."

"Oh, God, I was afraid of something like that."

"Why?" Gabe asked sharply, clearly wondering if the woman had reason to think something might have happened. But Laura's answer was much simpler.

"Because she loved it here, and it didn't seem like her to just stop coming without a word."

"The police looked for her for months, but no one knew to come up here," Cara said.

Laura frowned. She glanced at Gabe. "But…didn't you tell them?"

His jaw tightened. "I didn't know she'd ever set foot here."

Laura's gaze suddenly narrowed, as if she were pondering all the reasons Hope might not have told him about her apparently regular trips up here.

"Nor did I," Cara said quickly, sensing Gabe's reaction to the sudden suspicion in Laura's face. "Or her parents, as far as I know. For some reason, she kept her trips here a secret."

"Why would she do that?"

"That's what we'd like to know," Gabe said, his voice even tighter now. He looked strangely edgy, and Cara wondered if he hadn't expected this to hit him like this, not after all this time, or talking to people who had known Hope would make him so tense.

And she wondered how it was affecting him, finding out that there had been a side to his wife he'd known nothing about. She was shocked enough herself; she could only imagine how he must feel.

"Do you know…how long she'd been coming up here?" Cara asked.

"How long?" Laura seemed rattled by what they'd told her, and more than a little upset. "Let me think."

The little girl began to stir, and she shifted her against her hip. Funny, Cara thought inanely, how a woman could haul around twenty or thirty pounds or more of kid for hours and still be considered the weaker sex by some. Not to mention what they went through to get the kid here in the first place….

"At least a couple of years or so, off and on," Laura said at last. "She'd come every weekend for months, then not at all for months, then she'd be back." The young woman looked troubled; clearly she'd liked Hope. "I suppose that's why none of us realized she hadn't been back until a long time after that day."

It didn't take much thinking to figure out that Hope's trips up here likely correlated with Gabe's deployments; when he'd been home Cara knew Hope had never taken off for a weekend. She knew they'd spent every available minute together, until the time for his next departure approached, which was when she'd start getting moody again, calling Cara to complain.

The little girl woke up, opened eyes as dark as her mother's, saw she was among strangers, and promptly started to wail.

"Shh." Laura patted the little girl on the back, with no noticeable effect. "I need to feed her, and go pick up my son at school," she said. "I can't believe this. I'd just found out I was pregnant with him the last time I saw Hope. She was so excited for me. She said she was going to learn to knit so she could start making baby things."

"Thank you for talking with us," Cara said, trying without much luck to picture the energetic Hope settling down long enough to do something as calm as knitting.

"If you think of anything else," Gabe said, pulling out a business card with phone numbers on it, "would you call me? I'll be on the cell number for a while."

"Of course," she said, glancing at the card. "Redstone? So you really did leave the navy?"

"Yes." It was hard to talk over the yowling child, so Gabe left it at that.

"One other thing, if you could, before you go," Cara said. "Do you know why Hope started coming here? I mean, it's lovely up here and all, but we don't have any idea why here, specifically."

"To see her friend Miriam, I assume," Laura said, bouncing the child as if that would quiet her.

"Miriam?" Gabe asked, a little sharply; clearly this was something else he hadn't known about.

"Who is Miriam?" Cara asked.

"I'm afraid I don't know her last name. Hope just mentioned that she came here to see her. I don't think she lives right here in the village, because we're small and everyone knows everyone, and I didn't know the name."

The crying became a screech, and Laura apologized before heading off to deal with her hungry child, leaving Gabe and Cara standing on the sidewalk, both a little stunned by this development.

Cara looked at Gabe, who was looking after Laura Ginelli with an expression she couldn't define. But then, the man had just found out his wife, the woman he'd so loved, had apparently had a secret life and one he'd never known about, or even suspected.

She knew how she felt that her best friend had kept all this from her, but…the person you married, were supposed to share all with…how could Hope have kept this from Gabe?

Why on earth would she have walked out on you?

For someone else?

Their earlier exchange echoed in her ears, and for the first time she wondered. Just because she couldn't imagine anyone cheating on a man like Gabe….

"Rethinking whether she was having an affair?"

Gabe's quiet words yanked her out of her thoughts, unsettling her with their accuracy. He was looking at her curiously. She would have thought he'd have been more upset at having to seriously consider the idea, but if he was, it didn't show.

But then, hadn't Hope always said ramrod-straight Gabriel Taggert would never betray something like real emotion? Cara thought of his laughter earlier, when they'd talked about Mr. Woodruff before they'd met him. That was emotion, wasn't it?

Not to Hope, she realized. To Hope, emotion meant angst, anger or tears. She would have to think about that, later. Right now Gabe was studying her a little too intently for her comfort, awaiting an answer.

"For an instant," she finally admitted. "But no, I still can't believe it. For all her sometimes capricious nature, Hope wouldn't do that."

"I tend to agree," Gabe said, in an emotionless tone that had Cara wondering again about Hope's complaint. But then, it had been eight years. Eight years of not knowing, wondering, had to wear out even the strongest of emotions. "Not clandestinely, anyway," he added.

"Exactly," Cara said. "She might walk out on someone, but only after a confrontation where she was able to present her grievances in the most dramatic manner."

Gabe blinked. She saw the corners of his mouth twitch, as if he were fighting a smile. "That," he said after a moment, "would definitely be Hope."

Pleased at his reaction for reasons she didn't want to examine too closely, Cara looked around at the main street of this little alpine-styled village.

"Maybe," she said, "if Hope used the post office, and spent time at the café, she did other things here, too."

Gabe's expression changed then, became more intent. "Good point." He looked up and down the street. "Shall we split up, cover more ground faster?"

Military efficiency, Cara thought, smothering a smile of her own. "But I have the photo," she pointed out. "Besides, between us we have...a bigger data base on Hope. Better chance something might register as significant."

The look he gave her then was admiring. "I always knew you were smart."

"That's me," she said, looking away then as voices from other days rang in her ears.

That Cara Thorpe, she's such a bright girl, too bad she's got no personality.

The little Thorpe girl, she's very clever, but far too shy.

Cara, you can't spend the whole summer living in the library! It's time to have some fun!

That last had been Hope, her one true friend for most of her life, based on the simple good luck that she was lively, outgoing, generous, and happened to live across the street. By sheer force of her considerable will, Hope had pulled the shy, protesting Cara into at least the periphery of her much more exciting life.

If it hadn't been for Hope, Cara thought, I'd still be that painfully shy, reclusive girl. She made me see I didn't have to stay that way.

So this was the least she could do for her missing friend.

We'll find out what happened to you, girlfriend. Somehow.

"I haven't even asked," Gabe said, sounding a bit embarrassed. "What are you doing, these days?"

"Using that marketing degree of mine, actually."

"Doing?"

"I run the PR and advertising department of a Web design company. It was just county-wide when I started five years ago, but we went regional last year. We're doing well."

Gabe's eyes widened. She smiled; she was proud of what she'd accomplished, and didn't mind letting it show.

"Good for you," he said, and there was a sincerity in his tone that warmed her. "Are you ever sorry you didn't go for law school?"

"Lord, no," she said with a laugh. "That was only a passing aberration, and rarely does a day go by when I'm not glad to not be swimming in that."

"You said you wanted to clean up that pool."

"That," she said dryly, "was before I realized it didn't *want* to be cleaned up. Too many of them like it that way."

He didn't dispute her words, just gave her a crooked smile that made her heart do a silly flip. Just like it always had when Gabe had ever deigned to smile at her. Which, she had to admit, he'd done often enough. He'd never been anything less than kind to her; it was her own silly feelings that had tangled things up.

And all this silliness she was feeling now had to be just a holdover from those days. Because nothing had really changed. Even now, after all this time, even with her best friend long missing, in her mind one thing remained unchangeable.

Gabriel Taggert belonged to Hope.

Chapter 8

Gabe rubbed the back of his neck, frowning.

"Are you all right?"

He looked at Cara across the table when she spoke. They'd finished talking to everyone they found on one side of the admittedly fairly short main street of Pine Lake, then had stopped for a meal at the café where Laura Ginelli had once worked. It was an odd hour, too late for lunch, a bit early for dinner, but they were both hungry since they'd skipped lunch in the effort to get here as soon as possible.

They'd found out quickly that Cara had been right. Hope, while not a local, hadn't been unknown to the people of Pine Lake. Her outgoing nature and charm, her vivaciousness, had made her memorable in the little village. They found several people who had stories to tell of the charming young woman who had been so easy to talk to.

None of them, however, had any idea what might have happened to the visitor to their midst. Nor did anyone, so far, know of a woman named Miriam.

"Just edgy, I guess," he said as he quit rubbing. "It must be the small town. I keep feeling like we're being watched every step of the way."

"Maybe we are," Cara said. "Although you'd think they'd be used to the occasional stranger or tourist coming through. They seem to want to attract them."

The feeling he'd gotten had been more specific than that, as if the watcher was intent on them in particular, but since he had absolutely nothing but this damned itch at the back of his neck to support it, he said nothing more.

"It's a pretty place," Cara said. "I can see the appeal. All this fresh air, the look and smell of pine trees, the quietness."

"So can I," Gabe agreed. "What I can't see is the appeal of it to Hope."

"I've been wondering that myself," Cara said. "She was a city girl, through and through."

"And not a designer shoe store in sight," Gabe said wryly.

Cara laughed; Hope's obsession with shoes had been legend. He himself had dress shoes in brown and black, running shoes, an old pair of lace-up military-style boots he'd held on to from the old days and deck shoes. Hope had had thirty pairs of black shoes he couldn't tell any difference between.

He'd figured it was a benign-enough obsession, and if it kept her happy he didn't mind. Although when she started creeping toward four figures for a pair of what she called "essential black pumps," he had started to wonder.

And packing them up for donation when he'd finally left the house they'd lived in had been one of the hardest things he'd ever done.

But right now, he was wondering again why he had never noticed what a great laugh Cara had. Had he not noticed, or had she simply laughed so little before, that he hadn't had the chance to notice? Had she been that shy around him?

Which brought him back to her confession of having had a crush on him.

"What?" Cara asked, making him realize he must have been staring at her.

"I was just thinking," he said hastily. "Back to the old days, when Hope and I used to talk about setting you up with one of my buddies."

Her eyes widened and her cheeks flushed. "You what?"

He wished now he hadn't said it. Not the first time since she'd dropped back into his life that he'd spoken before thinking, he thought wryly.

"We wanted you to be happy. She always knew you'd… blossom if given half a chance, that you were just unsure of yourself." He smiled at her, much as he had back then, when he'd tried to silently buck her up when he sensed she was panicking over some unwanted attention. "Obviously she was right."

"I…thank you. But did she really ask you to do that? Like a blind date?"

He nodded. "She was always after me to set up something with somebody I liked and trusted."

"How…awkward for you. I'm sorry."

He shrugged, but his mind was running as if it were an over-clocked computer. It had been a little awkward, especially since he'd never managed to come up with anyone, which had made Hope impatient. But not nearly as awkward as the realization that had suddenly struck him now.

He remembered going through a mental list, and finding some reason to discard each possibility. Karl Linden had been high on the list until Gabe found out he'd cheated on his longtime girl-friend. Then he'd caught Jim Hardy in a lie about something inconsequential, which had made him wonder about his truthfulness in important things. Darrell Watson had been a possibility until the MPs had had to go pick him up from San Diego PD after he'd gotten into a drunken brawl with a Marine down from Pendleton. And worse, had lost.

The bottom line was, and had been then, that he'd never done it because there hadn't been anyone, of all the men he'd known, that he'd thought good enough or trustworthy enough for sweet, innocent Cara Thorpe.

Inwardly rattled, he stared down into his cup of coffee. If he'd felt that way when she'd been a shy, withdrawn girl, how did he feel now about the vibrant, confident woman across from him?

"How did you do it?" he asked, wondering, as soon as the words were out, what the hell had happened to his usual caution in speaking his thoughts out loud.

She blinked. "Do what?"

"Change so much."

She smiled, and he thought he saw a touch of ruefulness in it. Her words proved him right. "You mean from the little shrinking violet I used to be?"

"Well…yeah," he said, feeling awkward all over again, but curious enough to ignore it.

"Hope," she said simply. "I wanted to be like her. And after she…was gone, it seemed even more as if I should."

He noted the hesitation, knew from it that she, too, had faced too often that confusion over what to say, how to characterize Hope's absence. He'd never, even when his brain told him with cool logic that it was true, been able to call her dead. Not without knowing for sure. And he'd often chosen the word Cara had used. *Gone*. It was as good as anything under the circumstances.

But that wasn't what had really caught his attention. "As if you should?" he asked.

She gave a one-shouldered shrug, accompanied by a self-deprecating smile. "I know it sounds ridiculous, but I felt like the world was a duller, less colorful place without Hope in it. And since I was as close as she had to a sister, it was up to me to…make it up to the world for losing her." The shrug came again. "Like I said, grief does crazy things to you. Makes you do crazy things."

He looked at her intently then, pondering her words. He saw the changes not just in her looks, but in the steady regard she returned, holding his gaze levelly, and in the refusal to avoid his eyes, as she once had regularly.

"There's nothing crazy about it," he said after a moment, meaning it. "Hope loved you like that sister, and trying to be like her is one of the most…moving tributes you could ever give her."

She blushed. That, at least, hadn't changed. "Thank you."

"But you're not, you know."

The color faded from her cheeks. "I know that. I could never be what she was."

She stopped when he held up a hand. "Don't. That's not what I meant. I meant you're not Hope, no one could be. But you shouldn't be, either. You're yourself, Cara, and that's enough."

"It is, now," she said. "But I wouldn't have gotten to here if not for Hope."

He shook his head. "You probably don't believe this, but it always was enough. You just didn't know it."

She stared at him. "Gabriel Taggert, that is one of the nicest thing anyone's ever said to me."

If he blushed, he'd be doing it now. He was thankful he wasn't prone to it. Instead, he rubbed the back of his neck again, wishing that annoying itch would go away.

"For what it's worth," Cara said, looking past him toward the door to the café, "at the moment we *are* being watched."

His fingers stopped. For a moment he was disconcerted that she'd noticed his action and correctly guessed the reason for it, but what she'd said was more important.

"By?" he asked, without looking around.

"There's a young woman over there near the door," she said, "talking to Mr. Woodruff, who must be on his lunch break since he has a cup of coffee in his hand. And he just pointed our way."

"Mr. Woodruff," Gabe said dryly, "appears to be local information central as well as gossip."

"Indeed."

She looked down as she dipped a French fry—some of the best he'd ever tasted and so probably fried in something artery-clogging—into a small pool of ketchup on her plate. She didn't wolf them down, he'd noticed, but savored each one with an enjoyment he himself hadn't applied to food in a long while. Then she looked over his shoulder again.

"Perhaps it was just coincidence," she said. "They're both gone from the doorway now, and I don't see her sitting anywhere."

"Or it wasn't us Woodruff was pointing at."

She nodded. "Possibly. Sure looked that way, though."

"Maybe we'll come across her when we start in on our canvass again. Would you recognize her?"

"Yes," Cara said. "She looked young, twenties. Very long, straight, dark hair. And she was thin, kind of angular. She looked...."

"What?"

Cara shrugged. "Just an impression. She seemed kind of... hyper. Her gestures were very quick, sharp."

"Interesting," Gabe said. Cara wasn't sure if he meant it, or if he was humoring her.

"I know it sounds silly to say, having only seen her from this distance, but—"

"It sounds observant," Gabe said.

She blinked. She hadn't expected that. "Well, I did get very good at that when I was younger."

"I noticed," Gabe said. "You were always watching people."

"You have time to do that when you don't talk much," she said wryly.

"I remember," Gabe said, "when you did talk what you said was generally well worth hearing."

"I...thank you."

"And you were right on about people. You knew Hope's supposed friend Jackie Carter was a phony the moment you saw her, even though Hope insisted she wasn't that bad."

"That's because she called me Hope's charity case, behind her back."

Gabe looked flatteringly offended. "You were never that. You should have told me. I would have dealt with her."

The thought of Gabriel Taggert leaping to her defense took her breath away. She scrambled to keep that image under wraps.

"Hope tended to see people the way she wanted them to be, not the way they were."

He lifted a brow at her. "Including me?"

She flushed, and for a moment she was that shy, quiet girl again, face-to-face with the man she'd fantasized about, terrified that somehow he might look at her and guess, and she'd be humiliated beyond belief. She fought down the old feelings, wondering if she'd ever be truly free of them, of that instinct to hide, to not draw attention, to stay safely hidden away and unnoticed.

"It might explain," he said casually, as if he hadn't noticed her reaction, "why she didn't deal with the reality of my life very well."

"Hope," she said, her voice a bit sharp with lingering embarrassment, "didn't deal with the reality well because she was more than a little spoiled. Her reaction to your career, and what it entailed, was typical."

He looked startled at her assessment. "Typical?"

"Hope's world centered around Hope. But she was so sweet and charming, most of us forgave her for it."

Gabe stared at her. "You certainly aren't the girl who thought she walked on water anymore, are you?"

The words stung a little, given the reason they were even together, but Cara had come a long way from that girl, and hiding her thoughts wasn't the way she dealt with things any longer.

"I love her like a sister, but like a sister, I'm not blind about her, either. There were things about her I didn't love. She wasn't perfect. And what happened to her doesn't make her perfect."

Gabe gave her a smile that told her he'd been down that road. "Hard to convince some people of that."

"It's human nature, when someone—"

When she stopped suddenly, Gabe's smile faded. "Dies," he said flatly. "That's what this is all about, isn't it? Proving that?"

"Yes," she said, admitting it aloud for the first time. "That's why it's hard to say anything…unflattering about her."

"I know." He stared down into his half-empty coffee cup.

"Let's just leave it at the fact that we both loved her. And we need to know what happened to her."

"Yes," she said quickly, thankful for his words. But she also felt the need to elaborate on what he'd said before. "But I haven't been that girl who worshiped Hope, not really, since she started giving you so much grief. You were honest with her. She knew what she was getting into when she married a naval officer, and she had no right to complain she hadn't."

"I did tell her it wouldn't be easy," he said.

"I know. So did I. But she loved you so much…I understood why she went ahead."

Cara lowered her gaze to her nearly empty plate then, afraid she'd gone too far this time, that he would read in her eyes the real reason she understood exactly why Hope had wanted to marry her dashing officer.

"Hope just didn't have the resources to deal with being alone," she said hastily, anything to keep him from seeing the truth. "She needed people around her to charm."

"She needed her husband around," Gabe said.

His tone was so flat Cara's gaze shot to his face. And for the first time she saw a trace of bitterness there, and more than a little self-blame.

"It wasn't your fault," she said quickly. "Hope couldn't grasp the concept of something bigger than herself, something that's worth sacrificing for. In that way, she was… shallow, I guess."

His expression changed then, became thoughtful, considering. "But you grasp it, don't you?"

"Yes," she said simply. "I'm just sorry others got in the way of it, for you."

It took a moment, but the smile that eventually curved his mouth was the most wonderful thing she'd ever seen. It was genuine, real, and went all the way to his eyes. He opened his mouth to speak, and she held her breath, thinking that if whatever he said matched that smile, she was going to be—

His gaze shifted as something caught his attention through the café window. His eyes narrowed, and he frowned.

"Long, straight, dark hair, you said?"

It took her a second to make the shift. "The woman? Yes. In a braid. Why?"

"She's across the street trying to get into my car."

Chapter 9

The woman took off the moment she spotted them coming out of the café. Gabe ran for the street, but she darted into an alley. By the time he'd dodged an oncoming lumber truck, she was out of sight. He raced toward where she'd disappeared, but stopped in his tracks when he reached the end of the short, narrow alley and there was no sign of her.

The alley wasn't wide enough for a car, and he hadn't heard one start anyway. It was more of a gap between buildings, and it opened onto another street at the other end. She could have gone either direction after that. Or into any of the buildings. If she was a local, she probably knew all the places to go if she didn't want to be seen.

He was standing in the alley, looking around in frustration when Cara caught up with him.

"It doesn't look like she got into the car," she said.

"That'll teach me to use the alarm, even up here," he muttered almost to himself, although he doubted he could ever get into the habit as the thing going off for no real reason annoyed him so much. He scanned the empty alley once more. "I wonder what she was after."

"I suppose it's too much to think she just wanted to look at the fancy car," Cara said.

Her tone was so glum Gabe knew she didn't believe it. It also told him she knew as well as he did that this was a development neither of them had expected.

"Especially after she apparently asked the helpful Mr. Woodruff about us."

"Maybe she just asked who owned the car in front of his post office," Cara suggested. "You can't tell me one of those babies shows up here every day."

"Maybe," he said, but he didn't quite believe it. "Sexist of me, I suppose, but I'd be more likely to believe that if it were a guy."

"Hey," she said in mock offense, "I'd stop and look at it, and I'm not a guy."

"Well, I am, so believe me, I noticed that."

She didn't answer, and he wondered if it was because his voice had sounded as grim as he thought it had. He didn't dare look at her, but with that peripheral vision of his, he saw she was looking at him rather oddly.

"Cara—"

"Shall we start on the other side of the street now? Or do you want to look for her?" Her tone was brisk, businesslike as she gestured down the alley.

Nice work, Taggert, he told himself. *You compliment her, but you sound like a growling bear doing it.* At least, he'd meant it as a compliment. But it had come out sounding like a warning.

And apparently she'd taken it that way.

Or had it been more of a warning to himself? Here they were, trying to track down what might be the only clue they'd ever really found to his wife's fate, and he was noticing another woman?

But it wasn't another woman. It was Cara.

His wife's best friend.

What that made all this, and the fact that he'd meant to compliment her at all, he couldn't begin to figure out right now.

Task at hand, Taggert, he told himself. *Focus.*

"Let's finish what we were doing," he said, striving for a normal tone of voice this time. "Maybe we'll come across her."

"And we can ask about her, too. Somebody's bound to know who she is."

Gabe nodded, grateful she didn't seem to be holding his gruffness against him. They started where they'd left off for lunch, working their way down the single main street. They'd fallen into a routine of Cara speaking to the women, Gabe to the men, because they'd found it more efficient. Cara said it was because it took the male-female thing out of the equation, and she didn't seem bothered by it at all.

Gabe thought it was simply that no man could resist flirting with a woman like Cara, and that would cut down the ease of the process.

He still marveled at the change in her. She'd become a very self-sufficient, confident woman, in addition to having left her quiet, plain appearance behind.

He thought suddenly of what she'd said just before he'd spotted the woman at his car.

Hope just didn't have the resources to deal with being alone....

Cara had loved Hope, but clearly she hadn't had blinders on. And for all his understanding of what it took to be a military spouse, he realized he'd never really accepted that Hope simply hadn't been cut out to be one. That it hadn't been anybody's fault, really; it just wasn't who she was. Some of the old, familiar ache he'd been carrying around seemed to ease, and he glanced at Cara in wonder that in a few hours she'd managed to clear up something he'd been trying to understand for years now.

Hope couldn't grasp the concept of something bigger than herself, something that's worth sacrificing for.

Her words echoed in his head again. She'd spoken them with a conviction that told him she meant what she'd said. Cara Thorpe, he thought, would have what it took. In her quiet way, she was stronger than Hope had ever been. All Hope's verve and energy had sprung not from strength but from a need he hadn't understood until it was too late.

"—trouble, that Crystal. Nothing but trouble."

Gabe focused suddenly on the conversation going on at his elbow. He'd almost tuned out when it was clear the woman working behind the counter of the small, tourist-trap–style gift shop had been there only three years, so hadn't been there when Hope had been in town.

But apparently Cara had asked about the woman who had tried to get into his car.

"Trouble?" Cara's gaze flicked to Gabe, then back to the grand-motherly woman she'd been speaking to. "What kind of trouble?"

"You name it, that girl's been into it. Ungrateful, too. She'd be in jail, I'm sure, if people weren't so tolerant around here. Or if she were a better thief."

"So…we were right to be concerned when she tried the door of the car?"

The woman's brows lifted. "She try to steal something from you, too? Can't believe she still shows her face in town, she should be so ashamed."

"Do you know where she lives now?" Gabe asked.

The woman gave him a careful look, having to tilt her head back slightly to see his face. Finally she answered. "Last I heard, she was living at the old inn, on Big Tree Road."

"Inn?"

"A couple of miles out of town. Used to be a fancy sort of place, somebody had an idea we'd be the next Aspen or some-thing. Rose Terhune bought it ten years ago, although what a single woman needs with that much space I'll never know. But she's sort of an odd duck anyway. Those artist and writer types usually are. But to let that girl stay there rent free, when all she does is cause problems…."

It took a few minutes for Cara to extricate them from the woman's righteous indignation, but finally they were back outside.

"Well," Cara said, "wasn't that interesting?"

"Interesting," Gabe agreed, "but I don't know how helpful."

"Thinking now she might just have been trying to steal something out of an obviously expensive car?"

"Maybe," he said, having to admit the possibility had become more probable after the character assessment they'd just gotten. "But out there on the main street, with witnesses all around?"

Cara rubbed her arms as they stood pondering their next stop. It had clouded over, and there was a crispness in the air that hadn't been there when they'd arrived earlier that afternoon. Even he, who had a pretty wide comfort zone, felt a little chilly.

"Let's go back to the car for jackets," he said.

"Kind of you to notice," Cara said.

For a moment he thought it was a jab, that maybe she'd been cold for some time and he hadn't realized it, but there was no undertone to her voice and nothing but sincerity in her face as she looked up at him.

"Gabe?"

He realized he'd been staring at her; he didn't know for how long. He snapped out of it with a start and a mental chiding; he didn't understand why he was having so much trouble focusing on the task at hand, something he usually excelled at.

"Sorry," he muttered. "Let's go."

When they got back to the car he opened it, reached in and grabbed the fleece jacket he'd given her back at the boat. He held it for her as she slipped her arms into the sleeves. She pulled it close around her gratefully, and thanked him for the small courtesy with no sign of offense. It was clearly too big for her, but she snuggled into it as if grateful for the warmth.

She'd let him open doors for her, too, he thought. But then, just as often she opened them for others in the same way, so he put that down to basic good manners. His mother had been big on that, and it was a lesson pounded into him from an early age. For her, as for his father, the phrase "an officer and a gentleman" had had true resonance. He kept up the practice now in her memory, even if it earned him puzzled looks or teasing, and the occasional snide remark.

They had about a quarter of the main street left to go. Gabe was beginning to doubt they would find out anything useful, but it simply wasn't in him to leave the job three-quarters done. He suspected Cara would feel the same way.

But if he was right, and they finished the task they'd set and found nothing, then what? Give up and go home, after a simple if lengthy walk down the single main street of the town Hope had visited on the last day anyone had seen her?

"You're frowning."

He blinked. "Sorry. Thinking."

"About Hope." It wasn't a question, but an assumption.

"In a way," he said. "But more about what happens if we don't find anything down there." He gestured toward the portion of the street they hadn't covered yet as they started walking that way.

"I've been thinking about that," Cara said. "I want to look around more, off the main drag, see if maybe I can find someone who knows who Miriam is."

He nodded in agreement. "She's the key."

"I took a couple of vacation days to deal with this, but I realize you probably need to get back to work," she said. "So I can just come back in my own car tomorrow."

"Actually, I was thinking of staying, if that little motel has room."

She looked relieved. "If I could have figured out a way to get home tomorrow, that would have been my first choice. You're sure you can be away? On no notice?"

"One thing about Redstone, if you need personal time, you get it."

"Just like that?"

"Josh makes it so easy that nobody much abuses it."

She looked thoughtful. "I think that says as much about the caliber of people he hires as anything."

"Perhaps. He doesn't often hire bad apples. And when they do turn up, they're dealt with in short order. Josh is an amazingly generous boss, but he won't be taken advantage of. Not for long, anyway."

"I'd like to meet him someday."

"You'd like him." He stopped walking as they neared the general store where Mr. Woodruff reigned. "And he'd like you. And what you've accomplished."

She grinned suddenly. "Maybe I could interest him in a new Web site."

He smiled back at her, but that grin had taken the breath right out of him. Somehow he managed to say, "Maybe you could," before they went inside to purchase what they would need for an overnight stay.

"Call me fussy," Cara said, "but brushing my teeth is a requirement."

"Me, too," Gabe said with a laugh. They split up inside and found that the little store, amazingly, held all the basics they'd hoped for. They dropped the bags off at his car—with Gabe setting the alarm this time—then resumed their original quest.

They stopped in front of a chalet-style building that, according to the sign in front, housed the chamber of commerce, the community center and the library. It was the latter that was their goal; Hope had been a fairly voracious reader, and she loved libraries.

The librarian startled them. At first glance Gabe would have put him at maybe eighteen, but the freshly minted college degree on the wall behind the checkout counter that was crammed into one corner of the larger of the two rooms that made up the library told him the kid had to be at least twenty-two. Unless he was a child prodigy of some sort. Which seemed possible; under a mop of hair almost the same color as Cara's, intelligent and lively eyes looked back at him.

And looked at Cara with an appreciation that made age irrelevant.

"Hi, I'm Greg Mercer. Before you ask, yes I'm really the librarian, and yes, I'm old enough."

He said it with such a wide grin Gabe knew he'd heard the

inevitable questions often. That he'd decided to handle them with humor was something Gabe respected.

"So how'd it happen?" Cara asked with a laugh that made the young man's grin widen.

"Harry Potter," he said succinctly.

"Never underestimate the power of a good book," Cara said, earning another grin.

"Especially at a very impressionable age," he said. He glanced at Gabe, then back to her. "So what can I help you with?"

"Unless you were working here eight years ago, I'm not sure you can," Gabe said dryly, annoyed with himself for finding the instant rapport Cara seemed to develop with the young man irritating.

"Obviously I wasn't," Greg said. "But I did practically live here. I've got three younger siblings, and this was the only place where I could read in peace."

"You grew up here in Pine Lake?" Cara asked.

Grew up? Gabe thought. *Still waiting on that.*

Greg nodded. "And came back after college, amazingly enough. But I had a built-in job. Mrs. Barker, the old librarian, promised me I'd get it when she retired, if I wanted it. She even held off retiring until I was done with school." He gestured at his small domain. "It's not big, and it doesn't pay a lot, but it's a start."

Cara took out the photograph. "Do you happen to recognize her?"

The boy's eyes widened. "Er…yeah, I do. I mean, I don't know her, but I remember seeing her."

"You're sure?" Gabe asked. "It would have been a long time ago."

"I know it was. But it's not as if a geeky kid like I was would forget seeing a woman like that in the little old Pine Lake library."

"She was in here?" Gabe's voice sharpened. He couldn't help it.

"I think I remember seeing her a couple of times. I hung out in the kid's section—" he gestured toward the secondary, smaller room at the back "—mostly, but she came in there once. Looking at picture books."

"Laura's baby," Cara murmured.

"Did you ever talk to her?"

"Me?" He looked startled. "Never. I was just a stupid kid, she was this gorgeous, totally hot woman. I thought she'd crush me like a bug if I tried to talk to her."

While Gabe wrestled with the image of a young teenager with hormones running amok ogling his wife, Cara smiled at the young man.

"She wouldn't have," Cara said. "She would have been very nice. And," she added, "I doubt you were ever stupid."

He was still young enough to blush. And Gabe felt like a cranky old man for his reaction to the kid. How had he gotten to feeling this way, so old at thirty-eight?

"The old librarian," he began, making sure his voice was level.

"Mrs. Barker? She was nice. Let me hang out even after hours while she closed up sometimes, as long as I was reading."

"Does she still live here?"

The young man shook his head sadly. "No. She died last year. Right after she retired. I'm telling you, don't ever retire, it'll kill you."

"I'm sorry," Cara said.

"Me, too. She was okay. She was the first person I ever knew, I mean really knew, who died."

Okay, so that's why I feel so old around him, Gabe thought. I *am.*

"That's always hard," Cara said sympathetically. "It's always a shock to find out…what forever really means."

Young Greg blinked. "Yes. That's it, exactly."

With that possible trail gone, Gabe thought it was time they moved on. It was Cara who asked about Miriam. Gabe hadn't even been going to bring it up, but the moment she did he realized he should have thought less about the boy's age and more about the fact that he'd grown up here in Pine Lake.

"You mean Miriam Hammon, our most famous resident?"

Cara drew back slightly, clearly as startled as he was. If she was so famous, why was this the first person they'd found who'd ever heard of her?

"Famous?" Cara said tentatively.

"Well, she was. She's not working anymore, at least not writing. I think she's painting now."

"She's a writer?"

"She was. Fairly successful in her day. I remember Mrs. Barker was all excited when she moved up here. I looked at her books, because I thought I wanted to be a writer, but there were no magic or wizards, so I didn't care, then."

Cara lifted a brow at the last word. "And now?"

"I've read them. Woman's stuff, mostly, but I need to know about that, too. She really was good. Too bad she's not writing anymore."

"Is that why no one else in town seems to know who she is?" Gabe asked.

Greg's brow furrowed. "Everybody knows about her."

Gabe's gaze narrowed. "Then why did everyone we asked say they'd never heard the name?"

The young man's expression cleared. "Oh. That's it. She didn't write under her real name. She wrote as Rose Terhune."

Gabe went still. Cara glanced at him. Hope's friend was the woman who had given refuge to the troublesome woman who had tried to break into his car?

All of a sudden things had gotten complicated.

Chapter 10

"That has to be the place," Gabe said.

"Yes," Cara agreed. "It looks like it could easily have been a small inn, once."

The big house, which sat amid a cluster of small buildings that looked as if they could have been guest cottages once, looked expansive and inviting. It seemed a bit out of place among the more rustic and cabinlike structures they'd passed, most of them finished in natural woods, some of them with A-line roofs that gave them that mountain feel. This place had a steep roof—for snow, she guessed, although as a Southern California girl through and through she'd never seen much of the stuff—but was painted a soft yellow with bright white trim. It stood out among its camouflaged neighbors, but not in a bad way. It looked….

"Cheerful," she said.

"I guess," Gabe said neutrally.

She squelched a smile; Gabe had always had a typically male wariness about assigning emotions to color. In fact, he'd had a certain wariness about color, period. Once, on a rare occasion when she'd felt brave enough, she'd asked him teasingly if the navy had regulations that applied to his civilian clothes as well, if that was why he rarely wore anything other than grays, blacks, or blues. Hope, whose own favorite color was a vivid purple, had joined in. Shortly thereafter Hope had bought him a shirt in that shade. Cara had guessed he only wore it to please Hope, and please her it had.

And any other female who saw him in it, Cara remembered. The color had set off his dark hair and tanned skin in a way that caught the eye of any woman in the vicinity who was still breathing.

"Quite a garden," Gabe said.

"Glorious," Cara said, "even though it's not in full bloom yet."

"Good planning," Gabe said. "Things that are interesting even in winter."

That, too, was very Gabe, she thought. He appreciated the bones of things, the design, the foundation that made them work. She supposed it was part of what had made him like the navy; he'd known his ship from the keel up, the design, all the systems, everything that made it work.

They followed the pleasantly curved pathway through the garden. Cara saw shady places where there was snow still on the ground, but spring was beginning to win the yearly battle. The walk was intriguing, with new sights at each turn, a shrub with striking red stems here, a pyramidal trellis there, and a bed of brightly purple crocuses still hanging on to blooms there. Other plants were budding madly, and Cara imagined that in just another month the place would be in furious growth, and in two months would be spectacular.

"A lot of work goes into creating this kind of random effect," she mused aloud.

Gabe looked at her sharply. "I was just thinking that. That for all the casual effect, this was very carefully planned."

His surprise that they'd had the same thought made her smile. "I wonder if it was already here, or if it's our writer?"

"Let's ask," Gabe said, and only then did Cara realize he was looking past her, toward the house.

She turned. The woman approaching them, a questioning but not unfriendly expression on her face, looked to be in her forties, although from glancing through the books Greg had shown them, Cara was sure she must be older. She was about Cara's height and had that trim, wiry appearance that promised she would probably look much the same into her seventies.

She was wearing a crisp, long-sleeved white blouse tucked into faded but clean jeans, and a leather belt with what looked like real silver conchos threaded through the belt loops. Her hair was cut short and liberally streaked with gray amid the darker strands. She seemed utterly unselfconscious about it, and that coupled with her relatively unlined face made her seem much more youthful than the gray suggested.

"Hello," she said. "Can I help you?"

Her voice was pleasant, even welcoming. Cara had been so distracted by the enchanting garden she hadn't really thought about how to approach this.

"We were admiring your garden," she said, while she tried to decide how to bring up Hope. "It's beautiful even now, and it must be amazing later in the spring."

The woman's golden brown eyes lit up. "It is. I'm very proud of it."

"I can't imagine how much work it must be, to keep it from going crazy," Cara said, smiling as she waved at the profuse plantings.

"It is that," the woman said. "I had to bring in some help, or I'd never be able to keep up with it and my work, too."

So was she still writing after all? Cara wondered. "You work here, at home?" she asked, still unsure of what approach to take with this alert-eyed, kindly seeming woman.

"Yes, I do. I paint."

Greg had said that, Cara recalled. "You certainly have a lot of subject matter," she said, glancing around. "Your garden, the mountains, the trees…" She stopped suddenly, then couldn't help laughing at herself. "Assuming that's what you paint, of course. Which I shouldn't have done."

The woman responded with a smiling laugh of her own. "I'm very much a beginner at this, so I wouldn't dare claim to paint anything anyone might expect to recognize."

Even Gabe chuckled at that.

"I'm Cara Thorpe," she said, holding out her hand.

The woman took it. Her grip was definite, but not forceful. "Miriam Hammon." As she said it she was frowning, not in anger but as if she were puzzled. "Cara Thorpe," she repeated.

"Yes. I'm a friend of—"

"Hope!" the woman exclaimed suddenly, smiling widely.

"Yes," Cara said, relieved.

Miriam's gaze shot to Gabe. "Gabe Taggert," he said.

Miriam's smile widened even farther. "I wondered if that was you! You don't look much different than in the photograph Hope showed me. Tall, dark and handsome, she used to say."

Gabe shifted his feet as if he were uncomfortable. Cara felt the urge to laugh at his discomfiture. Didn't the man have a mirror? she wondered.

But the urge vanished at Miriam Hammon's next words. "It's been so long. How is Hope? I hope she's well, I've missed her visits."

Cara opened her mouth, but no words came. After a moment of silence that brought a frown to Miriam's face, Gabe said quietly, "We were hoping you could tell us."

The woman drew back slightly, obviously puzzled. "Me? But I haven't seen her for…oh, several years now."

"Eight?" Gabe suggested.

"I suppose it could have been that long. I'd have to check. But…what are you saying? That *you* don't know where she is?"

Cara finally found her tongue. "She went missing eight years ago."

Miriam gasped. "Missing?"

"No one's seen or heard from her since," Gabe said.

"My word," Miriam said, her hand going to her throat as if she were having trouble taking in enough air. Cara knew the feeling.

"But we've recently discovered she was here in Pine Lake on the day she disappeared," she said.

"You'd both better come inside," Miriam said. "I'll put coffee on."

She led them, not to the big front entrance, but to a smaller doorway that led directly into a large, country-style kitchen.

"I'm afraid what used to be the lobby is now my studio," she explained. "It has the best light."

The kitchen was warm and welcoming, in the same yellow and white color scheme as the exterior of the house, with touches of a deep green that echoed the fir trees outside. Copper pots and pans hung from a rack over a large, commercial-style range with six burners and a grill in between them.

"Lovely," she said, looking around as Miriam gestured them to two of the stools pulled up to a huge island topped with a granite slab that was polished to a high sheen.

"This was a bed-and-breakfast place before I bought it," Miriam explained as she scooped coffee into a filter and put it into a coffee maker that sat next to the big, stainless-steel refrigerator. "A bit bigger than most, with space for a dozen guests, and they fixed breakfast in here."

"Good space," Gabe said.

He could, Cara noted, easily reach the hanging pans she'd have to stretch for. As would Miriam, she thought.

"Too bad it's wasted on me," Miriam said with a quick smile that Cara thought charming. "I'm not much of a cook."

She got three mugs from the cupboard above the coffeemaker. They were utilitarian, heavy stoneware, but each was painted with a different design in the same deep green on white, making them clearly part of a set yet not numbingly the same. The very kind of thing that would appeal to Hope, Cara thought.

"Did you paint these?" Cara asked.

"Why, yes, I did," Miriam said.

"I like them."

"Thank you, dear. I've always dabbled, but only lately did I realize that the time was now or never, if I wanted to truly learn to paint."

"So you quit writing?" Gabe asked.

"Oh, no. I will always write. I write for myself, and short stories occasionally, and I'm working at my own pace on a children's book. But I put an end to the book-a-year grind about three years ago, yes."

When the coffeepot was full, she filled all three mugs, slid a container of sugar across the counter to them, and got a carton of milk out of the refrigerator.

She sat down herself as she poured a dollop of milk into her own mug.

"Now, let's get to it," she said briskly. "What on earth happened?"

"I wish we knew," Cara said. "May I ask how you and Hope met?"

"She wrote me a fan letter." The woman's golden eyes flicked to Gabe. "After a book I wrote that featured a woman married to a military officer. It was a lovely letter, but it was also filled with such anxiety that I urged her to get help. To contact Family Services at the naval base. I knew from my research that there were resources available to her."

"I told her the same thing," Gabe said, an echo of frustration in his voice. It was tinged with a note of despair that dug at Cara's heart. "But she never did it. I asked one of the fleet and Family Services counselors to contact her periodically, to make sure she was all right. She wouldn't even talk to him."

"She told me she felt she didn't fit in with the other families, the other wives," Miriam said.

"Hope wasn't much for fitting into a group," Cara said, still disturbed by how Gabe had sounded, as if this were all somehow his fault. "She was used to being the star."

"She had that quality," Miriam agreed. "Everyone was drawn to her, to her beauty, her charm. In any case, she wrote to me again, thanking me for my concern. After my next book was released, she wrote again, via e-mail, and we began to correspond regularly."

Miriam's expression changed, became thoughtful. "Excuse me a moment, please. I want to check on something on my computer."

Cara looked at Gabe as the woman left the room. "You had no idea about this?"

"None," Gabe said grimly.

"Neither did I. Not that she had to tell me everything, but…."

"She always did."

"I thought so, yes," Cara admitted. "We shared so much. I thought we knew everything about each other."

"So did I," he said. "Obviously I was wrong."

She reached out and laid a hand over his on the granite counter. "Maybe she would have, eventually. Maybe she just didn't want to take up the precious time you had together talking about other things."

"Something important enough for her to make the trip up here so often? You don't think she should have told me about that?"

"Should have? Of course." Cara lowered her gaze. "But then, Hope always did say I had some funny ideas about relationships."

"Funny? To tell your spouse the truth?"

"She didn't lie," Cara said, feeling stirred to defend her dearest friend. "She just didn't share this part of her life. Maybe there was a reason."

"Yes," Gabe said, sounding grim. "Maybe there was."

Chapter 11

Miriam came back moments later, interrupting what had threatened to become a difficult conversation. Gabe kept thinking of what Cara had said, that maybe Hope had had a reason for keeping this from him. None of the reasons he could come up with were particularly pleasant.

"I remembered what I was working on the last time I saw Hope," Miriam said, thankfully derailing his tangled thoughts. "She had dropped in unexpectedly, as she often did, and I let her read the opening chapter of the book I'd just started. I just pulled up the copy I archived, and it says the file was created just over eight years ago."

"Over?" Gabe asked.

"By about three months."

"How long had she been coming here, by then?"

"A couple of years, I think. We met when she came to a book signing. Her visits here began after that."

Gabe went still. "Wait. She told me about that. That she'd gotten a book autographed by her favorite writer."

So Hope hadn't kept everything a secret, he thought.

"But she was here after that," Cara said. "She mailed a postcard from here almost exactly eight years ago."

Miriam shook her head. "I didn't see her. I remember because she said she was going to come back every month, to read what I'd written. She wanted to follow the entire process. But she never did."

Gabe felt his jaw clench as he struggled to wrap his mind around this side of his wife he'd known nothing about.

"Why?" he asked. "I don't mean to be insulting, and I can understand anyone's interest in knowing a real writer, but—"

Miriam studied him for a moment. "You didn't know, did you?"

"Apparently there's a lot I didn't know," Gabe said, his voice tight again.

"It must have been hard, you being away so much," Miriam said. "I told her she should talk to you about it. About her dream."

Gabe was about at the end of his patience. Cara seemed to sense that. "Dream?" she asked.

"After we'd corresponded for some time, and she'd made a couple of visits up here, she confided that she'd been thinking she would like to try writing."

Gabe went still. "She what?"

"She said she'd always kept journals, which is not a bad first step. And her letters, and later e-mails, were always very readable and as vivid and vivacious as she herself was. So I saw no reason to discourage her. I thought there might be potential there."

"Hope wanted to be a writer?"

Gabe knew he sounded astonished. Only the fact that Cara looked as if she were barely keeping herself from echoing his words eased his discomfiture; how had he not known this?

"She didn't know what she wanted to write," Miriam answered, "but yes. I suggested, given the nature of her letters, that she try feature articles, perhaps starting out on Web site publications, then on to magazines or newspapers."

Gabe let out a compressed breath. Cara was shaking her head.

"I gather neither of you knew this?" Miriam asked gently.

"No," Cara said. "And we should have."

"Sometimes," Miriam said, "when people have a dream they think will never come true, they keep it hidden, for fear of being thought foolish."

"And Hope would hate looking foolish," Cara said.

Gabe's gut knotted. Had he been so judgmental that his wife couldn't even share a dream like this with him? Had she thought he would laugh, or in fact consider it foolish?

Would he have?

He didn't think so. He wanted to think he would have supported her wholeheartedly, but that was easy to think now, driven by guilt.

Miriam studied them both for a moment. "Perhaps it's the writer in me, but I can't help noticing…you're both using a combination of past and present tense."

"A battle I've been fighting for eight years," Gabe said, suddenly feeling utterly weary.

"So it's true, she simply…vanished?"

Gabe said, "She's never been found."

Miriam looked up at him at that. "Is there a difference?"

"Yes." It nearly burst from him, with a sense of urgency he couldn't seem to keep under wraps.

"Of course there is," Cara said. "Especially to a logical mind. Vanished is…inexplicable. Mysterious."

Gabe drew back slightly in surprise. He hadn't expected her to understand that. It made it easier to go on more calmly.

"No one just vanishes. There's an explanation, always. It may never be found by those left behind, but that doesn't mean it isn't there."

"A logical mind," Miriam echoed with a knowing expression that made Gabe wonder just what Hope had told her about him.

"Didn't you wonder, when you didn't hear from her?" Cara asked.

Miriam nodded. "Of course. I kept e-mailing her for some time, after she quit coming. She never answered. I always thought that she'd simply changed her mind about writing. I never lied to her about the difficulties of achieving success, or keeping it once you got there."

"Reality again," Cara murmured, then winced.

The knot in his Gabe's eased a little as he read the meaning behind Cara's quiet words and her own reaction to them. *Another dream world destroyed for Hope by reality?* he guessed she had thought. Followed quickly by guilt as her conscience told her she shouldn't be thinking that way about Hope, not now. It was a process he himself was far too familiar with.

"Then I wondered," Miriam went on with a look at Gabe, "if something had happened to you. She was always afraid of that."

Gabe drew back slightly. "She was?"

"Of course she was. Given your work, how could she not be?"

"We all were," Cara put in. "No matter how many times you told us you were perfectly safe."

"She never said a word," Gabe said, sounding a bit lame even to his own ears. Cara looked as if she were going to laugh, in spite of everything. "Neither did you," he felt compelled to point out.

"It hardly seemed necessary to dwell on the obvious."

"Men," Miriam said with a shake of her head.

Cara did laugh then. Gabe shifted uncomfortably; the looks the two women exchanged made it clear that any woman would understand the layers of that simple exclamation.

And then Cara reached into her purse and pulled out the postcard. She handed it to the older woman.

"She had tried to call me that morning," Cara explained, "but I wasn't there. I called her back when I got the message, but it went straight to her voice mail."

Gabe stifled a twinge at the mention of Hope's voice mail. He'd checked it periodically, hoping to find something, anything, that would help, until the number was finally unavailable. Cara, he'd found, had called many times. He'd wondered if she did it just to hear her friend's voice on the cheery greeting. He'd found it nearly unbearable, after a while, but Cara had kept on.

Miriam read the message on the card and smiled. "It's very much Hope, isn't it?"

"Yes."

The woman looked at the card a moment longer, then her brows furrowed. "But if you had this, then you knew she'd been here at least once."

She'd been quick to pick up on that, Gabe thought.

"That's just it. I didn't have it," Cara said. "It was just delivered to me yesterday."

"Yesterday?"

Miriam looked at the card again to confirm the date on the postmark, just as he had done, as Hope's parents had done, as Cara herself had no doubt done.

"It came sealed in an envelope from the post office, with a letter of apology. I had moved, and somehow the forwarding order didn't work on everything, and only when I moved again and put in a second one, did this catch up with me."

Miriam's eyes widened as she looked up from the card to Cara. "So you've heard nothing for all those years, and then out of the blue this arrives?"

Cara nodded.

"That must have stopped your heart for a moment," Miriam said, reaching out to put a hand over Cara's where it rested on the granite countertop. The gesture was simple, comforting, and gave Gabe a clue to what Hope had found here with this kind, intelligent woman.

"And as for you," Miriam said, looking at Gabe thoughtfully, "I'd wager you're not at all sure how to feel."

"I haven't been," Gabe admitted, unable to dissemble at the moment, "for eight years."

Miriam shook her head. "This is a fresh shock for me, since I've just learned of it. But after all those years, you must have assumed she was dead."

"Eventually, it seemed the only conclusion, yes," Cara said, flicking a glance at Gabe.

Miriam looked at the card once more. "I don't understand. If she was here that day, why didn't she come to see me?"

"You weren't expecting her?" Gabe asked.

"No, but she often liked to surprise me and just pop in."

"That's quite a drive, if you happened not to be home."

"But I'm always home. Or not far away," she said. "I traveled the world for too many years, doing research, searching out new settings for books." A flicker of sadness crossed her face, and Gabe wondered what she had to regret about a life that many would covet. "I swore that someday I would settle in and stay put, and when I came here I did that. Hope knew that."

The woman's expression of sadness deepened then, she blinked rapidly for a moment, and Gabe guessed the reality of the news they'd brought was at last setting in.

"I shall miss her, tremendously. I never forgot her, even after all this time. I should have known she wouldn't simply forsake our relationship without a word like that."

"I'm sorry," Cara said, leaning forward and putting her hand over Miriam's in turn. "And thank you for being her…mentor."

"Mentor? I suppose I was. But she was just as important to me." Miriam looked at them both as if considering whether to go on. "I lost my only daughter to cancer twenty years ago. She was only sixteen. It destroyed my family. My husband left soon after. Hope…eased that pain. She was like Lorna in many ways, bright, beautiful…."

"I'm sorry," Gabe said.

A thud cut off whatever Miriam had been about to reply. The sound made them all turn toward the back door that had just slammed open against the wall.

Gabe sensed rather than saw Cara tense.

It was the woman with the braid who had tried to break into his car.

And she was glaring at them.

Chapter 12

"Ah, there you are," Miriam said. "This is Crystal Lowden. She helps out around here, with the house and the garden."

The young woman continued to glare at both her and Gabe. Angry, she thought. This was a very angry person.

"Come in," Miriam said. "Meet Cara Thorpe and Gabriel Taggert. My friend Hope's best friend and husband, respectively."

So she'd known Hope, Cara gathered from the form of the introduction. If she was right about her age, she would have been about sixteen when Hope was last here. She could—

"*That* one? Thought that was over and done," the girl said sharply, cutting off her speculation.

"Manners, Crystal," Miriam said without heat. "They're guests."

"Guests?" Crystal nearly snarled the words. "They staying?"

"We hadn't quite gotten to that point," Miriam said, apparently oblivious to the rudeness, "although I was about to make the offer, since it's getting late to be just starting the drive down the mountain."

She turned back to them. "Will you stay? I would love the chance to talk with you more, about Hope."

"We couldn't inconvenience you like that."

Cara's response was automatic and polite, but the moment she said it she sensed Gabe tense, and wondered if he wished she hadn't made it. Fortunately, Miriam didn't take the refusal easily.

"My dear, if you'll recall, this used to be an inn. Two people are not an imposition. Besides—" she lifted a hand to her eyes, wiped at them "—I've only just learned Hope is gone. I'd like to talk to the people closest to her."

"And I'd like to get to know you," Gabe said. Cara flicked a glance at him, wondering if he was silently adding *because I should have known all along*.

It wouldn't surprise her. He seemed determined to take so much of the blame on himself for Hope's disappearance, even for the state of their marriage before she'd gone. Maybe this would help him to learn more about the reason she'd left home that day, to know for sure that she hadn't intended never to return.

"Then it's settled," Miriam said, clearly genuinely pleased. "Crystal, will you get the blue and green rooms ready?" She looked back at them, ignoring the near-growl that emitted from the young woman's mouth. "Although if you prefer, you could have two of the cottages. Most I'm afraid I've taken over for storage, but there are a couple I keep clear for guests."

"Whatever works best for you," Cara said, and felt Gabe relax as he saw she wasn't going to resist staying here. She glanced up at his face, and saw something there that told her there was more to this than simply wanting to get to know someone who had clearly been important to Hope.

Her gaze flicked to Crystal, who looked mutinous as Miriam reconfirmed her first request.

"Those rooms, then, Crystal. Thank you, dear."

Miriam was as polite as the younger woman was rude. Crystal fiddled with something in the pocket of the denim bib overalls, what looked like the handles of a pair of garden clippers. For a moment Cara wondered if she'd refuse the request. But finally and without another word the woman turned and stalked out a different door, slamming it behind her even more loudly than she'd shoved the exterior door open. Cara couldn't help the expression of puzzlement that crossed her face.

"Don't mind her," Miriam said. "Crystal has had a very rough life, for all her youth."

"And how much of that has she brought on herself?" Gabe asked wryly as another slam echoed from somewhere else in the house.

Cara wondered if Miriam would take offense at the question she, too, had been thinking, but only he had the nerve to voice. The woman's smile told them she wasn't as unaware as she'd seemed.

"A lot," Miriam admitted. "She has a very difficult time trusting anyone or anything. I don't know her whole story, but what I do know is frighteningly ugly."

"We saw her, in town," Cara began.

Miriam sighed. "And heard about her, I'm sure."

"Yes," Gabe said.

"I know the reputation she has. And that most of Pine Lake thinks I'm crazy for letting her stay here."

Concern for this woman who apparently lived alone and had been important to Hope filled Cara. Did she really know Crystal's reputation, and choose to ignore it? Had the woman in the gift shop been right about Crystal's stealing?

"We saw her trying to get into Gabe's car," she said.

"Oh, no. She didn't take anything, did she?"

"She didn't actually get in," Gabe said.

Miriam frowned. "I'm very sorry. I thought she'd finally broken that habit."

"She has a habit of breaking into cars?" Gabe asked. His tone was mild, but Cara sensed he was suddenly fully alert. And she had a feeling it had little to do with the actual threat to his expensive car.

"No, but of trying. She used to survive on the streets that way, finding unlocked cars, pilfering small things she could use or sell for cash for food. But she doesn't take anything, not anymore. At least, she hasn't. I think she does it now just to…keep her skills sharp."

"Keep her skills sharp," Cara echoed, a little incredulous at the analogy.

Miriam nodded. "Some lessons, especially painful early ones, can't be unlearned. She expects to be back on the street at any moment. Even though she's been welcome here with me since she was sixteen."

Cara felt Gabe's tension go up another notch. She thought she knew why, certain he'd done the same math she had. Then he spoke softly and she knew she'd been right.

"While Hope was still coming here."

"Why, yes, they did meet, but only two or three times." Miriam smiled ruefully. "And Hope thought I was as crazy as you do, taking her on."

"You have a generous spirit," Cara said, all the while trying to figure out what this might mean in light of why they were here.

"Perhaps. My son says I'm trying to make up for losing Lorna by taking in strays."

Cara wasn't sure she didn't agree with that assessment. "Your son?"

"Lawrence. He lives down in San Bernardino." She shook her head. "He never understood my moving, either. That I wanted to get away from the place where Lorna had grown up. He got very upset when I mentioned selling the house, so I gave it to him when I moved up here."

"He and his sister were close?" Cara asked.

"Very." Her face changed then, took on an expression of sorrow so deep, so harsh, that for a moment she looked like a different woman, much older, much more worn and tired. "They were twins. Even though they obviously weren't identical, he was never the same after she died."

"Some wounds never really heal," Gabe said. "Nor should they."

A shiver went through Cara as she heard him speak in a quiet, soothing voice she hadn't heard since the time he'd comforted her when her favorite aunt had died the year before he and Hope had gotten married. It reminded her forcefully that there was another side to this man than the coolly analytical side, a side he didn't often show, but when he did, the effect was remarkable. There was something about such a strong man who could be so gentle that was incredibly moving.

She should have kept in touch after Hope disappeared, no matter what, she thought again. Neither of them should have had to go through that process alone, not when Hope was so dear to both of them. But her feelings for him had kept her from doing so, and she supposed she would always regret that.

Miriam was looking at Gabe with a new respect. "Thank you. You're exactly right. Some wounds shouldn't heal, not completely. What would it say about my love for my daughter if I simply got over losing her?"

Cara had never thought about it in quite that way, but she certainly couldn't argue the point.

"Now," Miriam said briskly, "you're welcome to dinner, but I tend to eat late. I usually don't even think about it, I'm afraid, until it's dark and I lose the light. Since sunset's at sevenish this time of year, it's usually eight or nine by the time I get around to actually eating."

Cara glanced at her watch. It was just after six, which startled her. The nearly four hours they'd been here had flown, it seemed.

"We actually just had a late lunch at about three," she told Miriam.

"Then nine should be about right for you," Miriam said, refusing to take the explanation as a decline of her offer. She seemed genuinely pleased at the prospect of their company. Cara looked at Gabe, who gave the slightest nod of his head; he wanted to stay. She understood. Of course he wanted to talk to this woman who, unbeknownst to him, had clearly been a big part of Hope's life.

"I warn you, however," Miriam added with a smile, "if you

want a decent meal you'll have to pitch in. I tend to throw together what's handy and quick."

Cara smiled. "I'll be happy to help."

"Why don't we go to the market and pick up some things?" Gabe suggested. "And we'll cook *you* dinner."

Miriam's smile became a grin. "And he cooks, too?"

Gabe shrugged, but Cara saw one corner of his mouth lift. "I've been known to, on occasion."

"I suppose it's rude to have your guests cook for you, but the thought of eating something I didn't have to fix myself and that didn't come out of a drive-through bag is far too tempting."

Cara grinned back at her. She *liked* this woman, and would have even if not for the connection to Hope. "It's not rude at all," she said. "We're taking up your time and space, it's only fair."

Miriam shook her head. "You're Hope's people. It's no trouble."

Cara noticed Gabe checking his car out before they got into it to head to the small grocery that Miriam had warned them closed at eight.

"Thinking Crystal was busy again?"

"Just checking," he said.

"Maybe the sight of this car was just too much temptation. I'd guess this would be a lush target, back in the days Miriam spoke of."

"Could be," he agreed.

"Which would mean," Cara said once they'd started down the narrow lane back to the main—which meant two narrow lanes—highway into town, "that it has nothing to do with why we're here."

"Not everything has to," he admitted. "That's the problem when you're so focused on a mission, you have to fight the tendency to assume everything that happens is somehow connected to it."

A mission. Cara pondered his choice of words. A holdover from his training, she supposed. Although she couldn't deny that the words fit; wasn't that exactly what they were on?

"What you said before, about some wounds shouldn't ever completely heal," she began.

Gabe glanced at her, but only for an instant; the narrow winding road required his attention. "What about it?"

"I never thought of it that way," she said. "It's sad, but kind of…welcome at the same time. Sad to think you'll carry it forever, but welcome because it means you'll never forget someone who should never be forgotten."

"Exactly."

"That's…very wise. Hard, but wise."

That earned her another glance. "Wisdom doesn't generally come easy."

"No. No, it doesn't."

She didn't tell him he'd surprised her with it. It was hardly flattering to know someone is surprised that one had such depths. But she had been, and she supposed that said more about her than him. She thought back to the days when she'd been in the throes of her crush on him, the days when she had suffered through feeling like that fifth wheel—not through anything he or Hope had said or done, but through her own insecurities—just to be around him. She remembered how she had surreptitiously watched him as much as possible, learning by heart the way his mouth quirked when he was mildly amused, the way his eyes crinkled when he smiled, the way he tilted his head slightly when he was curious or intrigued.

That last thought made her breath catch.

She couldn't help looking at him full on then, thankful the steep, curving road kept him focused on driving.

He had, she had just suddenly realized, been looking at her that way all day long.

Chapter 13

They'd gone into the market without a real plan, but after discovering that the little market had an actual butcher—a man they chuckled to find was the brother of Anson Woodruff and as opposite the voluble postmaster as it was possible to get, communicating mostly with grunts and hand gestures—they'd come out with a paper-wrapped stack of thick, wonderful-looking steaks.

Local grown, they'd managed to pry out of the taciturn Woodruff brother. Guaranteed.

"I wonder if he's like that because he was never able to get a word in edgewise around his brother?" Cara had said as they returned to the car.

Gabe had laughed out loud at the image that was summoned up in his mind. And realized, not for the first time, that despite the relative grimness of their task here, he'd laughed more today than he had in some time.

And he had the sudden thought that this, all of it, the drive here, the search, everything, would have been much, much grimmer had he not had Cara to share it with. He would have done it, certainly, there had been no choice about that, but the entire expedition would have been one of silent, enduring determination without her.

Distraction, he told himself as he put the dish now holding the steaks in the big fridge. That was the key, distraction.

They'd purchased a marinade Cara had recommended, and after testing the artfully combined flavors with a finger dipped in the blend, he'd seen why. The meat had a couple of hours to nicely soak up those flavors.

He'd liked the way she'd teased him about the manly art of grilling, seemingly quite happy to turn that part of the prep over to him when the time came. While she'd prepared greens for a salad he'd chopped an onion, and when she'd remarked on his technique—he'd gone to a cooking class with Hope once, in an effort to spend more time with her when he was ashore—he didn't even feel the pang he usually did when he thought of those times.

Yes, she was the perfect distraction, he thought again. Not someone brand-new that you felt awkward around, which would have only added to the stress, but at the same time, so much time had passed since they'd seen each other that there was plenty to talk about. That's all it was.

Be glad of the diversion and quit trying to analyze it, he told himself.

They'd brought in the personal necessities they'd bought at the near-miraculous general store, and Miriam, after declaring the steaks to be perfect, had shown them upstairs to two adjacent rooms.

The minute the doors swung open Gabe saw why they'd been named the green and blue rooms; they were identical in furnishings except for those colors. Miriam showed them the bathroom in between the two rooms, with access from both sides, and in the surprisingly spacious room the two colors collided in a cool blend of jewel tones.

"It's our family suite, so to speak," Miriam said with her charming laugh. "The most practical to keep available all the time."

"Efficient," Gabe noted.

"As is Crystal," Miriam said as if in further defense of her choice to keep the young woman around, indicating the tidiness and readiness of the rooms, "when she wants to be."

"It's good of you, to help her like this," Cara said.

"She earns her keep, contrary to appearances. And considering the life she's had, a runaway from an abusive home at fourteen, finding even worse on the streets for two years, being kidnapped, assaulted and dumped up here in the dead of winter, it's amazing she functions at all."

Gabe felt a spark of remorse at his reaction to Crystal. But at the same time, his suspicions sharpened; with that kind of history....

"I'll leave you to get settled in," Miriam said. "I hope you don't mind sharing the bathroom."

"Of course not," Cara said.

Gabe thanked Miriam, all the while keeping Cara in his peripheral vision. If she was actually bothered at the idea of sharing the bathroom they were standing in, it didn't show. She simply set down the toothbrush and small tube of toothpaste she'd purchased, then turned to look at him.

"Color preference?" she asked with a smile. "Or shall I just assume you want blue, for the sea?"

What I want would shock you, Cara Thorpe.

The words echoed in his head, and for a moment he held his breath, afraid he'd unknowingly spoken them aloud, so suddenly had they come upon him. As had the sudden vision of the different conversation they might be having if there weren't two rooms at the ready. The different conversation they might be having if the rest of the vivid images that had disquietingly popped into his head were more that just imagination.

Talk about shock. What the hell was he thinking? This was Cara.

And Cara was standing there looking at him, puzzlement beginning to show in her face as he didn't answer what must seem to her a simple question.

He quashed the unexpected, unwanted, and unwelcome—it

was all that, wasn't it?—response and reached for the cover of long-ago training in keeping his thoughts hidden. He leaned against the doorjamb and looked at her, noting he was managing to smile pleasantly.

"There are places," he said, "where the sea is as green as that wall is."

The smile she gave back, one of warmth mixed with appreciation and what seemed to be a touch of longing, blasted his attempt at cool nonchalance to bits. "And you've seen them all, haven't you?"

"Not all," he said, having to work to hide the sudden quickness of his breath as his usually steady, unflappable pulse took a leap. "Many."

"I'd like to hear about them, someday."

"I'd like to tell you about them. Someday."

And to his surprise, he meant it. He meant it, because he knew that in Cara he would have a listener who truly wanted to hear the tales, not one who would hear them grudgingly, resenting even as he spoke that those places he talked of had kept them apart.

Initially, he thought, it had been flattering that Hope had missed him so much. But what had been attractive in the beginning had eventually begun to wear him down; the constant feeling of guilt at abandoning her had gnawed at him relentlessly.

Hope just didn't have the resources to deal with being alone.

Cara's observation, and that she'd made it at all, had surprised him. As so many things had surprised him since Cara had reappeared in his life.

This afternoon.

That realization stunned him. Had it really only been a few hours? It seemed much longer. As if they'd picked up where they'd left off.

Well, not exactly, Gabe muttered inwardly. *You never had thoughts about her like you just had before.*

"The blue will be fine," he said abruptly, before any of those thoughts and vivid images could creep in and take hold again.

He turned as if to go toward the room he'd chosen, but stopped when Cara put a hand softly on his arm. He looked back at her.

"Thank you, Gabe."

His head drew back a little in surprise. "For what?"

"For being willing to do this. To go through this. For not just wanting to…ignore that card, when that would have been the easier thing to do."

He looked down into those vivid blue eyes. Saw the warmth and emotion there. His gut knotted up all over again, but this time for entirely different reasons.

"Easier, perhaps," he said, aware his voice sounded a bit rough, but unable to help it, "but at the same time, impossible."

"Yes. Impossible."

For a moment she just looked at him, and then an almost inaudible sigh escaped her. It was a tiny sound filled with so much remembered pain. With a sudden awareness that they were two people who had suffered a huge, mutual loss, he found himself doing what he hadn't done all those years ago, hadn't been able to do because he was so curled in on himself, smothered in pain and confusion and guilt.

He put his arms around Cara and pulled her into a gentle hug.

"If the answer's here, we'll find it, Cara," he said.

She had gone very still at his embrace, but when he spoke she relaxed, leaned against him, into him, taking the comfort he'd belatedly offered. The shared contact, the warmth, eased the old pain even more, and Gabe wondered that he hadn't realized it would do that.

"I should be thanking you," he said, lifting her chin up with a gentle finger. "For still caring so much after all this time."

"It could have been twice as long," she said. "It wouldn't make any difference."

He knew, saw in her eyes, that it was true. Cara Thorpe was loyal to the bone, and mere time could never change that.

He didn't even realize what he was doing until his lips brushed hers. It hadn't been a conscious decision, couldn't have been, for it was one he never would have made. But she was there, so close, looking up at him with that unwavering steadiness he realized he should have appreciated more, would have appreciated more had he known how important it was, back then.

And the next thing he knew, he'd done it. He'd kissed her.

And he couldn't regret it. Even when she backed away, startled, mumbled something about freshening up for dinner, and darted into the green room, closing the door behind her.

He stood there for a long moment. It hadn't really been a kiss, he told himself. Not really. Not a serious one. It had been more in the nature of a thank you, just a bit stronger than words. That's all.

She wasn't perfect. And what happened to her doesn't make her perfect.

He wasn't sure why Cara's words about Hope hit him just then, but they rang in his mind as if she'd still been standing here and had spoken them again.

"So we agree she wasn't perfect," he muttered as he turned and retreated to the blue room Cara had chosen for him. "That doesn't mean we give up trying to find out what happened."

He gave a sharp nod to the empty room, as if for emphasis. And ruefully recognized the voice in the back of his head saying, *That doesn't mean carte blanche for you to get crazy over Cara Thorpe, either, buddy.*

No, he thought, it doesn't.

But the acknowledgment didn't tell him how to deal with the unwelcome fact that Cara Thorpe had somehow stirred the first real interest he'd felt in a woman in longer than he cared to admit.

Thanks.

That's all it was, all it had been, no question. Just thanks, right? Hadn't he said as much? Hadn't that just been a hug shared between two friends who'd lost someone very special in their lives? And that kiss, it hadn't really been a kiss, not a romantic one, but just…something that meant more than words?

Hadn't it all, as always, been about Hope?

If there's no question, why are you asking so many? Cara wondered in rueful silence.

"Because he just blew you out of the proverbial water," she answered aloud, needing to hear the words, needing the sound to emphasize the absurdity of her own reaction to the barest brush of his lips over hers.

It was in thanks, nothing more, get that through your head, she ordered.

She busied herself with setting out the other things she'd bought, a large T-shirt to sleep in and a tiny bottle of soap to wash her underwear for the morning, checking her makeup, what little she wore, and, to her embarrassment, pulling, out of her hair a pine needle she'd obviously picked up somewhere.

She pulled her purse across the top of the dresser, and dug into it to bring out the folding hairbrush she carried. She used it thoroughly, in case there were more needles she couldn't see. The tree in front of the library building, she guessed, vaguely remembering a branch brushing her head.

She was this gorgeous, totally hot woman....

Greg's words came back to her now, doing more to clear her head of any silly ideas that that brief, startling kiss had brought on than any self-lecture had. For on some level she suspected the truth was that that hug, that kiss, had been more than just thanks.

It had been a way for Gabe to feel close to Hope again.

She stopped brushing. And for a moment she just looked at her reflection in the mirror. Yes, she looked better these days. More than acceptable.

But she was no Hope Taggert. She never would be.

And that, she told herself, was something she would do well to remember.

Chapter 14

For all his traveling the world, Gabe wasn't used to waking up in strange places.

In the service, his tidy, utilitarian quarters aboard ship had been his home away from home. Now he woke up inevitably in one of only two places, either his somewhat Spartan, if spacious apartment near the marina, or more often since she'd been launched, the new Redstone flagship.

He'd laughed at himself when he'd had to admit, after some good-natured teasing from the crew, that he was spending more time there than at home. He'd told himself the understated but definite luxury of the boat had lured him into the soft life, then had smiled because he didn't regret it.

But he knew it was simply being back on the water that had lured him. It was, he knew, in his blood, and likely would always be. And he would be forever thankful to Josh for giving him a chance to put the sea beneath him again, for as long as he wanted; he still oversaw the marine division of Redstone, but Josh was more than happy to let him do it from the bridge of the sleek, subtly elegant boat.

But when he woke up this morning, it wasn't simply the unfamiliar surroundings that disconcerted him. It wasn't even that the startling sound of a neighboring rooster had acted as an alarm clock.

It was the dream that rooster's raucous call had jolted him out of.

"Hope," he whispered.

Unlike so many mornings after her disappearance, he didn't say it with sadness, longing, or grief. Because this time, his dream had been different. This time, he'd dreamed of rising this morning, going downstairs to Miriam's cheerful kitchen, and finding his wife sitting there, alive, well, and none too happy to see him.

"Can't you take a hint, Gabe?" she'd asked, not bothering with a greeting first. "If I'd wanted you to find me, I would have left a trail."

He sat up, running a hand through his hair, then rubbing at his eyes. He hadn't slept well anyway, and this was just the capper. It was early, not even six, but he knew there was little chance he would go back to sleep, not now.

It wasn't the first time he'd dreamed of finding Hope. It wasn't even the first time he'd dreamed of finding her and discovering she'd walked away intentionally, without a qualm, wanting simply to be rid of him.

But it was the first time he'd dreamed it with the annoyingly tempting Cara Thorpe in the next room.

Tempting? Cara Thorpe?

The words seemed to glow in his mind as he swung out of the bed he'd had to sleep diagonally on; a double bed just wasn't enough for his height.

He rubbed his stubbled jaw as he headed for the bathroom. And stopped dead as he realized he'd been about to walk, buck naked, into a bathroom he was supposed to be sharing with that same, tempting, Cara Thorpe.

He fought down the images that thought brought on. Retreated and grabbed his jeans, yanking them on with little heed for other things that had risen at that thought. If it took a little pain to get himself back in line, so be it.

The bathroom was empty. The door to Cara's room was closed, and he walked over to click the lock so she wouldn't walk in on him the way he would have.

But she probably doesn't sleep naked, he thought.

And groaned as he had to start the quashing procedure all over again. And ordered himself not to speculate exactly what Cara slept in. Or not.

When he finally got around to standing in front of the mirror with the disposable razor and the small can of shaving cream he'd purchased, he thought he was back under control. They would talk to Miriam again today, he thought as he started to shave, and he would probe a little more into the irascible and more than a little suspicious Crystal. Despite Miriam's assurances, her attitude, apparent history, and the fact that she and Hope had been here at the same time was enough to put her on his list of inquiries.

It occurred to him suddenly that this was an area where St. John might be of help.

He finished quickly, toweled off the remaining specks of the shaving cream, checked for spots he'd missed and found none. Then he went back into the cool, blue room and picked up his cell phone. It was early, but everyone at Redstone knew that whatever hour you called, chances were St. John would be there. It was part of the legend that had built up around Josh's mysterious right-hand man.

And in fact, the man answered in the middle of the second ring. With Gabe's name, gleaned obviously from the caller ID.

"Taggert."

"Yes," Gabe confirmed, probably unnecessarily; the guy no doubt recognized his voice already. He paused for a split second, then remembered whom he was talking to and got right to business. "I need someone checked out."

"Go."

He gave what little information he had. "I don't know if that's her real name, or exactly how old she is, but she may have a criminal record. Car burglaries or the like."

"Description?"

St. John certainly hadn't become loquacious overnight, Gabe noted with a quirk of his mouth. He recited Crystal's hair color, height, and approximate age and weight, but ran into a problem when St. John wanted eye color and any identifying scars or marks. He'd been too focused on the young woman's attitude and obvious anger to notice.

Gabe heard a sound in the bathroom; Cara was apparently up. He hoped he hadn't disturbed her at this early hour. But then it struck him she might have noticed more than he had about Crystal; women tended to, didn't they?

He walked over and tapped on the bathroom door. There was a moment of silence before she called out an answer to the knock. She didn't open the door, and the question of exactly what stage of indecency she might be in battered at him anew.

"I'm talking to St. John," he said through the door. "He's going to check out Crystal, but he needs more description than I can give him. I thought maybe you noticed something I didn't. Like her eye color, at least."

"Oh." He heard some rustling, and then the door opened. "Brown," she said. "Very dark brown."

He realized now he'd seen her nightwear. He'd thought she purchased the souvenir T-shirt to wear today, but apparently she'd slept in it. The image emblazoned across the chest was actually of the lake a few miles away, but declared the village of Pine Lake the Gateway to Fun. The fact that the image also rested directly atop Cara's nicely rounded breasts didn't escape him.

He hadn't intended to but he handed her his cell phone. He didn't trust himself to say another word at the moment, not when his mind had just connected Cara's breasts with the words *"Gateway to Fun."*

She looked startled, but accepted the phone.

"Mr. St. John?"

It only took a moment for her to fall into the rhythm he guessed most people did when talking to the man. In self-defense, he supposed.

"Yes, dark brown." There was a pause just long enough for St. John to say his usual single word. "There was one thing. She had some marks on her left arm. A row of dots. Could have been scars. Like she'd had stitches at some point, or maybe screws holding a break." Another pause. "Yes, we'll try to find out. No, nothing else. Thank—"

Cara stopped mid-phrase.

"You," she finished to the air as she flipped the phone shut and handed it back to him. She lifted a brow at Gabe, the corresponding corner of her mouth quirked upward in an expression of bemusement.

"An experience, isn't it?" Gabe said, well back in hand now.

"One of a kind," Cara agreed.

"If he lives up to even half the reputation he has at Redstone, we'll have her entire history by this afternoon."

She smiled. Then took a step back. "I need to get ready."

It took him a moment to realize she meant he should back up and let her shut the bathroom door again. And he realized with a little jolt he had felt comfortable standing here like this, talking to her in what, to anyone, would seem like very intimate circumstances.

He backed up hastily. The glimpse he caught as she turned and closed the door reminding him of something he'd always known but had forgotten: Cara had legs that went on forever. She was at least six inches taller than the petite Hope had been, but it hadn't been until one day at the beach that he'd realized the difference was practically all in those long legs.

But they'd been skinny then, he thought. Now they were just…luscious.

He groaned inwardly at his own unruly thoughts and turned away.

He sat down on the edge of the bed to pull on his shoes and socks, concentrating as if he were a five-year-old who'd just learned how to do it. As a device to keep his thoughts in control, it didn't work very well. Hope had always said his ability to compartmentalize made her crazy, that she hated that he could just stop thinking about one important thing to focus entirely on another. It was, she admitted, more efficient, but she herself simply couldn't stop worrying about everything at once.

You'd laugh at me now, he said to the image in his mind. And then went still.

He doubted very much Hope would laugh if she knew the reason he was having so much trouble just now. And he wondered, if that dream were to come true and he went downstairs to find her alive and well in Miriam's kitchen, how would he feel?

He'd always assumed his life would right itself, instantly and automatically, the way a Coast Guard motor lifeboat did when capsized by heavy surf.

Now he wasn't so sure. *Especially* now.

Because if they found Hope, then what he'd been thinking and feeling about Cara Thorpe were completely out of line. And that the idea of Cara simply dropping out of his life again bothered him a great deal more than it should only emphasized that he was in water that was deeper than he'd realized.

Much deeper.

"Good morning to you both. Did you sleep well?"

The cheerful words of Miriam's greeting matched the sunlit kitchen today. But there was a sadness in her expression that told Cara she hadn't at all forgotten why the husband and best friend of the girl she'd taken under her wing were here.

"Fine," Cara said, noticing that Gabe didn't speak but let her answer stand for them both.

Efficiency again, she told herself, trying to quash the thought that popped into her head, of what it would be like to have first-hand knowledge of exactly how he'd slept.

It was just that moment this morning, when she'd had to open the bathroom door. She'd thought about running into the bedroom and quickly dressing, but from what he'd told her, the mysterious St. John wasn't someone you wanted to keep waiting. So she hadn't, and while Gabe had been scrupulously polite, she'd been very aware she was standing there in nothing but panties and the T-shirt she'd slept in.

And even more aware of the broad expanse of his bare chest, and the pattern of hair she'd never forgotten, tapering downward over his belly in a path she hadn't even known enough to want to follow when she'd first seen it, all those years ago.

She knew enough, now. And the idea took her breath away.

She was sure she'd been imagining, because of her self-consciousness, that his gaze had lingered on her breasts. Then again, he was a man—most definitely—and perhaps unable not to notice. It wasn't specific, it wasn't her....

Satisfied that she'd resolved that embarrassment, she gestured at the stack of papers sitting beside Miriam on the kitchen counter. "What's all this?"

"You said at dinner last night you hadn't seen any of Hope's work."

"No," Gabe said, and Cara heard the edge that came into his voice whenever this heretofore secret side of his wife's life came up, although it seemed a bit less strident this morning, as if he were gradually adjusting to the idea. As she hoped she herself was. They had talked at length last night about Hope's hidden—from them, at least—interest, and had found themselves fascinated by Miriam's stories of her career. If it were true Hope had harbored such a dream, it was easy to see why she would have been drawn to this woman.

Miriam gave Gabe a curious look. "She must have kept copies of her work at home, for herself?"

Gabe shook his head. "She had her own laptop. It disappeared when she did. And I...when I was home, computers weren't what I was home for."

"I see," Miriam said. "In that case."

She nudged the stack of printed pages toward them. The obvious indication that these were Hope's writings gave Cara a chill. She gave Gabe a sideways glance. He was staring at the half-inch stack of pages with an odd expression, part anticipation, part apprehension and something else she couldn't name. Considering her own tangled emotions as she looked at those pages, she wasn't surprised he was feeling something similar.

But before either of them could bring themselves to look, there was a bang as the back door slammed open. Crystal again.

"Still here."

It wasn't really a question, and since the answer was so readily apparent, no one, even Miriam, seemed to feel compelled to answer it. Nor did Crystal seem to expect an answer; she just strode through the kitchen toward them.

Cara felt Gabe tense beside her, and wondered what he was thinking. Did he feel the rough-edged, angry young woman was really a threat?

Crystal skirted them almost warily, as if she'd sensed Gabe's sudden alert readiness. Perhaps she had; if she'd lived on the streets as Miriam had said, then she likely had some finely honed survival instincts. And anyone would be well advised to be wary of Gabriel Taggert on alert, Cara thought.

The young woman, wearing worn jeans and a denim jacket over a cropped T-shirt that revealed a rather sloppy circular tattoo of barbed wire around her navel, stopped beside Miriam. She crossed her arms in front of her, in a stance that was almost aggressive. In an odd way, it seemed as if she were putting herself between the woman who had taken her in and these two intruders, as if she felt they were a threat.

Miriam smiled at the angry young woman as if she were a well-behaved, charming daughter.

"Yes, dear?"

"Finished the shed."

"Why, thank you, Crystal."

"Found that broken easel. I'll work on it."

"That would be very helpful." Miriam paused, then gestured at Gabe and Cara. "Isn't there something you'd like to say?"

For an instant surprise registered on Crystal's sharp features. "What?"

"It was thoughtful of them to include you in their dinner plans last night, don't you think?"

They had discussed that when they'd bought the steaks. Cara had finally suggested they buy enough to include Crystal, and if there were leftovers, steak and eggs in the morning was always an option. With a comment about feeding the bears in the woods, Gabe had agreed. Crystal had, in fact, not joined them, but she had taken the extra steak and vanished to wherever it was she holed up.

"Oh."

When nothing else came, Miriam prompted gently. "One usually thanks people for such thoughtfulness."

Crystal flicked a glance at Miriam. Cara watched her expression, looked for anything that indicated emotion behind the stiff facade. She saw nothing—no gentleness, no affection—for this generous woman who had taken her in.

But there was no anger, either, not like the kind she'd seen directed at everyone else. Cara supposed that was something.

But when Crystal looked back at them, the usual resentment was in place as she glowered. "Thanks for the food."

Without another word she turned sharply on the heel of her run-down motorcycle boot and stalked back out the way she'd come in. Miriam didn't comment further on her appearance or manner, so Cara assumed what they'd seen was typical.

Perhaps Gabe was right to be on guard, she thought. That woman could definitely be trouble.

And then, far too belatedly, something struck her. Was Gabe thinking much more specifically than just a general wariness of this woman?

Was he thinking she had something to do with Hope's disappearance?

The possibility that had always and ever hovered, like a threatening thunderstorm, that Hope was not only dead, but had been murdered, slammed into Cara's consciousness with a fierceness that nearly made her gasp. Involuntarily she turned to look at the door Crystal had exited through.

Could she?

No doubt.

Would she?

Maybe.

Had she?

Cara shivered.

And suddenly the pleasant kitchen didn't seem quite so sunny.

Chapter 15

Cara was still shivering in response to her own thoughts about Crystal when, unexpectedly, she felt Gabe's hand at her back, warm, strong, comforting. As if he'd felt her reaction and wanted to ease it. She barely managed not to turn and look at him.

"You take a look at these, and I'll fix us some breakfast. The least I can do after that lovely dinner last night," Miriam said.

Cara took a seat on the same stool she'd used before. Gabe sat beside her, still looking warily at the papers Miriam had printed out, as if they were a coiled snake. Cara understood the feeling, felt more than a little of it herself, but curiosity finally overcame it and she began to read.

The pages contained, as Miriam had told them last night, short character sketches and *slice-of-life* pieces. The images they brought up were vivid, and Hope's charm and liveliness fairly leaped off the page. Cara smiled as from one she recognized Mr. Matton, their mutual sixth grade teacher; the portrait was sharp and funny, and she thought that anyone reading it would understand what it was like to have been in his overbearing grip.

She set the pages she finished in front of Gabe. It took him, she noticed, until the third one to actually pick up the first and start reading. But he did, and she wondered if that meant he'd won the battle with himself, or lost it.

Miriam set plates of eggs and ham before them, then discreetly left them to their task. They ate, but their attention was focused on the papers. It was as if Hope were there with them, so clearly did her personality show in the writing.

"Her parents," Cara murmured as she began the next set of pages. And when she'd finished, she looked up at Hope's husband. "Oh, Gabe, they must see this. It's so full of her love for them."

He took the pages she held out, and this time began reading immediately. She watched him, the memory fresh in her mind of what had been written on the page about the solid, steady pair who had raised and loved their beautiful little girl. She knew where he was in the piece by the way he smiled here and there, knew he'd gotten to the part about their unconditional love by the way he swallowed as if his throat were tight.

"You're right," he said softly when he finished. "They have to see this."

Pleased, she returned to the next in the stack. And then her breath caught as she realized what it was, a paean to Hope's best friend.

Cara felt her insides knot as she read Hope's words. *Cara's my rock. She's always there for me. She doesn't just listen to me, she hears me. She always has.*

She read on until the words blurred, as if the printed ink had smeared.

"Cara?"

Gabe's voice was gentle, and she realized that tears were streaming down her face.

He slipped from his seat on the stool beside her and put his arms around her. She leaned into him, heedless of anything except that, at this moment, she needed this comfort so desperately it didn't matter that he was the husband of the very woman who'd brought her to this state.

"I miss her," she choked out. "So much."

"I know," Gabe said softly.

She leaned against him, trying to control her weeping. Finally, she managed to choke back the next sob, then the next.

"I'm sorry. I didn't mean to—"

"Shh. I know."

She lapsed into silence then, her head still pressed against his strong, broad chest. Gradually she became aware of the comforting warmth of him, and that she could hear the solid, steady thud of his heart.

The heart Hope had joked never beat faster than sixty-two beats per minute, no matter the provocation.

"Never?" Cara had asked archly.

Hope had grinned at her, not missing the implication. "Well, there's always one exception to prove the rule."

In that moment Cara had regretted her own teasing. The innuendo was clear, and it had given rise to images in her fevered, infatuated imagination that she would rather not have had. And she'd seen just enough of Gabe, on the occasional trips to the beach where at Hope's insistence she had joined them, to fill in the blanks. Vividly.

Those images flooded her mind now, as clear and vivid as they had been back then. More so, in fact, since at the moment the star of those images had his arms around her. And she'd recently seen that broad, bare chest up close and personal.

The fact that he was trying to comfort her despite emotions of his own that had to be roiling with the discovery of these papers, the fact that he was the husband of the woman who had been her best friend and who had written this glowing testament to that friendship, the fact that they were 'till no closer to knowing what had happened, made her own reluctance to pull away from him seem embarrassingly inappropriate.

He's Hope's, she said silently, then repeated it with more emphasis. It had been the only thing that had worked, back in the days when she'd found herself looking at him with such longing she was terrified it must show. It would work now, she told herself.

Except…she wasn't who she'd been, back in those days.

And Hope isn't here.

The words ringing in her ears as if she'd spoken them, felt like a betrayal, especially coming on the heels of reading the piece that Hope had written about her, about her best friend, the one person she trusted more than anyone in the world and always had.

Fine way to deserve that trust, Cara thought as she pulled out of Gabe's embrace abruptly. He seemed surprised at her sudden movement, but he didn't try to stop her.

She fought to steady herself. "I'm all right. Thank you."

It came out stiffly, formally, as if he'd been a stranger who'd held open a door for her. She tried for a more normal tone. Gestured toward the pages she'd dropped when she'd no longer been able to read through her tears.

"It was just that she wrote this about me and it…."

"Caught you off guard?"

Glad he seemed to have accepted her explanation, she nodded. "I'll…finish that one later." *When I'm alone and can cry my eyes out and not turn to my best friend's husband for comfort.*

"May I read it now?"

Oddly, he sounded as stiff and formal as she had moments ago. She hesitated; Hope's praise—and her prediction of what Cara could become, if only she had more confidence—had been unstinting. Almost embarrassing, because no matter how far she'd come, she couldn't believe she'd come far enough to fulfill Hope's vision. But Gabe already had the pages in his hand, and she didn't feel she had the right to ask him not to read it, even though he'd asked. If anyone had the right to any and everything Hope, it was Gabe.

She gave up on finishing breakfast and pushed the plate out of the way still half-full of food. She had the feeling Miriam would understand.

She looked at the next page, the start of a story of Hope's first hair-raising drive up the mountain, and how she'd gradually become used to the steep, curving roads and come to love the adventure of it enough to seek out other roads to follow, to explore. Cara remembered their own drive up, and Hope's descriptions were so vivid it was like doing it all over again.

Gabe would like that one, she thought as she passed it over to him to read. He was still reading Hope's essay about her. And he was smiling, even nodding slightly. In agreement? she wondered. That thought took her breath away all over again, and she told herself he was simply responding to the fact that the words had been written by Hope.

She stared down at the next page she had, unseeingly, as Gabe continued to read. But after a moment something drew her attention and she focused on the printed words before her.

The next sketch was about Gabe. It was his name that had caught her eye.

She looked away quickly, not sure she wanted to read this. Then back at the page, which began with the words, "Only love can make you so happy and so angry at the same time."

She glanced at the rest of the first page, saw the description of Gabe, the "tall, dark and handsome" cliché plus a string of other descriptors like smart, sexy, brave, and generous. None of which Cara could argue with.

But Hope had also expressed anger here, and hurt, bemoaning his long absences and describing him as stubborn, single-minded, and sometimes thoughtless. Cara couldn't argue with those, either, although she would have amended the last to "belatedly thoughtful" rather than thoughtless; Gabe might be late in understanding sometimes, but once he did, he moved fast to catch up. How often had she envied Hope the way Gabe admitted minor offenses by going overboard to make up for them? How often had she wanted to tell Hope she was a fool, to zero in on such small failings when there was so much more that was positive?

And how was Gabe going to feel to read this?

She gave him a sideways glance. But he wasn't looking at her, he'd finally moved on to the next piece, so she slid the essay about him down to the bottom of the stack. She wouldn't hide it from him, but she could delay it.

When he put down the pages he held, he looked both thought-ful and…weary, Cara realized suddenly. And she realized she, too, was tired, not physically, but in that way that made even the simplest thought difficult.

"I need to clear my head," Gabe said, just as she'd been about to say something very similar.

"Yes," she agreed. "There's been a lot to take in since yesterday."

"I want to go down the mountain a bit. To that gas station we passed."

"You think she might have gone there?"

"It's the only one around, as far as I could tell. Chances are she did at some point."

They explained to Miriam before they left, who, as Cara had expected, understood. "It must be painful to read those. It will be for me, too, now." She shook her head sadly. "The writers I know tend to be introverted, solitary types. Hope was such a breath of fresh air."

Gabe asked about the gas station and Miriam nodded, confirming his guess that it was the only one in or near town.

"I remember at least once Hope saying she needed to fill up before she started home. And Stan's owned that place since it opened." She smiled. "He's also a bit of a harmless flirt, and I can't imagine he wouldn't have flirted with a woman who looked like Hope."

Gabe said nothing to that, merely nodded. Perhaps he'd been used to such things, Cara thought. If you married a woman like Hope, she supposed you would have to be.

By tacit agreement they left their things at the inn, meaning to come back. "I want to finish reading," Cara said as they got into the car, "but it's…too much right now."

"I know," Gabe said. "It's like she was there, in the room, looking over my shoulder."

"Exactly," Cara said, glad she didn't have to explain why she felt she had to take a break.

Gabe fastened his seat belt, and Cara pulled hers out to do the same. As she twisted to do so she saw, just past the corner of the inn, Crystal standing with a man she'd never seen before. As usual, she looked belligerent, while the man looked annoyed.

"It must be awful to wake up like that every day," she said when she saw that Gabe had noticed them as well.

"I'd be careful, if I were him," Gabe said, sounding as if he were only half joking. "She's armed."

Cara blinked, then realized he meant the pair of garden clippers the woman held. As she pointed them at the man in an angry gesture, Cara's own earlier thoughts about Crystal's potential for violence came rushing back to her. But in that instant the woman turned on her heel and stalked away. The man she'd been talking to glanced around, shaking his head as they had more than once after running afoul of Crystal's unpleasant demeanor.

As they left the little town, she tried to remember exactly how far down the gas station was. She remembered noticing it—and the higher prices that no doubt reflected the difficulty of getting the commodity up here—but couldn't recall how much farther it had been before they'd hit the main street of Pine Lake.

"I wonder if he thought Pine Lake would eventually spread this far," Gabe said, as if he'd been thinking similar thoughts.

"Maybe," she said. "Or maybe he picked the spot to serve more than just Pine Lake."

"Could be," Gabe agreed. "There's that place we passed the turnoff to, on the way up here. The one Hope mentioned when she wrote about driving up here."

He spoke evenly, as if he were referring to nothing more than some travel guide. And in the face of the neutral tone, Cara couldn't think of a thing to say.

"I want to check that out," Gabe went on. "She said it was one of the first places she went exploring."

"I wondered about that," Cara said. "If we should go there and do the same thing we did in Pine Lake."

"I think so. It's someplace she actually went, so she might have talked to people there."

"Hope always talked to people," Cara agreed.

"I think we should—"

He stopped suddenly, frowning. His hands shifted on the steering wheel. Tightened around it.

And then he swore, low and harsh under his breath.

"What?" Cara asked, turning in her seat to look at him.

"The power steering just went out."

Cara's eyes widened. She remembered once trying to steer a car with a dead battery down a driveway, how next to impossible it had been to control without the assist of the power steering.

She looked around. Her heart began to hammer in her chest.

They were on a steep, curving mountain road. With drop-offs that took your breath away.

In a car that was going to fight making every turn.

At least he had brakes, Gabe thought as he muscled the vehicle he'd bought as a road car but now couldn't help thinking was a brick with wheels, into the next turn.

The smart thing would be to stop right here and now…except they were on a narrow, blind curve that could get them killed as quickly as going over the edge. And after that came another curve, back in the other direction, this one masked with trees that would make it nearly impossible for a car traveling at normal speed to see them in time to stop or dodge.

The wheel jerked under his hands as they went over an uneven stretch of road. He was aware of Cara's tension, but thankfully she said nothing as he worked to find the balance; the slower they went, the safer, but at the same time the slower they went, the harder the car became to steer.

He considered again simply stopping, but as if in answer a big sedan came ripping up behind them, at what appeared to be a frightening speed now that they'd slowed. It darted around them with horn blaring, cutting it so close Gabe heard Cara smother a gasp. He quickly activated the hazard lights.

Down on the flat, it wouldn't be a problem; the car was hard to steer but not at all impossible. Up here, on a narrow, steep road, control was critical.

He felt the tension building in his shoulders and hoped he was right in his guess that the gas station was close. They rounded two more turns, the usually responsive car protesting every inch of the way.

And then there it was, the brightly colored Plexiglas sign of the station. Gabe let out a compressed breath as he wrested the car off the road, lined it up with the single service bay beside the main building, and finally, gratefully, put full pressure on the brakes.

A man in a surprisingly clean uniform shirt bearing the name "Stan" and a handlebar moustache that Gabe figured he had to have been growing for years was headed toward them before they came to a complete stop.

"Problem?" the man said as Gabe hit the hood release before he opened the door and got out. "She looked like she was turning a little sluggish when you pulled in."

Flirt or not, the man got credit for noticing, Gabe thought. He obviously knew his stuff.

"Power steering went out," Gabe said, walking around to the front of the car and lifting the hood. For a moment what he was seeing didn't register. He blinked, shifted his angle, but that didn't change what he now had to accept. The reservoir that should have been full to the marking on the side was empty.

"That's not good," the moustached man said. "Nice car like this, too." There was a hint of censure in his voice, as if he suspected Gabe wasn't worthy of driving it.

"What is it?"

Cara had walked to the front of the car to join them. Stan looked up from the engine compartment, and at his first glimpse of Cara, a wide smile appeared below the carefully cultivated moustache.

"Well, now," he said.

Gabe hid his annoyance; he couldn't blame the guy, after all. "Power steering fluid's gone," he said in answer to her question. "And it was fine on Sunday. I check fluids every week," he added pointedly, with a sideways look at Stan. It didn't matter, the man was so intent on Cara that Gabe doubted he heard a word.

After a brief hello, and a smile that made Stan's widen, Cara leaned to look into the engine compartment. She quickly found the plastic reservoir, he noticed, and frowned as he had when she saw it was empty.

"Isn't that…unusual?" she asked.

"Very," piped up Stan.

Something caught Gabe's eye, made his gaze narrow. Something glistening, wet where there shouldn't be any wetness; the road had been dry all the way. He backed up and dropped to the ground, scooting underneath the car to search for further sign of the gleam he'd seen.

He didn't have to look far. Something had sprayed all over the underside of the engine compartment. He reached up, ran a finger over the nearest piece of sheet metal, collecting some of the liquid. He already knew, but seeing the reddish cast of the fluid confirmed it.

"Flashlight," he said, a little sharply as something else caught his attention. "In the glove box."

He heard somebody move, then Cara's slim arm stuck the small light within his reach.

"Thanks," he said as he twisted it on. He looked, touched, and clenched his jaw.

He worked his way out from under, handed the flashlight to Stan. Something in his expression must have gotten through to the man, because he quit flirting with Cara and without another word duplicated Gabe's actions and got under the car.

When he came out, he looked as grim as Gabe was feeling.

"No doubt?" Gabe asked, looking at Stan.

"No doubt," the man said flatly.

"What is it?" Cara asked, looking only at Gabe. He hesitated, but then gave her the truth.

"The line was cut."

Chapter 16

"St. John says her real name is Linda Sparks. She's twenty-four. The story's pretty much as Miriam told us."

"Grim," Cara said.

"Yes," Gabe agreed.

But the grimness of the young woman's story didn't change one simple fact. Less than fifteen minutes after they'd seen her with garden clippers in her hand, they came near to having what could have been fatal trouble on a steep mountain road because of a cut fluid line.

The sheriff's deputy who had come out to look agreed with them that the line appeared to have been cut. He also, as Gabe had expected, said just seeing Crystal—or Linda—with a pair of garden clippers wasn't enough evidence. Not, he admitted, that he'd be surprised; he'd had a run-in or two with the woman himself. He'd look into it, he promised, and file the report, but he couldn't promise them any action in a hurry. They were still on their own, and Gabe wasn't sure he wasn't happier with it that way.

He'd gotten the call about Crystal from St. John, who'd given the information in his usual manner while Stan had been working on the car. Replacing the entire line was far more complicated than a simple fix, Gabe thought, but he didn't want to take any chances with a temporary repair not holding, not on these roads. And Stan seemed efficient and knowledgeable enough, once he'd stopped flirting with Cara.

Gabe looked over at her, sitting on the bench outside the gas station office. The sun had come out, and she'd turned her face upward as if welcoming the warmth in the brisk mountain air. She'd closed her eyes, so he felt he could look his fill.

The sunlight washed over her, and coppery sparks glinted in her hair. Now, in profile, he could see the slight upward tilt of her nose, the long sweep of her lashes, the set of the chin he'd thought of back then as so determined for such a quiet girl.

So different from Hope, he thought, but in a subtle, restrained way and now just as attractive. Hope had been right about that.

Gabe heard the clank of metal on metal. Stan muttered something from under the car, but kept working.

Stan had remembered Hope, of course. *Gorgeous little blonde,* he'd said. *A real charmer.*

All of which was true. Unfortunately, that's about all Stan remembered. She'd been in a couple of times for gas, and Stan, gentleman that he was, had waived the self-serve policy to fill the tank himself.

No sense a pretty girl like that smelling of gasoline, he'd said.

The one useful thing he'd been able to tell them was that Hope had asked about Morton's Corner, the place he and Cara had just been talking about.

"Told her there was nothing there but a little general store and a tavern, but she wanted to go," Stan had said, shaking his head. "Said she was exploring."

Another mutter came from under the car now, but Gabe saw that he had the old line out and was starting to put in the replacement. Gabe was grateful that Stan's repair bay was well stocked, and even if it wasn't a dealer-supplied part, he'd had something that would fit.

And next time he parked the car, even at a seemingly safe place like Miriam's, he'd set the car alarm no matter how much the thing irritated him when it went off. Not that it would help if the tampering was confined to the exterior; because the alarm annoyed him, he'd had the dealer set the sensitivity very low.

"Do you think she did it?"

Cara's words startled him; he'd thought she was just soaking up the sun. He should have realized she'd never stopped thinking. This was Cara, after all.

"I don't know."

That her mind had gone the same direction his had didn't surprise him. They'd been in synch on so much of this. She opened her eyes and turned to look at him then.

"What now?" she asked.

He'd been thinking about that. "I think when Stan's finished, we continue over to Morton's Corner." He gave her a sideways look. "And we take our time about it."

It didn't take her long. "And then, when it's been long enough that…whoever did this thinks they succeeded, we go back to Miriam's?"

He nodded, pleased but not surprised at her quickness. "And watch for reaction from Ms. Lowden-Sparks."

Cara nodded. "All right." Then, after a moment, she said with a note of sadness, "If she did do it, it's going to be very painful for Miriam."

"I know." He hesitated, decided it was nothing Cara hadn't already thought of, and added, "And it will be even worse for her if it turns out she had something to do with Hope's disappearance, too."

"She looks familiar," the woman putting boxes of macaroni and cheese on a shelf said as she peered at the photograph Cara held. "But she's not from around here."

"No," Cara agreed. "She would have only been visiting. But she wrote about coming here."

"Don't get many tourists out this far," the woman said. "Almost all of my business is locals, that's the only reason I remember her at all. Sorry I can't be more specific. But eight years ago...."

She left the obvious unspoken. But she was clearly not without sympathy. And, Cara thought as the woman eyed Gabe, appreciation for a fine-looking man.

"You could go talk to Charlie Taylor," she said. "He was the deputy sheriff around here for twenty-five years. He lives just up the hill. Drove all the way down on the flat to the sub-station to work, but said he loved it here too much to move closer. But him being the kind who notices things...."

They found the retired sheriff on his back deck tying fishing flies. He looked younger than Cara had expected, perhaps mid-fifties. He had salt-and-pepper hair cut in a short, brush cut Cara guessed he'd probably worn for decades. But on his upper lip was a moustache that made her wonder if he was competing with Stan for who could grow the longest handlebar.

He wore aviator-style glasses, but behind them his dark eyes were quick and alert as he looked at the photograph. "No, afraid she doesn't look familiar. Not a woman I'd forget, either." His gaze shifted to Gabe and he added in a tone that was more specu-lative than envious, "But if you were married to her, I reckon you're used to hearing that."

"She usually made an impression," Gabe said, apparently taking no offense.

"You say she came up here a lot?"

"To Pine Lake," Cara answered. "We're not sure if she came here more than once. We only know because she mentioned coming here, when she was writing about exploring the area."

"Exploring?"

Gabe began to explain, and Cara looked around. The deck they stood on was large and took advantage of the contour of the mountain to gain a view over an expanse of trees and sky. It must be lovely to just sit out here and soak it in, she thought. There was a fireplace built into one end of the deck that would let you be outside in all but the worst weather, she thought, and that sounded lovely as well. She'd lived as near the water as she could afford most of her life, but she could feel the appeal of this quiet, peaceful place.

"—roads. Happens all the time. Sometimes we never find them."

Cara abruptly tuned back in, feeling she should have been paying more attention.

"Never?" Gabe was asking, and there was an edge in his tone that told her this could be important.

"Sometimes," Taylor repeated sadly. "We'd get calls, about a crash in the night. Sound carries funny up here, echoes off the mountains, and if it's foggy it's even worse. You'd get a half-dozen calls about the sound of a crash, and every one of them would give you a completely different location, each one positive that's where it was. We'd check them all, but sometimes we never found a thing."

Cara stared at him. "You mean there could be people who were never found?"

"Can't say it doesn't happen." he shrugged at what Cara thought was a horrific idea. "More often, there are accidents where people went on their way. We'd find skid marks on the road sometimes, but no sign anybody didn't just drive away under their own power. That's not to say there weren't times we found nothing."

He seemed to realize Cara was aghast, and smiled at her. "Sorry, miss," he said. "It sounds callous, I know, but when you've been at this as long as I was, thirty-five years if you count my time down on the flat, you get to where you can't work up a sweat over things like you used to. Usually means it's time to get out."

"Is that what you did?" she asked.

He nodded. "It's a job where you had to care. I was too close to not being able to."

"Then congratulations on knowing when you had to get out or lose yourself," Gabe said. "It's a tough call."

Cara went quiet, knowing Gabe had spoken out of a fellow feeling Taylor would surely understand. The older man looked at Gabe, and after a moment nodded.

"That it is."

Even Cara could sense the quiet understanding that passed between the two men. Two men who, while wearing different uniforms, had held similar goals; the protection of those they served. Instead of feeling excluded by the masculine camaraderie, she felt uplifted, as if the world could never be a truly out-of-control place with men like this in it to stand against those who favored chaos.

They were back in the car and headed down Charlie's steep hill before Gabe said quietly, "I'd give a lot to know what you've been thinking."

Caught, Cara flushed. "I…it wasn't about this. Looking for Hope, I mean."

"I'd still like to know."

"I…" Lord, she was going to sound so corny. But he'd said it so quietly, so gently, that she couldn't doubt he really meant it. "I was just thinking about you and Deputy Taylor…and others like you. Who take a stand, I mean. You're why the world doesn't just…spin out of control."

Gabe slowed the car at the stop sign marking the intersection with the road that led back to the highway. When they were at a halt, he looked over at her. There was something warm and welcoming in his eyes, and in his voice when he said, simply, "Thank you."

"We—I mean the people you do it for—we don't thank you enough."

"You pay the price," he said, and turned back to his driving.

And Cara knew they were suddenly back to Hope, who, whatever her lack of understanding or appreciation for the bigger picture, had indeed done just that. Isolation and unhappiness had been the two things Hope had been least equipped to handle.

That there had been resources available to her wouldn't have mattered, Cara thought in one of those moments of assessment that made her feel so guilty now that her friend was gone. But she knew it was true; Hope wanted what she wanted, her husband with her, and no amount of assistance in how to cope with his absence would have changed that. In fact, Cara realize now, she probably would have resented it.

"She never should have married you," Cara said, voicing what in her heart she'd known for a very long time. "It wasn't fair to you."

"I can't argue with the first part," Gabe said, that harsh edge creeping back into his voice. He made the turn onto the winding road that had brought them to Charlie's.

"Then don't argue with the second, either. It's true, Gabe. You were honest with her, you told her what it would be like. If she chose to ignore all that, that wasn't your fault."

He glanced at her then, and she saw something in his expression she'd never seen before, a sort of speculation that made her pulse pick up speed.

"What would you have done, Cara? In her place, if you felt the way she had?"

In her place? Where I wanted to be with all my silly, young heart? I wouldn't have felt that way, she thought. *I would have been so proud of you it wouldn't have mattered.*

"I would have been first in line at the fleet counselor's office," Cara said, knowing he was waiting for an answer. Her mouth quirked. "I probably would have had a little trouble with the rank thing spilling over onto the families, but…."

She shrugged. She was afraid to go on, afraid she'd slip and let out how much she had longed for exactly that, to be in Hope's place, how furious she had been with her best friend for how she was reacting, how she'd barely managed to keep from erupting at her more than once, probably doing irrevocable damage to the friendship.

So instead she'd held it in, tried to speak of it only when she thought she could maintain control, and tell Hope she should be thankful, not resentful, that Gabe was the kind of man he was.

"It's a unique world," Gabe admitted as he slowed for a particularly sharp curve in the road. "And sometimes the unwritten rules are more important than the things in the regs. Hope always struggled with that. She hated that she couldn't even go to the doctor without having to give them all my information. Said it made her feel like an appendage, not an individual."

"I know. I heard all about it. I tried to point out they had to keep track of things somehow, but she didn't want to hear that."

Gabe said nothing to that, but Cara thought he was focused on driving at this moment. They were at a place she'd noticed on the way up, where the road nearly doubled back on itself in a rather hair-raising switchback. She remembered being glad then that she hadn't been the one driving. She wasn't particularly afraid of heights, but it was a scary spot.

She thought of what Deputy Taylor had said, and as she looked over the side into thick trees that somewhat masked what she knew had to be a horrendous drop-off, she suppressed a shiver. It would be so easy to go over, and in a little car like Hope's, the trees would just close back up around you, hiding you as surely as if you'd vanished underwater.

And if their own power steering had gone out now....

"That'd be my pick," Gabe said grimly when they were through the turn.

It took her a moment to realize his thoughts had gone in the same direction hers had.

"'Times we found nothing,'" she quoted softly, her throat tight.

Cara said nothing more, because the look on Gabe's face told her he was wrestling with images similar to the ones racing unstoppably through her head, none of them pleasant, some of them horrific.

He didn't speak again until they were at the main road, where the road to Morton's Corner met the highway, at the intersection where Stan's gas station stood.

"I need to make a call," he said, and turned once more into the station and parked. "I couldn't get a signal up there."

Stan again approached immediately, and Gabe quickly assured him things were fine, and thanked him once more for a job well done. Another customer drew the man to the gas pumps—self-serve was apparently open to interpretation for Stan—and left them alone.

Cara wondered if there was someone he wanted to call, after what could have been a narrow escape. Since they had a cell signal here, she would have thought he would have called before, while the car was being worked on, but maybe he had wanted to calm down first.

As *she* should, she told herself, embarrassed at how the idea of him with someone else still had the power to unsettle her. Just because he hadn't remarried after Hope didn't mean he wasn't involved. It might have been awkward, when Hope had never been declared legally dead, and as far as she knew he'd never filed for a divorce on whatever grounds he had, under the circumstances, but what woman wouldn't put up with a few complications for a man like Gabe?

"Do you want privacy?" Cara asked, one hand on the door handle, when he didn't use the hands-free phone system on the Lexus.

Gabe blinked. "What? No. I'm calling St. John." He saw her glance at the controls for the hands-free system. "I only use that when I'm actually driving," he explained. "Feels too weird talking into space if I don't have to."

"Oh. I thought maybe...."

Her voice trailed off. *Now that was awkward,* she thought, and felt her cheeks heat.

"No," he said, in an odd tone that made her wonder just what she'd sounded like. "There's...no one to call. Not like that. I—"

He broke off as the call went through. Cara was grateful for the distraction, wondered if she'd ever stop feeling like a fool in front of this man.

In the brief, succinct manner Cara imagined was typical for anyone talking to St. John, Gabe explained the situation. When he disconnected less than two minutes later, without a goodbye, Cara waited for and got the bemused expression again, the expression she imagined most people wore after a conversation— if you could call it that—with the man.

"He said they've got something that will help," Gabe said as he closed the phone. "He'll get back to me."

"Only he said it in five words or less?" Cara suggested.

Gabe looked at her. One corner of his mouth quirked upward in that lopsided smile she'd always loved.

"'There's something…be in touch,' I think is how it came out," he agreed.

"Amazing," she said as he put the phone away and put his hands back on the wheel.

"Now," he said with a grimness that wiped away the touch of humor, "let's go see if Crystal-Linda is surprised to see us alive."

Chapter 17

Cara didn't question him when he parked out of sight down the road from the inn, in the driveway of a small cabin that looked as if it hadn't been lived in for years. And he didn't bother to explain; it seemed clear she understood he wanted as much of the element of surprise as they could manage, and they had a much better chance of that if no one saw them drive up and stroll through the expansive garden.

She kept up with him as they made their way up the hill, and he noticed he didn't have to shorten his stride much for her to do it.

"There's a gate around on the side there. Looks like it goes through to the back, where the shed is," Cara said as they neared the wood fence that ran along the edge of the old inn property.

"Good idea," he said, and they changed direction.

The gate was a rather elaborate wrought-iron affair Gabe imagined required a bit of upkeep. Upkeep that hadn't been done, he thought, as he noted rusty patches on the bottom crossbar, and one spot where it had rusted completely through.

But his observations of the gate were cut short by the sound of voices. Raised voices. One of them male.

And the other was Crystal's, he was sure of it.

He saw Cara glance at him, but she didn't speak, just waited. He leaned forward to where he could see into the yard behind the old inn. The people talking weren't visible, but the voices seemed to be coming from the vicinity of the garden shed that sat across from the back door Crystal had come through when they were in the kitchen. He couldn't hear the words, just the angry tone.

He reached out to the gate's latch; it lifted easily. He nudged at the gate, testing for noise, but the tiny squeak didn't seem as if it would be audible beyond a few feet. Certainly not as far away as Crystal and her companion were, and not over their raised voices. He pushed it open the rest of the way.

Without comment Cara kept close, understanding the need for silence to get the result they wanted. Keeping to the edge of the path rather than the stepping stones, they made their way along the side of the inn toward the voices. With a quick glance and a nod at each other, they rounded the corner of the building together, then stopped.

It was definitely Crystal. She was up in the face of the man standing opposite her. The same man, Gabe noted, that she'd been arguing with before. And she was furious. So angry her face was distorted with it, red and blotchy. At this moment, there was no doubt in his mind that this woman could do something ugly.

And in that moment she did. She swung the handle of the rake she was holding at the man before her, with clear intent to do, at the least, bodily harm. Gabe heard Cara suck in an audible breath, weighed his options for a split second, decided there really were none, and moved.

In the same moment Cara moved with him, and he said under his breath, "Let me take her."

She didn't argue, apparently seeing the sense in him tackling the woman with the big stick and she the man who, while unknown, would presumably not fight with a woman, not to mention a total stranger. He spared a brief thought for the fact that she was—not surprisingly—cool in a pinch, and then he was focused on disarming the enraged Crystal.

If he'd wanted to know if she'd be surprised to see him, the look on her face gave him the answer. He realized, however, that it could be simply that, in her view, he'd appeared out of nowhere and wrenched her weapon out of her hands. She swore at him at the same moment he heard another oath from the man she'd been yelling at, who was no doubt wondering who they were.

"What the hell?"

He couldn't look at the man, not when Crystal was over her initial shock and glaring at him.

"Let go of me!"

For a moment he held on, looking down at her. The anger was still there, mixed with the surprise he had no way of knowing whether was because of their sudden appearance, or their appearance at all. And under it all, a touch of something it took him a moment to recognize through the rage.

Fear.

The moment the word formed in his mind, the moment he realized she was, in some way, afraid, he let go. It was instinctive, involuntary; it just wasn't in him to forcibly hold on to a frightened woman.

Crystal turned and ran, disappearing into one of the cottages closest to the garden shed, slamming the door behind her and, Gabe guessed, locking it.

"—guests of Miriam's, and we've seen Crystal's temper," Cara was saying soothingly to the man as Gabe turned that direction. He seemed calm enough now, although still a bit stunned at their unexpected intervention.

"I…thank you," he said. "I had no idea she could be violent. She caught me completely off guard."

He seemed to shake it off, and offered his hand to Gabe. "Mr. Taggert, I'm Lawrence Hammon. Miriam's son."

"Gabe, please," he said automatically.

The man looked to be in his mid-thirties, maybe a little older, and other than the golden brown eyes, he saw little resemblance to their hostess. Lawrence Hammon was taller than Cara, who was a tall woman, but shorter than his own six-one. He had the pale complexion of someone who spent most of his time inside. Worked in an office, Gabe guessed. His hair, lighter than his mother's, was longer than his own, but neatly styled, if a little thin on top.

"Mom told me she had some guests. I'm sorry we had to meet this way."

He glanced off in the direction Crystal had gone, frowning. Gabe could see the resemblance to Miriam now, more in profile than head-on. The nose, and chin, and when he turned back, it was there in the gentle smile.

"I worry about her," he said, and Gabe knew he wasn't talking about Crystal. "She's always taking in strays like that, thinking she can help."

"Maybe she does help," Cara said.

His brows furrowed again. "I'm not sure that one can be helped," he said frankly. "I get up here as often as I can, but I can't be here all the time. I wish Mom would move back down to civilization."

"I can see why she loves it here," Cara said, her tone a bit cautious, as if she didn't want to tread on any toes.

"She could come up here any time, I'd make sure of that. But I hate worrying about her here all alone, so far from help if she needed it."

Gabe could see his point, although Miriam certainly seemed healthy enough. He sympathized; he couldn't imagine what it must feel like. The admiral was hale and hearty and indomitable at sixty-one, and foolish though it was, Gabe couldn't picture him any other way. He supposed Miriam's son was worried about injury more than illness.

And after what they had just interrupted, Gabe didn't think Crystal's presence was of much comfort to him.

"So what was that all about?" he asked, indicating Crystal's cottage.

Lawrence frowned again. He hesitated, as if uncertain he should discuss it with strangers. Gabe guessed that their intervention, saving him from possible injury, decided him.

"I'm afraid she's been stealing again. Some valuable antique watches that belonged to my grandfather are missing. She says she doesn't know anything about it." He grimaced. "That was just before she took that swing at me."

"She's an angry young woman," Gabe said.

"Very," Lawrence agreed somewhat urgently.

"Are you going to report it?" Cara asked.

Lawrence blinked. "What?"

"It was an assault," Gabe pointed out. "If you want her out of here, I'm sure calling the sheriff would help."

"Oh. Yes." He'd obviously been more rattled than Gabe had realized by the near miss with the rake handle. Then he brightened, smiled at them. "And I have witnesses, don't I? My two Good Samaritans."

Cara smiled back, and Gabe couldn't help noting the appreciation that came into Lawrence's face as he looked at her.

Lawrence glanced toward the cottage again. "I don't know. If it were just me, I would, of course. But it would hurt my mother…she's so certain she can save that woman." He sighed. "I'll have to think about it."

Gabe's cell phone rang. As he pulled it out of his pocket, Lawrence excused himself, saying he was going inside to talk to his mother. Cara stood watching him go as Gabe glanced at his phone. The caller ID screen told him it was St. John, and he answered accordingly.

"Taggert."

"Airport, east end of the lake. Meet the Redstone chopper at Callahan Aviation. One hour."

Gabe opened his mouth to ask for details, remembered who he was talking to, and stopped himself. "Got it," he said instead. "Anything else?"

"Not at the moment." Then, because, based on St. John's reputation, he knew the man who was both legend and mystery at Redstone was still digging, he added, "Our woman with the alias took a swing at somebody with a rake handle when he accused her of stealing from her benefactor."

"Touchy."

"Very."

"True?"

"Don't know. Wouldn't surprise me."

"You?"

It took Gabe a moment. "No, the son of the woman we're here to see."

"Name?"

"Lawrence Hammon," Gabe said, starting to feel a bit like a billiard ball in play.

"Be in touch."

The conversation ended on that, leaving Gabe a little unsure whether the last had been a promise or a request. He shook his head.

"A challenge, as always?" Cara asked.

She was smiling at him. Much more warmly than she'd smiled at Lawrence. He felt a bit like a high school kid the moment the assessment formed in his mind, but he couldn't seem to help it. He smiled back.

"As always," he agreed.

"I'd like to meet him someday," she said. "Just for the experience."

"It is one," he said. And quashed the sudden image that hit him, of introducing her to St. John and everyone else at Redstone. Quashed it because in his imagination, which had recently become annoyingly overactive, he was introducing her as *his*.

"We have an hour to get to the airport at the east end of the lake," he said, his tone sharper than he'd intended in his effort to control his own thoughts.

She glanced at the main building, where Lawrence had gone inside to speak to his mother. "I suppose our little experiment was inconclusive, given the circumstances."

"Afraid so."

With a nod, she turned and started to walk back the way they came, toward the car. She didn't speak again until they were outside the gate once more.

"So why are we going to the airport?"

"To meet the Redstone helicopter."

She took that in stride, merely lifting a brow. "Because?"

"I have no idea," Gabe said.

She laughed at his wry tone. "And that bothers you?"

"It doesn't you?" he countered.

"It would have, once," she admitted. "I liked having everything planned out, knowing what was going to happen and when."

Just the way he liked things, he thought. *Or always had.* He'd learned to let up on it a little, since he'd left the service. But it was still in his nature, and he didn't know if he could change it much more.

"Why'd you change?" he asked, genuinely curious.

"Hope," she said simply. "Life's too uncertain to miss out on things that could be wonderful just because it wasn't in your plans."

The uncomplicated truth of that hit him like Crystal's rake handle. He was vaguely aware that Hope had tried to tell him just that, in some form, many times. But he hadn't listened. Or at least, he hadn't heard. Hadn't understood. But now.

Was it that Hope wasn't here to say it that made it register now, when it never had before?

Or was it that Cara was?

He wrestled silently with both the idea and his guilt about his own response to it, throughout the drive to the airport. The GPS system had quickly given them directions to the mountain airport, about fifteen miles away. He shut off the voice commands; he didn't want them intruding. On what, he wasn't quite sure, since he seemed incapable of conversation at the moment.

And Cara didn't seem to mind. Unlike Hope, she apparently didn't feel the need to fill the silence with chatter. He'd learned to tune it out, sometimes to his detriment, such as when Hope had realized he wasn't paying attention and threw in something about an encounter with aliens that he hadn't noticed.

No, there were many things about Cara that were different. He'd always assumed it had been Cara who had gravitated to the outgoing, vivacious Hope, basking in the reflected glow, as it were. But now…now he was beginning think it might have been the other way around as well, that Hope might have needed Cara just as much, or even more. Cara was the kind of person you could always count on, a solid, steady, unwavering center that the brilliant star Hope could orbit around.

As they skirted the north shore of the lake, catching impressive vistas through the trees whenever the landscape would allow, he nearly snorted aloud at his own ridiculous musings. But the image wouldn't leave him, and he couldn't seem to stop himself from wondering what it would be like to have that solid, steady, unwavering center for himself.

Get your head out of the ozone, Taggert, he ordered silently. *Don't drive right past the damned airport.*

And yet again he wondered what the hell had happened to his vaunted ability to focus.

Chapter 18

Gabe seemed distracted, as he had most of the drive, and Cara was about to point out the sign that indicated the airport was to their right when he spotted it himself and made the turn they needed.

The airport was small, a single runway aimed directly at the easternmost point of the lake. That made it easy to find Callahan Aviation Services, although the moment she saw the gleaming, red and gray helicopter she guessed they were in the right place.

The burly, jovial man who greeted them introduced himself as George Callahan. He had known Josh, he told them, since he'd been just a lanky kid with a drawl and a dream.

"Your chariot awaits," he said with a laugh, gesturing toward the chopper before he left them. "And your pilot. Couldn't believe it when a woman got out. Not many female chopper pilots. But if Josh says she's good, then she's good. That thing came in and set down like a feather."

He apologized then for not being able to stick around, but he had a plane to ferry to an airport down on the flat for some repairs to the fuselage that they weren't equipped to handle.

" 'Down on the flat' seems to be the term for it up here," Cara remarked as they walked toward the helicopter.

"I noticed," Gabe said.

As they neared the sleek craft glistening in the early spring sun, a figure walked out from behind it. Wearing the red shirt with the Redstone logo like Gabe had had on, but with unmistakably female curves, the woman was a couple of inches shorter than her own five-nine, with dark hair in a short, tousled cut that seemed to emphasize huge, dark eyes. Her bone structure was exquisite, with high cheekbones that gave her a stunning, slightly exotic look.

Then she smiled as she spotted them, and even from thirty feet away Cara felt the warmth of it. She gestured over, and they kept walking.

"Tess Machado," Gabe murmured.

"You know her?" Cara asked.

"Of her," Gabe said. "She's a legend at Redstone. Been there longer than almost anyone. She's Josh's personal pilot."

"I thought he was his own pilot."

"He was, up until a few years ago. Now most of the time he has too much to do, and needs to work in flight. She's the only one he'll surrender the controls to."

Impressed, Cara looked at the woman with respect. And with an instinctive liking; that smile was killer. She wondered how old Tess was; maybe late-thirties, although Cara guessed she'd look much the same twenty years from now.

The brief introductions corroborated Gabe's guess about her identity.

"I've heard of you," Gabe told the woman.

"Back at you," Tess said, the smile widening. "How's that sweet new boat?"

"Sweet," Gabe confirmed with an answering smile. He glanced at the chopper. "Not the same one you flew out of Colombia under fire, I hope?"

Cara smothered a gasp. Under fire? But Tess merely lifted a brow at him. "Heard about that, huh?"

"All of Redstone's heard about that," he said. "You don't rescue the head of security and Redstone's chief point man through a hail of gunfire without word getting around."

She shrugged, as if it were all in a day's work. There was, Cara thought, more to working for Redstone than she'd ever realized.

"You're safe," she said, the smile becoming a grin. "Different bird."

"Does Mr. Redstone design helicopters, too?" Cara asked.

"No," Tess said. "About the only thing he doesn't."

There was admiration, respect, and something more in the woman's voice.

"Yet," Gabe said, and Tess laughed.

"Good point," she said. Then the smile disappeared as she looked at them seriously. "I know this isn't going to be pleasant for either of you. I hope we're able to help put this to rest once and for all."

"Thank you," Cara said, meaning it.

"Let's go. Ryan Barton's already on board. Redstone tech-head," she explained. She said it with respect, not mockery, Cara noted.

"St. John sent a tech guy?" Gabe asked.

Tess nodded. "With Ian Gamble's latest invention."

Cara sensed Gabe react to the name. She glanced at him. "Redstone's resident genius inventor," Gabe said.

"He is that," Tess agreed. "You want anything from a prosthetic foot that responds like you were born with it, to an explosive-sensitive paint, Ian's your guy."

The range of those ideas left Cara a little stunned as they headed toward the helicopter. It was much bigger than it had appeared to her at first, and she couldn't help feeling a bit nervous.

"Never been in an egg-beater before?" Tess asked cheerfully.

"No," Cara admitted. "I try to stay away from machines that seemed designed to tear themselves apart."

Tess laughed, a genuine, warm laugh that made Cara smile despite her unease.

"The opposite, actually," she said. "It's the design that keeps them from tearing themselves apart."

As long as nothing breaks, Cara thought, but didn't voice the words. But if this woman had done what Gabe had said, rescued two people out of some Colombian jungle or wherever, with people shooting at them, she could no doubt handle something as routine as this.

"Get seasick?" Tess asked.

"No," Cara said.

"Then you should be fine," Tess said blithely.

Cara wasn't so sure, but she didn't see that she had much choice at the moment; she let Tess lead the way to the door of the waiting aircraft.

"Just what is this new invention?" Cara asked as she climbed aboard. Gabe, she noted, didn't wait and let Tess board before him. Some captain-of-the-ship last protocol? she wondered.

"I'll let Ryan explain," Tess said when she'd joined them. She glanced toward the front of the craft, where Cara guessed a co-pilot would sit if there was one. A young man with short, spiky hair bleached blond at the ends sat checking the stability of a large, complicated-looking device that appeared to be bolted to the helicopter's floor, if that's what it was called.

"In terms we can all understand," Tess added with a grin at the young man.

He smiled back at her. Cara imagined it would be hard for anyone not to.

"It's a pulse induction metal detector," Ryan said without bothering to introduce himself. Apparently he assumed Tess had already handled that, or it wasn't worth his time; he was obviously focused on the machine before him. "It's pretty standard for the most part, really. It fires a high-voltage pulse, and measures the time it takes for the voltage to drop into the target. If there's metal, it takes longer."

"For the most part?" Gabe asked.

The smile widened. "Well, it is a Gamble variation. What Mr.

Gamble did was amazing. He came up with a way to amplify and narrow the pulse so it could be used at a distance. Usually you have to be right on the ground for a metal detector to work."

Gabe's brows rose. "An airborne metal detector?"

"Yep." The young tech looked as excited as if he'd invented the thing himself. "And it's tied into a GPS system, so that if you can't land in the vicinity, people on the ground can find the exact spot. He's still fine-tuning it. It won't find small things yet, only things bigger than, say, a lawnmower, but something like a car? Easy."

"Ryan," Tess said softly. The young man looked at her, then colored fiercely. Cara guessed he'd just remembered exactly why they were looking for a car, and what else they might find if they located Hope's.

"I'm sorry. I get sort of excited."

"It's all right," Cara said, putting a hand on the boy's—he seemed like one to her now—arm.

"I hope you're still as enthused after we've found a dozen or so but not the one we're looking for," Gabe said, his casual tone easing the boy's discomfiture.

"We'll find it," Ryan promised.

"Yes," Gabe said with a level, quiet determination. "If I have to check every chunk of metal bigger than a lawnmower in these mountains."

"We," Cara said softly.

Gabe looked at her then, and some of the grimness faded from his eyes. "Yes," he said simply, and Cara felt a tightening in her chest when he didn't dispute her. They took their seats behind Tess and Ryan, and Cara spent a long moment fussing with the harness that seemed ominously more complicated than an airplane seat belt. Finally Gabe helped her, and she wondered if he'd logged some hours in navy choppers.

An hour later, she was wondering if perhaps Tess had been a bit optimistic in her prediction that Cara would be fine. She'd never been on a ride like this one. No roller coaster or thrill ride could ever have prepared her for this. The chopper lifted, dived, hovered, and sometimes seemed to spin in place, with a swift nimbleness that took her breath away and more than once sent her stomach plummeting.

And Tess Machado did it all without fuss, with a smooth, casual ease that Cara marveled at even as she fought the occasional blip of motion-induced nausea. Cara had given up trying to figure out how the thing worked; all she was sure of was that it took both hands and both feet, working in concert in a way that only increased the admiration she already felt for the woman. She tried to tell herself it was like driving a car, it became automatic after a while, but she wasn't convinced.

Despite her seeming complete focus on the controls—two foot pedals and two hand controls she called the collective and the cyclic—Tess noticed Cara's scrutiny.

"Somebody," Tess said, her voice coming clearly through the pair of headphones she'd given them all, "once said flying a helicopter was like standing on a greased beach ball while playing the drums."

Cara laughed, and her nervousness eased. "Where did you learn?"

"Josh taught me."

"Himself?" Gabe asked, hearing the conversation on his own headset.

"Yes. He said there were Redstone operations in places a fixed-wing couldn't get to, so I'd better learn."

"You obviously took to it," Gabe said.

"I can fly," she said simply.

Cara thought about that while Ryan interrupted, directing Tess toward something he'd seen on the screen. The words were just that, simple, but the world of quiet confidence behind them made her smile, and want to get to know this remarkable woman better.

Tess followed Ryan's directions, as she had three times already, bringing the chopper down low enough that Cara felt her heart start to hammer all over again. Even she, who knew nothing about helicopters, could see that this was some tricky flying in narrow, dangerous quarters. Yet Tess never turned a hair, just did it, brought them in close, and this time as once before, let the rotor wash part the trees they hovered over enough for them to see that this time, unlike last time when it had been an abandoned tractor, it was indeed a car.

It was not, however, Hope's little red coupe.

They lifted away.

"You're marking these, right, Ryan?" Tess asked. "We'll turn it over to the sheriff's office when we're done. They can check them out, make sure there's no one else going through this unnecessarily."

Cara went still. "I…hadn't thought. I'm glad you're doing that."

"It's the Redstone way," she replied.

Cara glanced at Gabe. He smiled at her, his expression confirming Tess's simple declaration. And Cara realized then that, even if he missed the navy, Gabe was happy where he was. And that eased a pain she hadn't even realized she was carrying.

A few minutes later they again followed Ryan's directions. They made a note of the location when Tess finally announced the power lines nearby made it impossible for them to get close enough; they'd check that later from the ground if necessary.

By the time they were heading up a small ravine near where Gabe had said would be his pick, Cara was thinking she might almost be getting used to this. Then Ryan spoke, and before she could brace herself the bottom dropped out again.

Nope, she thought. *No way I'll get used to this.*

But at least she hadn't humiliated herself by having to reach for the airsickness bag Tess had discreetly and kindly pointed out to her. *Yet,* although if this kept up—

Her thoughts cut off as Gabe went rigid beside her. Tess dropped down a little farther, trees whipping beneath them. And finally, as she followed Gabe's gaze instead of looking randomly, she saw it.

A flash of red at the bottom of the ravine.

"Tess," Gabe said, his voice tense.

"Got it," Tess said.

And, impossibly, they dropped farther. Cara would have sworn they were going to hit the trees and go careening down the mountainside. But Tess held them rock-steady as Gabe leaned forward, at his eyes a pair of binoculars Tess had retrieved for him before they'd taken off.

"It's oxidized a lot, but I think it's the right color," Gabe said. "Size looks right. Can you give me a bit to your right?"

"A bit," Tess said. And the helicopter obediently shifted. The wind of their presence gave them a slightly better look. Cara's pulse was racing now as she peered at the obviously battered vehicle below.

"It didn't burn," Gabe whispered.

Cara's breath caught; she hadn't allowed herself to consider any details, but now that he'd said it the possibilities flooded in. At first she was relieved, but what if Hope had been injured, and had lain helpless and in pain, what if—

She felt Gabe's hand on hers.

"Don't," he said. "We don't even know yet."

She suppressed a shudder, but with a strength he seemed to have loaned her, fought down the images.

"We're not going to land just yet," Tess said on the intercom, sounding regretful. "No place even close to set down."

"I've got the coordinates," Ryan said.

Tess took over then, as if she sensed both Cara and Gabe were too shell-shocked. Cara vaguely heard her giving the information to someone and instructing them to call the sheriff's office. Heard her say this was positive enough they were going to suspend the search awaiting confirmation. Heard her tell them to use all the weight the Redstone name could bring to bear to get them moving quickly.

Through all of it Cara sat strapped in the helicopter's passenger seat, trying not to think. But somewhere, deep inside, in the part of her heart that had always belonged to her dearest friend, she knew.

They'd found Hope.

And now they would know for sure that they'd lost her forever.

Chapter 19

After the initial reaction, Gabe thought, it was all oddly anti-climactic. As if finding Hope had merely put the period at the end of a tragic story already read. Still sad, still painful, but inevitable.

Because he was sure. Just as Cara was; he could see it in her eyes.

They had gone back to the airport, setting down at Callahan's and taking up residence in the comfortable lounge Mrs. Callahan showed them to.

"Any friend of Josh's is a friend of ours," she declared, and proceeded to brew up a fresh pot of coffee for them.

A while later, after having seen to the care and feeding of her aircraft, Tess joined them. Ryan, she said, was still aboard, processing the data they'd gathered on other vehicles to turn over to the authorities.

"St. John will get the call, and he'll call me," she said. "I gave the job to him. He's the best at exerting Redstone pressure if necessary."

"I can imagine," Gabe said.

"What's his story?" Cara asked, as if looking for distraction. Gabe listened curiously himself, figuring Tess, being so close to Josh and having been with Redstone for so long, would know if anyone did.

She didn't.

"Not a clue. I mean, I know the basics, that he's been with Josh nearly since the beginning, that he's actually known him since childhood. Longer than any of us, really, even me and John Draven, who have been with Redstone the longest."

"No idea why he's...." She stopped, and Gabe knew she didn't want to insult the man who was doing so much to help them.

"The way he is?" Tess asked with a smile. "No. Rumors abound, but the truth? Only he and Josh know for sure, I'd guess. Maybe not even Josh knows it all."

Gabe listened as the two women talked, although he wasn't fully tuned in. He noted they seemed to find a lot in common, including a shared interest in reading—in particular, they both admitted with a grin, mysteries and thrillers.

Time ticked on, an hour, then two, and as the twilight started to deepen Gabe barely managed to restrain himself from pacing. Soon it would be too dark, if it wasn't already in that deep ravine. If they didn't get there and report back soon, it would be tomorrow before they knew.

As if she'd sensed his edginess, Tess tried to draw him into the conversation.

"So what's your passion, besides the sea?" she asked.

It was all Gabe could do to keep from looking over at Cara. He chewed on himself a little, asking what the hell he was doing thinking about Cara and passion and the inevitable scenarios that juxtaposition put in his head, when they likely had just found his dead wife.

"I always thought about learning to fly," he said, almost desperately, figuring that would get Tess going. It did. And saved him from his own thoughts as well, as he and Tess settled into a pilot-to-pilot discussion of the differences and similarities between ships of the sea and the air, finding more in common than he would have expected. Cara listened with every evidence of interest.

"Flying this high in the mountains is different," Tess said. "The winds can be really tricky. Those ridges at the north end of the airfield can really keep things stirred up."

"Wind shear?" Gabe asked.

She nodded. "Fortunately it's pretty calm today. And cool, so density altitude isn't an issue."

"Density altitude?" Cara asked.

"When it's warm, like in the summer up here, the air mass expands, the molecules moving farther apart. Makes the air thinner, and flying in it an interesting thing."

"Both helicopter and fixed-wing?" Gabe asked.

She nodded. "Different, obviously, but—"

She stopped as her cell phone rang. All three of them froze, and no matter how Gabe tried to tell himself it could be anyone calling her, he knew it wasn't. And when she looked at the caller ID screen a second more than was necessary, he knew he was right. He saw that Cara knew, too; she rose and walked over to the window, looking out at the airfield as if turning her back on what was happening could stop it.

"Machado." A pause. "Yes, they're here." Another, even briefer pause, telling Gabe it was likely St. John himself. "All right. Any details?"

After another brief pause she, as had St. John no doubt, hung up without another word. Gabe read the news in her face before she said gently, "It's confirmed. The license plate matches, and…there are human remains."

Cara made a tiny sound that wrenched at him. He couldn't stop himself from going to her. She turned and came into his arms without hesitation, leaned against him, and he felt the quiver that went through her.

Tess spoke again, in the manner of someone wanting to get

it all said fast. "They're recovering everything. It will take some time to get the car out, but…the body is already on its way to the county morgue below. They know what happened with your car, so they'll be looking very carefully. He'll call with anything new."

Gabe nodded. Tess whispered, "I'm sorry. Both of you."

"Thank you," Cara said, her voice breaking between the words. Tess nodded, turned and silently left the room.

Gabe just stood there, holding her, unexpectedly finding comfort of his own in the gesture he'd meant to give to her. He felt another quiver, then another, then realized she was crying. He opened his mouth to say something, anything, then shut it again, thinking there was nothing to say, not really.

The quiet weeping eased sooner than he'd expected. But then, Cara hadn't been what he'd expected from the moment she'd walked back into his life.

"I thought I was prepared," she said. "It's been so long, she's been missing from my life for so long, I didn't think it would hit me so hard."

"That doesn't mean it still isn't a shock," he said. "I've known for a long time something like this was probably the answer, but…."

"I thought I'd just feel…at peace," she said. "To finally know, for sure."

"It will come," he said, wishing he believed it.

"I know," she said, as if she did. "But right now, it's hard."

"Yes," he agreed. And kept holding her.

They stood together to watch Tess take off into the darkness, flashing red lights the only thing they could see to tell them where the sleek chopper was. Then the bright headlight swept over them as the bird lifted and turned practically on an axis, and wind swept over them as it soared into the night.

"I like her," Cara said.

"Me, too. I can see why Josh relies on her."

It was a moment before she asked him, "Now what?"

He let out a compressed breath. "Until we hear if there's any evidence of tampering, I'm not sure there's anything we can do but wait."

"And tell Miriam," she said softly.

"Yes." His reluctance was clear, but she knew he wouldn't shirk the task.

"Shall we go back there now?"

"Might as well," he said. "Get it over with."

They talked little on the drive, each absorbed in their own memories of the golden girl they'd both loved, and both lost. When they arrived back at the inn, Cara noticed Gabe set the alarm on the car, a simple action that still made her shiver.

Telling Miriam was difficult, as Cara had expected; they'd had eight years to expect this; Miriam had now learned Hope was missing and now dead within two days.

By tacit agreement they didn't mention Crystal; there didn't seem any point in adding their suspicions to her grief, not yet. And after a while, Miriam got out a bottle of a sweet almond liqueur Hope had liked, and poured them all enough to toast.

"To Hope, who touched us all, and will never be forgotten," she said simply.

The sound of their glasses clinking together seemed like a death knell to Cara, an audible acknowledgment of the truth they'd learned today. And when Miriam insisted it was far too late to drive down the mountain, they agreed, for her sake as much as theirs, to stay another night.

"Do we need to watch out for Crystal?" Gabe asked casually, as if he were only concerned with avoiding the cranky young woman.

Miriam frowned. "I don't know. She left this afternoon, and I haven't seen her." She sighed. "I'm afraid she and my son simply do not get along."

Cara just managed to stop herself from saying *Hard to believe*; sarcasm didn't seem appropriate just now.

"I'm sure Lawrence is just concerned about you," she said instead.

"Yes," Miriam agreed. "He always worries. But sometimes I have to remind him who's the parent."

Cara smiled at that.

Later, as they were going upstairs to their respective rooms, Gabe said thoughtfully, "Well, that's three of us who don't trust Miss Crystal."

"Yes," Cara said.

She opened the door to the green room, then turned back to say goodnight, only to find Gabe standing much closer than she'd realized. Something in his face, some shadow in his eyes as he looked down at her, made her instinctively reach for him, put her arms around him.

"I'm sorry, Gabe," she said quietly.

He said nothing, but after a moment his arms came around her in turn. For a long time they just stood there, taking comfort, warmth and support from each other.

When Gabe bent his head and pressed his lips to her forehead, her heart leaped at the contact.

Stop it, she ordered herself. *It's the kind of kiss you'd give your sister.*

With the idea of forcing herself to stop her own silly thoughts, she made herself look up at him, knowing she would see only the friendly concern she'd always seen in Gabriel Taggert's eyes. Knowing that would quash these impossible longings where nothing else could. She was just the old Cara to him, glamorous, glorious Hope's quiet, shy, studious friend, and she always would be.

What she saw in his eyes burned away all pretense.

Cara's heart slammed in her chest. Never in her life had she thought any man would look at her like this. As if she were the only water in a lifetime of thirst, as if she were the answer to prayers he'd never dared to pray.

That it was Gabe made her forget how to breathe.

She opened her mouth to speak, but no words came. There was only a niggling fear that if she spoke she would ruin this moment, and never, ever know if he really meant it.

Gabe made an odd sound, something like a groan that rumbled up from deep in his chest. He seemed to take her parted lips as invitation, and lowered his head.

The moment his mouth closed over hers, any idea she'd had that he looked at her as a sister vanished, seared to ash in the sudden heat. As did all the imaginings she'd ever had about what it would be like to be kissed by this man. As the girl she'd been, she'd had little to judge by. As the few men in her life had come and gone since, she'd told herself the fire she'd imagined had been only that, a girl's dream, that no reality could measure up to her imaginings about Gabe. She'd loved her fiancé, but that had been a quiet, solid thing. Not this. Not fire.

She'd been wrong. And right. Reality could measure up. But only if that reality was Gabe himself.

His arms tightened around her as he deepened the kiss, and the pressure as he tested the softness of her lips was somehow the most arousing thing she'd ever felt.

No, it was the taste of him, of his mouth, and the heat, the incredible heat of him.

No, she thought foggily then, it was the feel of him, of his tall, hard body against hers, not a fraction of space between them. That was the most arousing thing she'd ever felt.

A moan escaped her, a sound unlike anything she could ever recall making before. But she was helpless to stop it before the onslaught of sensations being unleashed in her.

The reality was definitely living up to the dream.

When at last he pulled back, she whimpered a protest, unable to form a coherent word.

"Cara," he whispered. "Stop me now."

For a moment she just stared at him. Why on earth would she want to stop him, when she'd dreamed of this for years?

"Why?" It was the only word she could manage.

"So many reasons," he said, but he didn't let go of her, and the feel of him swamped any vestige of rationality left in her brain. On some level she knew he was right, there were so many reasons she shouldn't do this.

"But only one reason matters to me," she said softly.

He went very still. "What?"

"I will regret it the rest of my life if we don't."

She meant it. She would forever regret if she didn't—even if it was just this once—find out what this man really meant to her.

He groaned, louder then, and his arms tightened around her. She heard a sound, realized with a little shock that somehow they were in her room and he'd shut the door behind them. And then she was up against that closed door, the raised panel digging into her back as his mouth closed hungrily over hers once more. And then she felt nothing but him. His mouth on hers. His hands on her, stroking, exploring, learning. And he did learn; despite the fact that she could barely think, he was learning every spot that made her gasp, every caress that made her quiver.

For a moment she thought of Hope, and guilt surged through her. But, oddly, the thought was of Hope complaining about Gabe's ability to compartmentalize, to focus on one endeavor to the exclusion of all else, while she, Hope, could only scatter her attention amid everything before her.

Cara's last rational thought was disbelief; how could Hope have ever complained when it meant this could happen? When it meant this kind of fierce, intense, single-minded attention, as if you were the only person who existed for him?

When it meant that he could make you feel that you were the absolute center of his world?

Any lingering idea that she would feel as if she were stealing something from her best friend turned to smoke when his hands found her breasts, cupped them, lifted. It took a moment for her dazed mind to realize she wasn't feeling his touch through layers of clothing. And she didn't care that he'd lifted her shirt, unclasped her bra to bare her for his caress, leaving her only with the gold chain with the carved, pale green jade initial *T* she wore—for Thorpe, she always said, although in her heart she'd often thought of Taggert as well—all with her being only faintly aware. Not only did she not care, but she found herself arching her back, pushing herself into his hands, offering in a way she'd never wanted to before.

Gabe swore, low and harsh. And then, in a move so effortless she nearly gasped, he swept her up in his arms and carried her to the bed with the sea-green comforter. With that same ruthless efficiency he stripped the rest of her clothes off, and Cara helped him with an urgency that would have embarrassed her with any other man.

He kicked off his shoes and yanked his own shirt over his head. Cara smothered a gasp; the thought had just hit her that she was about to have the chance to fulfill her imaginings, and follow that trail of dark, crisp hair downward.

He paused with his hands on the button of the black jeans that had so taunted her since he'd put them on.

"Stop me now, Cara," he said again, then added the ultimatum, "or never."

"I choose never," she said, before second thoughts could invade, before anything could interfere with the dream come true before her.

The sound he made then was more growl than groan, and he shed the rest of his clothes in a rush. She had a split second to realize he was even more beautiful than she'd imagined before he was beside her, and the feel of him pressed to her, skin to skin, sent her mind reeling and seemed to end her capacity for thought altogether.

He was everywhere, caressing her not only with his hands and that incredible mouth, but with his entire body, rubbing, stroking, until she was unable to do anything less than ripple beneath the assault on her senses. It went on and on, and she heard herself cry out again and again. With every touch she felt a wondrous, stunning clenching inside as need gripped her in a way she'd never known.

"Gabe," she whispered finally, desperately. "Please."

"I thought you'd never ask." His voice was gravel-rough and sent a shudder through her.

And then he was over her, reaching to guide himself as she opened for him, lifting her hips, wanting, needing this man inside her more than she needed to breathe. At the first probing touch she smothered a gasp. As he slid forward, his way eased by her own slick readiness, she cried out at the delicious stretching sensation.

He stopped. "Cara?"

She couldn't speak. Could only moan. She reached for him then, grasped his lean hips and urged him on without the words she couldn't seem to form.

He surged into her then, and she cried out anew with the glorious shock of feeling him deep and thick and hot inside her. For a moment they froze, as if in wonder at a sensation as old as time and yet a new discovery for them both.

And then, with a heartfelt, shuddering oath, Gabe began to move, slow at first, and then faster, until Cara thought she would die from the sweet friction. She savored every involuntary sound he made, every shiver that went through him. And then, when he shifted his position slightly and she felt his body stroke hers in that swollen, critical spot, she gave up her grip on awareness and clung to him as the pressure built unbearably.

And then he said her name on a gasp, slammed into her hard and deep, and she cried out his name in turn as the hot, pulsing convulsions took her.

And she knew that, for once, it was the dream that didn't live up to the reality.

Chapter 20

The ring of his cell phone brought Gabe out of the soundest sleep he'd had in recent memory. That abrupt awakening was followed by the equally jolting realization that he wasn't alone. He was in bed, naked, wrapped around the equally naked but much softer and lovelier Cara Thorpe.

Some part of his mind that wasn't numbed by that shock was registering the number of rings, and considering where his phone was—in the pocket of the jeans that were several feet away on the floor—he calculated he wasn't going to get there before it went to voice mail, so he didn't even try. He wasn't sure he could move anyway.

He was in bed with his wife's best friend.

"Phone's ringing," that friend said sleepily.

"It'll stop," he said, wondering if he sounded as gruff to her as he did to himself.

For a moment it didn't matter that Hope was gone, had been gone for eight years.

Dead, he reminded himself grimly. There was no longer any doubt about that. He didn't need the coroner's ID to tell him; he knew in his gut, had known since the moment he'd seen that flash of faded red through the trees in that ravine.

The phone did indeed stop ringing. Nothing else changed. His wife was dead, and he was in bed with her best friend. Not only in bed with her, but becoming aroused all over again at the memories of the night they'd just spent, spent with a passion he hadn't thought himself capable of anymore. The first time had been amazing enough. But when he'd awakened some hours later wanting, needing more, she hadn't protested when his touch disturbed her sleep; instead she'd turned to him willingly, welcomingly, and it had been even more incredible.

But nothing had been as incredible as the moment when her soft, curious touch had awakened him, and the thought that shy little Cara wanted him enough to wake him from sleep had been the most potent of aphrodisiacs.

He was pretty sure he'd shouted her name that time.

His phone chirped, the announcement that he had voice mail. The slant of sunlight through the window told him it was later than he was used to sleeping. He'd taken off his watch, not wanting to risk scratching her silken skin, and there was no clock on the bedside table as there was in his room.

No, there was, he realized as he glanced that way, she'd just turned it away.

Now that was something he couldn't understand. If he woke up in the night, that was the first thing he did, check the time. It was instinctive, natural, he thought, and he didn't quite understand how you could not want to know what time it was.

"You're frowning," she said, and he realized she'd come fully awake and was looking at him. And he felt her retreat from him, even though she moved only slightly in his arms.

"Was I?"

She lowered her eyes, and he thought he felt a tiny sigh escape her. "I was afraid you'd regret this."

It took him a moment to understand what she meant. Before he could speak, she went on softly.

"I understand. It's Hope. She'll always be there, won't she." It wasn't a question. And then her gaze came back to his face. "I don't regret it, Gabe. I can't. But I understand how you feel, really."

"I'm not sure I do," Gabe said honestly. "But that wasn't what I was frowning about. I was trying to figure out what happened to the clock."

She blinked. "The clock?" Then her expression cleared. "Oh. The clock."

Clearly she wasn't at her usual peak first thing in the morning, Gabe thought. He was telling himself he'd have to remember that before he realized the implications of what he was thinking.

"I turned it because it's very bright," she said. "It was annoying."

He felt oddly relieved at that. And that, plus the knowledge that he'd been thinking he would even need to remember she woke up more slowly than he did, was unsettling enough to drive him out of bed and over to the phone that had just chirped again.

He dragged the jeans back on before he pulled the phone out of his pocket. It was time for some fresh clothes, he thought as he pushed the appropriate button, glad he'd grabbed socks and that pair of boxers in the little store, even if they were a rather startling shade of St. Patrick's Day green.

He sensed Cara getting up, but didn't look at her. Didn't dare; if he got a glimpse of that lithe, lusciously curved body in the morning sun, he was liable to swoop down on her and take her right back to bed. Not something he wanted to do before he had a chance to think about what had happened between them. To figure out if he'd made one of the bigger mistakes of his life last night.

If it had been any other woman, he wouldn't be lost in this quagmire of confusion. But it wasn't. It was Cara.

As he zipped the jeans he wondered a little that she hadn't complained at all—Hope would have been frantic—about heading into the third day in the same clothes. Although he'd never have known it to look at them. He'd noticed yesterday morning that she'd washed her underwear; it had been hard to miss the silky bikini panties and matching, lace-trimmed bra hung over the shower enclosure, even if she hadn't blushingly apologized for the "extra décor" when she'd later found them where he'd laid them on the counter to keep them from getting wet from his shower.

She disappeared into the bathroom while he worked his way through the voice mail menu. He hadn't told her, of course, about the effect those intimate articles had had on him. Not, he thought as he remembered last night's fierce passion again, that it would come as any surprise to her now.

He finally got to the actual message. He listened, at first mildly amused by the fact that St. John was reading something to him, and therefore actually using complete sentences. But his amusement faded quickly, and when he disconnected he saw that Cara was back, wrapped in a bath towel, looking at him.

"St. John," he said. "Speaking in full sentences, for once."

Her brows rose. "Why?"

"He was reading the preliminary report from the first-glance inspection of the car."

She said nothing, just waited; obviously she'd accepted that Redstone got results fast, even from law enforcement. He recited what St. John had said, the words already etched deep into his mind.

"They said that the deterioration after all this time was severe, but the car had landed at an angle that had somewhat protected the undercarriage. It will take closer scrutiny in the lab to be sure, but they think there are tool marks near where a brake line would have been secured to the frame."

She got to it as quickly as he had. "It was no accident."

"Any more than ours would have been."

Cara drew herself up then. Any semblance of sleepiness had vanished. Her eyes seemed to have turned a even more vivid blue as her gaze narrowed. A fierce anger seemed to radiate from her, and even wrapped in just a bath towel, with her copper hair tousled around her head, she looked suddenly more like an avenging angel than the soft, eager woman whose slick heat had taken him in and sent him flying.

"Crystal," she said.

"And her clippers," Gabe agreed.

"Coincidence?"

"That she was here both times? That she carries those things like some women carry a lipstick? And that she's a snarly, short-tempered, angry—"

He stopped when Cara held up a hand. "I get it."

"I don't believe in that much coincidence."

"Nor do I."

"But why?" Cara asked. "Hope would have been kind to her, as kind as Miriam. You know she would, she wanted everyone to like her."

He'd been thinking about this since long before he'd heard what the sheriff's office had found. "Maybe Miriam is the key."

Cara thought about that for a moment before nodding slowly as she said, "I've noticed that, for all her nastiness, Crystal seems almost…protective of her. Maybe she was afraid Hope would be competition for Miriam's help and attention."

He hadn't thought of it exactly that way, but now that Cara had put it into words, it had the ring of logic.

"She had a cushy nest here, and she thought Hope threatened that for some reason."

"Because," Cara said slowly, thoughtfully, "Hope and Miriam had something in common that Crystal could never share."

"The writing," Gabe said instantly.

Cara nodded.

"It's still just speculation," Gabe warned her.

"I know. But it makes sense, doesn't it?"

"Perfectly."

"Do we tell the sheriff?"

"We do," Gabe said. "But I'm not about to leave it to when-ever they can get to it. Especially knowing they likely can't make a move until they have the final report on the possible tampering."

"Let's go," she said abruptly, turning back into the bathroom.

"Go?"

"Find Crystal," she said, as if it were obvious. Since that was exactly what he'd planned on, he supposed it was.

"Let me handle this, Cara."

She turned back. "What?"

"If she did this, she could be dangerous."

The anger that had ebbed slightly flared in her eyes once more. "I'm in this, Gabriel Taggert. It's why I'm here. Don't think because of that—" she gestured toward the bed and its tangled, tossed covers "—you get to order me around."

He opened his mouth to say that had nothing to do with it, but he wasn't sure it was true so bit back the words. "'That?'" he quoted back instead.

With a look of pure exasperation she put her hands on her hips—those beautiful, womanly hips he'd had his own hands on not so long ago, as he'd pulled her atop him for a ride unlike anything he'd ever felt before—and glared at him.

"It's time to finish this, for Hope. We can talk about *that* later."

She closed the bathroom door in his face. He had no doubt she had used the word again simply to prod him. And once again he realized Cara Thorpe was unlike any woman he'd known. He couldn't think of one he'd ever been intimate with who wouldn't have wanted to dissect what had happened between them down to the last detail.

He gathered up the rest of his clothes and darted, half-dressed, back to the blue room.

Retreated, you mean.

This time, despite the situation they were in, the little voice in his head made him smile.

When did you turn into such a bitch? Cara asked herself. The guy was just trying to protect you. It's who he is, what he does.

But she couldn't be left out of this. After eight years they were close, so close to finding out exactly what had happened to Hope, and there was no way she was going to sit on the sidelines.

She gave herself a little shake, and with no small effort managed not to look at her tangled bed while she considered her clothing options. The T-shirt she'd slept in was wrinkled, but in better shape than the green blouse she'd been wearing.

And of course, she hadn't worn it last night, she thought wryly as she lost the battle for a moment and looked at the bed where she'd learned she really knew very little of how things could be with the right—or in this case, likely very wrong—man.

A shiver went through her at the memory. She made herself move.

She rolled up her blouse and put it in the bag from the general store. She'd like to steam the wrinkles out of the T-shirt, as she had with her blouse and pants yesterday, but Gabe was in the shower now and there was no way she was going in there. That she had the implied right, after the night they'd spent, and that she wouldn't see anything she hadn't already explored with great detail and delight, was something she tried not to dwell on.

She pulled on the T-shirt. Body heat would smooth it out a bit, she told herself, then groaned inwardly at her own choice of words. *Body heat, indeed.*

Miriam was in the kitchen when they got downstairs. Her expression was rather bleak, but she gave them a smile anyway. And handed them a folder full of printed pages.

"I couldn't sleep, so I went back and pulled up Hope's letters and the rest of the stories she sent me. I thought you might like to have them."

"Thank you, Miriam," Cara said, reaching out to touch the older woman's hand.

"Yes," Gabe said, his voice suspiciously tight, as if the single syllable was all he trusted himself to say.

"Where's Crystal this morning?" Cara asked. "I hope she'll be here to keep you company after we leave."

Gabe went still, as if he hadn't expected her to jump right into today's order of business, but Cara didn't see any point in wasting time. She felt a little guilty not telling Miriam the truth, but on the slim chance they were wrong, she didn't want to hurt the woman's feelings unnecessarily.

"She'll be back later. She went down to the store in town, to get…some hardware thing she needed, I forget. But Lawrence is still here. He was going to leave last night, but decided to stay when he heard the news. He knew I was upset."

Cara wondered where he'd stayed, since Miriam had indicated the two rooms they'd been using—well, one last night, she amended silently, fighting the heat that threatened once more—were the only ones kept ready for guests inside the main building.

"I'm sorry if we evicted him from his usual room."

"He prefers one of the cottages, actually. He's sleeping late, as usual, I'm afraid."

Cara glanced at Gabe. "I'm not sure who put the morning people in charge, and Lawrence has my empathy."

One corner of Gabe's mouth twitched upward. "No sense waiting until the day's half-gone to get started," he said mildly.

"Hmpf," Cara said.

They waited for a while, forgoing Miriam's offer of another full breakfast and sitting down instead with some English muffins and coffee, but Crystal didn't return. Finally Cara looked up at Gabe, and saw he was thinking the same thing she was, that Crystal had taken to her heels for good, once she'd learned Hope's body had been found.

Eventually they said goodbye to Miriam, who elicited a promise from them that they would keep her apprised and come back to visit. They walked out to the car, where Gabe proceeded to go over it inch by inch, top and bottom, looking for any sign of tampering.

"Nothing," he said finally, sliding out from under the car and getting up off the ground, dusting off what he could of the debris his clothes had collected. Instinctively she moved to help, brushing pine needles off his shoulders and studiously avoiding those that were clinging to his temptingly muscled backside.

"Thanks," he said when she stepped back, and the husky note that had come into his voice reminded her of how he'd sounded in the dark. Which reminded her of how he'd felt in the dark. How he'd made her feel.

The heat rose yet again, and she spoke quickly. "I suppose we should check around in town, just in case she's really there."

"Yes. If we don't find her, I'd say we call the sheriff's office, tell them Crystal may have taken off. Might be enough to tip them into seriously considering her a suspect."

Cara nodded in agreement.

"But first," Gabe said, "I think I'll call St. John. See if there's anything in the facts he dug up that might indicate where she'd go."

They got into the car, and since he was driving he used the hands-free system as they started down the mountain. Or perhaps it was just as much so that she could hear, and he wouldn't have to repeat everything.

Not that there was much to repeat, given he was talking to St. John.

After the amazingly short conversation about checking into where Crystal might run to, St. John changed the subject. To one even less pleasant.

"Prelim from the coroner. Want it?"

Cara went still. Gabe glanced at her, and she read in his face that he would tell St. John to hold it for him, if she didn't want to hear it. And she didn't, God help her, she didn't. But she had to. She had to as much as Gabe had to. She gave a short, sharp nod.

"Go ahead," Gabe said, his voice flat.

"Broken neck. Death instantaneous on impact."

Cara let out a breath. How could such awful, brutal detail be a relief? But it was. It was. Her worst imaginings weren't true. Hope hadn't suffered, hadn't lain there, trapped, forgotten, to die a slow, awful death.

"Thank you," Gabe said softly.

As usual, St. John let no emotion show. Perhaps the man truly didn't feel any. "Search help," he said bluntly.

"We're calling the sheriff next," Gabe said.

"Undermanned."

"Probably."

"I'll see who's available."

The click of the disconnect echoed in the car's quiet interior. With a rueful shake of his head, Gabe made the call to the sheriff's office next. He found out in relatively short order that the case had already been transferred from missing persons to homicide, a fact that encouraged Cara even as the words sent a wave of renewed grief through her.

He gave the somewhat harried-sounding investigator what they knew and what they suspected. The man asked enough questions that Cara felt comforted that he wasn't blowing them off. When he disconnected that call, Gabe nodded as if in satisfaction.

"Sounds like he's taking it seriously."

"Yes," Cara agreed.

"Difference between just another missing person and a murder victim."

Cara sucked in a breath. Murder victim. Hope.

"I'm sorry, Cara." Gabe's voice was even grimmer than it had been. She felt his hand on her shoulder, felt the heat of him, took comfort from it. "I was talking in the abstract, I didn't think how it would sound."

"But you're right," Cara said, her voice unsteady. "Hope was murdered."

"Yes," he said.

And in that one syllable Cara heard everything she needed to hear. Gabriel Taggert would never, ever stop until whoever murdered Hope was caught.

They were back on the main road to Pine Lake before she spoke again, more to distract herself from the steep drop-off at the side of the road and memories of what that had meant to Hope than anything else.

"What did St. John mean by search help?"

"I suppose that he'd send Redstone people to help, if necessary."

She shook her head. "I'm beginning to understand what an amazing place that must be to work."

"More than amazing." He glanced at her. "That boat I'm on? Anyone with Redstone has access. Down to the guy who cleans the floors at Redstone Headquarters. Took him out deep-sea fishing last week, with his family, including his little boy who has leukemia."

"Deep-sea fishing? On that gorgeous boat?" Cara asked as she gauged they were a couple of sharp bends out of Pine Lake now.

"Josh's orders. It's what the kid wanted to do."

"That's wonderful," she said, meaning it. "It must be gratifying to—"

"What the hell?" Gabe said sharply.

The crash and the hard jolt came simultaneously. Cara heard a startled gasp, realized it had come from her.

And then she couldn't breathe at all.

They were skidding out of control toward the drop.

Chapter 21

Gabe fought the instinct to hit the brakes just as he fought the wheel of the car. It jerked under his hands as he tried to force it into the skid. His peripheral vision told him they were getting close, too close, to the edge. He wasn't going to have room or time.

Utterly focused, he made a snap decision, the only thing he thought could give them a chance. This was the most solid car he'd ever driven; he was going to have to count on it. The instant he saw road instead of trees through the windshield he hit the accelerator. The powerful motor roared. The rear wheels spun, and for a moment they kept sliding sideways. Then the wheels dug in. For an instant they seemed frozen, motionless.

They shot forward. Not away from the drop. Beside it. Wrong side of the road. Skating perilously close to the edge. But not over it.

He'd gladly settle for that.

When the drive wheels were safely back on asphalt, he steered them back to the right side. There was, thankfully, room on the shoulder, and he pulled off there, with the suddenly comforting mountain beside them rather than the harrowing drop. He applied the brakes carefully, not wanting to hear even a hint of tires spinning on the loose gravel.

Only when they were finally stopped did Gabe look over at Cara. She was pale and wide-eyed, and as he looked he saw her take in a breath and relax a clenched jaw. And then she looked at him.

"Thank you," she said.

He hadn't expected that. "What?"

"For having a cool head and getting us out of that."

He tried to smile, wasn't sure it was more than a grimace. "That wasn't cool. Just instinct. Training."

"Whatever. We're here, and not—" she gestured across the road toward the drop with an eloquent shudder "—down there. No thanks to whoever hit us."

"And contrary to their hopes," he said grimly.

He saw Cara's mouth tighten, knew he didn't have to sugar-coat it, she knew perfectly well this hadn't been an accident.

"Did you see them?" was all she asked. *Talk about cool heads,* he thought in silent salute. "I didn't. I was oblivious, chattering away when I should have been paying attention."

"Paying attention was my job, I was driving," he pointed out. "And I didn't see the truck either, until it was on us."

"Truck?"

"Yes," Gabe said. "A brown pickup. And it was timed perfectly. Just after we rounded that sharp turn. The perfect spot. Steep drop, and not enough straight road behind us to see them coming."

He waited, knowing she'd get there, and quickly. She did. "A brown pickup, like the one at the inn. And someone who knows this road. Well."

"Exactly."

"Crystal," she said.

"My guess," he agreed. "Although I couldn't see the driver. Truck was there so fast all I saw was the front end in the back window."

"And she just kept going."

"She must have been sure she'd taken us out."

"She had reason to be. We couldn't have come much closer."

He saw a faint shiver go through her and knew she was thinking, just as he had, of Hope.

"She must have been so scared, once she knew," Cara whispered.

"It would only have been seconds," Gabe said, reminding her of what St. John had told them.

"An eternity, when you know what's happening."

He couldn't argue with that, so didn't even try.

"But if Crystal was already in town, how did she end up behind us?" Cara asked.

He thought about that for a moment. "Maybe she wasn't in town. Maybe she was along the road somewhere."

"Waiting?" Cara asked, her voice tight. He knew how she felt; lying in wait took it out of the realm of crime of opportunity and into full intent.

"It wouldn't be hard to guess that we'd be leaving Miriam's this morning, now that…we found Hope."

"But if Hope's already been found, why go after us? The sheriff already knows, she couldn't think we hadn't told them."

"But don't forget," Gabe reminded her, "she has no idea we even suspect her."

Cara nodded slowly. "That fight between her and Lawrence. We never did confront her about the cut steering line." She looked out at the road where they'd very nearly replicated Hope's fatal plunge. "Did the truck keep going toward town?"

Gabe's mouth quirked. "I didn't notice. I was a little busy."

She looked back at him quickly. "Saving our lives. I know. It was a rhetorical question, since I was useless in that emergency."

"You didn't shriek," he said. "Believe me, that was useful."

After a moment she lowered her gaze and smiled. A warm smile that sent his blood pulsing through him in hot, heavy beats. And suddenly he wanted this over, so he could focus on what this woman had so quickly come to mean to him. He wanted this over, and her safe, so they could talk. The irony that he wanted the kind of talk men usually ran from in abject terror wasn't lost on him.

But it wasn't over. They were in the middle of it, and it wasn't getting any safer by them just sitting here. It was time to get moving.

He got out to assess the damage. Cara joined him, lending her quick eyes to the task. After a few minutes of inspection, including moving the seriously dented right rear quarter panel—the point of impact—away from the tire with the pry bar from the trunk, he patted the solid coupe on the roof and thanked its makers fervently. He'd have to have it checked, of course, but right now it was drivable.

"Stan?" Cara asked.

"Before we start down, yes," Gabe agreed. "Just to make sure. While he's looking at it, we'll decide what to do."

"And call the sheriff?"

"Yes."

"What if she made a U-turn while we were…spinning, and went back to Miriam's?" Cara asked. "Should I call her?"

"I don't want to tip Crystal off," Gabe said.

"I could make up something."

"But if she finds out you even called, she knows we're not at the bottom of the mountain. And she might run."

Cara nodded in understanding. "But…is Miriam safe?"

Gabe considered that. "I think so. This whole thing seems to be centered on keeping her place with Miriam. So why would she hurt her?"

"That's logical," Cara said. "But is Crystal?"

The truth of what she was saying was undeniable. He'd been thinking as if a woman who had killed once and just now tried again, was rational. Big mistake.

"You're right," he said. "Let's get back to the inn. We'll make calls from there."

She gave him a look he couldn't quite interpret, but said nothing as they got back into the damaged but life-saving car and headed back the way they had come.

* * *

Cara was glad to be sitting down. She felt more shaky after their near miss than she wanted to admit. Oddly, she felt safe enough in the car, with Gabe at the wheel at least. He'd said something about the power and suspension saving them, but she knew it was more his skill and reactions than anything else.

She stole a sideways glance at him. His jaw was set, and he was clearly on hyper alert.

And he'd changed his mind.

She hadn't expected that. She'd been concerned about Miriam, but he'd seemed to have his plan set, and she hadn't thought he would change it to indulge her worries. It was one of the things Hope had always grumbled about. Once he made up his mind, Hope had said, she could rarely get him to change it.

They started out slowly, and she suspected he was testing the car, making sure there wasn't damage that they hadn't found.

"Feels like it's been knocked out of alignment, but other than that, it's amazingly normal," he finally said, picking up speed a little.

"Thank you," she said.

He flicked a glance at her before turning his gaze back to the road and asking, "For what, now?"

"For changing your mind, and going to check on Miriam."

His brows furrowed. "Why wouldn't I? You were right."

"Hope always said…" Her voice trailed away, and she wished she hadn't said it as he glanced at her again and she saw his face.

"Hope," he said carefully, "would change her mind at the drop of a hat. She'd want to back out at the last minute of things planned long ago, where other people were counting on us, simply because she didn't 'feel like it.' Sometimes—" He stopped, as if he were trying to decide whether to say what he was thinking.

"We agreed she wasn't perfect," Cara said, her voice quiet. "And that her being dead, if she was, wouldn't change that. Now that we know it's true, it still doesn't change that."

He didn't comment on what she said, just went on with what he'd started. "Sometimes, she did it just to see what I'd do. To see if I'd give in to her whim, without reason. As if she wanted to see how much control she had over me."

Cara winced, because somewhere in her gut she knew it was true. Hope had played those kinds of games. "She...did that with me, too, sometimes. I never thought about it as a control thing, though. It was just Hope."

They slowed for the turn to Miriam's, and as they sat waiting for an approaching delivery van to pass, he looked at her. "You had a good, solid and logical reason to want to go back to Miriam's. Changing my mind was no problem."

Cara pondered that as they drove toward Miriam's. They once more parked down the road, determined this time that if Crystal was there, they'd catch her alone.

"I don't want Miriam getting in the way or hurt," Gabe said. "If Crystal gets desperate, she might do anything."

Cara nodded, liking his concern for the woman she'd come to care about.

They walked toward the front of the inn, watchful for the bitter young woman. They didn't see her, but spotted the brown truck. They couldn't see any fresh damage from here, but they couldn't see the front end, either. And it was parked, not in its usual spot on the driveway where any new damage would be easily spotted, but up toward the garden shed.

Crystal's territory.

Cara nodded silently as they headed back to the gate they'd gone in before. There was no one in sight this time, so they slipped in and followed the same path they'd taken then.

At the corner of the main building they paused, and Gabe gestured at his ear. Cara's brow furrowed, but then she heard the faint, arrhythmic sound he'd heard.

Clippers. Garden clippers.

Gabe crouched, darted his head around the corner for a quick look, so quick Cara was amazed he'd seen anything.

"She's right there, in the roses," he whispered. "By the first guest cottage."

She kept her voice just as low. "Alone?"

He nodded. "If we split up—" He stopped, looking sorry that he'd said it.

"What?"

He shook his head. "Too dangerous."

"What?" she asked, as insistently as she could in a whisper. When he didn't answer, she looked around. "You mean, while I confront her you go around and come up behind her? In case she tries to run?" He looked startled enough she knew she'd guessed right. "Good idea," she said.

"Rotten idea."

She ignored him. "Go. I'll give you two minutes to get around the other side of the main building. Then I'll go greet her as if nothing were wrong. And we'll see how she reacts."

"Cara—"

"Go," she said. "We'll never have a better chance. I promise, I'll stay more than an arm's length away from her and her clippers. Or rake, if she has it handy."

She wasn't sure what decided him, but something did. He leaned down, planted a quick but luscious kiss on her lips, and then he was gone.

She was so startled—and her response to that kiss so hot and swift—it was a moment before she thought to start tracking that two minutes she'd promised. But when she was sure it had passed, she took a deep breath to steady herself, and began to move.

She went quickly at first, her eyes on Crystal, who was intent on pruning back the rosebush that was nearly waist high and showing spring growth. She was barely ten feet away when Crystal noticed her, and she instantly slowed to a casual stroll, and put a smile on her face. And put out of her mind that she was looking at the woman who had killed her best friend.

"Why, good morning," she said cheerily, all the while watching Crystal's face.

The woman was surprised to see her, there was no doubt

about that. But surprised to see her alive? Cara couldn't tell. And Crystal recovered quickly.

"Thought you were gone," she snarled.

"I'm sure you did," Cara said. "How was your trip to town?"

The young woman looked puzzled. "Useless. Didn't have what I needed."

The expression looked genuine, Cara thought.

Crystal went on bluntly, as if to say they weren't welcome any longer, "Miriam didn't expect you back. Had me strip the rooms." She gave Cara a look she couldn't quite interpret. "Not that you used both of them last night."

Cara felt color rise in her cheeks, the last thing she wanted when face-to-face with this woman. Especially since she'd just seen Gabe, just beyond the arbor a few feet behind Crystal.

"Don't blame you," Crystal said. "He's a hot one."

Cara blinked. And Crystal smiled. A real, sincere smile, and it changed the hard, set lines of her face. For that moment, she looked her age, instead of eons older. And for that moment, Cara had no idea what to say.

But the smile vanished quickly, and Crystal's face settled back into her usual sullen expression as she tossed her thick braid over her shoulder and went back to her pruning. With those clippers.

"Yes, he is," Cara finally managed, carefully avoiding another glance at Gabe. "I feel guilty, though. Hope was my best friend."

"She's dead, I hear. Sorry."

Cara took a deep breath. "Are you?"

Crystal gave her a sideways look. "Not really. All flash. Didn't like her."

Cara caught Gabe's movement. She wondered if he was closing in because of what Crystal had said, or because she was getting close to why they were here.

"So you wanted her to go."

"Wasn't sorry."

"Because she shared something with Miriam you never could."

Crystal shrugged, as if indifferent. "They were tight."

"And you felt threatened."

Crystal looked at her then. "By her? She'd no more do what I do around here than fly."

"But she took up Miriam's time, and attention. Weren't you worried she wouldn't have any left to give you?"

Crystal laughed. It wasn't a pleasant sound, and the suspicions that had wavered slightly came flooding back full force.

"You think I was looking for a mother figure or something? Hell with that. They're overrated. I get food and a roof here. Miriam doesn't give it. I earn it."

This was getting her nowhere. Crystal was back at the roses, so Cara glanced over at Gabe. He nodded, and she knew he meant she should just cut to the chase.

"So why would you risk that? We were leaving anyway. Why try to kill us?"

Crystal's clipping stopped. She turned her head to look at Cara. Better than lunging at me, Cara thought. Not that she'd have gotten away with it; Gabe was moving now.

"What the hell are you talking about?"

"You trying to kill us like you did Hope," she said, with a bluntness that more than equaled Crystal's usual tone.

Crystal backed up a step. Then another.

"Going somewhere?" Gabe asked pleasantly.

Crystal yelped, jerked, turned as if she were going to run. But Gabe was right there, blocking her retreat.

"It's over, Linda," Gabe said, and Cara saw the woman pale as he said her real name.

"You're crazy," she said. "Both of you. I never killed anyone."

"You sent Hope driving down the mountain to her death," Cara said.

"But you and your truck didn't succeed with us this morning," Gabe said. "You should have stuck around to be sure we went over the edge."

Crystal frowned then. "Truck? I haven't driven that truck in a month."

"Nice try. You already admitted you went into town."

"I walked." She looked from Cara to Gabe and back again. "I don't have a driver's license."

"So law-abiding citizen that you are, you don't drive? Please," Cara said.

"It's over," Gabe said again. "You got away with killing my wife for eight years. You tried to kill us, twice, because we got too close."

Crystal burst into motion. She bent, grabbed a pruning saw Cara hadn't seen from the ground beside her, and in the same movement lunged at Cara.

The glint of the nasty blade left little doubt in Cara's mind.

Crystal would kill again if she had to.

Chapter 22

Gabe's heart slammed as he saw Crystal grab the wicked little saw and lunge toward Cara. Adrenaline poured through him as Cara darted to one side, putting the rose bush and its thorns between her and her attacker, and giving him the split second he needed.

He tackled Crystal. They went down in a pile of bark mulch. Rolled. Gabe tried to dodge the nasty blade. Crystal tried to hack off whatever she could reach to escape. Gabe felt a sharp rush of pain as the blade connected with his left shoulder. He tried again to pin Crystal, this time taking no care; female or not, she was dangerous, and had to be stopped.

Crystal suddenly yelped in pain of her own. She recoiled, giving him the leverage he needed. In the next second he had her face down, pinned with his knee. And over them both stood Cara, Crystal's rake in her hands, ready to jab again if necessary.

"Nice work," Gabe said.

Cara didn't smile. "You're bleeding," she said anxiously.

He tested his arm, his hand. It hurt, but everything worked. "It'll keep for the moment."

"Hey!"

The shout came from behind them, and they both looked that way in time to see Lawrence Hammon trotting toward them, a look of shock on his face.

"What's going on? What happened?" He paled slightly at the sight of Gabe's bloodied arm. "My God, she's finally done it, hasn't she? I knew it."

His gaze was fastened on Crystal, who was busy trying to spit out pieces of decorative bark.

"You knew what, Lawrence?" Cara asked as Gabe got Crystal to her feet, keeping her under control with an arm twisted behind her back.

"I knew she was crazy. Dangerous."

"Dangerous?" Gabe asked.

Lawrence looked at him. "I didn't know who you were related to, when we met before. But I was here, the last time your wife was here."

Gabe went still. Crystal twisted, her eyes fastened on Lawrence now as she spat out, "Yes, you were, you son of a bitch."

Lawrence ignored her. "I'm sorry about her, by the way. She seemed nice, the few times I met her." The banal nicety sounded oddly out of place in the current circumstances. But Lawrence soldiered on. "Now it all makes sense. I caught her—" he gestured toward Crystal "—messing around with your wife's car, that last time."

"You're a damned liar!"

Lawrence ignored Crystal's shout. "I thought she was just trying to steal something. That's what she usually does. But she had those clippers, like she always has."

Crystal let out a string of epithets that would do the saltiest sailor proud.

"Now I realize what she was really doing." He shook his head mournfully. "I've tried over and over to get Mom to do the sensible thing, and get rid of her. But that soft heart of hers…."

"Damn you!" Crystal shouted. She twisted in Gabe's grasp. He tightened his grip, ignoring the jab of pain from the slice on his shoulder; the bleeding had mostly stopped, so he knew it wasn't serious.

"I'll call the sheriff," Cara said, taking her cell phone out of her pocket. At least she'd thought to do that, Gabe thought. His was stupidly still in the car.

"You're believing him, aren't you?" Crystal said. Rage reddened her face. "He's lying through his teeth and you believe him."

Cara flipped open the phone, but looked at Crystal before dialing. "Lying about what?" she asked.

"Everything!" Crystal seemed to make an effort to steady herself. "Look, I know what you think of me, what everyone around here thinks of me. But Miriam's been good to me, one of the only people who ever has been, and I wouldn't do anything to someone she cared about. Unlike *him*," she finished with a vehemence aimed at Lawrence that startled Gabe.

Lawrence backed up a step, looking at Crystal much like Gabe would imagine he'd look at a coiled rattlesnake.

"Nice try," Gabe said. "But what reason would he have to hurt my wife?"

"And a friend of his own mother?" Cara added.

"Exactly," Lawrence said.

"I'll tell you," Crystal said. "In one word. Lorna."

Gabe blinked. But before he could ask Crystal what she meant, Lawrence took a step toward them. Gabe felt Crystal tense, as if she expected a physical attack. He wondered if he was going to end up in the strange position of protecting the woman who'd murdered his wife.

"Don't you dare! You're not fit to even speak my sister's name."

"There!" Crystal said. "You see what I mean?"

Gabe frowned. So did Cara, as she said, "No. What do you mean?"

"Don't you see? He's crazy! He's obsessed, he's never let go of his dead sister."

"That's ridiculous," Lawrence said. "Are you calling the sheriff, or shall I? I want her gone from here."

Crystal glared at him. "You think I'm blind? That I didn't see or hear your fights with Miriam?"

She looked at Cara, apparently thinking she was her best chance. A torrent of words poured out, more than they'd ever heard from her before.

"He was convinced Hope was trying to become a replacement for his dead sister. That she was taking Lorna's place, in Miriam's heart. They were getting too close. You were right about that, they shared something Miriam and I never would. That didn't matter to me, she was already giving more than I'd ever had in my life. But he—" Gabe still had her arms pinned, so she kicked toward Lawrence "—was the one who was threatened by that. So he decided he had to get rid of her."

"Can't you shut her up?" Lawrence said to Gabe. "This is absurd, having to listen to this."

"I'm the one who caught *him* messing with Hope's car," Crystal said. "Right before she left that last time." She looked at Lawrence again. "*He's* the one who was driving the truck this morning. I saw him get out of it when he came back."

"That's preposterous," Lawrence exclaimed.

"Ask Miriam. She knows I've been out here working all morning," Crystal said, looking from Cara to Gabe and back, a pleading in her eyes Gabe would have never expected to see there. And he remembered that moment in the kitchen, when Crystal had seemed protective of Miriam.

"Gabe," Cara said softly. "The story. The last one she wrote, before that last trip here…."

Gabe's brows furrowed. He'd automatically looked at the dates on all the writings Hope had sent Miriam, remembered the one that had been sent right before she'd come up that last time. The one that had puzzled them, because in it Hope had made no mention of an immediate visit, had only said she'd see Miriam next month, as planned.

And then it hit him. That was the story where she'd mentioned Lawrence. That he'd driven into Pine Lake behind her as she headed home.

The story where she'd jokingly mentioned that you could surely tell Lawrence lived down on the flat, because he drove like a city maniac, tailgating all the way, not easygoing and courteous like all the mountain residents were. He was the exception to the village friendliness, she'd written, the only truly unwelcoming soul she'd found here. And then she had, Hope-like, forgiven him, because he was such a lost soul, still grieving fiercely for his long dead sister.

Tailgating.

Unwelcoming.

Grieving.

Cara's words came back to him in a rush. "Grief does crazy things to you," he said softly.

"Yes," Cara said.

"What are you wasting time for?" Lawrence demanded.

They both turned to look at him.

"Call the sheriff," he said. "Or I will. Don't you want her to pay for what she did?"

"Did you try to run Hope off the road the way you did us, first?" Gabe asked; he wasn't sure he believed it, but he watched Lawrence's face as he went on. "And when that didn't work, you cut her brake line?"

Lawrence paled. And backed up a step. "Don't be stupid."

"And was Crystal just handy?" Cara asked. "A likely scapegoat that no one would believe anyway?"

Lawrence switched his gaze to Cara. "You can't be taking her seriously! Look at her. She's nothing, a stray, a step away from jail all her life."

"Is that why you didn't try to kill her?" Gabe asked. "She was no threat, not like Hope, who shared a talent and a love of writing with your mother?"

"He did try."

Gabe looked at Crystal. He still had a firm grip on her, but she'd quit fighting the moment they'd started to listen to her. He'd noticed, and it had been part of the reason he'd turned the probing questions on Lawrence.

"First he tried to buy me off. Offered me money to leave. Then he tried to drive me away. General nastiness, pranks, then he really got ugly. Tried to poison me, with stuff from his own mother's garden shed."

"That's a lie!" But Lawrence was backing up quickly now, his eyes darting around nervously.

"What would your sainted sister think of you now, Larry?" Crystal sneered.

"She'd understand," Lawrence spat back at her. "She always did. She was the only one who ever did."

Gabe was expecting it when Lawrence broke and ran. He'd already made his decision, and he let go of Crystal and went after Lawrence. Cara reacted almost as quickly, grabbing up Crystal's dropped pruning saw and darting toward him, making him reverse course. It was just the split second Gabe needed and he took the man down with a knee-popping tackle.

They scuffled, Lawrence flailing wildly. He landed a lucky hit on Gabe's cheekbone but then suddenly stopped, curling up like one of the sow bugs that populated the garden debris, screaming, "Stop, stop!"

Gabe rolled off the man. He looked at the new assailant; Crystal had finally gotten to put her rake to use. He let her get in a couple of good licks before he gently stopped her.

"Enough, Crystal. He'll get his, now."

She delivered one more blow to the quivering Lawrence, but then she backed up and dropped the rake.

Cara reached out and put a hand on Crystal's arm. Somewhat to Gabe's surprise, the woman didn't shake it off.

"Now I really will call the sheriff," Cara said.

"You believed me," Crystal said, sounding astonished.

"Yes," Gabe said.

Crystal looked from Cara to Gabe. And for the first time since they'd known her she looked, not angry, but genuinely troubled. "I'm sorry," she said. "I was sure he'd done it, but I had no way to prove it. And I knew no one would believe me."

Gabe imagined apologizing was not something Crystal did often. "I understand," he said.

Cara paused in the act of dialing the phone. "Why did you stay, after he tried to poison you?"

"Miriam," Crystal said simply. "I couldn't be sure he wouldn't get even crazier and decide she deserved to die for trying to replace his precious sister."

This time it was Gabe who reached out and put a hand on her arm. "Crazy indeed. You can't replace someone you loved."

Cara made a sound, then finished dialing the call to the sheriff.

"I've never loved anybody like that," Crystal said, "but that doesn't mean I don't know how it works." She glanced at Gabe's bloody shoulder. "I'm sorry about that, too."

At the second apology in as many minutes, Gabe smiled. "It's all right." He glanced at Lawrence, still curled up in a fetal position on the ground. "He's lucky he didn't have the guts to take you on face-to-face. You would have taken him out in a minute."

She gave him the first real smile he'd ever seen on the young woman's face. And for an instant he saw what she might have been, had her life gone differently. A sudden idea occurred to him, and he made a mental note of it.

"It just never occurred to me," Cara said softly.

"What?" Gabe asked.

"That he meant Hope, too, when he talked of his mother taking in strays."

Gabe winced inwardly. "Me, neither. If it had, I might have thought of him sooner. But this explains why he reacted that way when we broke up that fight between him and Crystal. I thought he was hesitating to talk about something personal, when in fact he was trying to think up that lie about the antique watches."

Things happened quickly after that; a single sheriff's deputy, a young man who looked barely out of the academy, arrived to assess the situation and quickly call for backup and a supervisor when Gabe informed him he needed to take custody of a murderer. While he handcuffed Lawrence Hammon, Crystal went inside to find Miriam, insisting on telling her herself. Miriam was writing again, behind closed doors, and could tune out the world, Crystal told them.

"If she's going to hate me for ratting him out, then I want to know now," she said.

"Gently, Crystal," Cara said. "He's her son."

"And a pitiful excuse for one."

"Perhaps. But still…."

"I'll be gentle." She glanced at both of them. "I can be, if I want to."

"I think," Gabe said quietly, "you can be a lot of good things, if you want to be."

That startled her. So much that twice on her way into the house, she turned and looked back. And when Gabe glanced back to Cara, she was smiling so warmly it took his breath away.

Cara and Gabe followed as the deputy put Lawrence into the back of the black-and-white car parked in front of the inn. There was no sign yet of Miriam, and for that Cara was thankful. There was no way this couldn't be awful for the kind, generous woman, and Cara regretted that. But they'd had to do it. For Hope.

While the deputy was in the middle of taking their statements, still waiting for his sergeant to arrive, a big four-wheel-drive crew cab pickup with the name "Callahan Aviation Services" written on the side pulled up in front of the inn. Two men got out and walked toward them. Neither was the man who'd met them when they'd gone to the airport, George Callahan. Not that she could figure out why he'd be here anymore than these two strangers. Although one of them did look vaguely familiar, she thought.

Both were tall, one about Gabe's height with close-clipped dark hair, the other, the one that seemed familiar, even taller, with longer dark hair faintly touched with silver at the temples. The first man strode toward them in a way that reminded her of Gabe. The taller, lanky man seemed to simply stroll as if they had all the time in the world and yet, she noticed, had no trouble staying even.

"Holy—" Gabe bit back however he'd been going to finish the exclamation. "Talk about sending out the cavalry."

"What?" Cara asked.

"I don't know who the other guy is," he muttered, "but you're about to get your wish to meet Josh Redstone."

Cara smothered a gasp. That was why he'd looked familiar; she'd seen his picture several times in various business publications. The articles had always emphasized his unassuming demeanor, his casual approach, but the photographs had always seemed stiff and formal. Now, in reality, he looked like nothing more than what some detractors—jealous rivals, she'd always thought—called him, a cowboy with freakish luck.

As if you could build an empire like Redstone on just luck, she'd thought then.

And now, as the two men stopped before them and Joshua Redstone turned a pair of steady gray eyes on her, she knew she'd been right. When he spoke, she also understood why those detractors had fallen prey to their own misconceptions.

"Gabe," Josh said, holding out a hand, taking Gabe's in a firm shake. He raised his other hand as if to clap Gabe on the other shoulder, noticed the blood and pulled his hand back. His expression quickly morphed into a frown. "What's this? St. John didn't say anything about you being hurt."

"He didn't know. It's fine. I'll get it cleaned up and be good to go."

Josh seemed to assess that for a moment, then accepted it. He gestured at the man who'd come with him.

"Gabe Taggert, Noah Rider."

Cara saw Gabe's eyes widen. "Rider? Redstone's premier point man? What are you doing here?"

The man grinned as Cara tried to figure out why just as Josh's face had seemed familiar, this man's name did. "I happened to have the good fortune of being in Josh's office when he got word you might need some help up here. I sort of invited myself along to escape the boredom."

"And Paige will have my hide when she finds out I let you hitch a ride into what turned out to be a murder case," Josh said, his mouth twisting wryly.

Rider laughed. "Don't forget my wife and I met during a terrorist hostage-taking."

Cara felt the urge to gasp again, but quashed it. She'd read about that incident at the Redstone Resort in the papers, where guerrilla rebels from a neighboring Caribbean island had taken a school full of children hostage. And this was the man who'd saved them, all of them.

And, she realized belatedly, he was probably the point man Gabe had mentioned before, the one Tess had flown out of the Colombian jungle under fire.

"You must be Cara," Josh said, jerking her attention back. He held out his hand, and as she took it, Cara thought what a crazy turn her life had taken in the past three days, to end up standing here shaking hands with multi-billionaire Josh Redstone. "I'm Josh Redstone. This is Noah Rider who, no matter what he says, could never be bored, not married to Paige and with twins on the way."

"Congratulations," Cara said, looking at Rider. Then, to Josh, "I…can't believe you came yourself."

He shrugged, as if it were nothing. "Gabe needed help. I was the one not doing anything important at the moment."

"And the one who could fly," Rider put in.

Josh grinned. "There is that. And I had just been into that airport not so long ago."

"I hope you were gentler with Reeve than you were with me," Rider said, but the smile on his face belied the complaint. "But it seems we're too late to help much."

"You can save us from spending hours giving statements of the same thing over and over again," Gabe suggested.

"Now that," Rider said, "I can do."

And in that moment, what she saw in the man's eyes made her very confident that somehow, the law enforcement maze would be threaded more easily.

Josh's expression turned serious then. "Can I talk to you for a minute, Gabe? Privately?"

They walked away a few feet, and Cara saw Josh put a hand on Gabe's arm as he listened intently. After a few words Gabe went very still, paled slightly, and Cara's stomach knotted. She didn't know what Josh had told him, wasn't sure she wanted to know. Perhaps it wasn't anything to do with this, perhaps it was something work-related, some bad news there. Because what on earth could be worse than knowing Hope had been murdered?

She found out a short while later, when Josh and Noah Rider had gone off to smooth a path for them and they were about to go inside to face, reluctantly, the woman whose son they'd just had arrested.

But on the wide front porch of the cheerful yellow inn, Gabe stopped. Cara looked up at him. Then, bluntly, in a flat voice unlike any she'd heard from him, he told her what Josh had told him.

"St. John pulled some more of his strings."

"And?" She held her breath, waiting.

"Hope was pregnant."

Before Cara could even absorb this shock, a gasp from the doorway turned them both around. Miriam stood there, staring at them.

"Oh, my God. It's my fault," she said.

Chapter 23

"It's my fault. It's all my fault."

"Stop that, Miriam. It's not your fault."

Gabe and Cara stood in the kitchen, watching Crystal try to comfort her benefactor.

"She's right," Cara said gently. "Lawrence made his decisions, he's a grown-up. You had nothing to do with it."

"I didn't mean Lawrence," Miriam said, startling them all. "I…can't deal with that, not yet. I meant Hope."

Cara glanced at Gabe, saw by his furrowed brows that he had no more idea what Miriam meant than she did.

"How was what happened to Hope your fault?" Cara asked gently.

"You said she was pregnant."

Cara didn't dare look at Gabe again, she didn't want to see what might be in his face, his eyes. His beloved Hope had been carrying his child, a child he'd obviously never known about, a child who had died with her.

The second miracle, Cara thought with an ache in her chest.

"What does that have to do with what happened?" Gabe asked. His voice was level, even, and only the tightness of the muscles along his jaw told Cara what an effort it was.

"I made her promise me that if it ever happened, I'd be the second to know. After you."

Gabe let out a compressed breath. "And I was deployed," he muttered. "It could have been days before we could talk."

Miriam rubbed at her reddened eyes as tears brimmed once more. "Why didn't she just call me?"

"She would have wanted to share it in person," Cara said of the friend she'd known so well.

"I shouldn't have made her make that promise. But I told her that, after losing Lorna, this would be as close as I'd ever come to having a daughter to share that with. She promised. And died trying to keep that promise."

Miriam broke down then. Crystal never left her side, and urged her gently into the other room to lie down.

"She must feel destroyed. First her son, now this," Cara said.

Gabe said nothing, and finally Cara looked at him. He said in that same, flat voice, "Redstone will help, if we can. Anything she needs."

"I hope that's short of a slick lawyer for Lawrence," Cara said.

Gabe said nothing, didn't even react.

"I'm sorry, Gabe," she said. "I can't even begin to imagine how you must feel. First Hope, then…a child you never even knew about? I'm so sorry."

When he still said nothing, Cara reached out and touched his uninjured arm. It was rock-solid beneath her fingers. And still he didn't react.

"Gabe?"

He wouldn't even look at her. Cara's heart sank. Somehow in the past few minutes, everything had changed between them.

What did you expect? He just found out he would have been—

should have been—a father. A child with Hope, the woman he had loved. And probably still loves.

Gabe's words to Miriam came back to her, painfully.

You can't replace someone you loved.

She didn't have the heart or the time to press further. Josh and Rider descended on them, having organized things in an almost frighteningly efficient manner. The statements they'd already given would stand for now; the sheriff's office would contact them later for more. Gabe's car would be towed down for repairs, Rider told them, while the two of them flew back with him and Josh in the jet Josh had flown here. The *Hawk III*, he said, the only one that could handle the limitations of the high-altitude airport's runway length.

"Do you want me to call Hope's folks?" Josh asked Gabe as they drove in the big pickup back to the airport, Cara and Gabe in the backseat of the cab.

"No."

Cara had known that would be his answer. He would never let someone else do a job he felt was his responsibility.

Josh nodded in understanding, as if he'd never expected anything else. The fact that he'd made the offer anyway told Cara that the stories—legends, really—about this man were apparently true; if you worked for him, you were family.

"We'll get you back home," Rider said as they pulled in once more at Callahan Aviation. There on the apron, where before the Redstone chopper had sat, was a sleek little private jet in the same colors. "And once we're there, if I can help, you just say so. Anything you need, Gabe, to make arrangements, you've got it."

Rider and Josh got out of the truck, leaving them alone for the moment. And Cara belatedly realized Rider had meant arrangements for some kind of funeral for Hope. And for the first time the utter finality of what she'd always suspected but apparently never completely accepted hit her. Tears welled up suddenly. She fought not to break down sobbing, but it was a useless effort. She felt the urge to lean into Gabe, to seek comfort with the man who had given her such joy, but he'd made it clear he wanted nothing to do with her right now.

Maybe ever, she thought. *Maybe it was just too much to overcome, Hope, this news, all of it.*

So instead she leaned against the door of the truck, trying to keep the weeping she was helpless to stop as quiet as she could.

And then Gabe was there; he'd moved closer, awkwardly put his arm around her. Pulled her close where she'd wanted to be, leaning against him, taking strength and warmth from him. For a long time they just sat there, Cara weeping, Gabe holding her, until she couldn't stop herself from looking up at him through the tears, wondering what he was feeling.

The moment they made eye contact, he drew in a deep breath.

"What Hope went through," he began, then stopped as if it were beyond words.

"Yes," Cara said, steadying herself with an effort; if Gabe was ready to talk, she had to be ready to listen. He deserved that. "But now we know. Why she was here, and what the second miracle was."

"Yes," Gabe said. Then, after a moment, he went on. "I can't picture the guy I was then as a father. Not a good one, anyway. I was too young, too focused on my career."

"But maybe Hope would have been…happier."

"Maybe."

They sat in silence. Once, Cara looked out to see Josh talking with George Callahan, whose crew was readying the red and gray little jet for flight.

"I still can't believe Josh Redstone himself just hopped in one of his planes and flew up here to help."

"That's Josh," Gabe said. "Rider surprised me more."

"So, is everybody who works for Redstone like you two, and Tess and Ryan? So loyal and dedicated?"

"Pretty much," Gabe said. "He inspires it."

Cara thought later, after they'd landed and taxied over to the Redstone hangar, that she wished she had been in a better frame of mind to enjoy this. The *Hawk III* was something: sleek, quick, and elegant. And Josh Redstone was obviously a pilot who knew what he was doing; she'd never had such a whisper-soft landing.

The rest was a blur; Josh himself cleaned up Gabe's shoulder, and offered him a clean shirt from a locker inside the hangar. Rider drove them back to the marina, where it had all started what seemed like ages ago, and where Cara's car was parked. Through it all, Gabe and Cara never spoke, at least, not to each other.

The boat Gabe commanded now sat docilely at the dock, yet still looked as if it could fly in its own way as gracefully as the *Hawk III*. Cara wondered idly if there was any end to the designs the fertile mind of Josh Redstone could come up with.

Gabe gave Rider a quick tour of the boat, then the Redstone point man left with a promise to be in touch to see what was needed.

And then it was only the two of them, standing in the boat's salon in almost exactly the spot where they'd first seen each other again. For a long moment silence spun out between them.

"Cara—"

"Gabe—"

They both stopped, looking rueful.

"Awkward," Gabe muttered.

"Yes."

He reached out then, put his hands on her shoulders. "I'm not that kid I was with Hope anymore. If I met the both of you for the first time now, I'm not sure it would be her I'd be looking at."

Cara's breath caught.

"I want to see you again, Cara. I want you in my life. I want more days, and—" his voice went husky "—nights."

She hadn't thought, hadn't dared to think of this as a possibility. Those words, coming from this man, were a dream come true. But it was a dream she'd never had the right to dream. And even now that she knew Hope was truly gone, she wasn't sure she could bring herself to take what had once been hers. And he was in turmoil, coping with confirmation of their worst fears, and the shocking knowledge that Hope had been pregnant. The loss had to be astounding, and she suspected that was behind his words.

"I...not now, Gabe. It's not the time." She could hardly believe she was saying it, turning away what she'd once longed for so much. But she couldn't do anything else. "I won't be a consolation prize, Gabe. And I could never replace Hope. I won't even try."

He released her abruptly, took a step back. For a moment he said nothing, then, slowly, "I understand."

And that was it. The last words between them, except a forced casual goodbye as she got into the car she'd parked there—had it really only been three days ago?—and drove away. She forced herself not to look in the rearview mirror at him. What had brought them together again, their love for Hope, now lay as an impassable roadblock between them.

Chapter 24

"What's going on, Cap?"

Gabe turned to look at his first mate. "No idea. Josh said head to these coordinates and wait, so that's what we're doing."

It had taken him a while in the beginning, to get used to explaining things like that. In the navy, a captain didn't usually explain a simple order. But then, in the navy, the first mate likely would never have asked. But now he did it without much thought; this was a different world, and in the end, he valued it just as much, if not more.

"Weird," Mark said, but in a tone that was more conversational than judgmental. "Just sitting here, a couple hundred miles out. But if it's what the man wants…."

"Exactly."

Mark grinned. "Not like anybody's gonna argue with him, even if they wanted to, which nobody does."

"Exactly," Gabe repeated, managing a brief smile back.

It was all he could manage. He hadn't been in a smiling mood for five weeks now. Ever since the day Cara had gotten in her car and driven out of his life as abruptly as she'd dropped back into it. He'd only seen her once since, at Lawrence Hammon's court appearance. They'd barely acknowledged each other.

"Sir?"

He refocused on Mark, realizing he'd lost it again, standing here on the bow staring out at blue water unseeingly, he who once would have seen every swell, every ripple that indicated current, every wind wave that told him how to adjust the boat to maintain the position they'd been sitting in for several hours now.

"About your wife. I'm really sorry."

Mark's tone held genuine sympathy, but also trepidation, as if it had taken him this five weeks to work up the nerve to speak about it. That was what made Gabe force himself to respond.

"Thank you." He sounded a bit sharp even to himself, so he added, "It's been a long time. It's not…raw. But thank you."

Mark nodded, and lowered his gaze as if afraid he'd offended his boss. Gabe took pity on him and said in a near-normal voice, "Check for any new weather advisories, will you? I want to be sure that front isn't coming any farther south."

"Yes, sir." Mark turned smartly on his heel and left.

He'd driven the crew hard in the last five weeks. The first two were spent pushing the boat to its limits, and true to most Redstone designs, she'd held steady and firm, requiring only small adjustments here and there as things settled in. The last three had been spent fine-tuning the crew in much the same way; for all the relaxed atmosphere, Redstone vessels were run at utmost efficiency. The ease aboard ship didn't come easily.

He'd driven himself even harder, overseeing everything personally, until he was fairly sure most of the crew wished he would back off. But they'd never say anything, not when they all thought he was grieving for his murdered wife.

Too bad he himself wasn't convinced of it. But it was hard to sell the idea that he was grieving for Hope when all he could think about was Cara.

I won't be a consolation prize, Gabe.

Had he given her the idea that he was trying to replace Hope? he wondered. That he'd wanted her because she'd been Hope's best friend? Had he made her feel that her connection to his dead wife was the only reason he wanted her?

Was it the truth?

He'd been wrestling with that for five weeks now, and was no closer to an answer. Countless times he'd wanted to call her, just to hear her voice, but his doubts had stopped him. Above all the doubt that she would want to talk to him, if that was how he'd made her feel.

"Sir?" Mark was back.

Gabe gave himself an inward shake. "What is it, Mark?"

"You've got a call on the bridge. Mr. Redstone."

Gabe nodded and started back toward the outside stairs. "Maybe now we'll find out why we're here."

A few minutes later, he had a partial answer, and sent Mark to round up the helipad crew to get it ready for an incoming flight.

"You've got about an hour," Josh said.

"All right."

"How are you, Gabe?"

"Fine." He almost, instinctively, added a "sir" but held it back. "We'll be ready," he said instead.

"Good. And don't worry about Cara. If she needs anything, we'll see she gets it."

Gabe went still. "Cara?"

"I'm sure she'll be fine. But if she needs special care, Redstone will—"

"What's wrong?" Gabe cut off his boss without a thought as his heart began to hammer in his chest.

"You haven't talked to her?"

"Not since Hammon's arraignment. What's wrong?"

"I don't have all the details. Just that she's not doing well."

Gabe felt a queasiness in his stomach as a sweat broke out on his body. "Josh, I—"

"I've got to go, Gabe. I'll see if I can find out more and let you know."

With that Josh hung up as abruptly as his right-hand man, St. John. Gabe just stood there, his hand clenched around the handheld microphone that accessed the Redstone satellite com system.

He sat down abruptly in the captain's chair. *Cara.* What was wrong? Hideous possibilities raced through his mind in rapid succession.

"Sir?" Mark's voice held genuine concern this time. "Are you all right?"

No, he thought as his heart hammered as if it were trying to beat its way out of his chest.

Definitely not, he added, suddenly aware he wasn't breathing so much as gasping for air.

He couldn't just sit here and wait to find out. If he wasn't bound by Josh's orders to stay put, he'd already have this boat headed to port.

He was thinking about it anyway.

He told Mark he was fine and to give him a minute, then be-latedly grabbed his cell phone. It wouldn't work out here, but it had Cara's number. He got it, then picked up the more private, receiver version of the satellite phone and dialed.

It immediately went to voice mail, telling him the phone was turned off. He shivered at the sound of her voice on the record-ing, wondering how he'd gone so long without hearing it. He left a message he was sure was disjointed and confused, but he hadn't thought beyond calling to what he'd say.

She's all right. She has to be. I can't lose her, too.

It hit him then, that somehow, on some level, his mind, or his gut—or his heart—had been working on this. And now the answer was perfectly clear; Cara Thorpe was no replacement for Hope. And she was certainly no consolation prize. She was the woman he'd been waiting for, and looking for. The one with the solid, steady center Hope had lacked, the one with the resources to handle whatever life threw at her with style and grace.

He began to pace the bridge, barely managing to resist calling Josh back and telling him he couldn't wait here, he had to get to Cara. And then it occurred to him that he could hitch a ride back in the Redstone chopper and get to shore a lot quicker than by riding this boat back. Whatever this VIP guest needed could be handled by the crew he'd drilled so relentlessly the last three weeks. And if Josh didn't like the desertion of his captain, well....

Over the next half hour he tried Cara's cell every few minutes. Then he gave up and went to stand on the stern deck near the raised helipad, trusting Mark to hold the boat steady into the wind for the landing. He put on the headset that would allow him to talk to the incoming pilot. The two-person crew responsible for keeping the helipad safe and bringing in aircraft kept giving him curious looks, but he said nothing. All the patience he'd ever learned seemed to have vanished.

"Incoming!"

The voice came over the PA, and he and the two crew members scanned the horizon. Patty spotted it first, and yelped the sighting. Gabe followed her gesture and spotted the helicopter heading toward them.

It was the same chopper that had flown them through the mountains, Gabe thought with a qualm. And judging by the way the pilot negotiated the headwind, bringing the craft to a hover just in front of the pad, then backing down to a whisper-soft landing even on a pitching target, Tess Machado was likely at the controls.

"Nice landing," he said into the headset.

Tess's voice came back at him. "It's like rotor-heads tell the starch-wings who think they're better pilots— 'Yeah, but how fast can you fly backwards?'"

He could see her grin through the bubble, and managed a smile; something about Tess's grin was infectious even through his worry. And today there was something even more delightful about her usual cheerful expression.

The rotors began to slow as she disengaged. She left the engine running as she got out, telling Gabe she was planning a quick departure. He wondered if he should tell her now that she was going to have a passenger on the return trip.

"Got a present for you," she called, and opened the passenger compartment door, where someone was just getting free of the harness. A woman, who slid out of the helicopter in an obvious hurry.

Cara.

He gaped up at her. She spotted him and froze, staring back.

He stood stock-still, unable to believe she was there at all, let alone apparently perfectly healthy. The breeze from the slowing rotors was still enough to stir her hair, and it glinted bright copper in the sun. She had one hand to her mouth as she stared at him in obvious surprise.

"Cara," he said.

She couldn't hear him over the chopper's engine. Finally galvanized he started up the steps just as she started down. They met on the third step and he grabbed her, letting out a heartfelt oath at the feel of her in his arms again. He swung her down to the deck and leaped down beside her.

"I thought you were sick!"

"Josh told me you were hurt!"

"I'm fine."

"So am I."

"No, you're not," Tess said from above. "You're two stubborn, wary people and you're letting history get in your way. Anybody who's seen you together knows you belong that way."

They gaped at her in unison; they had obviously been had, in a big, Redstone-style way.

"You're clear to head in, now, Gabe," Tess said with a grin. "We figure it'll take you about eight hours to get to port since Josh forbids you to run at top speed. Enough time even for you two to work things out."

Before they could even react to that, Tess was back aboard the chopper. The rotors picked up speed, their pitch changed, and in moments she was lifting off as smoothly as she'd landed.

In the silence Tess's departure left behind, Gabe was vaguely aware the deck had suddenly become deserted. There was no crew in sight, and he wondered if Tess or Josh had manipulated that, too.

Not that it mattered. The only thing that really mattered was that Cara was all right, and here in his arms.

"I was about to get on that bird," he said against her hair. "I didn't care about my job, this boat, anything except getting to you."

"I did get on that silly bird," Cara said, "even though I swore I never would again. I was afraid otherwise I might not get here in time."

"We," Gabe said wryly, "have been had."

"Yes."

He looked down at her. "But with the best of intentions."

"Yes," she repeated.

He hesitated for a moment, then decided to hell with it, he'd waited long enough.

"You were wrong, Cara. I never, ever thought of you as a replacement for Hope. How could I, when you fill places in me she never did?"

He heard her draw in a sharp breath, saw her eyes widen, and knew he'd somehow found the right words.

"And you could never be any man's idea of a consolation prize. *You're the* prize, Cara. And I'll do whatever it takes to win."

"Too late," she said.

Gabe's breath died in his throat. Had he left it too long? Then she smiled at him, and he could take in air again.

"That contest," she said, "is already over."

He pulled her tighter and took her mouth with a ferocity that had five weeks of longing and aching for her behind it. And when, later, he introduced her to the captain's quarters and they locked the door, he barely noticed that there still wasn't a crew member in sight.

Epilogue

Cara looked down at the small, richly bound book in her hands. The gold lettering embossed on the cover and spine gleamed in the California sun, catching the light. Another glint caught her eye, and she smiled as she looked at the diamond on her left hand. This was the last day her engagement ring would be on her finger by itself.

As she watched Gabe drive the expertly repaired Lexus, she thought about the last time they'd made this trip. It had been the last of three destinations, the one they'd feared the most.

The first, a quick flight to Oregon—thankfully too far for the chopper, meaning she got to enjoy this trip on the bigger *Hawk IV*—netted them the surprised but pleased approval of her parents, especially her father, who appreciated Gabe's respectful request for his permission. The second had been to see the Admiral, whose approval was gruff but not grudging; "You'll do," he said to Cara after they'd talked for a while, and Gabe had later told her that was the highest praise the man ever gave.

No, the difficult part had been the third visit, one they had put off. But they discovered they'd both decided independently it needed to be done, which made it an obligation they couldn't ignore.

So they'd gone to the quiet, suburban home of Gwen and Earl Waldron, where just months before they'd gone to give them the news they'd expected but dreaded, but also the closure they'd needed. They'd thought about waiting, giving them more time, but Gabe finally said time wasn't going to heal this wound, and they'd gone ahead.

And found, amazingly, that although surprised, Hope's parents welcomed the news.

"It feels right," Gwen said. "You're the two people closest to our little girl, and we know you'll never forget her."

"We never could," Cara had told them gently. And someday, she'd thought, if there was a little girl in their lives, perhaps her name would be Hope.

And now they were back again.

Earl opened the door to Gabe's knock, and stared in surprise. Gwen came up behind him, and her brows rose in a surprise that echoed her husband's.

"Well, now, I figured you two would be busy as bees, today being the day before your wedding. In fact, I was about to call and see if there was anything I could do to help."

"Thank you," Cara said as the pair ushered them inside, "but there's not even much for me to do, except show up."

"Redstone has the wedding thing down pat," Gabe said with a grin. "They've had lots of practice recently, it seems."

"Besides," Cara said, "we wanted to bring you something."

"Us?" Gwen asked.

"It's…well, sort of our wedding present to you."

"Well, that's a twist," Earl said.

Cara glanced at the man who, this time tomorrow, would be her husband. Gabe nodded, and she held out the small book, bound in Hope's vivid purple.

Gwen took it, a puzzled look on her face. Then she saw the title and name on the cover and gasped.

"We thought you should have these," Gabe said. "Hope's personality, her heart, is all over them."

"And know that our own copy will come along wherever we go, so that we will always have Hope with us, too," Cara said.

Hope's parents stared down at the little book of their daughter's stories, including the ones Ryan Barton had been able to recover from the hard drive in Hope's laptop, which had somehow survived with data partially intact. Gwen traced the golden words, *Always Hope*, that gleamed on the cover.

Cara felt her own eyes brim at the raw emotion on those two much-loved faces. And was flooded with gratitude that Gabe had instantly agreed with her idea about this book, and in fact had found the self-publisher himself, through Redstone. Of course.

At that thought, she wondered for a moment how Crystal was doing in her new life; it had taken only a word from Gabe to his boss and an entire new life had opened up for the young woman. She'd hesitated to leave Miriam, but the woman had encouraged her to grab the opportunity; you didn't often get the chance to pick and choose your place in an organization as incredible as Redstone. *The golden touch balanced by the golden rule,* Gabe had told her, the phrase coined in a news magazine about Redstone, was, in fact, true.

She felt Gabe's arm come around her and leaned into him. She remembered when she'd made him read Hope's piece about him, remembered the odd combination of relief and pain that had shown in his face as he did. And how he'd responded when she told him, with every bit of the emotion she was feeling, that what Hope had seen as failings, she found reasons for pride and respect.

And wondered what it was going to be like to be, as Josh had told her she would be, married to Redstone.

Married to Gabriel Taggert, literally the man of her dreams.

She couldn't wait to find out.

* * * * *

THE BEAST WITHIN

BY

LISA RENEE JONES

Lisa Renee Jones is an author of paranormal and contemporary romance. Though she's always lived in Austin, Texas, Lisa will soon be making a new home in New York. Before becoming a writer, Lisa worked as a corporate executive, often taking the red-eye flight out of town and flying home just in time to make a Little League baseball game. Her award-winning company, LRJ Staffing Services, had offices in Texas and Nashville. Lisa was recognised by *Entrepreneur Magazine* in 1998 for owning one of the top-ten growing businesses owned by women.

Now Lisa has the joy of filling her days with the stories playing in her head, turning them into novels she hopes you enjoy!

You can visit her at www.lisareneejones.com.

Thanks go out to:
Diego – for taking me to Brownsville and helping this idea take form, not to mention inviting me into the world of paranormal. I had no idea what I was missing!
Roberto Harrison – for the endless stream of cultural and historical support!
Cathryn Fox – for the great input and reading the same pages over and over.
My editor Ann Leslie Tuttle – for her belief in me and the Knights and for her valuable editorial support.

Legend of the Beasts

Sentenced to an eternity on earth for killing his brother Abel, Cain became angry and sought the good graces – and powers – of the underworld. By doing so, it is said that he was granted magical powers and given leave from the physical plane. But his gifts came with a price. Cain now rules an army of beasts who walk the earth, stealing souls and delivering them to the underworld.

Though Cain was allowed to get away with his actions, over time, the scale of good and evil began to tilt. The Angel Raphael, the healer of the earth, was given the duty of balancing the scale again. To do this, he assigned Salvador, his most trusted companion, the duty of saving those souls worthy of serving good against evil. These unique men are given back their souls and enlisted in an elite army… the Knights of White.

Prologue

Angel or demon?

She sat astride him, long blond hair flowing around her creamy white shoulders in a veil of silky perfection. She visited his dreams often in recent days, but never often enough. He both desired her visits and dreaded them. Dreaded them, because he knew instinctively she led him to the forbidden. Like the devil in the disguise of a beautiful woman, she lured him to temptation. To a place sure to damn his soul.

With a seductive rhythm, her hips arched into his body, swaying with delicious invitation. Everything about her made him burn. Her smell. Her full bottom lip. Her full breasts as they bounced, nipples peaked with arousal. Begging for his hands. For his eyes.

With each stroke of her wet heat along his body, he yearned to be deeper. To take more of her. To become lost in her until he forgot the burning need threatening to surface. A need, relentless in its demands, threatened his control. A desire to claim her very essence. To go to a place he'd never dared go. But if he did, would he stop there? Or would the beast then take control? Would he be lost to a lust for more than physical satisfaction?

Would he then become one of the soulless fanged monsters—the ones he had come to know as "Darkland Beasts"—who had taken his wife, Caron, and his life, two centuries before? The ones that had destroyed everything he'd called his world, and lurked just beneath his human shield, ready to claim the part of him still a man.

He felt the beast move in him, calling his name, calling for ownership and command. Felt it trying to pull him into darkness beyond human comprehension, pressing him to act on primal instincts.

And there seemed only one answer. One way to resist the beast.

He had to get lost in this woman. To sate his lust with her body, not her life. She held the answer. Though part of him screamed in warning, screamed she was his demise, another part knew her as his salvation. It was always like this with her. Confusing. Conflicted. Better not to think. Just…feel.

Using her hips as leverage, he arched upward, thrusting his body deep, and pulling her hard against his pelvis, trying to get lost in lust. He was far too close to the edge. Too close to the beast. It wanted him, just as he wanted this woman.

He wanted her like he hadn't desired another in a hundred years. Not since his wife. But that had been another life. Another world. Staring at the blond beauty atop him, for just a moment he pictured his Caron, dark hair and dark eyes. For just an instant, he flashed back to a time of the past. So real was that image that he squeezed his eyes shut, confusion raking through his brain.

A soft moan of pleasure escaped her full lips, drawing his gaze again. He watched her lashes flutter, searching her features. Another moan filled the air, pulling him into the present fully again. Arousing and sweet, the sound hummed along the rawness of nerve endings. He struggled against his urges…fighting…resisting.

As a serpent might its prey, she seemed to play on his weaknesses. Yet, with his every attempt to hold back, this woman, this temptress, seemed to draw him out more. It was no use. Desire controlled him now. Release was his only salvation. It was hers, too. Release would stave off the beast.

He thrust into her, but she arched backward, holding him back, not allowing him to become lost in the burn. He had to find release…release would save them both. Without it he would take more than pleasure, without it… He told himself to shove her away. To ignore the erotic feel of her body squeezing his.

But she seemed to sense his resistance. Bending forward, she pressed those lush, full breasts against his chest. Her lips brushed his jaw. His neck. His ear. Teeth scraped his lobe. A rush of heat surged through his veins, and a low growl escaped his lips. His mind clouded. He could only feel. Only need. And what he needed was…*to devour her.*

The thought screamed with warning. He had to end this now, before it was too late. Before he did something he'd regret. But even as he willed himself to end this craziness, his hand slid around the curve of her perfect, round ass. With a hard thrust, he lifted his hips and pulled her against his cock. At the same time, his other hand found her breast, palming it, pinching the nipple with rough demand. His mouth found hers, and he drank her in, desperate to sate the ravenous hunger only this woman created.

This hunger that reached beyond the pleasure shared between a man and woman.

"Take me," she whispered, pulling back to stare into his eyes. "I already belong to you. You know I do. I know what you want, and I give it freely. Take all of me."

Her words rang in his ears, and his wife flashed in his mind again. He was so confused…so aroused. So… The sight of her elegant, white neck as she shoved aside her hair made her intent clear. She couldn't know what he was, yet her actions, her invitation, said otherwise. And, Lord help him, he wanted to take what she offered. To drink of the sweet liquid that ran through her veins. Only he wouldn't stop there. The taste of her would bring out the beast. And the beast would drain her dry.

"Take me," she said, sitting there on top of him, looking like a goddess. All that creamy white skin against his darker coloring aroused and tempted.

"You have no idea what you suggest," he murmured, fighting a moan as she glided along his length.

A slow smile slid onto her lips. "Oh, but, I do. I know exactly what I suggest." She leaned over him and brought her lips just inches from his. The warm tickle of her breath caressed his skin. "And I give it to you freely."

"You don't or you would know how dangerous—"

Taking the role of aggressor, she kissed him, cutting off his words as her tongue slid past his teeth. Her body rocked atop his, demanded he move with her. His head spun with the impact of her words. With the soft pressure of her mouth upon his. Reality seemed a distant place. What happened here and now became fantasy.

Her cheek rested against his. "I am yours." There was a soft, angelic promise to her words. "Take me." Hands pressed into the mattress, on either side of his head, she leaned back enough to once again bare her exposed neck. "Drink."

His cuspids extended as if answering her demand. An unconscious action. What was happening to him? The beast stayed buried deep inside, out of reach. Even in battle, he controlled the primal side of his being. But not now. Not with this woman.

Jag squeezed his eyes shut. *No!* The word screamed in his mind. This wasn't real. It was a dream. What happened here didn't matter. But some part of him rejected the thought. This seemed like it was really happening. His lashes lifted, fixing on the beauty rocking atop him. She looked and felt real. And the thirst she induced did, as well.

With a low growl, he reacted, rolling her to her back, determined to reclaim his control. To put this yearning for the forbidden in a safe place. He'd never taken from a human, and he wouldn't now. Deep down he knew he was a monster. But he still possessed his soul, unlike his enemies, the Darkland Beasts.

He could resist temptation. He *must*.

Raised up on his hands, he stared down at the puckered nipples of the woman beneath him. Licking his lips at the delicious sight they made, he thrust deep, watching her breasts jiggle with the action. He pounded into her. Once. Twice. Over and over.

With each stroke, each grinding of their hips, he focused on the immediate pleasure, rather than the temptation to taste blood. Yet, it burned inside him. Begged to be fed. He just wanted to find an escape. To get lost in pleasures of the flesh. To forget temptation.

Soft moans and words of praise slid from the lips of his seductress like a sensual song. And no matter how much he took of her, she took more. She kept wanting.

"Deeper," she begged, fueling his fire. "Harder." Again and again he drove deep into the wet heat of her depths. Her legs wrapped his calves, her hips lifting to meet him stroke for stroke.

He claimed her mouth, and with hungry laps of his tongue, he tasted her, praying it would sate the building flame inside wanting to explode. But kissing her only made his body yearn at new levels. He couldn't get enough of her. He molded his body to hers, skin to skin. She clung to him with something just shy of desperation. Wildly, they bucked, rocked, and moved as one. Trying to get closer. Yes. He. Had. To. Get…closer.

Burying his face in her neck, he acted on instinct. Never before had sex pushed him to this level of absolute lust. He couldn't think. He thought passion had been the answer, a way to forget the need for her blood. But it only seemed to fuel the fire. Her body squeezed him, short, hard spasms milking him.

"Take me," she whimpered. Then, louder, almost a demand, "Do it!"

He had no comprehension of what made him act. No instant of decision. No reason why he understood what she wanted him to do. He simply slipped into the moment. Control, the very thing he valued the most in this eternal life of hell, perhaps the only thing he still valued, simply failed him. He could hear her blood rushing through her veins…calling to him. His nostrils flared, hunting for the scent of the crimson liquid not yet free.

With raw hunger, he turned his mouth to her shoulder and sank his teeth deeply. She stiffened and made a low sound as he began drinking, taking her in. His mind reached for hers, helping her calm, feeling her muscles ease.

The bittersweet, metallic flavor of her blood touched his tongue like a perfect drug. He felt a rush of power beyond anything he'd felt in all of his two centuries of life. Still hard, buried deep in her body, he felt a primitive need to thrust. It overpowered the fear that he might begin to change physically, to take on a monstrous form. The one who had saved him from the beasts had told him he couldn't transform. But then, he had also warned him to never taste blood.

But none of this mattered. He could only think of the need to sink deep to her core. To pound her as the crimson delight slid down his throat. His body shook with the ecstasy of the combined pleasures, and he moaned as he drank in her rich flavor. He spilled himself with one final descent to her depths, seeing darkness with the utter, complete ecstasy of the moment.

As his body slid into a relaxed mode, he felt the slow return of reality. His teeth eased from her shoulder and a combination of confusion, fear and guilt took hold. He looked at her first, trying to confirm her safety. She sighed in satisfaction and smiled as if nothing was wrong. Frantically he held a hand up to view it, looking for signs of his body's change to beast. But there were none.

She looked up at him, her soft fingers caressing his cheek. Her eyes were an amazing color. Sky-blue with a hint of green. How had he missed them before? Why did he notice them now?

"You only did what had to be done," she whispered.

He didn't even know what to say. She made no sense. Or maybe he was going crazy. Maybe he heard what he wanted to hear, not what was really spoken. He buried his face in her neck, desperate to hide from the trust in her eyes.

Desperate to wake up from the dream…now a nightmare.

With a gasp, Jag came awake. He shoved away the cool, white sheets and sat up in his bed. His eyes traveled his sparsely decorated bedroom in the ranch he considered a sanctuary of sorts. It was here he hid from the world. Here he trained others like himself. Here he pretended he belonged. But at this moment, it offered none of the calmness it often brought. Not when his heart beat in his chest like a drum.

The instant he confirmed he was alone, no seductress to be found, he reached for the sheets again, wildly looking for the bright crimson tint of blood. There was nothing. Yet…it had seemed as real as anything else he'd ever experienced. His eyes darted around the room, to the left and then the right, confirming no one lurked in the shadows.

But like all the times before, it had been just a dream. She wasn't real.

Jag's hand ran over the dark stubble of his jaw. It had been nearly two centuries since he'd had a dream. Not until three weeks ago when his sleep had become haunted by a blond beauty who took him to bliss and back. Night after night, she teased him with her body and drew him into some emotional climax he didn't pretend to understand.

But tonight, she'd offered more than mere pleasure. He bit his bottom lip, certain he could still taste her. What had been a dream felt far too real. He'd stolen her blood to feed his own needs.

He'd become the very thing he hunted—a Darkland Beast who took the lifeblood of humans.

He felt the words like a hard punch in the gut. No… Never. He pushed off the bed and walked toward the shower. Long ago, he'd learned never to take surface answers. The obvious would be to assume these dreams were simply about his own battles with who and what he was. But it felt like more. Like a warning.

When he'd taken on the role of leader to the "Knights

of White," he'd sworn an oath to protect humanity and his men. He couldn't ignore a possible message. He gambled with his own existence but not with that of others.

He looked down at the ring on his finger, touching the engraving, a five-pointed star given to him by the one who had saved his soul. He needed answers, and there was only one place he knew to get them…back to where he had left his prior self behind. Back to where a man he knew only as "Salvador" had given him a new life and a new name. To where he had become simply "Jag" for Jaguar, named by Salvador after a creature of great speed and skill.

To the immortal who had taken a monster and turned him back to a man. At least, part man. The beast still lived inside, and Jag never forgot this fact. He led others like himself, fighting to destroy the Darkland Beasts. It was all he had left. All he lived for.

And he couldn't allow anything, or anyone, to stand in his way.

Most certainly not some seductress who was nothing but a dream, and a bad one at that.

Chapter 1

The sound of her bedside hotel phone ringing startled Karen Gibson awake. She blinked into Caribbean sunlight beaming between the sheer white curtains of the French doors, which opened to a beachfront patio. The luxury hotel was one of many stops she'd be making while on assignment for *Vacation Fun* magazine.

Normally she called her life one of pleasure and fun. Yet, deep down, especially lately, she knew it only sheltered her from the realities of her past. Waking here alone bothered her today. Bothered her a lot. Reaching for the phone, she fumbled with it, almost dropping the receiver, as she sat up and shoved it to her ear.

"Yes," she managed hoarsely, shoving a long strand of blond hair from her eyes.

"We have a telegram for you at the front desk. Shall we bring it up?"

Karen's blood went cold, her chest tightening. Sleep had been fitful at best. She'd tossed and turned with an odd feeling of dread. Somehow, she'd known something dark was coming. "Send it up, please."

A flash of a dream came to her. Of a man who stood well above her, broad-shouldered, with long dark hair. So familiar. But how did she know him? She reached for the images floating in the back of her mind but couldn't manage to draw them forward. But she felt comfort in this man. Comfort she needed right now. If only she could find that dream right now. To remember what it held.

Barely able to breathe, Karen realized she still held the phone and settled the receiver in its place. Having lost her parents years before in a car accident, bad news brought fear for her sister, the only person she had in this world.

Guilt took hold. If something had happened to Eva, she'd never forgive herself for leaving her back in Brownsville. Eva might be a grown woman, now married, but she'd always been a bit needy.

Karen's own feeling of something missing in her life had driven her to travel, searching for an elusive secret to life she'd never found. The feeling had always been inside her but it had grown stronger after losing her parents. Years of traveling, of searching, had revealed nothing. In the end, she felt just as lost. Just as empty.

Karen knew she needed to reevaluate her decisions and make changes in her life. She needed to go home and see her sister and reestablish their relationship. And she would. She'd go home and she'd fix things. If…it wasn't too late. As she tied a knot in the sash holding her robe in place, she couldn't shake the feeling of doom taking hold.

A knock sounded and she darted for the door, eager for answers. Fighting her desire to know what the telegram said, she hesitated, hand on the handle, eyes lifted upward, and said a silent prayer. *Please let Eva be okay.*

With shaky hands, she accepted the telegram, signing a form the doorman handed her. She never looked at the man's face, only mumbling a thank-you.

She ripped open the envelope, removing the single sheet of paper with a short, typed message. "Mike's dead."

Nothing more. Two words. No signature. No explanation. Not so much as an "I love you." Just a short note informing Karen that Eva's husband was dead. Oh, God. How? How did he die? Was Eva hurt, or in some sort of danger? Eva. Poor Eva. Why hadn't she called instead of sending a telegram.

"Everything okay, miss?"

The hotel employee's voice drew Karen out of her inner turmoil. "No." Her hand raked through her hair. "I mean, yes. I, ah, I need to get to the airport."

The man, near sixty judging from the solid gray hair and deep wrinkles in his forehead, offered her a concerned look. "I can have a shuttle ready in fifteen minutes."

She couldn't think. "I…never mind." Booking an international flight needed to be her priority. "I'll call downstairs after I talk to the airlines."

Karen processed for all of a minute before darting

toward the phone. She dialed the operator and gave her Eva's number. Ten rings later, she heard the operator's voice again, telling her that no one was picking up.

"I need the police department in Brownsville, Texas," she told the woman.

Ten minutes later, Karen hung up, with the news that Mike had been involved in a car accident. The same way their parents had died. God, what Eva must be going through.

Karen had to get home, and she had to get there now.

Only hours after deciding to visit Salvador, Jag arrived at his creator's home. Deep inside the valleys of Mexico's Sierra Madre ranges, this was where Jag had first trained with Salvador.

Jag pushed open a steel gate covered in jasmine and stepped into a courtyard filled with flowers and trees. He felt none of the peace most would feel here. He preferred the ranch, preferred his place by his men's sides. But Salvador limited his exposure to the Knight, his existence cloaked in mystery, even to Jag.

Here, deep in these mountains, the Darkland Beasts had destroyed his world. This was the place the beasts had taken homage and fueled the evil of their dark world. And it was here where Jag had first hunted his prey.

Here he had first trained to be the destroyer of the Darkland Beasts. Where he had gotten so lost in vengeance, Salvador had been forced to pull him back to reality. Forced him to see the colors of the world around him, beyond the red of burning anger, the black of painful darkness.

It had been many years since he last visited this place, but he came today in hopes of finding answers. To understand the meaning of his dreams. Yet coming here held repercussions as always. Images of the past danced within his mind, taunting him with memories of destruction. With the reality of his wife's blood-drained body. And of her pale, lifeless face.

Jag hated this place. Hell, he hated…life.

Staying so close to this place came from necessity. Otherwise, he'd be on the other end of the continent. The small border town of Brownsville remained a haven for the Darklands, and he had become its protector.

A wooden atrium covered in greenery stood before Jag, and he could see Salvador in the center. His mentor stood there, dressed in loose-fitting gray pants and a shirt, hands on his legs, eyes shut. Clothes worn for meditation. And though Salvador seemed unaware of Jag's approach, it was a mere illusion. Salvador knew Jag was here. Salvador *always* knew. Exactly why Jag rarely sought out Salvador for guidance. Salvador saw beneath his exterior, to the inner turmoil Jag hid from others. Facing Salvador meant facing far more than the mentor who'd trained him to face the Darklands. It meant facing himself.

And that, he didn't want to do.

As Jag walked up the three wooden steps leading to the core of the structure, his nostrils flared, taking in the essence of sage and rosemary in the air. Incense and candles often donned the areas of Salvador's presence. Salvador called them cleansing. Today, they burned in lanterns hanging from each corner of the building.

But nothing could make Jag clean, and he knew it. He suspected Salvador did, as well. He'd been tainted by battle and touched by death. No one could cleanse the blood from his soul.

The sultry scents lifted with a breeze and enhanced the memories already in the forefront of his mind. Forcing them aside, he studied the man before him, the one who had both saved and created him two centuries before.

Tall and lithe, with high cheekbones, a strong jaw and light brown skin, Salvador hadn't aged, just as Jag had not. They were immortal, and for them, time had stood still. At least, in the physical form. But each day felt like a lifetime.

Drawing to a halt a few steps in front of Salvador, Jag watched as the other man opened his eyes. Eyes like emeralds, so intensely green they never failed to take Jag by surprise. For long moments, Salvador stared at Jag, taking him in as if he memorized every pore and line of Jag's face.

"Your heart is heavy, my friend," Salvador said in the soft yet commanding voice Jag had come to expect from him. Salvador motioned to a bench positioned along the atrium railing, and together they moved toward it. Jag didn't want to sit, feeling anxious about what he had to discuss, but he did.

"What troubles you?" Salvador asked, once they were settled.

Jag wasn't fooled by the directness of the question. This conversation would not be straightforward and easy. With Salvador, everything came in riddles and word games. Just one of many reasons Jag dreaded

coming here. Frustration always came with these meetings. Worse, Jag got the feeling Salvador knew why he
was here before he told him. Regardless, Salvador
would make him work for the answers he sought.

The sooner he got this conversation over the better.
"I've been having…dreams. The first since…" His
words trailed off. They both knew since when. Since
he'd become the leader of the Knights of White. He
wanted to stand, but he forced himself to remain still.
Telling Salvador, he'd dreamed of bloodlust didn't
exactly come easy. Avoiding detail for as long as possible, he did a verbal sidestep. "They mean something,
these dreams. I just don't know what."

Seconds passed and Salvador didn't respond. Finally
he broke the silence, disappointment heavy in his voice.
"You still do not accept your destiny. I'd hoped you
would have by now."

As expected, the riddles were already starting. Despite frustration, Jag kept his voice controlled, speaking
through clenched teeth. "I hunt. I kill. My destiny is
clear. I get that. What I *don't* get is these dreams."

"And you want me to explain them to you?"

"Yes," Jag said. "Why else would I be here? I came
here for answers."

Salvador pushed to his feet and crossed to a corner
where a hanging shelf held an array of knives and
swords. The scrape of metal filled the air as Salvador
withdrew a sword from its sheath and then moved to the
center of the atrium. He faced Jag, his blade in front of
his body, its steel glistening in the sunlight trickling
through the crisscross of the cover overhead.

"You say you want answers, but I see only one thing inside you, Jag. I see a desire to fight." Salvador spit the words out, goading him with their truth. "I have never denied you what you seek. So stand and fight."

Jag narrowed his gaze on Salvador, the man who had not only fixed his bleeding body when the Darklands had destroyed it, but taught him to wage a war against them, as well. A man who could raise a hand and change a person's fate, with the power of good behind him. A power he refused to explain to Jag, and that did nothing but piss him off. How did he know Salvador was good and not evil? Okay, he knew. What he didn't know was if he, himself, could ever be anything but dark.

Sometimes, he wished Salvador would have just killed him instead. That he had allowed him to live made Jag angry. Furious even. He pushed to his feet, feeling the thought like hot flames licking at his body. Without hesitation, Jag turned to the weapons rack, found a sword, then turned to face Salvador.

If Salvador wanted to fight, they'd fight. Fighting was all he knew. It's how he dealt with everything in his life. He fought. He killed. He slept. He woke up and did it again.

He hadn't asked to be the leader of the Knights. He hadn't asked for any of this.

Jag bent at the knees, one hand in the air, sword in ready position, matching the stance Salvador already held. Then, Jag touched his blade to Salvador's, the action announcing his readiness to press this challenge onward.

Silence fell between them as seconds passed, their gazes matching in a mental war of sorts. Without warning, Salvador moved, scraping his blade along Jag's in an aggressive action that demanded response. Jag double-stepped and blocked the move, returning it with a swipe of his weapon, but something made him hesitate to go fully on the attack.

Blade to blade, Salvador and Jag held them steady, moving in a circle, again in a mental war. "What are you waiting for?" Salvador prodded. "I offer you what you seek. I give you a battle to fight."

"I do not seek a battle. I seek answers."

Salvador made a disgusted sound. "You aren't ready for answers."

"Why must everything be a word game with you?" Jag demanded. "Why?"

"This is no game, I assure you," Salvador replied, his sword hitting Jag's.

The clang of metal against metal filled the air for several minutes, but it didn't provide an outlet for Jag's frustration. With his chest rising and falling, his breath heavy, not from activity but emotion, Jag finally understood what was happening. Salvador simply played with him. The man was an expert swordsman who taunted and teased Jag with well-conducted maneuvers, just as he had his words.

"Enough," Jag said, taking a step backward, and dropping his weapon from ready position. "I'm done."

Salvador followed suit, lowering his weapon. Jag bowed his head, inhaling, feeling defeated with no place to put all the emotions and confusion rolling within him. Jag wanted to stay angry with Salvador. Wanted to blame him for this life he led. But deep down, he knew Salvador hadn't created this hell he lived. No. Salvador had simply given him a way to fight back against those who had.

"The war you fight is necessary," Salvador said, all challenge gone from his voice. Now it soothed, like a soft, musical instrument. "The skills to win that war are gifts. Until you see who and what you are, you will never be as strong as your enemies."

Jag shook his head at Salvador. "Why can't you simply say what you mean?"

Salvador rid himself of his weapon before returning to Jag's side. "You say you came here for answers, but you already have them. They are inside you, ready to be found."

This was crazy. Why had he bothered to come here? A flash of anger ripped through him. Jag wanted to raise his weapon and fight again. To force Salvador to tell him what these dreams meant. Every instinct he owned told him trouble was coming. Something beyond anything he'd ever known. He needed Salvador to give him answers.

"In other words," Jag said through clenched teeth, "you won't help me."

Salvador seemed unaffected by the contempt and accusation in Jag's tone. "Not won't," Salvador said. "Can't." Silence fell, implication in the air. "*You* must find your way down this path on your own. Trust your instincts. If they tell you these dreams mean something, then they do."

Jag's grip on the sword's handle tightened. It had

been difficult to come here and it had been for nothing. Absolutely nothing. "That's it? Nothing more?"

Salvador extended his hand and motioned toward the weapon Jag held, as if he knew Jag itched to raise it in battle. He stared at Salvador's hand and slowly handed over his sword.

And just like that, in a flash of movement, Salvador acted. With a step backward, the blade sliced through the air and stopped at Jag's throat, a hair from cutting through his skin.

Jag's breath lodged in his throat, shocked at the aggressive action of this man he trusted so completely. Somehow, he didn't move. Didn't flinch.

"I could take your head," Salvador said. "I could kill you with one flick of my wrist."

Calmer now, air trickled past his lips, rational thought returning. "But you won't," Jag said quietly, half wishing it weren't true. Whatever agenda Salvador had, killing him was not it.

"You're sure?" Salvador inquired in a low voice laced with a hint of threat.

For an instant, just one, Jag doubted Salvador, his mind going to his dream. Of how he'd drank of the woman and enjoyed the liquid sweet flavor of her blood. Perhaps, he was turning into a true beast and Salvador had to kill him… He considered this, and reached deep for Salvador's intentions.

"You won't kill me," Jag said.

"You're certain?" Salvador questioned. The blade touched Jag's skin and pricked it. A trickle of blood oozed down his neck. "Do you still believe I won't kill you?"

"Not today."

"You know this?"

Even the cold steel at his neck didn't change his answer. "I know."

Still, Salvador persisted. "How?" he demanded, his voice raised. Harsh.

Jag was getting pissed all over again. He just wanted answers, not these crazy head games. "I just know!" he shouted back. "What do you want of me Salvador? What?"

One second. Two. Salvador lowered the blade. Then, his voice free of all harshness, he said, "I want you to trust your instincts. You knew I wouldn't kill you. Look beyond the surface and find the truth."

Jag understood what Salvador was trying to tell him, but it wasn't an easy thing to do. "The dreams—"

"You think they hold a warning."

Jag gave a short nod.

"They do," Salvador confirmed, offering nothing more.

"And the woman?"

"She is important. Keep her close."

Jag's heart kicked into double-time as he realized the implication of Salvador's words. The woman was real. "Who is she?"

Salvador waved a hand with finality. "In time, you will understand. This is a journey you have started and must finish on your own." He turned and started down the stairs, ending the conversation. Jag didn't call after him. There was no point. Salvador had spoken and would say no more. He knew this from the past.

Jag was on his own, no closer to answers. And no closer to understanding why a seductress born of his dreams now haunted his waking hours, as well.

With a flash of light, Marisol, an immortal Healer who served under Salvador, appeared in the simple room of silver, gray and white, responding to Salvador's mental call to her. With long, raven hair and dark eyes, she appeared human, but her gifts were those of an angel. In the fifty years she'd been assigned to Jaguar Ranch, it was the first time he'd done such a thing without warning.

Salvador wouldn't have done so now if there wasn't trouble.

Marisol found him sitting in the center of his meditation room, deeply focused; legs crossed, his body draped in a white robe. His eyes were shut, long black lashes resting on his perfect, light brown skin. He was a beautiful male in human form. The chosen warrior for humanity, he had walked this plane of existence for centuries, honored by the Archangel Raphael with this duty.

But she often wondered at the emptiness of the solitary existence he chose.

Salvador didn't immediately acknowledge her, but then he rarely did anyone who visited. She'd come to understand this was simply his way. Yet, she also wondered at the reason. Wondered if he searched his visitors' minds for their intentions and purity. No one fully understood the extent of his powers, just that they were many.

These thoughts made her uncomfortable, as she considered what he might find if he searched her mind. Would he figure out she'd gotten personally attached to one of the Knights of White? Or did he already know? Had he called her here because of this?

She stood there, waiting. She scanned the room, eyeing the darkness falling outside, the sun sinking between the mountaintops. Salvador lived in a secluded house with nothing but nature around him. He allowed himself no luxuries. No company between the visitors he mentored. The Healers in training. The Knights he created with a magical touch.

Her skin tingled with awareness the instant Salvador fixed her in a stare, his green eyes taking her in from head-to-toe. No matter how many times she visited him, his attention still undid her. There was something so pure, yet so sensual about the man. And knowing. He knew things others didn't.

Did he know the young Knight named Rock had her feeling emotions that were forbidden? Her stomach knotted. To be granted human form meant proving one was above the temptations of the flesh. It had taken Marisol centuries to obtain her spot to serve on the physical plane, and she had thought herself ready. She had trained, studied, meditated. But none of it had prepared her for what it was like to touch, taste and smell again. For the pure divinity of life. But she'd shoved temptations aside, no matter how difficult. All, except for this crazy need to protect Rock.

She fidgeted, shifting her weight from one foot to the next, trying to wipe her mind clean. Salvador was too intuitive. These thoughts would give her away.

"You are looking good, Marisol," Salvador commented, finally breaking the silence. He motioned her forward. "Your assignment seems to suit you."

Marisol felt her cheeks flush as she settled down on the floor. She loved her faded jeans and scuffed boots but wondered if Salvador approved. There hadn't been time to change before coming here. "Thank you. I enjoy helping the Knights."

"Good," he said, "because I need your help in a sensitive matter."

She swallowed, an alarm going off in her head. She'd been right to assume there was trouble brewing. "I'm listening."

"Jag is being tested."

"By you?"

"I do not test any of my people. I simply guide."

She knew what that meant. "Evil is at work?"

"Evil is always at work, my dear. You know this. Sometimes it simply screams louder for notice."

"And now is one of those times," she confirmed.

"Now it shouts for attention and we shall give it what it wants." He smiled. "But make no mistake, little Marisol. We will win."

Chapter 2

Karen finally felt the 727 touch down near her home-town of Brownsville after twenty-four hours of travel, including two canceled flights and a cluster of bad luck. When she'd finally boarded the last flight in her passage, she'd thought the trouble had ended. Not so. She and a hundred and twenty other passengers had sat on the runway two hours before takeoff. Two hours with no circulation and a plethora of nasty moods.

She was beginning to feel like some evil force was working against her getting home to her sister.

But finally, she was on the ground, only an hour's drive from her destination. Now, if she could just get Eva on the phone. So far every attempt had come up dry and it had Karen tied in knots inside with worry.

"We're here, pretty lady."

"Yes," Karen said, teeth grinding together. "We are, indeed, here."

The announcement came from Bob, her travel partner by seating default, and the final test of her composure on this incredibly long and frustrating trip. Good ol' Bob who had forced his life story on her. She now knew he was forty. Divorced. An insurance salesman. The list went on. He'd talked while downing four of those miniature bottles of rum, each one making him more obnoxious and flirtatious. The fifth bottle had ended up in her lap, her thankfully dark-colored slacks still damp from the mishap.

"How are you getting into Brownsville, sugar?" Bob asked, leaning his arm behind her seat, crowding her as he had for the past four hours. He smiled, his eyes glazed from too much booze. "My car is here. I can drive you into town. Maybe buy you dinner."

Like she'd get in a car with a drunk. "No. I have a rental car I plan to make good use of." She reached inside her purse trying to find her phone to no avail. "Damn." She started digging in the cushions.

"What'd you lose?" Bob asked, his voice slurred as he started trying to assist.

"My phone." A moment later, their heads connected and pretty darn hard for that matter. Her hand went to the spot of impact. "Ouch."

Bob reached out to touch it, as well. "Let me see," he said. "I'll rub it and make it feel better."

She pulled back, almost hitting her head on the window this time, biting back a remark. With the luck the past day had delivered, biting remarks were more likely to excite anger than restraint on Bob's part. Still, when his hand touched her hair, she wanted to scream. "No." The word was crisp. "Stop." A whiff of rum invaded her nostrils, and she inwardly cringed at the scent. Bob was a prime example of why she stuck to Diet Coke when she traveled. "I'll find it when we get up. After everyone gets off the plane."

A few minutes later, as she followed the signs directing her to the baggage-claim area, recovered phone in hand, Karen dialed her sister's number. Unfortunately Bob was still by her side. He'd insisted on helping her find her phone, thus leaving her with a problem she didn't have time for…getting rid of him. After ten rings and no answer, Karen hit the end button on the phone, upset her sister still hadn't answered.

She sighed as Bob pointed out their luggage area, feeling both tired and defeated. There was no escaping the man, shy of being rude. She could only hope her luggage would come soon and Bob would leave sooner.

At times like this, Karen could almost wish for a knight in shining armor. But only for a minute. Bob coughed and stumbled, and she grimaced at the walking, talking proof, there was no such thing in her future. Not that she'd ever thought as much. For some reason, Karen had always felt she wasn't meant for the traditional happily-ever-after, so she'd never wasted time thinking about it. But Eva had. Eva had wanted marriage and kids and the white picket fence. Mike had wanted the same things.

Karen's chest tightened at the thought. A buzzer

sounded and the conveyor began to move. Relief washed over Karen, urgency building inside. She needed to recover her bags and make fast tracks to her sister's side. That meant getting rid of Bob with whatever means necessary. She hated being rude but at this point, unless some other brilliant plan slid into place in the next few minutes, she saw no other option.

Bob had to go.

Jag stepped off the exit walkway from his plane, his visit with Salvador behind him, but without the answers to the questions he'd sought. Why he'd thought this trip was a good idea he didn't know.

With rapid steps, he walked past rows of gates, yearning for the sanctuary of the ranch, the place that brought him the closest to peace he ever found…which wasn't saying a lot. The plane ride had certainly held none.

Sleep had come halfway through the flight, but it did not deliver rest. It had delivered yet another dream. The darkness of slumber, the comfort of darkness…they were no more. This dream had been more confusing than the others. It had been of Caron, of his wife. The dreams of the past few weeks were always erotic, but this was the first involving his wife. The first where the woman had taken on Caron's appearance.

Without any luggage to claim, Jag started to bypass the collection area when he caught a glimpse of a woman standing beside a conveyor belt, her profile in view. Long blond hair, slim with sultry curves in all the right places. Recognition slammed into him, stopping him in his tracks. His heart pounded against his chest, a drum beating loudly in his ears as the sounds around him blanked. Someone barreled into him from behind, but Jag remained unmoved.

"Hey, buddy, watch it," the man said from behind, but Jag didn't even bother looking at him. The vision before him had him spellbound.

The impossibility of her presence clung to a moment in time, stilling him into a frozen state. Yet, it was true. The woman from his dreams was here, now, in this airport. He'd suspected she was real, of course, just based on the few hints Salvador had given him about her. Still, seeing it, confirming her flesh-and-blood presence, delivered a jolt.

Shock behind him, Jag started toward her, acting on instinct, ready to confront her. Before he could get to her, a man stepped to her side, complicating Jag's plan of attack. Slowing, he stopped a foot away, within hearing distance, pretending to watch bags pass on the conveyor. Watching her interact with the stranger, sensing her discomfort with the man before he ever heard her words. Feeling an instant need to protect and defend her. An ironic feeling, when for all he knew, she was the devil in disguise. A seductress bent on calling him to evil.

"No," she said to the stocky, bald man, "I don't need help." She stepped toward the conveyor. "Excuse me. I need to grab my bag."

"I'll get it for you," the man said, his words slurred as if he'd been drinking. He moved forward at the same time she reached for a small leather bag passing by. The two collided and she stumbled backward.

Jag double-stepped, finding his way behind her just

in time to catch her before she completely lost her balance. His hands went to her shoulders stopping her fall, his chest and body protecting her softer one. The heat of arousal darted through his body like an electric charge. Instant. Scorching. Her intake of breath told him she felt it, too.

The scent of jasmine flared his nostrils, familiar, strong, delivering memories with its impact. She smelled exactly as she did in his dreams. For a moment, his eyes shut, images of her ivory naked perfection flashing in his mind.

He leaned down, whispering in her ear, "Are you okay?"

"Hey, you, let go of her." The bald man's breath, thick with the scent of rum, was suddenly close. "The lady's with me."

Jag ignored his more primal instinct, the one that wanted to yank the man by his poorly knotted necktie and then toss him a few feet.

Responding before Jag could, the blond seductress shoved out of Jag's grip and turned to face him. Her skin was pale ivory perfection that contrasted with her full, red lips. And her heart-shaped face held an angelic quality. The minute her gaze locked with his, he saw her blue eyes go wide with surprise that quickly turned to confusion. The same reaction he'd had when he'd first noticed her. Either that or it was a damn good act. The latter had to be the case. Meeting like this couldn't be a coincidence. And if he didn't plan their encounter, surely she had.

"I'm fine," she said, responding to his inquiry, running her hands through her hair as if trying to ensure it was in order. Her gaze never left his face. "Do I know…?" She glanced at the bald man and stopped midsentence, her attention returning to Jag, a pleading look on her beautiful face. A plea that made sense as she said, "I thought you'd never get here."

Jag's brow inched upward as understanding took hold. She wanted to be saved from the drunken man. Fine. He'd save her. Then he'd get answers. In agreement, he gave her a subtle nod.

In a flash, she was standing next to him, arm linked with his. "Thanks for everything," she told the bald man. "My fiancé's here now, though, so I'm all set."

Jag wasn't sure who was more surprised by the announcement—the drunk, bald man or himself. Either way, a grumble later, the drunk was gone and Jag went into motion, revolting against the crazy warmth her words had evoked. What the hell was wrong with him?

He grabbed her hand and led her toward the escalators. "What are you doing?" she asked, protest in her voice. "Hey!"

Jag didn't respond, stopping just out of hearing range of the crowd and pulling her into his arms. One hand went to her lower back, melding her close, while the other went to her cheek. To most it would seem a happy homecoming, two lovers saying hello after too much distance. Too much time.

To Jag it was an effort to control her. "I don't like games," he said. "Who are you?"

"Games? Excuse me, but you're the one who just

dragged me across the airport against my will. You're lucky I didn't scream."

"Why don't you?" he demanded but he didn't wait for her response. "That wouldn't serve your agenda well, now would it?"

"Agenda?" she asked. "Are you crazy or something? I didn't scream because you seem familiar. Who are you?"

"Who are you?" he countered.

"I asked first. *Who the hell are you?*" she demanded, her fingers digging into his chest. "Talk fast or I'm going to scream. How do I know you?"

Her bottom lip trembled, perhaps in anger. He didn't know. He didn't care. It became an invitation, drawing his gaze, his body hard with her nearness, his emotions tangled with some strange burning beyond the physical. A burn that frustrated him. He didn't like being controlled, nor did he like being toyed with.

"I'm only going to ask one more time," he warned. "Who are you?"

"Let me go and I might tell you."

An odd sense of pleasure rushed over him at her challenge. He enjoyed this matching of wits, and he didn't know why. Insanity was the only thing he could call it. Maybe magic of some sort.

"I'll let you go when you tell me who you are and why you're here."

"You first. And this is *your* last warning. Start talking or I'll call for security." She shook her head. "No. I'll scream. I'll scream at the top of my lungs."

He narrowed his eyes on her, a flash of memory darting through his mind. Of a day so long ago when he'd snuck into Caron's family's stable to ride her father's prized horse, Diablo. Of her threatening to call for help. Of how he'd responded…just like now.

"Scream you say?" His eyes narrowing on her, he decided she just might do it. "Then I better give you a good reason," he said, kissing her as he had his wife to be so many years before, not thinking, letting his emotions and instincts take hold.

Jag pressed his lips to hers, her body stiff, her protest quickly turning to a sigh of surprise. The kiss was gentle, nothing more than a whispered touch of his mouth to hers. Ah, but he felt it in every inch of his body and soul. Felt it with such intensity he couldn't pull away. He lingered, lost in the moment, pleased beyond reasons as she seemed to melt, easing against him.

But any real pleasure quickly ended as someone cleared their throat. "Excuse me, folks."

Jag and his seductress pulled away from one another, sharing a look of stunned disbelief at what they'd just shared. As they broke apart, no longer touching, Jag had the distinct yearning to pull her close again. The feeling of loss, he wouldn't try to understand right now. For that feeling had to be some spell, some form of manipulation by a woman who'd long haunted him. How else could Jag explain any of this? How else did he explain the fact that a security guard stood only a few inches away, too close for Jag to have missed his approach? But he'd been that lost, that out of the present.

The gray-haired man in uniform smiled. "I know

you two are happy to see each other, but we can't allow too much of that stuff in public."

His blond seductress smiled at the man, diverting her gaze from Jag's, suddenly acting nervous, hands sliding down her clothes as if straightening them. "Sorry about that." She smiled at the security guard. "Can you show me to a bathroom to freshen up?"

Jag considered following her but decided against it. At least obviously. He needed time to think and plan. He'd keep his distance for now and figure out how to fight the impact this woman had on him. Why did she have so much power over him?

Watching her walk away, he inhaled and then let the breath out. Now wasn't the time or place to finish this. As much as he wanted answers, he knew he had to be patient.

But not for long.

They would meet again, and next time, next time would be on his terms.

Karen rolled her bag toward the rental car van, an emotional roller coaster going on inside. Her sister was going through all kinds of trauma, and Karen had just acted like some sort of airport bimbo. It was bad enough that she'd lost an entire day to travel when she should have be with Eva, but to act as foolishly as she just had really topped it all off. Good gosh, she'd just kissed a stranger in the middle of the airport.

Clearly no sleep and a whole lot of worry had gotten to her. Clearly she wasn't thinking straight.

And he was still here. Oddly enough, she *felt* him.

The realization should scare her, but instead, it thrilled and enticed. His presence even seemed to comfort. Walking away, she'd wanted to turn back. Wanted to extend their time together.

As crazy as it was, for the first time in her life, a man—a stranger to boot—gave her a silly "knight in shining armor" fantasy. A crazy notion considering she didn't want such a thing, nor did his behavior merit such a comparison. He'd saved her from a drunk and then accosted her himself.

What the hell was wrong with her?

A tall, lanky man with glasses appeared in the rental-van doorway. "Can I help you with that?"

"Please," Karen said, welcoming the assistance. "Thank you." The man took her bag and disappeared inside the van to stow it.

Karen started to follow when a tingling awareness compelled her to turn to her right. And there he was, her stranger, standing beside a pickup truck, staring at her. She studied him, struggling with the familiar feeling he delivered. Trying to place him, frustrated when her dream came to mind again. A dream she couldn't quite visualize. Besides, dreaming of a stranger was impossible. And what a stranger he was. Tall and broad, his body rippled with muscle, his presence screaming of sex and desire, of a mighty warrior.

Still, searching his features, the dream continued to cling to her mind. The vision of pure masculinity he portrayed in real life the only thing clear in the array of blurry images of her sleep.

So damn familiar…his raven-colored straight hair

hung past his chin. Untamed. The word came to her from nowhere. Like a whisper in her mind warning her of wildness behind the deep, dark depths of those mysterious eyes staring back at her. A whisper she'd felt in his kiss, even now, in some unattainable memory taunting her.

"Ready to go?" the attendant asked, reappearing in the van door.

Several seconds passed before Karen could manage to force her gaze from her stranger. Air slid from her lungs, and she realized she'd been holding her breath. The urge to turn, to look for her stranger, begged to be answered, but she refused.

She nodded. "Ready," she told the employee, taking the first step into the van, determined to put her silly obsession with the "dream" man to bed. They'd shared a little flirtation, a kiss even.

So what?

It was over.

She had real life to attend to, not some silly fantasy of a dark stranger come to save her from all her troubles. That wasn't how things happened in her world.

She did the saving. And right now, she needed to go save her sister from heartbreak and pain.

Karen had to get to Eva.

Chapter 3

Adrian rested against the hood of his black BMW. His car, like everything he surrounded himself with, was a sign of power. He liked power and soon he would have more of it. When he led the Darklands to the destruction of Salvador's army, Cain would reward him. Cain, the ultimate force in the underworld, could offer him power and wealth beyond that of this existence.

Everything was going as planned. Jag would soon crumble and Salvador would soon follow. As expected, Karen Gibson had returned home to rescue her sister.

Soon he would unite the two soul mates. Jag would have his wife back through Karen, in soul if not body. And Jag's denial of the source of his strength, of his unique abilities, would be his demise. He'd crave his mate both in flesh and blood. Ah, but he would deny the needs, seeing it as evil. Jag would fight his urges until he couldn't control himself. Until he drained Karen dry, caving to the beast begging for life.

And if that didn't work, Eva would be insurance. If Jag claimed his wife, his mate, then he'd surely do anything to save her the pain of losing her sister. Yes. Eva was perfect leverage against Jag.

The elevator opened bringing Sherry Wright, the nurse he'd enlisted as his servant, into view. Her complexion was pale, the shadows of the hospital garage did nothing to hide the distress in her face. She worried for her best friend's life. The friend he'd kidnapped as motivation for Sherry to do his bidding. He needed her clear-minded. So he hadn't dared take her blood to submit her fully.

Sherry's distress, her fear, warmed his blood. He'd enjoy taking her beneath him and demanding her surrender.

When the petite brunette stopped a few feet away, Adrian didn't press her to move closer. But her fear raced through his blood and ignited his desire. Adrenaline coursed through his veins.

"You know what has to be done?" he asked.

"Yes," she said hoarsely. "When the woman, Karen, arrives, I'll make sure she goes to the doctor at Jaguar Ranch."

"Excellent," Adrian said, satisfaction filling him.

"But what if she doesn't come?"

"She will," he said. Adrian had made sure of it. Adrian had taken Eva's blood and controlled her now.

He ensured Eva's husband had died instantly in that car crash, just as he'd ensured Eva would follow his orders. She'd lead Karen where he wanted her to go. "This is the only hospital in the city."

"Then you'll release my friend, right?"

A slow smile slid onto Adrian's lips. "When I'm done with you." Which wouldn't be until she'd serve his pleasure. He was tempted to try her out now, but there were matters to attend. He needed to visit Eva one last time before her sister entered the picture. To ensure Eva was deep under his control, closer to death.

He pushed off the car, standing in front of her, his finger sliding down the woman's cheek. She shivered in response, already falling prey to his seductive powers. Unable to stop herself from desiring him. "Don't disappoint me," he said. "I'll be back for you." His eyes narrowed, a smile hinting on his lips. "Soon. Very soon."

And then he disappeared into the night, a flash of fire and smoke.

He was here again.

Eva Gibson uncurled her body from the fetal position she'd taken on the bed, thankful for the relief he would bring. She didn't want to see anyone but him. Only he brought peace. Adrian, he called himself. She called him an angel. *Her* angel. The only hope she had in this world. Endowed with a magical way of stealing her pain, he burned inside her. She longed for his presence and barely endured his absence.

It hurt when he left her alone.

Adrian called himself her guardian. Her escape from the loss of her husband, Mike. A gift granted to her in a time of need. It scared her that she couldn't remember why or how Mike had died. Yes. She was scared. Yet… Adrian said it was part of his role. To make her forget. To make her whole in a new and brilliant way.

He appeared in the doorway, broad enough to fill the entryway. Tall enough to almost reach the top. Eva sat up on the edge of the bed, her breath catching in her throat. Black leather hugged muscular thighs. A matching vest showed off defined biceps and powerful forearms. Long, blond hair swept his shoulders, so different from the dark-haired men of the Hispanic culture who had touched her world before him. She remembered how that hair smelled. How it felt to her hands. How it brushed her skin as he kissed her.

He was so different from Mike. Eva blinked, feeling a rush of panic. Mike. Why couldn't she picture Mike? But then, suddenly, Adrian was there, holding her. Touching her. "Fear nothing, little one. I am your salvation. I will heal you."

His mouth came down upon hers, his tongue sliding past her teeth in a long, sultry stroke. Everything sunk into a dim darkness, passion consuming her, blessing her with the oblivion of forgetting.

Eva was saved. From the past. From the pain. From the moment. *Adrian,* she whispered in her mind. *Take me.*

And he responded without words. *I intend to, my love.*

Karen walked up the porch to her sister's house, the wood creaking beneath her feet. Her stomach was balled in a knot of discomfort that matched the sharpness of her nerves.

Eyeing the pitch-black thickness of the woods surrounding the tiny little house that had once belonged to their parents, she shivered. It felt like something was out there in the midst of the trees... Watching.

Swallowing against the sudden dryness in her throat, Karen hesitated. Never, ever had she been scared.

Straightening, Karen willed herself to march up the steps, refusing to let her eyes travel away from her destination. But as she got to the top of the porch, something made her turn and look into the woods. There, deep in the coverage of night, two red eyes stared at her.

Karen jerked around and raced for the house, adrenaline pumping through her blood in overdrive. Logic said it was nothing but a deer or some other harmless animal. Instinct said the opposite. To run. To get inside.

She didn't bother knocking, twisting the doorknob and yanking open the door. Relief rushed through her as it turned. *Thank God.* In a flash, she was inside, scrambling to put the locks in place. Task complete, she turned and rested against the door, chest rising and falling as she drew air into her burning lungs and shoved it back out.

She laughed, a choked sound that filled the quiet room. This was nuts. Absolutely nuts. She didn't spook easily. But then this was an unusual day, she reminded herself.

Bringing the living room into view, the walls danced with the shadows of flickering candlelight, the light scent of Eva's favorite flower, lavender, lacing the air. Even with the familiar fragrance offering promise of Eva's presence, an odd feeling of uneasiness clung to Karen's emotions.

Surveying the room, she found everything as she re-membered, still decorated in the cozy furnishing their parents had adorned it with. Nothing seemed out of place. No turned over tables. No broken glass. Yet... Something didn't *feel* right though.

"Eva?" she called. No answer. "Eva?"

Still nothing.

Her brows dipped as a realization came to her. The door had been unlocked. Okay, something really wasn't right here. Eva always locked the door.

Karen eyed the room for a weapon. Her travels had taught her much about the world. Karen might be the more daring of the two sisters, but a fool she wasn't. She'd learned to defend herself, and had a few occasions to be glad for it. Like now.

Finding an umbrella by the coatrack, she grabbed it. Despite her frazzled state, she couldn't help but roll her eyes. Karen never had an umbrella when she needed it. Eva did, of course. She was always cautious *and* always prepared. The thought quickly sobered Karen again, as the cautious part reminded her of the unlocked door and eerie silence. A renewed determination to find her sister safe and well put her into action.

Cautiously Karen eased her way into the kitchen but found it empty. Next, she worked her way to the back bedroom. It was there that she found Eva sitting on the bed, staring toward the wall as if in a haze. At least ten candles flickered around the room, casting shadows on the walls.

Karen quelled the urge to rush toward her, not sure

what she was dealing with. Eva seemed to be awake but not. Like she was in a daze, perhaps having some sort of reaction to the trauma over losing Mike. Karen leaned the umbrella against the wall and then flipped on the light. Eva didn't move.

Walking toward Eva, Karen studied her, noting the paleness of her skin. Even her pupils seemed dilated, her normally gorgeous sea-green eyes nearly consumed by black. And oddly, she wasn't blinking.

Karen stopped several steps from Eva, and her brows dipped as she observed her sister's attire, an ultrasheer white gown that molded her overly slim body, so sheer that Karen could see the dark circles around her sister's nipples. Not an outfit one would expect from a grieving, rather shy and conservative, widow. This was a gown a woman wore to meet her lover.

Karen kneeled at her sister's feet. Feet, she realized, that were on the floor, fearless of what was under the bed. Eva was most definitely not herself. Not that Karen would know, these days.

A sick feeling of guilt gathered in Karen's stomach. Karen hardly even knew Mike, her travels had kept her so distant. No. She'd kept herself distant, she corrected.

Karen had gone away to college the instant Eva graduated. She'd tried to get Eva to go with her, but she wanted to stay with Mike and get married. Eva had clung to stability to survive, while Karen hadn't wanted any part of anything that might be taken away again. She'd done the happy family once. She had needed away from the loss she felt in this town.

But now she knew there was more to it than that. In

the back of her mind, she'd always been looking for something she couldn't quite put her finger on. Something elusive that she needed and wasn't able to visualize, let alone find.

What if that thing she sought had always been here, right in front of her face, by her sister's side? More than ever, Karen realized, she'd left her sister behind in her quest for the unknown. If she lost Eva, she'd crumble. Eva was all the family she had left.

Swallowing emotion, she tentatively touched her sister's knee, pulling back after that tiny contact, afraid of scaring her. When there was no negative response— no response at all, actually—she settled her palm back in place, feeling comforted by the touch. "Eva?"

Nothing.

She moved her hand to Eva's cheek. "Eva, sweetie? Come back to me."

Suddenly Eva blinked and focused. "Karen?"

Relief. "Yes, sweetie. It's me. I'm here. How are you?"

Eva grabbed Karen's hand from her cheek and held it in her lap, lacing her fingers with her sister's. "I'm… waiting. He will be back soon."

"Who?" Karen's heart tightened. This wasn't good. Eva clearly was in shock. No wonder she hadn't been answering the phone. They needed to go to the hospital. "Mike?"

"Mike?" Eva said, tilting her head to the side ever-so-slightly, puzzlement in her wide eyes. "Who is Mike?"

Oh, God. It was worse than she thought. "Mike is your husband." *Was,* Karen thought, painfully. "Don't you remember?"

With a childlike quality, Eva seemed to consider Karen's words, and a flash of pain darted through her eyes and then took root. "Where is Adrian? I need Adrian." She let go of Karen's hand and slouched, hand on her stomach. Her breathing became heavy. "He. Makes. The pain. Go away."

"What pain?" Karen asked, urgent. "Is your stomach sick?" She pressed her palms to Eva's face. Her skin felt so damn cold. More so with each passing minute. "Talk to me, Eva. Where do you hurt?"

Eva shivered and hugged herself. "I'm so cold." Her lips trembled. "Get Adrian. He will make me feel better." Her voice started to rise, and her body was shaking. "He promised to take away all this pain. I *need* Adrian."

Karen didn't know what to do. She pushed to her feet and yanked the blanket off the bed, pulling it around her sister. Once it was in place, she brushed strands of hair from Eva's eyes. "I'm going to get you some clothes, and we're going to the hospital."

Eva's hand shackled Karen's wrist. "No. Need… Adrian."

Karen's gaze caught on Eva's neck, and her breath lodged in her throat. With a shaky hand, she brushed Eva's hair aside. Surely she wasn't seeing what she thought she saw. She blinked several times as she inspected the four marks on her sister's neck. No. God. She was going insane because they looked like bite marks.

Stories from her youth, of monsters who preyed on women, biting them, taking sexual favors and then their souls, rushed at Karen.

"Eva." She swallowed. "What is that on your neck?"

Eva touched the spots Karen inspected. "Adrian. He's going to make me like him. Then he said I won't have this pain."

This couldn't be happening. The monsters were myths. Nothing more. She'd heard the stories over and over, for years, but they were just that. Stories. She eased Eva's hand from her neck so she could see the marks again. The visual clarified the need to act. They were going to the hospital.

Suddenly the candles flickered, as did the light above. Seconds later, what felt like a gust of hot air rushed over Karen. She stiffened, eyeing the bedroom door as the candles painted the hallway with a splattering of shadowy movement. Then darkness.

"Do you have a window open?" she asked Eva without looking at her, watching the doorway, not sure what she expected next.

"Window?" Eva whispered.

Karen shook her head. Of course Eva didn't know. She didn't know anything right now. "Stay here," Karen said, not that her sister was in any shape to do anything but that.

She crept toward the hallway, grabbing the umbrella along the way. Once there, she reached for the switch on the wall, half surprised when it illuminated the hall. Which was nuts since the bedroom lights were out. Still, she felt better already. No one had cut the power lines.

Cautiously she inched down the hallway, finding her way to the living room again. She took it in, nothing appearing different than before. To be safe, Karen walked over to the windows, testing the locks, finding them all sealed. So why the rush of air she'd felt… The air conditioner? No. It had been hot air she'd felt. But, then, maybe it was broken. Somehow, though, she didn't think that was the case. Right now, she just needed to get Eva to a hospital. Out of this house in general was a good idea, too.

She started back toward the bedroom, eager to get going, when a big empty space on the wall above a corner chair caught her attention. Karen froze, staring at that spot, knowing what belonged there. A picture of Eva and Mike had graced that wall. Her brows dipped. The memory must have been too great for Eva. Then the strangest thought came to Karen…had someone else removed the picture?

Where that idea came from Karen didn't know. What she did know was that the home that had always delivered comfort suddenly felt ominous. She was tired. She was worried. And it was way past time to get her sister to the hospital.

Three hours after arriving at the hospital, Karen stood outside the sterile, cracker box-sized room where her sister rested and pulled the door shut. She turned to face the doctor, a fiftysomething man with salt-and-pepper hair, who had asked to speak with her in private.

Now that he had her alone, he seemed to hesitate.

"What is it, Doctor?" she asked, urging him to speak. Her patience was wearing thin, fear for her sister driving her to push. She wanted answers and her nerves were frazzled, her body tired and in need of rest. Even a hot bath would help. She still wore the black jeans and a matching T-shirt with a pink glittery heart on it she'd started the day in. Thankfully for her tired feet, she'd changed from boots to tennis shoes.

"This type of thing is never easy to deal with," the doctor said.

Oh, God. "What is it?" Karen asked hoarsely, desperation evident in her voice, and she knew it. Her heart pounded in rapid pace, threatening to explode in her chest. "What is wrong with my sister?"

He cleared his throat. "We believe your sister is suffering from clinical depression. A loss of a spouse is a traumatic event. Intervention in these type of cases is quite critical. The best method to achieve this is a treatment center capable of nursing both body and mind back to a healthy place."

"Depression." Karen said the word in a flat tone. "What are you talking about? I'm here because of the injury to her neck."

"Yes, and you were right to bring her here. Self-inflicted injuries can be quite dangerous. With marks on her shoulder and one on her arm, she is at risk of infection, not to mention potentially cutting an artery. This kind of thing—"

"You think my sister hurt herself?" Karen asked, disbelief melding with a growing sense of anger. She'd come here for help, not this. Certainly Eva hurting herself had crossed her mind, but she'd inspected those wounds. No way were they self-inflicted. They were too precise. Too oddly placed. No, she didn't believe Eva made them herself.

The doctor laced his fingers together in front of his body. "I am quite certain Eva created those injuries herself."

Karen blinked and shook her head slightly, trying to get a grip on the situation. "Those marks on her neck… You can't tell me you believe she could do that to herself." It wasn't a question.

"It is normal to feel a bit of denial, Ms. Gibson."

The anger lurking beneath the surface pulsed to life, barely contained. Her lips thinned, eyes narrowing on the doctor's face. "Those marks were not self-induced. I brought Eva here for medical attention, not accusations. What is her physical condition?"

The doctor gave her a frustrated look. "As expected with such injuries, she is weak. She is dehydrated and her blood count is low. I'd like to admit her for observation. Once she is stronger, I hope you will consider allowing a transfer to a treatment center that can deal with her *other* issues."

Other issues. Karen could barely believe what she was hearing. Her sister *did not* hurt herself. "Those marks are not self-inflicted. They look like bite marks."

Laughing, the doctor crossed his arms in front of his chest. "What do you suppose would bite her neck?" he asked, amusement in his voice. "One of the Matamoros monsters?" He waved a dismissive hand in the air before and turned serious. "Making excuses for your sister does nothing to help her."

Damn arrogant bastard. She whispered the words in her mind to keep from saying them out loud. This was getting her nowhere fast. Karen had to act. She inhaled and then slowly let the air out, thinking. Debating. Lord help her, and Eva for that matter, but Karen knew deep down what had made those marks. It *was* a monster. The question was what did she do about it? How did she help Eva?

Karen thought of being back at Eva's house, of the flickering lights and gust of hot air. Going there wasn't an option. One thing for certain—this doctor, and this hospital, wouldn't offer her the help she needed.

Decision made, Karen fixed the doctor in an even stare. "Is she able to leave the hospital?"

"I don't recommend—"

"Can she leave?" Karen repeated through clenched teeth. "Is she stable?"

"Yes, but—"

She gave him a nod. "Do what you have to and check her out. I'm getting a second opinion."

"I really think she should stay the night," he said, his tone insistent.

Karen stiffened and firmed her voice. "Check her out."

He sighed and studied her, seeming to contemplate saying more. Then, with a shake of his head, he turned away. Karen watched him disappear around a corner. The minute he was out of sight, she let her back settle against the wall, tilting her head to rest against the wall and shutting her eyes. A mixture of exhaustion and fear coursed through her body, making rational thought a difficult task.

What was she supposed to do now? Staying here wasn't an option. They weren't going to help Eva here. That left trying to reach a local doctor on call or a drive to another city to find a hospital. Times like these, she missed her parents more than ever. Her father, for his steady voice of reason. Her mother, for her calming comfort.

"Excuse me."

The voice made Karen jump and push off the wall. A petite brunette wearing scrubs stood before her. "Sorry," the woman said. "I didn't mean to scare you."

"It's okay. I'm just a little jumpy."

The woman visibly swallowed. "I wanted to talk to you about your sister." She seemed to hesitate. "Only off the record."

A fizzle of warning went off in Karen's head. "Okay."

Leaning in closer, the woman lowered her voice. "There is a doctor at Jaguar Ranch that handles things like this."

Jaguar Ranch set off more than a fizzle of warning. It set off a full-fledged alarm. That was the place named in the monster myths. Of monster hunters, actually. The ones who killed the Matamoros Beasts.

Karen kept her expression indiscernible, but it took a heck of a lot of effort. "Like this? Meaning what?"

"There was another patient who had those marks. Her father was all freaked out. He disappeared for a few hours and then checked his daughter out. He said he was going to that ranch."

Karen couldn't believe she was entertaining this. Not that she was. Not really. "And what happened to the man's daughter? Do you know?"

"I saw her the other day in town. She looked fine." The woman exhaled. "Look," she said, "I know this is a bit crazy, but the drive to the next closest hospital takes you right past Jaguar Ranch. It might be worth stopping and seeing what they say."

Karen needed to think. This was all too much. It was overwhelming. "I'll think about it. Thanks."

The woman nodded and then patted Karen's arm. "Please don't tell the doctor I said anything."

"I won't."

"Good luck," she said, and turned and walked away.

Staring after her, Karen felt like she might be sick. Did she dare go to Jaguar Ranch? Eva was all she had left. She had to make the right choice.

And she had to do it now.

Chapter 4

She must be insane.

Nevertheless, an hour after leaving the hospital, Karen turned her rental car down the ranch road leading to Jaguar Ranch. The stories of Matamoros monsters had also come with tales of the men who hunted them. Those men lived and worked at Jaguar Ranch.

If Karen was to believe a monster had injured her sister—and Lord help her, but she did—then, she also had to have faith in the existence of the good guys who defeated the bad guys.

A glance at the clock in her car dash told Karen it was almost three o'clock in the morning. No wonder every muscle in her body ached. She'd been awake nearly twenty-four hours with no hope of rest anytime soon. Not until Eva was safe. She wasn't losing Eva.

Blinking against the heaviness of her lids, she focused on maneuvering the car over gravel and bumps, hating her weakness when Eva needed her. Sleep wasn't important.

On either side of the vehicle, wooded acreage enclosed the gravel path. The effect created a wall between her and the sky, shielding the moonlight from view and casting the car in an unnatural, deep darkness. The impact emphasized the secluded nature of the location, and Karen felt a shiver race up her spine. Perhaps a warning, but she pushed it away. Her gut said this was the right move, and she had to see it through. Besides, the ranch was on the way to the next town and closest hospital. It seemed worth a stop.

Karen could only hope.

A two-story house came into shadowy view, and Karen felt the flutter of butterflies in her stomach. Another few moments, and she found herself stopped in front of a huge gate, a clear message of deterrent. A hint of self-doubt invaded her resolve.

Karen couldn't help but wonder if that gate protected those inside, or was it the opposite? Did it protect foolish people like her who dared to come here? Darkness enveloped her, making her surroundings difficult to decipher. Karen knew the property stretched over miles and miles, much of it heavily wooded.

She put the car in Park and stared at the house ahead, visible but still a pretty good distance away. What now? If she was going to do this, she needed to act. With a sigh, she glanced at her sister, who slept with her head against the window. Karen tucked a blanket around Eva and then expelled another breath. Reaching for the door, she did the only thing she could think to do. She decided to walk the rest of the way, leaving Eva safe—relatively—in the car.

She had to save her sister, and no matter how scared Karen suddenly felt of what lay beyond that gate, she was more afraid of what would happen to Eva if she didn't find out. Every instinct she owned told her salvation lay ahead. She had to go through the gate to find it.

Jag dismounted his horse in the middle of a clearing and pulled off his gloves. Security monitors had alerted them to visitors. Beside him, Des, his most trusted Knight, did the same. Eyeing the car sitting in front of the gate, Jag noted the absence of a driver but he knew that car, that license plate. If they weren't standing in the direct light of the moon, he might not believe his eyes. But it was true. She was here.

The woman from the airport, from his dreams, was actually here, somewhere.

Jag eyed Des to ensure they were on the same page. Des gave him a nod. He, too, recognized the rental car as belonging to the woman they'd followed several hours earlier.

"You never told me who she is," Des commented, stepping to the front of his horse to stand beside Jag.

It was a question.

One Jag didn't intend to answer.

He didn't appreciate being pushed, and Des knew this well. Des also knew he was one of the few people who could get away with it. Jag kept his men in line. He had to. Their lives meant being prepared, being focused. Des had been with Jag nearly a century, though, and somewhere in that time, he'd slid past Jag's walls.

But not this time. Not about this.

Jag cut Des a hard look meant to cut the prodding short. "I'll let you know when I have something to tell."

Des wasn't detoured. "*Chingado,* Jag," he said, cursing in Spanish, as he always did when frustrated. "Don't treat me like a fledgling Knight. You knew enough to follow her." He narrowed his gaze. "Keep it real, man. We both know you just don't want to tell me, so say so."

Leave it to Des to tell it like it was. "I know she's trouble," Jag said, and that was as much truth as he had to offer right now. "That's enough."

"She's trouble," Des said, his tone flat. He snorted and patted his horse. "That's what you say about all women."

Jag maneuvered to face off with Des, squaring his shoulders as he prepared to issue a familiar reprimand. "Women are trouble and you'd best remember that."

This time Des's horse snorted. It was female, quite appropriate for Des, who loved the ladies. "Shh," Des said, sliding his hand over its nose. "He didn't mean it, *cariño.*"

Jag eyed his friend and shook his head. Des always found a joke to hide behind. Tall and dark, Des wore his reddish brown hair chin length and on the wild side. A scar above his lip drew the eyes. His half-Indian bloodline was more evident than his Spaniard side in his high cheekbones and chiseled jaw.

But it was the raw edginess Des wore as a second skin that made him so distinctive. His shield might be his easygoing exterior, but most sensed what was beneath, even feared it. Except women. They found it alluring. Des could bring a woman to surrender faster than he could a man in battle, which was pretty damn fast.

Jag grimaced. "You push your luck, my friend, and today is not a day to test me."

"You say *that* all the time, as well," Des countered, grinning, his bright white teeth glimmering in the moonlight.

Jag stared at Des, unmoving, half because of Des's dismissal of his warning, and half because he was still processing the implications of that car being here...of the woman who came with it.

"This is not jest, Des. You're headed for trouble." Silently he added, *I've already found it... A blond seductress after my soul.*

Des pinned Jag in a look, his voice serious. "You know why I am like I am. Sex calms the beast."

Many of the Knights felt this, Jag included—until these dreams. Still, some of the men, Des especially, sought that outlet too often. Too freely. Sex took the edge off, yes. But during...during the act it was volatile. The man didn't completely have control...the beast lived. They all knew it. Jag feared it for all of his men.

"If that were the case," Jag replied, "you'd be damn near comatose from so much activity." A vision of his dream flashed in Jag's mind. Of biting the woman's shoulder. A muscle in his jaw jumped as he delivered a warning he often did to Des. "One day it's going to backfire on you. One day you won't be able to stop at simple pleasure. Instead of calming, you will instigate. The beast won't stop at simple pleasures of the body.

It'll make you take more." He cut his gaze away, afraid the fear his dreams evoked would show in his face, afraid his voice held too much conviction.

Silence clicked like a timer in the air. One second. Two. Then, "You're avoiding the subject," Des said, doing the same himself about the topic Jag had just launched. "I held my tongue as we followed her today, certain you would tell me when the time was right. She's here now. The time is now right."

Jag didn't respond before, nor was he going to now.

Des refused to back down. "Who is she and why is she here?"

Jag shoved his gloves in the leather bag hanging from his horse's saddle. "Like I said, when I know more, I'll tell you." His tone was sharp, full of authority, irritation clear. The subject was closed. Jag jerked his chin forward. "Let's move." He started walking, and soon Des followed.

Once they were beside the car, Des peered into the passenger window as Jag did the same on the driver's side, both taking in the sole, unfamiliar woman inside. Straightening, Des eyed Jag over the roof. "If I open it, she might fall. She's leaning on the window."

Nodding his understanding, Jag opened his side of the car, wondering where the driver had gone. The engine was still running, the air blowing to keep the car semicool. Even with the sun down, it was close to ninety outside.

Jag leaned across the seat, inspecting the pale-faced blonde and noting the familiarity to his dream woman. The seductress he couldn't get out of his thoughts. The one who brought to mind sex, seduction…and trouble. The one who'd taste like heaven but dared him to hell.

This woman was thinner, but she shared the same bone structure, the same high cheekbones. Perhaps this was her sister. Yes. It had to be. At a minimum, a relative.

Reaching across the car, Jag eased the woman off the door, drawing a murmur from her, but nothing more. Her skin was cold. Too cold. That was all he needed to tell him why she was here. He stood and fixed Des in a look. "Check her for marks."

A moment later, Des stared at him over the rooftop again, and confirmed what Jag already knew. "She's been marked, claimed by a beast without question. Whoever brought her here probably saved her life." His eyes narrowed. "The Darklands want these women. Why?"

"I don't know," Jag said, and it was the truth. He couldn't have answered if he'd have wanted to.

Darklands often used humans for pleasure, keeping them in a trancelike stage until they were through with them. Until they killed them. That they picked the relative of the woman from his dreams by accident was unlikely. Then again, at this point, he wasn't ruling out a trap. For all he knew, the women were bait of some sort.

For now, he needed to deal with what was urgent. They needed to get the injured female to their Healer. "Cut through the woods and get her to Marisol while she still has a chance. I'll find the other one and deal with the car."

Jag turned off the engine of the car and pocketed the keys. If he had trouble finding the missing woman, she'd eventually come back to the car. If she could find it, that was.

With a low whisper, Jag called the horses forward.

He mounted Diablo, and leaned forward, patting the animal in reward for his response. Though he'd never told a soul, the name had meaning to him. It had been the name of the horse Jag had gone to ride the day he'd met Caron. The memories were all coming back to him with painful force. Memories he'd buried long ago.

Beside him, Des settled the injured visitor in front of him. She held herself upright as if awake, but she stared ahead, a blank look on her face.

Des eased his mare parallel to Diablo. "You want me to send a search party to help?"

"No," Jag said, shutting that idea down fast. "Just get her to Marisol."

Des stared at him a moment too long, and then kicked his heels, putting his horse into motion. Still, Jag sat there, unmoving. Thinking about the implications of the day's events. Thinking about her. The woman who had seduced him in his sleep. She'd taken him into submission and stripped him of the control he valued so completely.

What was this woman to be able to do such a thing inside his mind and make it feel so real? Salvador's words came to him then. *She is important. Keep her close.* Right. Keep a woman who is pure temptation close. A woman who makes him want things he shouldn't. A woman who could steal his soul if he let her.

Jag's nostrils flared with a gust of wind. With the scent of the woman so near, images from his dreams leaped into his mind. Of her naked, pressed close to him, full breasts bouncing as he moved inside her. And already, he felt the slight extension of his cuspids. Felt the hunger to taste her. The beast inside wanted to taste the blood of her flesh. To devour her. And from there, he knew what would come next. He would destroy her. Blood brought the rage to kill upon a beast.

This woman knew not what she asked of him in those dreams. If he took of her blood, he'd surely take her last breath. Now, she was here, alive. Real. And already he'd tasted temptation on her lips.

"Damn it," he murmured, giving the horse a slight nudge with his boots to start them in motion.

There could be no good come of this.

Karen wasn't so sure walking had been a good idea. The path was dark and no doubt snake infested. This was, after all, Texas, where rattlesnakes were darn near as common as dogs.

The sound of a horse approaching brought part relief and part trepidation as she turned toward it. Would the rider be friend or foe?

There wasn't time to decide what she would do if the latter was the case before a black stallion appeared by her side. Karen tilted her chin up to see the man riding it, taken aback by the sight he made, broad and strong, atop. She blinked up at him, taking in the long dark hair and the foreboding look in his piercing gaze. The word *warrior* came to mind. Her eyes narrowed on his form, cutting through the darkness as recognition took hold.

It couldn't be…yet, it was.

To her utter, complete shock, she found the man from the airport. His darks eyes met hers, and despite the shadows of night, she felt the contact from head to toe, the intensity of it quite frightening. A roller coaster of emotions overtook her. Lust, desire, fear, even disbelief, rushed through her like a wild gust of wind. In that moment, she could almost feel his lips against hers again. Almost smell his spicy male scent.

She took a step backward, forcing herself out of whatever spell his appearance, or perhaps lack of sleep, had cast. Logic said that this man meant trouble. He'd been following her. How else had he been at the airport? The coincidence was too much. Perhaps, he was actually involved in what was happening to her sister.

With that thought, she took action. She didn't think, just took flight toward the car. Adrenaline pumped through her body, her heart pounding against her chest with fast beats. She had to get to Eva and get out of here.

But she'd made it only a few feet when she found herself pulled tight against the hard body of the stranger, her back to his chest. She tried to kick and fight, but he held her with ease. Out-of-character tears burned in the back of her eyes, as fear—not for herself—but for her sister, took hold.

Suddenly the man's mouth was close to her ear. "When you're done fighting, let me know."

His words infuriated her, when they should have frightened. But anger felt better than fear, more empowering, and she clung to it, kicking with renewed energy. Energy that got her nowhere and quickly started to turn to defeat. She hated being out of control like this. Hated feeling as if she could do nothing to change the outcome of what occurred.

To her dismay, the stranger laughed. For some reason, she got the feeling he was angry with her. Not like in the airport. This was darker. Almost…condemning. Why, she didn't understand. But it was there, beneath the taunts. Beneath the low, sultry sound of that laugh.

She fought some more, giving her best effort to injure him and get free. Finally she had to face facts. This plan wasn't working. She stopped moving, still trying to think. Not an easy task with him holding her so close. He got to her, this man, and she felt ashamed. He might be the one who hurt her sister; he might be Adrian. Though, for some reason she couldn't begin to understand, she knew it wasn't true. She knew he wouldn't really hurt her. Still, she had to act on logic, not feelings.

"You have a temper that would be more fitting in a redhead," he commented, amusement in his voice. "But then, I like the blond. It suits you."

She drew a breath as a shiver raced up her spine, born of the impact of his voice, so deep and masculine, the velvetlike notes stroked her nerve endings. She squeezed her eyes shut, certain he used magic to manipulate her.

"Let. Me. Go."

"Not a chance," he said softly. "At least, not yet."

His hand rested on her stomach and she could feel his fingers spread. Again, she felt that familiar feeling. An image flashed in her mind. Of him naked, holding her. Touching her. Of him laughing at something she said. She wanted to melt against the stranger, to make it real. It felt…happy. She shook her head. No! It wasn't real.

She tried to shove away the images, tried to reject them. Still, the feelings they created lingered. "Why are you doing this?" she whispered.

He didn't respond immediately, instead his body seemed to absorb hers. To get closer. As if he, too, was seeing the images. Or perhaps focused on creating them. She didn't know. In that moment in time, she didn't care.

The scent of him, masculine and a bit woodsy, surrounded her with a familiar sense of knowing this man. Time seemed to stand still. A sizzle started low in her body, dancing along her thighs and building into an ache. Even knowing she was under some sort of a spell, the feeling of heat and desire began to consume mind and body. She felt like she was drifting into a fog. A lust-filled fog.

Then, abruptly, the spell was broken. He spoke, and this time his voice came out hard. Almost harsh. And the anger. She felt it again. "The girl in the car is safe. I had her taken to the house."

He let her go, the warmth of his body disappearing. She hugged herself as she turned, suddenly chilled without reason in the midst of a scorching Texas night. As she brought him into view, she found the stranger walking toward his horse. She stood there, staring after him, not sure what to do.

"You have Eva?" she asked. "You have my sister?"

Karen watched as he mounted the stallion, and then maneuvered the animal sideways to look at her. "Yeah, I have her." He stared down at her for several seconds and then held out his hand. "You coming or not?"

There was only one answer, and they both knew it. He had her sister. Of course she was damn well coming!

She started walking toward him, feeling like she was following the devil to destruction. She thought of all her monster lore, of how they could control a human mind. He'd done that to her. She was sure of it. Why else would a stranger have aroused her in such a way?

He had to be one of the monsters.

Still, she accepted his hand, willingly offered to follow. Because, Lord help her, as his dark eyes met hers, lust brimming from the rims, telling her he wanted her, she wanted him. She wanted to give herself to him. Her sister was perhaps lying dead, and she was feeling all wet and wanting over a man that might very well be the cause.

And somehow she knew nothing in this world would ever be the same again. Life had taken a drastic turn. Deep inside, she felt this night, these events, somehow played into the destiny she'd always searched for. The one that kept her traveling, kept her looking for what she couldn't touch.

All those years of feeling she was searching had somehow come back to the here and now. Back to her hometown.

A town tainted with blood. Would it now take hers?

Chapter 5

By the time Jag brought Diablo to a stop in front of the house, having had the soft curves of the woman from his dreams pressed tight against his body, he was ready to come unglued. He couldn't get away from her soon enough.

Two of his Knights rushed forward. "Take the woman," he ordered to the one who'd become known only as Rock. A mere fifty years old, though he looked not a day over twenty, he was the baby of the group and still needed a lot of grooming. Often Rock's hot temper got the best of him, and he acted before he thought.

"What's your name, sweetheart?" Rock asked her as he set her on the ground.

This time it might not be his temper that got him in

trouble. For some unknown reason, Rock calling this woman *sweetheart* bit at Jag's nerves. Dismounting from his horse, Jag stood beside Diablo. He shouldn't care that another man might find this woman attractive. But he did. Damn it, he did. The things she evoked within him, primal and wild, were dangerous for men like them. No. Beasts like them. He didn't trust her. He couldn't allow himself to trust her.

"Where is my sister?" she asked, fixing her attention on Jag, her voice just barely hinting at a tremble.

"The other woman is already with Marisol," Rinehart, the second Knight, offered, talking to Jag, not Karen.

"Meaning, my sister?" Karen asked, shifting her attention to Rinehart, a demand in her voice. All signs of fear were gone, determination filling her voice.

The look in Rinehart's deep blue eyes was stone-cold. A cowboy hat told of his good ol' boy upbringing, but the buzz cut beneath it bore the mark of a military man who didn't like disorder. He, too, felt these women brought trouble. Jag could see it in his expression.

"If the woman in the car was your sister, ma'am," Rinehart drawled, "then, yes, she's safe."

"Take me to her," she ordered, her attention going to Jag again, dismissing Rinehart as if she'd figured out he didn't hold the power. "I want to see my sister."

Rinehart answered as if she spoke to him, never one to be pushed aside easily. "If you want your sister to live, let our Healer work. She can't have distractions."

She ignored him but her fists balled by her sides, a sign of growing frustration. "Take me to my sister," she demanded through clenched teeth.

Silence followed as Jag locked gazes with her. The air crackled with expectation from his men. No one ordered Jag around. *No one.* He took control, and he saved lives doing it. He'd told her no. Everyone knew that was final. Everyone but this woman whose name he still didn't know.

Oddly enough, instead of anger at her demand in front of his men, he found himself admiring her courage. He could sense her fear. All the bravado in the world wouldn't hide it from him or his men. The Knights were animals in disguise. They could taste fear as easily as they could their own breath. And she reeked of it… Yet, still, she stood up to him.

As she stood there, so very brave, so determined to see her sister, Jag wanted to throw her over his shoulder and carry her into the house. To bury himself deep inside her warm, wet heat and make love to her until she screamed his name.

The thought, unbidden, thickened his cock and sent a rush of heat through his limbs. It reminded Jag of the temptation she represented, and the evil she'd brought out in him during his dreams.

She couldn't see her sister now. Not yet. Not until they finished what must be done. Besides, he still had no idea if she was friend or enemy. For now, she was the enemy. If she was somehow aligned with the Darklands, she could put his men at risk.

And in his dreams, she'd certainly tried to get him to do what only a Darkland would do. To bite her…and then who knew what might follow. Perhaps, he would kill her and his soul along with her.

"You'll see your sister when I say you see her. Let our Healer do her job." He turned away from her giving Rinehart an order. "Take her to a room and keep her there until I say otherwise." With the words, he started for the house.

"What?" she gasped, yelling behind him. "No! Take me to my sister."

The sound of a struggle followed, but Jag didn't look back. Didn't even consider responding. He needed space and time to think. Time without this woman making his body rage with lust.

Only minutes after leaving his men to deal with the blond spitfire, Jag reached beneath the long, leather-covered bar in the far corner of the den. Grabbing a glass, he filled it with Bourbon, and took a much-needed drink. The caramel-colored liquid warmed his throat and bit at his tongue, giving his senses something to focus on besides the stranger who'd invaded his life.

His eyes traveled the walls lined with rows of books. Unbidden, Caron came to mind. She'd collected personal travel journals from anyone who would give them to her, using them to imagine where her father, a part of LaSalle's explorations, might be. She would talk for hours on end about what she'd read, what she imagined.

He eyed the volumes of fiction, history, science around him, all of which he'd touched, read and studied. In his overly long life, he'd had plenty of time to look and learn. If only one of those books held the answers he needed. But none of them did. A world of knowledge filled this room, but not one bit of it answered the questions he needed answered.

A knock sounded on the door a second before it opened. It wasn't a surprise when Des showed himself, not bothering to wait for an answer. No other would do such a thing. Des strode into the room, quickly shutting the door again and crossing to the bar.

"Chingado," Des muttered as he walked, sliding onto a high-back stool and then pressing his hands onto the bar as if exhausted. "I need a drink." He shook his head. "Talk about wild. That blonde you hauled in is a hellion. Your horse might not deserve to be named after the devil, but that woman upstairs, *her* I'd call Diablo."

Jag tightened his grip on the Bourbon bottle. Of all the things for Des to call her… "Why do you say that?"

"Pour," Des said, motioning to the bottle, his brows dipping. When Jag didn't respond quickly enough, he motioned again. "I'm thirsty, man."

Jag ground his teeth and poured. "You think the woman is evil." It wasn't a question. It was a demand, urgent to be fulfilled.

"If kicking a man in the balls isn't evil, then I don't know what the hell is."

Des tipped back his glass, emptied it in a long drink and then set it on the bar. He motioned for a refill. It was hard for a Knight to get drunk, often taking double the alcohol it would a human, but occasionally, Des gave it a good effort. Apparently tonight was one of those occasions.

Jag poured. "She kicked you in the balls?"

"Not me," Des said with a disbelieving snort.

"Since when did a woman land a knee anywhere I didn't want her to?"

Jag understood. "Rock." The young Knight had a lot to learn.

"Shit, yes," Des confirmed. "Kicked him wicked hard, too." He grimaced and took a drink as if the thought made him need it. When he set his glass down, he held up two fingers. "Twice."

Jag and Des stared at each other and then, at the same moment, burst into laugher. Though Jag knew this wasn't the time to be joking around, he couldn't help responding. Des had that effect on him for some unexplainable reason. Nobody else had the ability to take the edge off his dark mood. And, as often before, the shared laughter with his most trusted Knight, offered a badly needed moment of escape from Jag's tightly wound emotions.

"That boy can find trouble, can' he?" Jag asked, shaking his head, and resting weight on the bar, palms down.

"Sometimes, I think he looks for it," Des said, and some of the playfulness slid from his voice.

"He's only been a Knight for twenty-five years." Then because, he knew it would bug Des, he added, "Believe it or not, you weren't so different in your beginning."

Des gave him a disbelieving look. "I'll pretend you didn't just insult me simply because we have business to attend to."

Jag let one brow lift in question, having no intention of giving away anything Des didn't pry out of him. How did he explain what he didn't understand himself?

"Who is she, Jag?" Des asked, getting back to the obvious question burning in his mind. "We both know this isn't some random Darkland attack."

"Probably not," Jag answered, knowing Des was putting together the pieces of the puzzle and he might as well just tell him what was going on.

"This has something to do with why you went to see Salvador." He let the words settle between them, then, "Because of that woman."

Jag gave him a quick nod but offered nothing more. "Right."

Des sat there several seconds as if he expected Jag to explain. Finally he cut a hand through the air in obvious frustration then pressed his palms to his jeans-clad thighs. "Okay," Des said. "This is like pulling teeth. Let's take this slowly. You went to see Salvador and you already knew about the woman."

"Right," Jag reluctantly agreed. "I knew about her but not the sister."

"How?" Des questioned, shooting the one word challenge back in a flash. "Who is she?"

"I've…" Jag hesitated.

He trusted Des, but this was complicated. As the leader of the Knights he had to be strong. To admit this woman haunted his dreams might cause concern or weaken him in their eyes. He couldn't allow that. His ability to lead helped keep them alive. No. For now he had to keep his mouth shut. Until he knew more.

Des motioned with his hand. "You've what?"

"Nothing." Jag said, and then grabbed control, sliding into leadership mode, the place he went to erect his walls. "For the moment, I want the two separated and under lock and key. No one goes near them unless absolutely necessary. And I need a report on the condition of the injured one ASAP."

Silence.

The two Knights stared at each other. Des searched Jag's face for long moments. Then, clearly deciding he'd pushed as hard as he could get away with, he stood up. "Just answer one question. What's our agenda with these women? Are we treating them as the enemy, or protecting them?"

"I'll let you know when I decide," Jag answered.

Des took the stairs to the second floor two at a time, feeling the pulse of urgency in his blood. What the hell was going on?

He needed answers. Something wasn't right with Jag. He'd sensed it earlier. He knew it now. Jag didn't shut him out like this. Not for years. He shut everyone else out but not him. Not Des. Not after the years of fighting side by side. Of watching each other's backs. Of nights when all seemed lost when they would find a bottle and spill stories of their pasts. Things they would swear weren't true in dawn's light but they both knew they were real.

They trusted each other.

And Jag didn't shut Des out.

Des ground his teeth. But Jag had shut him out. He damn sure had. Somehow, Des had been demoted to the same spot as sex in Jag's life…necessary thus tolerated. *Chingado,* he thought, trying to process the implications.

Sex might be the problem. His kind couldn't deprive their urges, or it made them a bit whacked out. It brought home the beast. Jag thought the opposite might just happen one day, so he hid from his needs. It was one of the only subjects he'd ever disagree with their leader on.

How long had it been since Jag had been with a woman?

Too long, for certain.

Taking the last step to the upper level, Des found Rock standing outside one of the spare rooms, door open to display Marisol, leaning over the sick woman.

Des's nostrils flared with the soft scent of candles burning. "How is she?" he asked, focusing on Rock again, not surprised he was here. It was obvious the young Knight wanted the Healer in a big way.

Like *that* was ever going to happen.

Healers had a higher purpose, and temptations of the flesh were forbidden for them. Des had known several Healers in his century of life. They tended to be rather secretive about those higher purposes, but all of them, every last one, treated the rules placed upon them like gold.

But this was Rock we were talking about. Lord only knew, he loved to break the rules. Rock might do his thing with other women, but only because he had no other choice. Des bet the sick bastard was even thinking about Marisol while he was with the others.

"The woman isn't responding," Rock said. "Marisol's concerned."

Great. She wouldn't be talking soon. Des needed something, anything, to go on here. "Do we at least know her name?"

"Eva," Rock said. A pounding on the shut door directly to Des's left started, and Rock groaned. "That one is Karen. The loud one I can't get to," he raised his voice, *"shut the hell up."* He returned to his normal voice. "You know Marisol needs quiet to heal." He leaned inside the room where Marisol worked and whispered an apology before pulling the door shut. "If Karen knows what's good for her sister, she'll zip it."

Des eyed the door where a new roar of pounding started. He walked to it, resting his palm on the surface, considering his options. Perhaps talking to Karen about her sister. About Jag.

But as he flattened his hands on the wood, he felt heat radiating through the door. Des pulled his hands away, realizing Karen had been touching the surface at the same time he had. Awareness and warning rushed through his body, like a red alert going off in his mind. Taking a step backward, Des was shocked at the magnitude of what he felt.

As a Knight, in battle, he often felt a force behind him. A power he didn't even try to understand. There was something otherworldly about who and what they were and they all knew it. Secrets surrounded them that even, they, the Knights of White themselves, didn't understand.

Yet, right now, with fire burning a warning in his veins, he knew something big was about to happen. Something beyond anything he'd faced as of yet.

And the woman behind that door—perhaps more beast than beauty—was at the heart of it.

Chapter 6

Jag found Rock standing guard outside Karen's room. *Karen.* He knew her name now. And it made him angry. *Karen.* His wife, an Italian immigrant, had been the Italian version, *Caron.* She'd settled in Texas in 1841, near his family ranch. Next door, in fact.

He'd never spoken his wife's name to any of his Knights…not even Des. Not to anyone but Salvador. It had been all Jag could do to hide his shock when Des had told him this new visitor's name. What kind of game was this and who was the instigator?

He wanted answers and he wanted them now.

Jag gave Rock a quick nod. "Is Marisol making progress?"

Rock's grim expression told the story before his words. "The girl won't respond."

Marisol had sent word through Des that she needed to speak to Jag. He assumed this was why. In the past, any human Marisol had healed had responded well. She'd done her job, wiped the person's memory and returned them to their home.

Somehow, it didn't surprise Jag that this new visitor wasn't so easily cured. Nothing about these two sisters fit the norm.

Jag looked at the closed door where Karen waited and then to the separate one where Marisol and the injured sister were. As much as he wanted to deal with Karen and get it over with, he should talk with Marisol first. Decision made, Jag gave Rock a nod and entered the room.

He found Marisol sitting beside the bed of the injured woman, her long raven hair spilling forward, her hand hovering over the woman's chest, a light spilling from her palm into Eva's chest. Jag stood back, watching, hoping for results. Giving Marisol the peace to do her work.

Jag's attention went to the pale woman on the bed... Darkness formed half moons beneath her eyes. No doubt, a beast had been feeding on her, taking her life force and using her body for pleasure. The threat to Eva was not the physical damage done by the bites. It was the state of limbo her soul was left in. Jag had been drained dry, his soul ripped from his body. With Eva, the beast was playing with her. Draining her slowly. Leaving her soul stuck between two worlds.

Biting the victim was a Darklands way of marking the woman. Eva had been claimed, first as an amusement, then most likely for death. Rarely did the Darklands convert a female. They preferred using women for pleasure. Humans who were easily controlled and then disposed of.

Her injury seemed to indicate these women were being hunted, not doing the hunting. But the picture was too uncertain, too full of questions. Willingly or not, these women were somehow connected with a Darkland plot to destroy the Knights. It was the only explanation.

Eva tossed her head from side to side, moaning as she murmured incoherent words. Aggressive, angry words. Almost as if she fought the Healer's efforts. Unlike the other humans they'd healed, Eva didn't act as if she wanted to come back to this world.

A frustrated sound slipped from Marisol's lips, and she dropped her hand. She fixed Jag in her emerald-green stare. Eyes so green they looked unnatural. So pure they made Jag feel his every ounce of darkness within.

"She won't respond," Marisol said.

Jag leaned against the wall, one booted foot against the surface, arms crossed in front of his chest. "You've had tough cases before."

"Never like this," Marisol argued. "She…" Her words trailed off as the Healer's gaze slid back to Eva.

"She what?"

Marisol seemed to reluctantly look at him. "It's like someone is pulling her away from me. I've never experienced that before. Someone…very powerful." She inhaled and let it out. "I tried to reach Salvador, but he won't answer."

For Marisol to call on Salvador, she had to be worried. "Do what you can," Jag said, knowing she couldn't transport to Salvador until he allowed her to do so. Until Salvador answered her call, Marisol was without his guidance.

"I will," Marisol said, nodding, her expression showing the same distress her voice did. "I'm sorry, Jag. I'm really trying."

Her desire to serve a greater cause never ceased to humble him. Marisol knew her purpose and lived it. He didn't know her past, nor did he know how she'd become what she was. But he didn't have to. She'd only been with him a few years, but Jag trusted her more than he did a few of the Knights who'd been with him far longer.

Jag forced himself to stare into those eyes of hers, so full of pureness and good. Windows into her soul, showing her to be so much different from himself. "If anyone can do it, you can," he told her, meaning it from deep inside. "I know you can."

She studied him a moment and then inhaled. "Thank you, Jag. Your confidence means the world to me. I'm going to consult the *Book of Knowledge*. Somewhere in it, perhaps, I will find a solution."

Every Healer brought with them a book with pages only they could read. Pages blank to the common eye. Jag pushed off the wall. "Do what you must. Have Rock stay with her. I'll see what I can find out from the sister."

With those words, Jag turned toward the hallway, toward the path to his dream woman. He could no longer put off this confrontation. The time had come to talk.

And as he reached for her doorknob, deep in his soul, Jag knew, once he walked into her room, once he faced her, life as he knew it would never be the same.

Marisol watched as Jag left the room, feeling heaviness in her heart. Whatever test Salvador had spoken of, whatever evil was coming, had arrived. She glanced down at the woman on the bed, knowing she was a part of some dark master plan of the enemies.

What she didn't understand was why evil wanted this particular woman so badly. And it did. Marisol had felt a dark force pulling the soul of this woman even as she had tried to rescue it.

Worse, the human felt drawn to this dark presence. As if she thought it held her salvation. As if Marisol was the enemy.

"Jag said you needed me."

Marisol looked up to find Rock in the doorway. Tall with light brown hair and a young, athletic body, he didn't look a day over twenty-five, yet, she knew him to be fifty.

Rock.

Her friend. Her temptation.

His words replayed in her mind. *Jag said you needed me.* Her stomach fluttered. Wanted was more like it. Only she was supposed to be above the temptations of the flesh. Yet, it went beyond such a thing. Her heart called to Rock, as did his to hers. She felt it. Even saw it in his eyes when he looked at her. Heard it in his voice when they talked. And they did that a lot. Long

hours of talking when everyone slept. Or they had.
She'd pulled back, knowing she was crossing a line.

There could be no future for a Knight and a Healer.
The very fact that she wished there was proved her
weakness. She was unworthy to be called Healer.

After all, she was here to prove she could move to
the next level of service. To prove she could aid in the
battle against those who destroyed her family, the Darklands, and still remain pure. She was here to heal and
guide, to support, while also making up for the vengeance she had once sought against another.

In other words, she had no room for failure.

"Marisol?"

Blinking, Marisol realized she'd drifted into her own,
painful reverie. She refocused on Rock. "Yes." Hesitation. "I'm sorry. I do need…assistance." Marisol pushed
to her feet, cutting her eyes from Rock's warm hazel
stare. She hated it when he looked at her like he was
now. So concerned. So caring. It made it hard to stay
distant from him. Already she'd crossed too many lines
with him. Now, in the face of evil, having just felt it in
the fight for this woman's soul, she knew she had to put
distance between them. "Can you stay with the woman
while I do a little research?"

"Of course." A moment of silence. "You are troubled."

She still couldn't look at him. Marisol started toward
the door, wishing she didn't have to pass him. Wishing
she could run out of the room and not look into his eyes
again.

But she couldn't. She knew this even before she
came shoulder to shoulder with him and felt his hand

lightly shackle her arm. Goose bumps covered her skin at the touch, her body reacting in ways it shouldn't. Inwardly she screamed at her own weakness. She didn't want to fail her test. She didn't want to let down those who depended on her.

"Marisol?" he asked, concern in his voice. "Are you okay?" Slowly she let her gaze lift to his, trying to prepare herself for the jolt of awareness she knew would come. And when their eyes locked, she felt the impact clear to her toes.

"Let go, Rock," she said, her voice holding an intentional chill, and hating what she had to do. Hating pushing him away, but knowing it was necessary. "I have a job to do and so do you."

A wounded look flashed across his face before he wiped his expression clean. It tore at her gut. Marisol knew his past. Knew how much pain he felt inside. The Knights, all of them, needed so much more than she could offer. Their souls were dark with the pain of the past, needing a kind of healing she couldn't offer.

But it was Rock's soul, his deep ache and loneliness that reached out to her like no other. She didn't understand why, only that it felt like she was meant to experience his hurt.

Like she was supposed to heal what she had no power over…his loneliness and torment.

Abruptly Rock dropped his hand, shutting himself off from her as if he'd closed a door. "Right. We have a job to do."

The loss of his touch, of his emotional connection to her, felt like a tear in her heart. Marisol swallowed against the emotion rising to her throat, and forced herself to step forward. Away from Rock. Away from temptation. There was more at risk here than his feelings or her own.

They were both on this earth to fight a war against evil. And fight they must. Win they must.

No matter what sacrifices or pain came with the battle.

Karen paced the bedroom floor, her stomach fluttering with a combination of worry and just plain sickness. She hadn't slept. Hadn't eaten. Hadn't stopped worrying since she'd gotten that telegram from Eva saying Mike was dead.

A rush of nausea came over her and Karen paused, pressing her palm to her forehead. *God.* She didn't have time to feel sick but her body wasn't cooperating. It wanted rest. If only she'd slept on the plane instead of worrying and working on her article.

Why wouldn't they let her see Eva?

She shouldn't have come here. She didn't even know if this Healer treating Eva was a real doctor. She had to get her sister to another hospital. Besides, something wasn't right here. What exactly had she walked into? How could the man from the airport be here?

Karen couldn't quite get her mind around his presence. Of course, her body had grasped the concept quite easily. Even tired, he'd drawn a sizzling reaction. A reaction she felt guilty as heck for. The man had her locked in a room, captive for all practical purposes, forbidding her from seeing her sister, and Karen had managed to get all lusty over him. How sick was that?

Karen sank onto the bed. She'd reacted to him at the

airport, too. That funny familiarity from her dream nig-
gled inside a bit stronger. Her mind played with some
distant image, trying to make it vivid and understand-
able, trying to grasp it. The clouds were thick and hard
to clear. She was just so tired. Maybe rest would make
her remember how she knew this man. Because to
dream of him, she had to know him.

As her lashes fluttered, Karen told herself to stand
back up. To get her blood pumping again. Her body just
felt so horribly achy and heavy. Yet, the very thought
of falling asleep while terrible things could be happening to her sister brought panic. What if this Healer did
more damage than good?

She had to stay awake. There wasn't another option.

Karen balled her fists in the dark brown comforter
on top of the mattress. Everything in the room was
brown. Brown curtains. Brown blankets. Brown carpet.
Brown. Brown. Brown. So incredibly dreary and dark.
And so was the future right now. Somehow, Karen realized, she'd taken a bad situation and made it worse.
Somehow, once again, she had failed Eva.

Karen looked skyward. "Mom. Dad." Her chest tightened painfully and she gave into the need to rest, easing
back to lay on the mattress. "I don't know how to fix this."
Her voice dropped to a whisper. "I have to save Eva…
I…"

A knocked sounded and Karen jerked up to a sitting
position. Before she could find her way to her feet, the
door flew open. In strode the man who seemed to hold
her destiny in his hands. As he had on their prior two
meetings, his powerful presence overwhelmed her, his

masculine beauty registering even when she wanted to
deny its presence.

But as he slammed the door behind him, locking the
door and turning to face her, the contempt and anger in
his deep, dark eyes were what took her breath away.
Whatever brought this man here now, it wasn't an
apology.

From the look in his eye, it appeared he wanted
more than a word with her… He wanted blood.

Chapter 7

Jag allowed anger to drive his actions as he entered the bedroom, shutting the door behind him, and locking it. Turning to face the woman he now knew as Karen, that anger coursed through his veins. How dare she come in here, taunting him with his wife's name, with her sacred memory?

It was bad enough this woman haunted his dreams. Now she dared to taint the name of his only love.

Unexplainably, as angry as he was, as full of fury, he managed to bite back his imminent explosion. He studied her, this woman who might well be his enemy, exploring her features. Searching for some unnamed something.

What he found was a look of concern and uncertainty so raw, so real, the power of his emotions shifted. Softened. Began to evolve into something just as powerful, but far more hungry. This woman did things to him he had yet to understand. Perhaps it was magic, certainly black magic if that were the case.

In her eyes, in her expression, he saw the same kind of honesty he sensed in Marisol. The same pureness. Surely, if it were an act, the animal in him would sense as much.

But it was too late to retreat, to rethink his actions. The beast still roared inside, needing an outlet for the anger of only seconds before. The beast he'd always controlled…until this woman. If she was so innocent, so honest, why did she bring it to the surface?

He watched her movements, the animal inside him purring with life, his body reacting to the vision she made. To the unintentional, yet, oh, so, seductive curves of her hips in the snug black jeans.

Her eyes narrowed on his face, and it was clear she searched for his intentions just as he did hers. Slowly she took several steps backward, putting distance between them. "How is my sister?"

"Who sent you here?" Jag demanded, ignoring her question, while refusing to let his reactions to this woman drown out his agenda.

"Where's my sister?" Karen demanded in turn, ignoring his question as he had hers. She crossed her arms in front of her chest. Over the top of those lush, full breasts that fit into his hands like they were made for him. He knew, because he'd seen and touched them so many times before in his dreams. Even knew that her nipples were a perfect rosy pink and that they were so sensitive, he could practically bring her to orgasm just by tasting them.

His gaze dropped, tracing each line of her body through the clingy material of her shirt. Fire burned in his veins, pushing him to claim her as he had so many times before this moment. In the dreams so ripe with reality.

He'd never met a woman who could do this to him. It went beyond reason, this need, this reaction. He couldn't be near her, or talk to her, without wanting her. "You didn't answer my question," he countered, wanting to know how this woman found him. Wanting to know a lot of things, actually. Questions flew through his mind.

She spoke through clenched teeth. "*Where is* my sister?"

Her fearlessness should have surprised him, but it didn't. In his dreams, she'd been brazenly direct. He expected nothing less of her in flesh and blood.

"You already know your sister's with our Healer," he said in a low voice. "But what do you know of me before this night?" That was the real question. One he wasn't going to find out on his current path.

"I want to see Eva," Karen declared as if it would make him oblige her wishes.

Jag noted the command in her voice, but he also sensed her fear. "You'll see her soon," he replied. Silently he added, *once I decide if I can trust you.*

"Not soon," she said, pointing at the ground and taking a step forward. "Now." Her lips thinned. "I want to see her *now.* We came here for help, not to be locked up like criminals."

His nostrils flared with the scent of woman, sultry and sexual, and it drew an immediate response from his body. Damn this woman. The one he knew far too well for a stranger. The one he'd lost himself in until he couldn't see straight. The one who had driven him to complete ecstasy and then, by doing so, delivered him to his darker side. She'd shown him his beast and taken him to the edge of the cliff, one step from the pits of hell.

A mere hair from snapping, Jag crossed his arms in front of his chest, mimicking her prior position. Trying to keep from claiming her. Knowing his physical surrender could be exactly what she wanted. Maybe she was a part of some master plan to destroy him. In his dreams, she'd certainly pushed him to the worst of places, using pleasure as her tool.

The thought brought a welcome jolt of reality. "And how do I know you aren't a criminal?" he asked. "You were trespassing."

Her eyes went wide. "I came for help and you locked me up. I call that kidnapping."

The fear and desperation in Karen's voice rang with sincerity. He wanted to believe she was a victim. He really did. But not once in his dreams had she come off as innocent. Not once. To trust her would be a grave mistake, and too many depended on him being cautious. His men. Their cause against evil, their fight for good. And evil, he'd long ago learned, could easily come off as pure as newly fallen snow.

The name Caron meant *pure* in Italian. He wondered if this woman knew that.

New anger formed at the thought of being manipulated and before Jag could stop himself, he closed the distance between them. He didn't give Karen time to protest, pulling her into his arms and staring down at her. Instantly he knew it was a mistake. He'd only meant to rattle her. To grab hold of the situation and make her tell the truth. He just wanted the truth. But everything inside him called to her. He wanted to take her. To taste her. To claim her right here and now.

His own inability to resist her hardened his voice, frustration at his lack of control burning inside him. Even her stiffness in his arms upset him. He was a wreck, and she was to blame.

"How did you even know about this place?" he asked, determined to find answers.

"I…"

"How?" His voice was rough. Harsh. He stepped backward with her, toward the wall.

Her hands were by her sides, her chin tilted up to study his face. As if she gaged his next move from his expression. "I…heard there was a doctor here."

"From who?"

Another step backward, his thighs against hers. And damn it, the friction shot through him like rocket fuel. His cock thickened, pressing against his jeans. Reminding him of her power and adding to his frustration and her lack of response.

"From who?" he repeated, his tone more forceful.

"A nurse." She sounded breathless. "At the hospital."

Her full bottom lip trembled as if in invitation. He wondered if she tasted as sweet as he thought she did. Like honey with a hint of cinnamon. That is how he remembered her. Unique but familiar. So damn familiar.

He'd wanted to know at the airport but hadn't dared taste her fully.

Fury blazed in her eyes as he flattened her against the wall, his knees caging hers. Ah, but there was more. There was lust in the depths of those perfect blue eyes. Knowing she wanted him, knowing that could not be faked, only served to fire his desire. It took every ounce of willpower he had not to ground his hips against hers. Not to palm those lush breasts.

His gaze dropped, and he could see her nipples pebbled against her thin T-shirt. He didn't have to see them to know they were rosy-red and plump. Or to know how she would whimper if he pulled them between his lips and suckled.

Her hands went to his arms as if silently begging him to stop. To look at her again. His gaze lifted, contempt in his voice as he broke the sex-laden silence. "You expect me to believe the hospital told you to come? You expect me to believe the hospital told you to come here?"

She stared up at him, and her deep blue eyes pulled him in, drawing him under her spell. Further into his sensual haze. But as seconds passed, he was amazed at what he saw in Karen's gaze. Beyond the lust, the exhaustion, the fear for her sister. Not of him.

In her eyes, he again, found that pureness, more subtle than in Marisol's but there. Or was it? Perhaps he just wanted it to be. Perhaps it was a trick. He couldn't let himself believe in her. He couldn't. His dreams had warned him of what she would do to him. Of where she would take him.

"Answer me," he ordered. "Why would the hospital tell you to come here?"

"The nurse told me. I shouldn't have listened. I shouldn't be here. I know that now. It was stupid. I just thought…" Her words trailed off as her gaze dropped to his chest.

She squeezed her eyes shut. "I thought you could help. I…needed help."

The pure desperation lacing her words reached out to Jag and made him snap and he kissed her. He slid his tongue past her teeth, tasting her like a starving man would food. She was stiff, hands pressing against his chest.

But Jag took with a ruthlessness that allowed no room for resistance. Taking. Taking. Demanding. Her resistance lasted all of a few seconds. Slowly she eased into the kiss, her arms sliding upward, over his chest and around his neck.

In his lust-laden mind, he justified his actions. She wasn't an innocent victim. Not at all. This woman had manipulated his dreams for what felt like a lifetime, controlling him with some unknown agenda. She'd used sex as a weapon. Sex to consume and devour his very will.

He'd come to her to talk, but to hell with it. She wanted to use sex against him. Well, no more. He'd use it against her. He'd make her need him. Make her beg to have him buried deep in her body. Make her beg. Yes. He liked that. And with each passing moment, she softened more, her body melting into his and she made a soft, whimpering sound. A sound that told of his success. Of his conquest.

Abruptly a knock sounded on the door. A knock that jolted Jag back to his senses. He pushed away from her, putting distance between them even as the knock sounded again. He wiped his mouth with the back of his hand, desperate to get the sweetness of her out of his system.

She collapsed against the wall, her chest rising and falling with heaviness. Her expression one of shock. Her lips parted and swollen from his kiss. The taste of her still lingering with him, driving him wild with the need to pull her close again.

"Jag." It was Des.

"Yeah," Jag called.

"We got a problem, man."

"Be right there."

He stared at Karen, lowering his voice for only her ears. "Why do I know that problem has something to do with you?"

"You're crazy," she whispered. "I only wanted help. Just let us go."

A smile touched his lips, but not one of pleasure or invitation. He didn't like being played with. She might or might not have started this game, but she was a part of it. And he intended to end it. No matter how good she was at playing the sweet, innocent, good girl, he'd seen another side of her in his dreams. He'd lived the temptation she offered in them. Even felt her press him to seize his dark side.

"Let me go," she whispered again.

"Not a chance in heaven or hell."

And without another word, he turned and walked

away, knowing she wouldn't follow. Wouldn't beg. And she didn't. She watched him leave in silence, not moving. Proof that he knew this woman, knew her well. Which meant he couldn't dismiss what the dreams had told him no matter how much he felt drawn to her. No matter how innocent she looked and even felt in his arms.

She wanted the beast in him. The dreams were proof.

The thought twisted his gut. Deep inside, Jag needed Karen to be innocent. She felt so perfect in his arms and he sensed a connection with her. But then, maybe that was the plan. The dreams, her presence, might well be a part of confusing him.

Still, he went back to one thing. She felt so damn pure and innocent. He saw it in her eyes. Felt it in her touch. But he knew her actions. He'd known she wouldn't follow him or beg. He could predict how she would respond. His dreams were the only way he could know her. And those dreams spoke of something dark and evil. Of his beast rising to the surface.

A beast he could never let have life. There was still too much unknown. He didn't dare trust Karen. Not yet, at least.

Maybe not ever.

Karen stared after the man who'd just left the room, hearing the door slam shut and the lock click into place with finality, signaling no hope of escape. Unable to immediately move, she just stood there, looking at the door, and feeling the emptiness of the moment.

What had just happened?

Her fingers slid to her mouth, touching where his

lips had. Not only had that man, her captor, kissed her, but she'd kissed him back. Worse, she had gotten all wet and warm in all the wrong places. Or right ones. Wrong because he was a stranger, and, quite possibly, now her kidnapper. But that fact didn't change her heated response to him. Nor could she pretend it didn't happen. The dull throb between her thighs lingered as proof.

And despite her inner voice of self-reprimand, she fought the urge to call him back to her. The man they called Jag, as in Jaguar Ranch. The name made it pretty obvious who he was. Of course, the way he bossed everyone around did, as well.

Easing herself onto the bed, her legs feeling weak, Karen sat on the mattress and tried to figure out what to do. Only, no answers came. Nothing. She felt weak and dazed which had to be partially from no sleep. Probably no food, too. The confusion over her response to Jag wasn't helping. She couldn't think straight, and she knew she had to give into a need for rest. Her body simply demanded it.

Still, her mind raced with worry, guilt and the dark and mysterious, and far too enticing, Jag. The one that set her on fire with desire and scared the hell out of her at the same time.

Slowly she lowered herself to her back, lying down with her legs still hanging off the side of the bed. She needed to be able to get up quickly. To respond if there was trouble. She needed…to rest just a few minutes. Her eyes were so heavy. Then, she'd be able to think about what to do. Then, she'd find a way to escape….

* * *

Karen was dreaming.

She was standing in Jag's room. How she knew it was his, she couldn't say. She just did. Just as she knew she was dreaming.

It was an odd sensation, really, feeling awake but knowing she wasn't. In fact, standing in the center of the open French doors, the wind lifting the sheer white nightgown around her ankles and legs, the moment felt quite real.

Her hair blew behind her, long and straight, and she could feel the strands flutter against her neck and face. On her feet, she wore sexy black stilettos. She didn't have to look down to know what they looked like. She'd somehow picked them before seeking out Jag. And she knew she wanted them because of how sexy they made her feel.

Everything about the moment, about her body, sizzled with an electric charge. With the potential of what might come from her visit. Even the breeze, warm and a bit moist, touched her with a hint of sensuality. As if it played with her, preparing her for what was to come.

Karen's nipples puckered against the thin fabric, friction melding with anticipation. Anticipation already turning to desire. Desire she'd felt before. For this man. For Jag.

Suddenly she remembered all too well. Memories rushed at her like a light turning on inside her mind. This wasn't her first dream of Jag. Seductive, sensual images flashed in her mind and burned a path through her body. This was one of many times, she'd come to him. No…that he had *called* her to him.

Jag had brought her here. No wonder he'd aroused her so before when he'd kissed her. No wonder he'd felt familiar. The thoughts rang in her mind as odd, though remote. She didn't understand how her waking and dream worlds seemed to be merged.

As she tried to understand, a soft sound drew her gaze from shadows cast by the flickering candlelight in the room. To the center of the massive four-post bed. To where the man who drew her there sat, chest bare, a sheet draped tantalizingly low on his hips.

But he didn't call her to him. He just sat there, staring at her. Though his expression was indiscernible, she sensed he was either nervous or uncomfortable. Maybe both.

"Do you wish me to leave?" she asked.

A choked laugh escaped his throat. "Yes," he said. "I want you to leave."

She tilted her head slightly, studying him. Rolling his request around in her mind, and then, deciding on a conclusion. He didn't mean the words. Instinctively she knew this. Still, they hurt. But there was a stronger feeling. One she couldn't ignore.

For some untouchable, imperative reason, she knew she couldn't allow him to send her away. And as if in confirmation of her thoughts, the wind blew harder and soft whispers came with it, filling the air.

He must accept you.

Claim him or the darker side will.

You are his salvation.

With the words, a power filled Karen. Suddenly she didn't feel scared or uncertain. Purpose filled her mind.

Love burned in her heart. For this man. A man she didn't know, yet…she did.

She reached far into her mind and almost found an image. Almost. It stayed just out of reach. Just beyond full understanding. Reality slipped away into the fog of the dream. All that remained was one certainty. Jag had to surrender to her. Had to claim her as his own.

Had to…claim his beast. She needed to make his beast come out, to show itself.

Yes. This was clear. And she knew how. Somehow, she knew what to do. Sure of what must be done, of her need to seduce Jag, Karen took a step forward. Her gown flowed against the action, behind her, the fabric clinging to her breasts and hips.

Karen watched Jag's gaze drop, following her movement. But even more so, she *felt* his gaze. Felt the heat of it. The potency and desire. Felt it as one might a touch. A caress. A lover's hand. It scorched her skin and created urgency. She wanted his body against hers. His mouth upon her mouth.

Karen stopped at the end of the bed, and knew he avoided eye contact. His admiration of her body went beyond appreciation or lust. He was hiding behind the physical.

Such a warrior he was, yet, he feared her. So powerful and strong on the outside. His body so perfect. Muscular. Defined. His soul…well, she felt it, too. The bravery. The willingness to die for his cause.

"Jag," she whispered, needing to see into his eyes. To the windows of that brave soul.

In response, his gaze traveled upward, lingering for

just a moment on her pebbled nipples. Finally he fixed her in a direct stare. "I told you to leave."

Karen could tell his words were forced. He didn't mean them. And his eyes…they held torment. Loneliness. Pain. Her heart squeezed with an ache that came from him to her. It hurt. It hurt so much.

Shaking her head, Karen discarded his words. "You don't want me to leave," she said, pulling her gown over her head and kicking her shoes off.

She climbed onto the mattress, and she saw Jag coming forward, reaching for her. He pulled her down onto the covers, sliding her beneath him. The warmth and power of his body enclosed hers only moments before his mouth claimed hers.

Karen moaned as the spicy perfection of his flavor took control, his tongue doing a sensual slide along hers. Her arms slid around his neck, as his cock settled between her thighs. Karen wrapped her legs over the top of his. Because she knew, no matter how willing he seemed to accept where he belonged at this moment, it would change.

Jag was going to make her fight for this. And she couldn't let him win. She'd claim him.

If it meant pushing him over the edge and then pulling him back, she'd claim him.

Lost. Jag was lost in Karen. Lost in the moment. He told himself not to kiss her. Not to touch her. Not to get lost as he always did when she came to him.

But even as the warnings went off in his head, his body burned for more. He palmed her full breast, filling his hand, then tweaking her nipple. She moaned into his mouth, and he felt the sound like an aphrodisiac. The scent of her, sweet and floral—familiar even—insinuated into his nostrils, potent in its impact.

He'd pulled her further beneath him, trying to maintain control. Right. Like that was possible with this woman. She had the power. She always did. The ability to tempt him to the dark side. To bring out his beast. The beast that would take his very existence. The beast that would claim her complete submission. It's what she came here for. It's what she demanded. He knew this.

So why, why, did he want her so badly he could barely breathe?

Already, he felt the animal within. The monster. Felt the rise of the beast as it pushed to the surface from deep in his being. Only this woman made him feel this. At the same time, she made him feel such a sense of belonging. He didn't understand. The two things conflicted, impossible to reconcile.

Karen arched into him, her actions begging him to do more. To slide deep into her core. Using his tongue to explore the rage of passion he felt, he tried to shackle the need of his body. But her taste was as sweet, as addictive, as her touch. It only made him want more. *She* made him want more. As if she read his mind, she pressed against him, hips lifting to bring her closer, her soft hands everywhere upon him. On his shoulders. His face. In his hair.

She tasted like honey. Felt like silk. Fit his body like temptation come to life. But this wasn't life. This wasn't real. *This* was a dream. Yes. *A dream.* What happened here didn't matter. He repeated this in his mind several times, falling prey to the calling of desire. Unable to hold back any longer.

He reached between them, his fingers finding the slick folds of her core, caressing her into a moan. Parting her for entry. She was ready for him. Beyond ready. Dripping with desire.

Desire he had to experience. Had to know.

He leaned back and looked into her eyes as he fitted the head of his throbbing length into position. Then, feeling the anticipation in the tightening of his chest, he sunk deep into her body. In one breath, or so it felt, they both moaned with the impact.

For several seconds they stared at each other, unmoving. "This is where you belong," she whispered. "Inside me."

It wasn't her words as much as the look in her blue eyes that took him by storm. Emotions erupted inside him. Turbulent. Dark. And there was hatred. For all he had become and all he could never be.

"You have no idea who or what I am," he said hoarsely, trying to stay focused on resisting not thrusting. But the look in her eyes, so trusting, only drew him deeper under her spell. Further into the passion.

"I know you, Jag," she whispered, lightly running fingers over his jaw and cheek. Then, in a darker, sensual voice, "And I know I want you to make love to me." Her hips rocked. "I need you moving inside me, with me."

Raising her head, she let her lips linger a hair from his, her breath warm and sultry on his mouth. "Take me," she demanded, and her tongue flickered over his bottom lip.

And just like that, Jag snapped. If she wanted to be taken, he'd take her. He'd please her until she knew no tomorrow. Until she begged for mercy. It was what she wanted, and be damned if he would deny her.

Suddenly they were kissing wildly, moving together in a frenzied slide of skin against skin. Her teeth nipped at his lip. At his neck. At his shoulder. The impact was potent, engaging the primal part of him. Begging him to respond, to bury his teeth in her neck…in her shoulder.

With each drive of his shaft to her core, she became a bit more demanding. The beast in him responded, his teeth feeling sharper, his hunger more alive. He pressed his face in her neck, thrusting fiercely, trying not to focus on the growing need to taste her.

Harder and faster, he pumped her, sliding one hand around her ass to leverage a harder thrust. A better angle. Her legs wrapped his, body lifting off the bed to mold into his.

"Yes," she cried out, as her hands traveled his back, his body. His chest. "Yes."

Jag pressed his fists into the mattress, raising up to rest his weight on his arms, staring down at her. Enjoying the pleasure of seeing Karen's body as he pumped in and out of her. Watching her breasts shake and jiggle with the pounding of their hips together.

She reached up and covered them with her hands, pinching her nipples and moaning. At the same time, she began bucking against him, wild like an animal, head tossing from side to side. It was his name murmured over and over in that sultry voice of hers that pushed Jag over the edge.

He needed…to taste her.

Fear enveloped him. Of what he might become. Of what he was feeling and could not control.

Letting his weight settle on top of Karen again, he hid his face, afraid his battle of beast against man might scare her. Did he look like the animal he felt? His tongue slid along his teeth, feeling for the elongated teeth of the Darklands, but his concern was lost. Lost to his arousal. Lost to how near release his body had become.

But Karen wouldn't allow him to back off. She nipped and licked even as she arched into him. "More, Jag. More." Then near his ear, in a husky whisper, "Take me, Jag. All of me. Anything you want is yours. I… Oh. I am—"

The words were cut off when her body clenched at his cock and demanded his release. Spasms of her orgasm gripped him, stroking his shaft with tight little squeezes. Drawing him into ecstasy. He could do nothing but accept the cry of his body. Accept there was no escape from it or what might follow.

Jag thrust into Karen, burying himself to her deepest point, and shaking as he spilled himself inside her. But with his pleasure came an urge, primal, refusing to be ignored, demanding he claim Karen as his own.

He couldn't think. Couldn't stop what he had to do.

Jag's teeth sharpened and he sunk them deep into her shoulder. Deep into the sensitive flesh of her body until he tasted the bittersweet proof of her life…her blood.

In his mind, Jag screamed with denial. No! He could not be this thing. He could not be a beast. He wouldn't…but he was. Lord help him…he was.

Chapter 8

Karen sat up with a sharp inhalation of air, her eyes darting around the room, searching for reality.

Outside the window, sunshine spilled through the gape in the curtains of the bedroom. Brown curtains. Her gaze dropped. Brown carpet. Same room in Jaguar Ranch.

Her hand went to her chest. It had been a dream. Just a dream. She blinked. An incredibly vivid dream. A strange dream. To have a little fantasy dream with Jag as the star didn't seem so hard to believe. The man was gorgeous, even if he was arrogant and bossy. Still, to do so under the circumstances…no, it was more than that. To have that dream.

To say it had been odd would be an understatement. But it had been more than odd. It had felt emotional.

Intense. Lord help her, hot. Really hot. Arousing. She could tell her jeans were damp from her body's reaction to the images in her sleep.

The voices in her head… She'd heard whispers.

He must accept you.

Claim him or the darker side will.

You are his salvation.

She could almost hear them in her head now. Like they were repeating over and over. She shook her head. This was nuts. She was going nuts.

Holding her hand out in front of her, realizing she was actually shaking a bit. Inside that dream she'd felt so involved, so urgently in need. For a moment, she just sat there, the dream replaying in her head. Her body feeling all warm and aware with the flash of naked bodies and sensual kisses.

Karen shook off the thoughts, laughing at herself, though even to her own ears, it sounded strained. She pushed to her feet, noting the doorway that she hoped led to a bathroom. This was ridiculous. She'd had a dream bred of circumstances. Even Jag biting her in the dream, and her actually liking it! The monster stories, this ranch and the arrogantly sexy man running it, her sister's bite marks…all of it combined was messing with her head.

And judging from the aches in her body, she hadn't even slept long. She shouldn't have slept at all. She needed to find out about Eva. Karen flipped on the light in the tiny bathroom and turned to face the mirror. Dark circles smudged her pale cheeks and worry laced her features.

And she was worried. About her sister. About her decision to come to Jaguar Ranch. Damn. About that dream. It still felt so a part of her. God. It was familiar, too. Wait. Her hands went to the plain white sink, the counter barely wider than her hips as she leaned into it. She'd dreamed of Jag before. Her head spun as images flashed in her mind. Images of him kissing her like he had in the airport, saying the same words…only, it hadn't been her he was kissing. It had been someone else. Yet, it *felt* like her.

Swallowing against the sudden dryness in her throat, she tried to make sense of the story playing in her head. Of the words that repeated once again in her mind.

He must accept you.

Claim him or the darker side will.

You are his salvation.

The words clung to her emotions, compelling and alive with meaning. Almost as if they possessed her. She balled her fist and pressed it to her chest, realizing her heart was pounding like a drum. Inhaling and then letting it out, she forced herself to calm. To process. She had to think. Panic wasn't her style nor would it get her anywhere now.

What did all of this mean?

What was happening to her?

Jag needed answers, and he needed them now. His heart pounded against his chest as he took the stairs to the upper level of the house two at a time. Either Karen was playing games with his mind while he slept, or someone was using her to do it.

Either way, it stopped now. This was *his* house—*his*. He would not be a victim under his own roof. If he couldn't control what happened here, how the hell would he control all the outside obstacles he and his men faced?

Rinehart stood outside the entrance to Karen's room, arms crossed in front of him, staring straight ahead. You could take the man out of the Army, but you couldn't take the Army out of the man. At least, not in Rinehart's case.

Jag walked past him, no explanation offered. He unlocked the door, and eyed Rinehart. "What's the status on the sister?"

"Same," Rinehart said, never a man of many words.

"Lock it behind me," Jag said as he turned the knob.

Without waiting on a reply, he stepped inside the room. No announcement. No knock. Finding the room empty, his gaze went to the bathroom at the same moment she appeared, a startled look on her face as she took in his presence.

Jag felt her presence like a charge of electricity. His body responded with memories of his dream. Of having touched her and tasted her. He was going insane over this woman. And just like that he snapped. He'd only intended to talk to her. To demand answers.

Instead he charged at her, unable to think beyond the moment and the two emotions clinging to him like a second skin. Desire and fear. Fear of losing himself to the beast. Driven by these feelings, Jag scooped Karen into his arms and carried her to the bed.

"What do you think you are doing?" she yelped, squirming in his arms to no avail.

Jag went down on the mattress with her, his legs

framing her hips, hands grasping her wrists over her head. He rationalized his actions and words. If he fucked her now, he'd defeat the power she possessed of him in his sleep. Yes. That was what had to happen. He'd take her now and prove to both of them that she couldn't push him to places he didn't want to go. He was awake, and nothing outside this room controlled his actions.

He stared down at her. "Here I am, Karen. Right here. No dream. If you want to mess with my mind, do it in my face. If you want to have sex with me, do it in the flesh."

Not giving her time to respond, Jag kissed her, his hands sliding to her face, his weight rested on his forearms. She was stiff at first, but in mere moments, she was whimpering into his mouth.

He felt her hands touch his shoulders, and then pull away, as if she fought her response. Jag didn't like that. He wanted her submission. Needed it, even. Here in flesh and blood, he needed to establish Karen's inability to control him.

He deepened the kiss, making love to her with slow, sensual slides of his tongue. Her scent, her taste, her very presence, filled him, pushing him to take more. And he did. He wasn't holding back. The beast wasn't coming out. Neither it nor Karen had a say in how this went.

Satisfaction filled him as her fingers glided up his arms, lacing behind his neck. Proof, she no longer held back. Proof he was breaking her, not the opposite. This woman might dominate him in his sleep, but not here, in the waking world.

Wildness formed between them, like two beings starving for what only the other could deliver. He cupped her ass, lifting her and molding her hips to his, moaning at the sweet pressure against him. Somehow, one of her hands found its way beneath his clothes, her soft palm grazing his back and side. The skin-to-skin contact scorching him, making him want more.

Still kissing her, he shoved her shirt up, finding the front latch to her bra and snapping it apart. He trailed his lips down her jaw, and neck, even as he filled his palms with her breasts. Jag wanted her shirt gone, over her head, but he was impatient. Instead he slid downward, his mouth finding her nipple and suckling.

Karen moaned, arching her back, fingers sliding into his hair. Her response drove him onward, and he swirled his tongue around the hardened peak. He took his time, licking and teasing, moving from one nipple to the next, feeling her arousal in her body's response.

But when he lifted his mouth to find hers, his gaze caught on hers and locked. In her passion-filled eyes, he found more than lust and desire. More than the arousal they shared. Lord help him, something deep inside him moved in that moment. Something he hadn't felt since he'd looked into his wife's eyes…since Caron.

He stared at her, wondering why she reminded him of his wife, why she did to him what only one other had done. Though there were no real answers to be found, her gaze held innocence and honesty. She wasn't plotting against him. If anything, she was more victim than him. After all, he knew the war being fought. He'd chosen sides. With these realizations came a heavy dose of reality. He couldn't do this. Couldn't take Karen out of anger and accusation.

Murmuring an apology, he rolled off of her, onto his back. He covered his face with his arm, and willed the rage of his body to calm. Everything inside him screamed to go back to her. To take her. He just needed to lay here a minute.

And not touch her.

He absolutely could not touch her again.

Karen scrambled to fix her shirt and bra, feeling her cheeks flush with the realization of just how willingly she'd given herself to a stranger. If he hadn't stopped… well, she wasn't sure she would have. She'd been shocked when he'd carried her to the bed. Even more so when he'd started kissing her. But her own reaction, her blatant lust, that was the kicker, and the thing, that had her floundering for what to say or do next. Karen had no business participating in some sex-fest when her sister might need her.

Clothes back in place, Karen sat there on the bed, staring at Jag. At the wild array of hair framing his face. At the dimple in his square chin. At his muscular forearm as it rested over his forehead.

Somehow, her gaze managed to settle on his stomach where his shirt was still pushed up from her efforts. On a thin trail of hair leading from his inverted navel to his waistband before disappearing in his faded Levi's. She swallowed as she thought of exactly where it might end and how much she wanted to find out.

She lightly shook her head, trying to get rid of the craziness of her thoughts. *Talk.* They needed to talk.

Karen diverted her gaze and pulled her knees to her chest, arms wrapping them. If she kept looking at this man, her mind would not be on talking. The urge to climb on top of him and kiss him again was all too strong.

She felt like she was in the *Twilight Zone.* Fear, not lust, should be her reaction to Jag, a man who basically held her captive. But she didn't fear him. Not at all. She made a face. That was obvious, considering she'd just gotten half-naked with the man.

Eyeing his unmoving form, she wished he would say something. But even now, with no words spoken, the feeling of knowing him was getting stronger. The dream—correction, the dreams, as in plural—of him seemed to indicate she, indeed, knew him, though she couldn't imagine any woman forgetting a meeting with this man.

Something Jag had said surfaced. He'd mentioned a dream right before he'd thrown her into a heated flurry of kissing him. Could it be possible for two people to share a dream? She didn't know, but one thing was for certain, whatever was between her and Jag seemed somehow linked to Eva. It had to be.

Growing up here, then traveling the world, Karen had heard superstitions and myths. She rarely gave any of them merit. But now, well now, the myths, the bites on Eva's neck, this ranch…it all seemed to add up. She drew a breath. If she said any of this out loud, she'd be called an absolute Fruit Loop. Still, her sister was affected by whatever was going on, and Karen had to keep an open mind. Before she told anyone else, she'd get proof. Somehow. Someway. She'd get proof. And she'd help Eva. She'd keep her sister safe.

Delicately, Karen cleared her throat. "Jag?"

Silence.

"Jag?" she asked, and touched his shoulder.

He jerked his arm away and turned his head to fix her in an accusing stare. "I'm hanging on by a thread here. Unless you want me to forget I'm a gentleman, don't touch me."

She frowned. Could this man really want her that much? Surely he had women lined up to please him. Besides, he'd put her through virtual hell in the past few hours.

"You're hanging by a thread?" she demanded, feeling fairly agitated at this point. "What about me?" Her hands dropped from her legs and she moved to her knees to face him. And as always, when she got angry, she was swiping her hand through the air. "You come in here, flinging accusations at me, after you've kept me from my sister, invaded my dreams and then made me act like a…a damn hussy or something." Feeling flustered, she paused, "I don't like it one bit."

He was sitting up now, and his hand shackled her wrist. "Oh, now you dare touch me?" Karen demanded. "Let go. I'm sick of being bullied by you. I want to leave. Let me have my sister and I am out of here."

"You had a dream about me?" he asked, urgency in his voice.

"Yes," she said, glowering at him. "I had a dream. I was trying to tell you that when you shoved me away."

He ignored her comment. "Have you had one since you got to the ranch?"

She nodded. "Yes, and you're squeezing my wrist too hard."

He loosened his grip but didn't let go or acknowledge the remark in any other way. "Have you ever dreamed about me before?"

"I would have said no this morning but now…now I think the answer is yes. The images are cloudy but I feel certain I've dreamed of you. Maybe many times."

Jag stared at her, his dark eyes intense. Potent. Unreadable. As abruptly as he'd grabbed her, he let her go. With an agile move, he was off the bed. He paced the room a moment, much like she had earlier, pausing with his back to her and running his hand through his hair.

Karen could feel his torment like a charge in the air. He was struggling with some unnamed emotion she wished she understood. Maybe it would give her insight into what was going on.

"I know you think you can't trust me," she said in a low voice, moving to sit on the edge of the bed. "Honestly I don't know if I can trust you. Still, it seems whatever is going on involves us both, and I think I deserve to know what it's all about."

Jag turned then, facing her and fixed her in a potent stare, his dark eyes holding a hint of darkness beyond their color. His hair was in wild array around his face from having both their hands all in it.

"You want to know what this is about?" he asked, but he didn't give her time to respond. "Us sharing dreams.

You say you dreamed of me since your arrival here. Well, I dreamed of you, too. What happened at the end of your dream, Karen?"

She didn't know what to say. Did she dare bring up him biting her? "You…"

"I bit you," he said. "Whoever is playing with our dreams wants that to happen. Once I bite you, once I cross that line, I become like the beast that hurt your sister. I lose everything I am." The words lingering in the air with implication. "So now you have your answer. This is about monsters, Karen. Real-life monsters like the one who bit your sister. Monsters that steal your soul and your life. They did mine."

She swallowed, fighting the emotion welling in her chest. His emotion as it reached out and wrapped around her. Of an odd connection that made her understand exactly what he was feeling.

"Jag—"

He cut her off with a swipe of his hand. "You were right not to trust me. I do fight those monsters but as you saw in your dream, I am not so different from them, either." His teeth clenched, a muscle jumping in his jaw. "But this ranch and my men are the closest thing to safety you have. If you leave, they *will* hunt you down and kill you. So choose to believe me or don't. It's up to you. Just know this—staying means you live."

She expected him to say more, but when he didn't, she realized he was waiting for a response. There really wasn't an option. Everything inside her said he spoke the truth, as insane as it would sound if she said it out loud.

"For how long?"

"You and your sister have become targets, and don't ask me why. I don't know." His lips thinned. "But I intend to find out."

She nodded, believing him. "We'll stay."

"There's more," he said. "The dreams won't stop. Whoever is doing this plans to push me to the limit."

"And you think they are using me to do it?"

"Do you know what my wife's name was?" he asked, but didn't give her time to answer. "It was Caron. C-a-r-o-n. The Italian version of your name."

Her hand went to her throat. "Those beasts killed her, didn't they?"

"Yes," he said, "and they'll kill you, too. Don't doubt it."

"How did you escape?"

"I didn't, Karen. Don't you get it?" he challenged. "I didn't."

"And they're still after you."

"Right," he said, his lips thinning. "And they're trying to use you to bring me down."

"Why me?" she asked. "I don't understand any of this."

He ignored her question. "I'll have you taken to your sister. You can move about the house as you please. I'll send the housekeeper up to show you around and make sure you eat." With that he started for the door. When he reached for the doorknob, he stilled, keeping his back to her as he spoke. "I can't be near you, Karen. Stay away."

Chapter 9

Adrian lifted his body, thrusting deeper inside the human female atop him. The windowless room, part of a facility buried deep beneath the earth, flickered with candlelight.

Black silk sheets covered Adrian's massive oak-framed bed and caressed his back. His newest servant, the nurse he'd captured and would soon convert, rode him, her wet core stroking his erection. He didn't remember her name. Alice. Sherry. Something like that. He didn't know, nor did he care. Humans were simply toys, lesser beings who served the greater beings like himself.

With a low moan, his servant sat up, slowing her movements as if she savored each slide of his erection inside her body. Palming her voluptuous breasts, she bit her bottom lip, and tilted her head back, lost in the pleasure Adrian delivered. The beast in him, primal and sexual, consumed humans, taking their satisfaction without acknowledging or allowing resistance. The beast fed off the power to take. To control. To devour.

His servant straddled him, wild with desire. Grinding the V of her body against him, matching his upward movement with a downward one. Sounds of pleasure slid from her lips, her body jerking and swaying like the animal in heat, desperate for release.

Adrian eyed his newest prize, enjoying the visual delight she presented. Her nipples, so plump and tight, peeked through her fingers and he wanted to taste them. To lap at them with his tongue. The thought thickened his cock, delivering what she wanted. What she needed…more. More of what only he, the ultimate beast, could deliver: absolute satisfaction.

All she had to do was give herself to him. And she had.

At first, she'd fought him, a crazed female ready for blood. He'd enjoyed it immensely. Breaking them always turned him on. But now, hours later, she'd forgotten her missing friend, the one he'd captured for bait. She'd forgotten the minute his tongue had touched her clit.

One long lick along the silky folds of her core and she'd shuddered into submission.

And now, his little nurse was panting and rocking, not an ounce of restraint in sight. With enjoyment he checked himself, not sliding into his primal side. Enjoying the show she delivered. He bored easily, disposing of his submissives when they no longer incited his interest. His lust. He'd thought to use the nurse for a night or two and then kill her. Now he wasn't so sure. She had potential, this one, her sexual nature making her a perfect playmate for a beast. He needed his sex and he needed it often. If she was this hot before he claimed her human side, he could only imagine how she'd respond when he did.

The thought pleased him and his hands went to her waist. He pulled her down harder against his hips, bucking upward, the pounding of their bodies driving him toward release. She cried out, arched her back, hands going behind her to brace herself on his upper thighs.

He pumped and pumped, driven now by the sight she made. Nothing but lust and burning satisfaction controlled him and his actions.

Hunger ate at him and Adrian sat up, wrapping one arm around her back and pulling the warmth of her human body against his colder one. He loved the feel of a living human in his arms. It made him feel so… alive.

He pinched one of her nipples and she made a sound, a mixture of pain laced with pleasure. Her head lifted so she could look at him, her brunette hair wild as it framed her heart-shaped face and draped her shoulders.

He pinched the erect peak again and she rewarded him with a yelp. A smile on his mouth, he bent his head, finding the nipple with his lips and teeth and then licking away the ache, stroking it with wet caresses. This time, she purred for him. Again, his teeth scraped, then nipped and she gasped.

But he didn't soothe her with his tongue as he had

before. Not yet. Adrian lifted his gaze to hers. "Does it hurt?"

"Yes," she whispered with a shuddered breath.

"But you like it, don't you?"

She cupped her breast, offering him her nipples again. "Yes."

He gave her what she wanted, suckling her rosy nipple deep into his mouth. But not for long. Adrian buried his face in her neck, pressing their bodies together and rocking. For several minutes, they moved together, toward satisfaction and release. Rising to the ultimate completion.

The instant her body clenched, biting at him with orgasm, he felt his own pump from his body, as well. He sunk his teeth into her shoulder, tasting the crimson pleasure of her blood as he spilled himself in the wet recesses of her body. She stiffened, gasping at the sting of his cuspids burning through her flesh. But only moments later, she sighed with bliss and called his name…*Adrian.*

And, that easily, her conversion began.

When he withdrew his teeth, he ran a finger across her wounds, sealing them, but not completely wiping them from view. He preferred his victims see the proof he'd claimed their lives, their very existence.

A knock sounded on the door, and he shoved the nurse off of him. When she protested, he sent her a mental command, ordering her to sleep. She sank onto the mattress, obeying as he knew she would, her soul, her mind, her very being, already sliding in between the living and the dead. Into his control.

"Come in," Adrian called.

The double doors opened, light spilling into the dimly lit room from the hallway. Beneath the ground, it always felt like night, but the beasts saw almost as well in the darkness as in the light.

Adrian's next in charge appeared in the entryway, shrinking it with his broad shoulders and muscular frame. Years before he'd been called Drake. Adrian simply called him Segundo or "second." It kept things in perspective. His Segundo would never be the "first." That was his role with Cain and no one else's. The last Darkland that tried to take his place lost his head.

Adrian waved a hand at the lamp on the nightstand, using one of his many magical abilities to illuminate the room in a dim glow, the act a subtle reminder of his higher rank and skill.

"Where the hell have you been, Segundo?" Adrian demanded, sitting up, unconcerned about his nakedness. "I've been trying to reach you for hours."

Segundo stepped inside the room, shutting the door and then taking a military stance, hand crossed in front of his chest, legs in a V. His chiseled, harsh features showed no reaction, his square jaw set and unmoving.

For a mere instant, Segundo's eyes flickered to the naked woman on the bed and then returned to Adrian. "The recruitment mission ran into difficulty."

"What the hell does that mean? What can go wrong with a simple *recruitment* mission?" Adrian's question came out an intentional demand, harsh and lethal. He felt the fury inside building. He sat up on the edge of the bed, not looking at his second as he waited for the answer. Instead he inhaled, fighting the urge to cross the distance and jack Segundo against the wall. Nothing was going to screw with his plans to take down Jag. Nothing.

And the damn silence was pissing him off. When he asked a question, he damn sure expected an answer. And he felt the uneasiness in his second. Adrian didn't have to look at the other beast, to feel the tension. The anger.

"Well?" Adrian asked, yanking open the nightstand and withdrawing a small Mexican cigar. He shoved it between his lips and lit it.

Finally Segundo spoke, his words tight and low. "A battle with the Knights means substantial loss of manpower."

Adrian drew deep on his cigar and then glanced at Segundo, taking his time to respond. Letting Segundo squirm.

His second came off as cold and callous to those around him. The scar that zigzagged down his right cheek along with his military-style buzz-cut haircut only serving to intensify the blackness of his deep-set eyes. But Segundo didn't even come close to matching how cold Adrian could be. His second would be smart to remember as much.

"So you thought you'd recruit to fill those losses today?" Adrian asked.

"Exactly," Segundo replied. "Preparing for the worst."

Adrian narrowed his eyes on the other beast, keeping his voice low. Lethal. "I expected preparation to be done—" he raised his voice "—in goddamn advance!

And there better not be a worst case. This better go so great that we are celebrating." His voice lowered and his tone took on an edge of menace. "Got that?"

The other beast cut his gaze to the floor as if hiding his reaction. "Yes, master," he mumbled.

With a mental picture, Adrian clothed himself. Black leather pants. Black T-shirt. Black boots. He stood, feeling the power running through his body. The power of anger, of anticipation, of thirst for Jag's destruction. Of the rewards Cain would give him for destroying the mighty leader of the Knights.

Segundo lifted his eyes. "Master—"

When Segundo opened his mouth to explain, it was the last straw. Adrian would have thought Segundo would know better than to make excuses by now.

Segundo managed two more words before Adrian acted. Those words, "My intention—"

Adrian bit the cigar between his teeth and held his palms up, stop-sign fashion. Segundo flew in the air and hit the door, his body pinned to the wooden surface, his muscles and even his vocal cords frozen. Adrian allowed him to breathe.

But just barely.

It had been far too long since he'd last reminded his second of just how potent his master's powers. Now, before they put their plans in play with the Knights of White, Adrian wanted Segundo to remember. To know just how painful Adrian would make his failure. He wanted Segundo to feel fear.

With a blink, Adrian flashed out of the room and

reappeared in front of Segundo. He took a puff off his cigar and then withdrew it from his lips. "I love these damn things," he said looking at the thin brown smoke between his fingers and inhaling the musty smell. "But I have some Cubans stored away to celebrate the destruction of Jag."

For several seconds, he stared at the face of his second. He respected Segundo more than most around him. This beast was one who lusted after power and control as Adrian himself did. Honorable qualities—as long as they were kept in check. Adrian eyed the scar on Segundo's face and then smiled.

Without warning, he shoved his lit cigar into the old wound. A wound born of Segundo's human days. Segundo's shock and pain ripped through Adrian's body, delivering a rush of pure pleasure and Adrian laughed with the high of it.

He pushed harder on the smoke, grounding it into the raw, now open skin. "Mess up my plans," Adrian said, "and I'll burn every inch of your body."

He pinned Segundo in a stare, searching his eyes, to be sure his second understood fully. When he was certain he'd made his point, Adrian stepped backward, tossing the cigar in the air. A second later it vanished.

Adrian held his palms up again and Segundo fell to the ground.

"Get up," Adrian said, feeling Segundo's anger and defeat charge the air. He motioned toward the bed where the naked servant lay. "Use the girl. She's a hot little bitch, eager to please. Work this out of your system because I won't deal with this on the battlefield." Adrian sneered. "Just not here." He hated intruders in his space. "We leave in three hours."

And then, he flashed the beast and the human woman out of his room.

Marisol entered the miniature cathedral-like structure nestled deep in the trees to the west of the main house. She had inherited it from the Healer who had served the Knights before her.

The Healer no one talked about, not even Salvador. A little detail that bothered her in a deep way. Had her predecessor met destruction—or salvation?

Resolved to control her own destiny, she stepped inside the octagon-shaped room she called "The Green Room" because everything inside was some shade of green. The walls, curtains, even the carpet. A color symbolic of rebirth and rejuvenation.

It was here Marisol often found solitude. Not an easy thing to come by with the Knights, and their big bodies and bigger attitudes at every turn.

Taking in the sight of the room, Marisol already felt calmer. She padded across the carpet to a small chest sitting beside the only real piece of furniture in the room, an oversize chair.

Marisol couldn't get to Salvador, so she had to face facts. She was on her own, her duty as her guide. Already, a human's soul threatened to slip away. And she couldn't let it happen. She could not fail.

On many occasions, she called souls back to humans, but this time was different. A powerful darkness held Eva's soul in its control. A darkness she had to stop.

With *The Book of Knowledge* in hand, Marisol sank into the familiar comfort of the chair. She pressed her palm against its surface, feeling an odd but familiar sense of power from holding it. She felt its weight where it rested on her lap, heavy with the wisdom it held. Wisdom passed on from Healer after Healer, century after century.

With resolve to find a solution to save her new patient, Marisol considered her book. The book she'd never had a use for before now, although she had studied from cover to cover, because until now, healing had come as easily as funneling her energy.

Marisol lifted the cover of the book, determination in her mind. She'd won her spot as Healer, a chance to make good on her past, and she wouldn't fail. Eva would be saved.

Chapter 10

It was an hour later when Jag approached the cathedral. Marisol knew it was him, just as she always did. Magic surrounded his presence, strong and forceful. Untouched, because Jag refused to truly accept all he could be.

On the outside, a warrior led the Knights. On the inside, she felt his fear. Fear of himself and what he had become. He'd been delivered into his destiny, while she'd chosen hers. Marisol understood his struggles. She also worried they would be his demise.

She put the book away, a plan formed to heal Eva. Just as she turned toward the door, Jag pushed it open, his expression guarded as always. "Any ideas?"

"Other than you finding the beast controlling her

and killing it?" she asked, but didn't expect a response. "Maybe. Or at least a way to hold her in this world until we can find another one."

Jag gave her a questioning look, one brow arching upward.

Still, she hesitated, knowing she was treading on choppy water. "I should be able to use her sister's love as a boost to my powers. That is, if I can get her to believe in the Darklands and in my healing abilities."

"She already knows the truth. She just hasn't accepted it." His lips thinned. "Make her. She's with her sister now."

This news came as a surprise. Just hours before, she'd expressed her concern over the sister's confinement only to be cut off cold. These women were victims, but Jag acted as if they were enemies.

"I should be there, too," Marisol said, starting for the door but forced to stop again.

Jag still blocked the entryway. He didn't move. Didn't speak. Yet, the air crackled with an electric current. With unspoken words.

"What is it?" Marisol said, feeling his tension, wishing she understood what was going on.

"Someone has been playing with my dreams." He hesitated. "Not just mine. Karen's, too. I need you to find a way to make it stop."

Marisol narrowed her eyes on him. "I'm confused. What kind of dreams?"

A muscle in his jaw jumped. "Just make them stop, Marisol."

"I don't know if I can," she said. "Salvador—"

"Isn't here," he finished for her. "You are."

This was way over her head. She didn't know enough information to start working this and Jag didn't seem to want to give any more, either.

"One more thing," he said. "I need to know Karen understands what will happen if she runs."

Marisol narrowed her eyes on his, searched the black depths of his unreadable stare. She also noted his use of the human woman's name. "Meaning the Darklands will hunt her down and kill her."

"Meaning I'll go after her."

That wasn't the answer she expected, and she tried to hide the surprise she knew had to register on her face. Who was this woman, and what did she mean to Jag?

"Because the Darklands will be after her, right? You'll go after her to save her," she said, her final statement not meant as a question…yet it was. Why was there a hint of threat in his voice?

But Jag didn't answer. He was already walking away.

Marisol had no option. She needed to talk to Karen.

Karen paced the bedroom again, needing somewhere, anywhere, to put all the confusion and emotion burning inside.

Jag's order to "stay away" replayed in her head, over and over, a loud taunt in the silence in the bedroom. Why did the words bother her so much? And if he wanted her "away," why'd he bring her here and lock her up in the first place?

His claim of "monsters" who would hunt her and Eva

down and kill them rang with eerie warning in her mind. Karen had seen the marks on her sister's skin. She'd heard the stories, the ones that claimed Jaguar Ranch to be the home of the monster hunters. She'd come here to heal her sister, to find help and even protection.

Protecting someone didn't mean making them a prisoner. She'd gladly leave if only she could.

But then, there lay a complication, and she knew it. Deep down, Karen wasn't so sure she really *did* want to leave. For some reason, coming here had felt the right choice. Being here now, despite the craziness of the event unfolding, felt right, as well. More than right. It felt like the way to save her sister…and maybe herself.

Karen prayed Jag meant his words, that she was now free to leave the room and see her sister. Seeing the proof, that her sister was okay, would help her solidify her choices. She should be with Eva, helping her through this. Surely Jag understood this.

How easily she used his name, Karen realized.

A sultry replay of her dream formed in her mind, engaging her with questions, and the need for answers. How could she have dreamed of Jag in the past, before meeting him? And why couldn't she remember them until now? Then there was the big question—why did she heat when he looked at her and downright melt at his touch?

Did she know Jag before spotting him at the airport?

Perhaps she did.

Somehow. Someway. Yes. She thought that must be the case. Maybe the memory was suppressed, hidden in dreams she'd buried deep in the night. Perhaps seeing him, being here, had brought them to the surface. It appeared the only logical answer.

People didn't dream of strangers they'd never set eyes on. She laughed, but not with humor, sinking onto the mattress as she felt her legs wobble a bit, exhaustion ever-present.

If she didn't know Jag before today, then meeting him in her dreams had to be…what? She laughed again, feeling a bit crazy as she formed an explanation.

Magic?

The word made her stomach lurch, as if her body knew a truth she hadn't accepted. Monsters and monster hunters…if she'd come here, daring to believe monsters might be true, then why not magic?

Running a rough hand through her tousled hair, Karen's nostrils flared with a whiff of spicy male. Jag's scent was all over her, teasing her with its presence. Reminding her of his kiss. Of his taste.

Karen paced faster, squeezing her eyes shut, and trying to block out the image of Jag's hand in her hair. On her body. In her dreams.

Karen's gaze jerked to the door as she heard it being unlocked. A second later, it slowly creaked open. One of the men who'd locked her away stood in the doorway.

Tall and broad, with ultrashort hair, a square jaw and a cowboy hat, this man was nothing like his boss. Nothing like Jag. No, this man looked and felt more "American Pie" mixed with "Bad Boy," as if he was a good guy trying to hide behind wild ways. Jag didn't hide. His exotic appearance spoke loudly of true darkness. He oozed danger. Darkness. Sensual power.

"Name's Rock, ma'am," her visitor said, his broad shoulders taking up the entire width of the doorway. "I'm here to take you to see your sister."

Relief washed over her. Getting to Eva was all that mattered right now and knowing her sister was safe. Pushing to her feet, Karen wasn't about to argue. "Great. Where is she?"

"Right across the hall," he said, motioning for her to follow. He started to turn, and hesitated, tipping his hat back with his index finger. "Sorry we got off to a bad start. I, um, know this thing with your sister must have you pretty raw."

His words surprised her. Karen searched his face, focusing on his deep-set hazel eyes, for the sincerity she heard in his voice. And she found it there. Found sincerity and more. For an instant—just one—she saw shared pain.

Rock understood her fear for her sister.

He'd lost someone he loved very deeply before that person's time.

Without another word, he moved to the hallway, and eager to find Eva, to see that she was safe and okay, Karen followed.

A few moments later, with Rock on her heels, Karen entered a dimly lit room, a plain white shade covering a lone window. Adjusting to the lighting, Karen brought the twin-size bed into focus.

The instant she saw her sister, Karen went cold inside, her chest tightening.

Gone was the vibrant woman she knew as her sister, the one so full of life and love, as well as fears. In her place rested a pale, unmoving stranger, dark circles under her closed eyes. Brownish black lashes framing her cheeks. Karen swallowed against a rush of emotion, barely able to breathe as fear tried to take hold.

She forced out the question she needed answered but was afraid to ask. "Is she…dead?"

"Sleeping," Rock said.

Relief washed over her. Karen stepped forward, easing onto the edge of the mattress and reaching for her sister's hand. "Eva?"

Nothing. Not even a hint of response.

Karen leaned forward and brushed her knuckles over her cheek. "Eva, sweetie. Come back to me." Tears burned in the back of her eyes. "Please come back to me, baby."

Swiping at the lone droplet that slid from her eye, Karen eyed the room. There was no sign of medical tools or machines. No hope of life support. She was crazy to be here. Crazy.

"Where is the Healer?"

"I'm Marisol."

Karen turned to find a young woman—not more than twenty-four or five—with long, dark hair standing just inside the room. Dressed to blend in with the surroundings, she wore faded jeans, boots and a T-shirt. With her heart-shaped face, pointed chin and luminous eyes, she looked almost angelic. Her youthful appearance gave her a childlike appearance.

Karen laughed, but not with humor. With disbelief

and a bit of panic for Eva's well-being. She pushed to her feet, facing the new visitor. "Tell me you're joking."

"I'm taking good care of Eva, Karen," the woman said in a low voice. "I promise you I will do everything in my power to bring her back to you. You have to trust me."

"Right." Karen raised her hands to the room. "You don't even have any medical supplies."

"Because that won't help your sister, and I believe you know that. You came here for a reason. You came because you knew she needed help she couldn't get any other place."

Karen rejected her words and glanced at Eva's pale features, noting again the dark circles on her pasty-white skin. It was time to stop this foolishness. Eva had gotten worse, not better, since their arrival.

"I want to talk to Jag, and I want to talk to him now." Her voice trembled with emotion, with fear and anger. "I will not stay here a minute longer."

She'd barely finished her sentence when Rock moved. He pulled a knife from Lord only knew where, and in a flash of movement sliced his palm deep. He held it out, blood trickling to the ground, the gouge of the wound evident.

Karen gasped, feeling like she'd been kicked in the chest. She sank back onto the bed, shocked and fearful of what he would do next.

The Healer looked at Rock with outrage. "Are you trying to scare the hell out of her?"

In response, Rock stepped closer to the Healer, his big body dwarfing her tiny one. He shoved his hand at the Healer, the knife still in his other. "Fix me."

With a deep breath, she grabbed his wrist. "Hold it open."

Karen watched in amazement as the Healer held her palm above Rock's, a glow spilling from her hand to his. A minute later, the Healer let go of his wrist. "Don't do that again," she said in reprimand.

"Whatever you say, Marisol," he said, his voice low. Then, he looked at Karen and held up his palm for her to inspect.

Blinking, Karen took in the sight before her. It couldn't be. She blinked again. The wound was healed. The huge slash in his hand was completely sealed. Remnants of blood stained his hand as proof that the wound had existed, but there was no other evidence at all.

Fingers digging into the mattress, Karen digested what had just happened. Either she was going completely freaking nuts, or she'd just seen proof that magic—miracles—existed.

Slowly her gaze turned to Eva, taking in her sister with a sickening feeling of loss. If magic existed, monsters did, too. Deep down, she already knew it was true. The Healer was right. Karen had come here for a reason. She knew this place, these people, were her only hope of saving her sister.

"I'll need your help to save her," the Healer said, her voice near.

Karen looked up to see the woman standing by her side. She drew a deep breath and reached deep inside for her response.

And then she took a leap of faith. "What do I need to do?"

Chapter 11

Jag was the leader of a bunch of immortal monster hunters. No. *Beasts.* Marisol had called them beasts.

From what she understood, there were about twenty "trainees" on the property, and a core group of five Knights who worked directly with Jag. Men he kept close, who helped him train and place other Knights outside of their facility. All those years growing up near this place, she'd thought it was a horse ranch, thought the rumors of the monster hunters living here to be silly.

Karen sat at a very normal-looking, wooden kitchen table, tucked in the corner of a very normal-looking kitchen. In front of her was a bowl of macaroni and cheese.

A quite normal meal.

But it was a facade.

This normal-looking room sat in the middle of a training facility for what she now knew to be the "Knights of White." After hours of talking with Marisol, hearing about the "beasts," Karen was quite certain nothing in life would ever be "normal" again.

Especially Eva.

Marisol had worked hard, with Karen's assistance to revive her sister. The results had been dismal at best. Eva had tossed and turned as Marisol had tried to heal her. And no matter how hard Karen had tried to calm her sister, she hadn't been able to.

Eva seemed lost, gone forever.

Marisol set a glass of soda on the table and then claimed the seat next to Karen. "I can feel your exhaustion."

Karen would have responded, but she had just shoveled a spoon into her mouth. The minute the food hit her taste buds, her stomach growled. It was as if it had gone into hibernation and just woken up. "God. I was hungrier than I thought. It's been forever since I ate."

"Makes mac and cheese taste like lobster, doesn't it?" Marisol asked, offering a smile.

"I love this stuff," Karen said. "I'd take mac and cheese over lobster anyday." She'd mentioned her travel reporting during their earlier talks. "None of my travel is in the States, so it's not easy to get some of the things I enjoy. The last time I was in the States, I packed Kraft Easy Mac to take on the road."

Marisol finished off a bite of food. "It must be fun seeing places and getting paid for it."

Karen shrugged, guilt stabbing at her gut and zapping her appetite again. "I guess. Maybe." She hesitated, needing a friend. Marisol already felt comfortable. Almost familiar. Much like Jag… Well, not like Jag, but familiar all the same. "It also took me away from my sister when she obviously needed me."

Marisol set her spoon down. "You didn't do this to Eva. The Darklands did."

"But—"

"There is no *but*. You feel the guilt because you love her, not because it's deserved. Besides, we aren't done fighting. If I can't fix this, Jag can."

Karen took a drink, trying to hide the way just hearing Jag's name affected her. For hours, she'd hoped to see him. She told herself it was to curse him for treating her as he had, but it was more than that. Even his name seduced her senses. Jag…did things to her.

"Talking about Jag makes you nervous."

Karen's eyes darted to Marisol's, surprised at her intuitiveness. "He locked me in a room. Nervousness is to be expected, isn't it?" She didn't give the Healer time to respond. "What can Jag do to help Eva?"

"If he can find the beast controlling your sister and kill it, then Eva will be free." She hesitated. "Karen, we need to talk about a few things and they need to stay between us."

Karen's eyes narrowed on Marisol. "Who would I tell?"

"I know things even Jag doesn't know I know. Things that have allowed me to come to a few conclusions I think you have a right to know."

"Like?" Karen asked, hoping for answers to questions she wasn't even sure she knew to ask.

"Jag had a wife once. Most know that, but they don't know her name."

"He told me," Karen said. "Caron. The same as mine."

Surprised registered on Marisol's face. "I don't know of anyone he's ever shared that with."

"He only told me because he wanted me to understand why someone is using me to get to him."

"Through your dreams," Marisol said, but seemed to already know.

"Right," Karen said, twirling the fork in her fingers, a bit uncomfortable. She liked Marisol, even felt instant trust with her, but this was confusing, and honestly, she didn't want to share the nature of the dreams. "Can you make them stop?"

"I don't know," Marisol said, her response a bit slow. "And I'm not sure I should even if I can."

Karen stiffened. "Why?" she demanded, her voice a bit rough and she knew it. "I don't understand?"

"I bet you didn't know that Caron's father was an explorer. He traveled the world and Caron wanted to do the same. She collected journals from him and from other explorers. She used to read them to Jag."

The words stroked something far in her mind. Something buried. Karen shook her head, wanting all of this confusion to end. "I don't see what that has to do with the dreams."

"You write for a travel magazine," Marisol said. "You travel the world."

Karen laughed, but not with humor. The words hit home, refusing to be ignored. "Surely you're not suggesting there's a connection between Caron and me?"

"I'm simply suggesting you open your mind to possibilities," Marisol offered. "Before we try to get rid of the dreams, make sure they don't hold answers we need." She considered a moment and then added, "*You* need. What if those dreams represent the path to saving both your sister and Jag?"

Before Karen could respond, male voices, followed by laughter, filled the air. "I'm freaking starving." Another bark of laughter. "First food. Then a nice long-legged blonde, I think."

A not so polite reply followed, and then the laughter seemed to fade. Karen and Marisol exchanged a look. "Sorry," Marisol said. "Living with a houseful of men you get that."

Whistling filled the air, a familiar tune Karen couldn't quite place. It ended abruptly as a shirtless male appeared in the kitchen. Karen's eyes went wide. This wasn't just a male. It was a large, incredibly sexy, half-dressed male.

The testosterone in this place was almost over-whelming.

Sweats hanging low on his hips, the newcomer displayed abs-of-steel, a broad chest, and defined shoulders. The towel thrown over his shoulder, his auburn chin-length hair barely contained in a tie at the back of his neck, suggested that he'd just finished a workout.

"Am I interrupting?" he asked.

"Yes," Marisol said, "but it's not like you care." She gave Karen a knowing look. "Meet Des, the Knight with the biggest ego."

Des winked at the ladies and yanked open the

fridge, pulling out a jug of milk and kicking the door shut again. "Confidence does not equal ego," he countered, grabbing a glass from a cabinet, biceps flexing with the movement.

Marisol rolled her eyes. "Please." She looked at Karen. "He's as arrogant as they come."

"And adorable," he said. "Don't forget adorable." With a loaf of bread, a jar of peanut butter and a knife in hand, Des sat down across from Karen. "She loves me. Can you tell?"

At closer view, Karen knew this man. Knew the scar down his cheek. Memories of being carried up the stairs by several men came back with a bitter bite. "You helped lock me away."

"Guilty as charged," he said, scooping peanut butter on a slice of bread. "You were too much for Rock and Rinehart, poor guys." He smiled. "Nothing personal. Just doing as I was told."

"By Jag."

He shrugged. "He's the boss."

"And you do whatever he says."

"Jag doesn't do anything without cause."

"He locked me up."

"He had a reason."

She wanted to scream. "Which was?"

"You tell me," he said, taking a bite of his peanut butter-covered bread and swallowing.

Karen leaned back in her chair as if slapped. The truth was, she knew why. She just didn't like it. That Jag treated her like an enemy, even now, upset her in a deep way. But yes, she knew why he'd acted as he had. The dreams...but she didn't create them. She lived them as much as he did. For all she knew, Jag had been the one... No. She knew that wasn't true. He feared those dreams. Maybe not inside them, but later, after. Karen didn't know what to think about all of this. Her mind raced with the implications of Marisol's words. She needed some time to think. To process. This was all too overwhelming.

"Love this stuff," Des said, slapping more peanut butter on his bread. "You know it's only been around about fifty years, and for the longest time, we couldn't get it in Texas." He looked at them and a light seemed to go on in his eyes. "Want some?" He lifted the jar toward Karen and then Marisol.

Marisol made a face at him. "No, we don't *want* some. And stop causing trouble. If you'd carried me to a room and locked me up, I'd be furious. It's a miracle Karen is being as accepting as she is. Poor thing has been through hell."

"How is the sister?" Des asked, his attention on Marisol, his mood suddenly serious.

Karen answered before Marisol could, not liking the way he talked about Eva like some "thing." "*My* sister isn't good at all."

"No, she's not good at all," Marisol agreed. "We need to talk to Jag."

"Talk to me about what?"

Karen felt the voice even before she saw the man. Jag stood just inside the kitchen, just as Des had only minutes before, but the impact of his presence yielded one hundred times the amount Des's had. He took over the room, took over *her,* his powerful aura like fire lighting the air with sparks.

Des scooted his chair around to better see Jag. In doing so, he put Karen in Jag's direct line of vision. Their eyes locked, and she felt the connection clear to her toes. Good Lord, a connection beyond this moment. A connection two people shared who knew each other well.

"It's Karen's sister," Marisol told Jag. "She's stable, but far from cured. I'm not sure how long I can bind her to this world."

But Jag's attention wasn't on Marisol, it was on Karen. His attention took control of her, making coherent thought or speech, impossible. The world was lost in the depth of Jag's heavy stare. So much so that, for a moment, she couldn't even breathe.

She cut her gaze from his, trying to get a grip on her reaction to him. Trying to reject what Marisol had suggested, what her mind wanted to turn to truth. She was *not* Caron, Jag's long-dead wife. It was insane. But then so were monsters and monster hunters, she reminded herself.

"This beast wants Eva and it's powerful enough to take her, I fear," Marisol added. "More so than any I've encountered. I don't understand why it's fighting for her like it is. Why not just choose a new human?"

"Karen?"

Jag spoke her name, willing her to look at him, and full of accusation. "What?" She ground her teeth at the implications in the air, her gaze heated as it darted to his. "Are you asking if I know why?"

Silence laced the air as they squared off, gazes

locked in war and confirmation of her assumption. He still didn't trust her. He was accusing her of Lord only knew what. Here she was, having everything sacred in her world threatened, even her own existence, and she couldn't get a little trust.

Frustration quickly escalating, Karen flattened her palms on the table. "How would I know why this thing wants her?" she demanded. "Until a few hours ago, I didn't even know these 'beasts' existed. I'm not the enemy here. I need to save my sister. Are you going to help me or not?"

"We *are* trying to help," Marisol said, her voice low. "Finding the one who controls your sister isn't an easy task. Maybe if you recap the events that brought you to the ranch in detail."

Karen drew a deep breath and recalled the past twenty-four hours, starting with the telegram. When she finished, a memory lodged in her mind just out of reach. Karen let her head ease forward, exhaustion and emotion, threatening to take control. "Eva called the thing…the beast by a name." She made a frustrated sound. Why couldn't she remember it?

"What name?" Des and Marisol asked in unison.

Karen lifted her head, her fingers digging into the tabletop, her mind hurting with the effort to recall. She was just so tired. "I can't seem to remember. I can't. I never forget things. I…just… I can't."

Marisol's hand slid over the top of Karen's. "I can feel your need to sleep. Rest will clear your mind. I bet you'd like clean clothes and a shower, too. I'll pull some of my things for you and bring them to your room.

Rock is with Eva. He'll alert us if there are any changes. She's safe."

Karen shook her head, discarding the suggestion and reaching deep for the name. It was so close to the surface of her memories. So close but out of reach. "You said you can't protect Eva much longer."

"Go rest," Des said. "Marisol's right." His voice softened. "I didn't mean to be an asshole, by the way."

She was surprised by his apology but didn't try to respond. She was too busy fighting the tiredness taking hold, wanting to refuse their suggestion of rest. But her body was starting to shut down, and she knew it. She had an amazing memory. Almost photographic. To forget a name in such an important situation didn't seem right.

"Please," Marisol urged, "go sleep a little while. I will keep Eva in this world, I promise. She's stable."

Karen fixed her in a stare. "Will you wake me in an hour?"

"Two," Marisol countered.

"Fine," Karen said in defeat. "I…my clothes. I have a suitcase in my car."

"We'll get it for you," Jag said.

Karen didn't look at him as she pushed to her feet. Her legs felt like Jell-O, her muscles aching. And now, when she felt she couldn't take any more, she had to walk past Jag. Worse, he'd be bringing her bag to her. Or even more unsettling, maybe he wouldn't. Maybe he really didn't want to see her. God, she needed rest, because she was insanely conflicted.

Just facing Jag here, with others around, felt overwhelming. He'd told her to stay away from him, but right now he appeared resolved to stay in her path, perhaps because Marisol and Des were watching.

He confused her, this man, this leader of the Knights of White. She didn't know why she was so drawn to him, or he to her. And he was drawn to her. She felt it. Even completely exhausted, she felt it. Could they really have been lovers in the past? Perhaps even married? A part of her screamed with the impossible, telling her, *yes,* they had been. The words from her dream came back to her, barely able to catch her breath with the impact of them playing in her head.

He must accept you.

Claim him or the darker side will.

You are his salvation.

She kept her gaze at chest level as she crossed the kitchen, but when she was directly in front of him she stopped walking and looked at him. Karen opened her mouth to speak, wanting answers, but then reconsidered. She was tired. There was an audience.

No, it wasn't the time or place. Still, a memory flashed in her mind. The one Marisol had sparked with her recount of the past. Karen was lying under a tree with a book of some sort in her hand—only it wasn't her in appearance—it was another. It was Caron. It had to be. Yet, Karen felt it like it was her. Knew the moment as if she'd lived it.

Her head was in Jag's lap as she read to him, his fingers stroking her hair. A tender touch filled with love. He whispered something to her and she looked up at him, taken aback by the love in his gaze. So much love.

The kind of love she'd never felt in this lifetime. It was a good memory. *Oh, God.* Crazy as it might make her, it did, indeed, feel like a memory. Her memory. Karen's chest tightened as the images slipped away. As they departed she wanted to call them back. It was as if something sweet was being stolen away, snatched without her regard.

She searched Jag's face, feeling warmth begin to flood her as she recognized his eyes as those in her memory. This time the warmth was not from desire, but from something much more heartfelt and tender.

"Oh, God," she whispered. "I think...it's true."

Jag narrowed his eyes on her. "What's true?"

Karen opened her mouth and shut it, becoming aware of their audience again. A bit happy for it, in fact. Some sleep would help her deal with this, make sure she wasn't simply delusional. That what felt real, really was.

Jag's hand snaked out and shackled her wrist, his voice hard. "What's true?" he demanded in a hard voice that contrasted with the gentle way he held her wrist.

He put on a tough show for the others, but she felt the carefulness of his touch. Jag would never hurt her. "That I need sleep," she said, feeling the most unbelievable urge to grab his hand and pull him with her to a quiet place and replay her memory. She cut her gaze away, afraid he would see there was more to her declaration than her words gave as reason. "I just need sleep."

She felt him studying her, and knew instinctively he didn't quite believe her. The minute he released her, she sidestepped him, and made her way from the room. But even in her retreat he haunted her, the spicy maleness of his scent chasing her, as did the vividness of her memory.

In that moment, she vowed to find out the truth about her dreams and how they connected her and Jag to the past. Because they did. She knew Jag before this day. She felt it with all of her being. If that memory had been true, they'd once been in love.

This wasn't over because he told her to "stay away." Not by a long shot. She didn't obey when ordered. If the Caron of his past had simply listened when ordered, Jag had a surprise coming to him. Sitting back and waiting for someone else to take action wasn't her style.

Karen found her way to the top of the stairs and had a choice of her room or Eva's. She chose her sister's. If she had to sleep, she'd do it there. If Eva woke up, she needed to know Karen was near.

Karen found Rock sitting in a corner of Eva's room in an armchair she hadn't noticed until now. He stiffened as she entered and pushed to his feet.

"I can watch her awhile," Karen said.

Rock gave her one quick nod. "I'll just be outside if you need me." He started for the door.

Why he needed to stay at all, she didn't know, but she didn't argue. Instead she walked over to her sister, and pressed a palm to her cold cheek. When she didn't move, Karen touched two fingers to Eva's neck, feeling for a pulse. She let out a breath as it beat beneath her touch. Relieved, she brushed her knuckles over her sister's cheek and let her hand drop away.

Karen took Rock's place in the corner chair. The

overstuffed brown chair was remarkably comfortable, or perhaps Karen was simply that tired. She took off her shoes and settled her legs to her side.

Once she got a little sleep, and was sure her mind was clear, she was going to talk to Jag. They were going to have a face-to-face and figure out what these dreams were really all about.

Instinct said she needed to get close to Jag and fast… before it was too late. Her head eased onto the cushion, her eyes drifting shut.

The minute Rock told Jag Karen wasn't in her room, he handed Rock her suitcase, cursing under his breath. Karen had to have been awake over twenty-four hours now, and the only way to save Eva might be locked in her memories. She needed rest, plain and simple. Eva's salvation might well hinge on a name Karen was too tired to place. If Jag knew the name of this beast, if it was recognizable, it might help him track it down and kill it.

Without allowing himself time to think, Jag acted, ignoring his own silent vow to stay away from Karen.

Charging into the room, he stopped dead in his tracks as he found Karen asleep in the chair, her hand tucked beneath her chin. Everything inside him went still and then warmed. So beautiful, so innocent.

Blond hair framed her face in wild disarray. Dark lashes rested on her porcelain-perfect skin. His heart squeezed at the vision of loveliness. At the tenderness it made him feel. Yet, he knew from the dreams, she could make him feel much darker, even dangerous. She could easily bring out the beast in him. Bring out the very thing he'd battled for several lifetimes now.

How could one woman bring out such softness in him, yet still tempt his darker side like no other?

But he knew now that Karen was a victim, not the enemy. Those dreams were warnings: not just to him, but to her, as well. He feared their message. Feared they might be a premonition of what would come if he dared give into the temptation Karen represented.

Yet, standing in the kitchen, watching her as she interacted with his people, he had felt her torment and pain over Eva. He wanted to soothe and protect her. To reassure. Not to hurt her. It had been near impossible to control those urges. But he didn't dare let her near. The dreams had been clear. Karen would lead him to the beast.

He had to stay away from her.

His chest tightened as his eyes swept her beautiful features. Why, then, did the idea of letting her out of his sight and direct care scare the hell out of him?

Chapter 12

Salvador flashed into the bedroom where Eva slept. He stood, invisible to human eyes, in front of the chair where Karen rested, and stared down at the woman who, unknowingly, held so many people's destiny in her grasp.

She was Jag's salvation, if he would accept it. And he in turn held profound influence over his men, an influence that would ultimately impact this war of good over evil.

Things were moving faster than expected, with the Darklands nearby and ready to attack. He'd hoped to allow Karen and Jag time to find each other again, to find their past, of their own accord. But he feared allowing things to progress too slow.

His Knights would need more power, more skill.

To receive it, Raphael had demanded the Knights be balanced with another pure soul, and that each Knight must accept her willingly. Karen would be the first of her kind; of the mates who would balance the dark side of the beast in his Knights and gift them with light. That Adrian had somehow found Karen first and plotted to use her existence against Jag, Salvador wasn't surprised.

In fact, Salvador suspected it was Raphael who'd allowed such a thing to happen. Raphael had made his position clear. Great powers awaited the Knights of White as rewards for proving their loyalty. It would be too easy for Jag to simply meet his mate and fall in love with her all over again, as he had in a prior life. Jag had to be tested. He had to taste his woman's blood and for once allow his beast to rise, to claim it and then take control.

Salvador found the plan distasteful. He understood the reasoning, just not the method. Had these men losing their families, all that was precious to them, not been enough torture?

Now Adrian played with Jag's mind, the dreams clearly a work of his creation. Adrian wanted Jag so confused that he would taste his mate's blood and go insane, devouring her and his own soul at the same time.

But it didn't have to be that way. Love would show Jag the way, if he dared feel it. Karen had to know what they shared to deliver him there. To assist Jag directly in this mission was forbidden, so Salvador had to find another way.

Salvador waved his hand in front of Karen's face.

"Awaken your past and let the memories fill the present. Let the light of day guide the way."

He let his hand fall to his side, satisfied as Karen murmured Jag's name that he'd achieved his goal.

He smiled and flashed from the room in search of Marisol's *Book of Knowledge*. If all went as planned, she'd need to understand the mating mark Jag would soon give to Karen.

Once he'd taken care of that matter, he moved on to dirtier business. On to the outskirts of the ranch where Adrian and his beasts prepared to attack.

It was time to teach Adrian a little lesson in fair play.

Segundo ordered his troops to take cover in the high grass just outside the boundaries of Jaguar Ranch.

Once they were settled comfortably in position, he eased further into the night, closer to the ranch, scouting. Lowering himself to the ground on all fours, Segundo eased forward, searching for any sign of trouble.

He found nothing but still, black night. Even the wind seemed to have vanished, the stars gone into hiding. The chatter of scattered crickets and a lone owl were the only signs of life.

Normally Segundo would have sent another beast to do this job. But not tonight. Not when his freedom stood at risk. No. More like his *existence*. If this mission failed, Adrian would cremate him. Literally. As in turn him to ash.

He was slave to that bastard, and Segundo hated it.

One day, somehow, he'd find a way around Adrian. Find his way directly to Cain. But he also wasn't stupid, like the last Segundo who'd literally lost his head by crossing Adrian.

Segundo would find Adrian's weakness—and he had one, everyone had one—and then he would use it to come out on top. To find it, Segundo knew he needed to stay tight with Adrian. To be the one who Adrian trusted to deliver results. Then Adrian would let down his guard, and Segundo would discover how to bring him down.

Taking his time, searching the parimeters, Segundo ensured he knew all of the entry points. Mentally he adjusted his attack plan ever-so-slightly, noting a fence he'd been unaware of on the west side of the property.

It was nearly thirty minutes later when he returned to the center point of command, where several of his most trusted beasts were. But before he could issue the slight change of plans his surveillance had made necessary, a flash of fire filled the air, and Adrian materialized.

Adrian's long blond hair flowed around his shoulders as the wind seemed to return, as if doing his bidding. The fair color of his locks was a drastic contrast to the battle garb of black vinyl-like pants and a matching vest: the same clothing all Darkland troops wore. Clothing made for protection in war, magically touched by Cain.

Beasts might not die easily, but the Knights knew well how to make them hurt.

A twenty-four-inch Rapier Sword, sheathed in a case, hung from each of Adrian's hips. Short and lethal, it could easily behead man or beast with one swipe.

Daggers were tucked neatly inside Adrian's vest, knives strapped to his thighs.

Yet, not once had Segundo seen Adrian kill with those weapons. No. Adrian killed with the flash of fire from his hand. He simply used his armory for torture and his own entertainment.

Adrian wouldn't lead the Darklands to the battle. He wouldn't lift his hand against those so beneath him as the Knights.

"We are behind schedule," Adrian said, crossing his arms in front of his broad chest, fixing Segundo in a stare as dark as coal, as deep as the fires in hell. "Is there a problem?"

Segundo motioned to the two beasts he'd been directing to stand at ready. They turned and faced Adrian, hands folded in front of their bodies.

"No, Master," Segundo offered, stepping forward, hoping to limit his exposure to Adrian's belittling in front of his troops. "There's a fence on the west side I had to adjust for. We're ready to move."

"I trust your men are well versed on tonight's objective?"

Segundo felt frustration deep in his gut and hoped Adrian did not sense it, as well. How many times would he be asked this question? For over one hundred years he'd led the army of the beast. He' trained and directed the Darklands with precision and skill.

"Yes, Master."

Adrian walked toward one of the beasts standing to Segundo's right. Grinding his teeth, Segundo vowed to one day leave this submissive role. To have his men questioned was the worst insult he could receive, worse than any physical pain Adrian had ever placed upon him. And there had been plenty.

"State the mission objective," Adrian ordered the beast.

The beast replied, "Staged kidnapping attempt, no injury to the human women. Kill the Knights, just not Jag."

Adrian stared at the beast, seconds passing, the air thick and hot, with his scrutiny. "As if you could kill Jag," he said, laughter in his voice. Then, abruptly he turned on his heels, rotating to face Segundo. "I expect nothing less than perfection."

The words seemed to lift in the air and linger. As though summoned, with a flash of light another man appeared, the air filling with a scent of some spice or incense that flared Segundo's nostrils.

"Salvador," Adrian said, his voice a low, half-growl. His beast surfaced almost instantly, turning his face animal-like.

Segundo had heard of Salvador, the equal to Adrian in power, but not skill—or so Adrian claimed—on the other side of the war. But he'd never seen the man and often wondered at his true existence. The green-eyed warrior, as myth called him, had never shown himself before.

Why now?

A thought came hard and fast. There would be no time better than this one, Segundo realized, to earn his rightful respect with Adrian. Taking down Salvador would be his ticket to trust.

He motioned to the two beasts to attack. Instantly they charged, half of each of their faces contorting to beastly images, fangs extending.

Salvador balled up his fists, extended his arms toward the two attackers, then gestured his fingers at the two beasts. And just like that, both were frozen, unmoving, as if turned to statues.

Segundo could barely believe his eyes. He blinked and refocused. Still, his beasts were completely, utterly still. Suddenly he realized Salvador wore no weapons. No armor. Black jeans. Black shirt. No place for hidden artillery.

And it appeared he didn't need any. He'd stopped Segundo's beasts with a wave of his hands.

Salvador had launched himself into the center of enemy troops and he had done so unarmed. Unafraid. There were at least thirty beasts within a mile, yet Salvador seemed to be fearless, even at ease.

"I see you didn't warn this newest second of my powers," Salvador commented.

"Why would I?" Adrian challenged.

"Or rather, why wouldn't you?" Salvador asked, a smile on his lips. "Perhaps you fear what weaknesses my power exposes in you, Adrian."

Salvador turned to Segundo and held out his palm. "Show your beast," he ordered.

To his dismay, Segundo felt his control slip away. His face contorted without his conscious decision to allow it, his heart kicking with the rush of adrenaline it caused. With his beast coming to life in physical form.

"That's better," Salvador said to Segundo. "Don't

you wonder why Adrian is showing his beast? We both know he's too arrogant to be in such primal form. So why now, in my presence, did he change?"

Segundo's mind raced with the implications of that question. Salvador was right: Adrian never exposed his beast.

Salvador continued as if he didn't expect a response. "While in my presence, I demand you show your true self." He eyed Adrian. "Your 'Master' didn't want me to force his to surface. That would have shown you the power I have over him."

In a flash of movement, Adrian disappeared and re-appeared in front of Salvador. He snarled. "You have no business here, Salvador."

"You're about to attack my Knights," Salvador commented, appearing more amused than threatened. "I'd call that my business."

"And you can't interfere," Adrian said, jaw tight, fangs exposed.

Salvador flashed out of sight and reappeared beside one of the frozen beasts, a saber sword suddenly at its throat. "Ask your 'Master' why I don't kill 'it' right now."

Adrian turned to face Salvador. "Because you're a pussy who hides behind rules."

"Rules you are bound to, as well," Salvador reminded him. "If you don't…we both know what happens."

In a blink of an eye, the sword disappeared and Salvador stepped to the side of the frozen beast. He leaned on its broad shoulder as if it were a wall, crossing his arms in front of his chest and then one booted foot over the other.

"You go to a hell even the mightiest of beasts would beg mercy from," Salvador said, and then fixed Segundo in a green-eyed stare that suddenly seemed to glow and go all white. Segundo felt a crushing feeling in his chest, and then the oddest feeling of having his soul ripped from inside.

The sensation crawled inside him and traveled to the exterior, his skin tingling and itchy.

Which was freaking insane. He had long ago given up his soul.

"The powers of good allow evil to exist on this plain of existence because it serves a purpose. True good must come from free will. But there are rules to this allowance. Rules that even your 'Master' cannot break. The one you will enjoy the most, 'Segundo,' is the one that makes you so necessary. See—" he raised a finger "—higher or lower beings not born of this realm cannot raise a hand in battle. Your boss, Segundo, cannot join you in battle."

A fireball shot through the air and straight at Salvador's chest. A flash of movement and Salvador caught it. An instant later it dissolved.

"Temper, temper," Salvador said to Adrian. "Shooting fire through the night tends to take away the advantage of surprise. Maybe you should just call Jag on the phone and announce your presence."

"What," Adrian said, fists balled at his sides, hair wild around his distorted face, "do you want?"

"I simply wanted the latest 'Segundo' to know the rules," Salvador stated, no hesitation. "Now he does. You can't win your war without him."

Adrian drew his swords. "You want a fight, Salvador. Fight."

Salvador pushed off the frozen beast but made no attempt to arm himself. He held his hands out to his side. "If we fight, it will replace tonight's battle."

"Don't hide behind your Knights. If you believe them so strong, let my Darklands face them. Our fight is our fight alone."

"That is the deal, Adrian." He walked toward him. "Take it or leave it." Salvador stopped almost toe-to-toe with Adrian, and with a flash, swords appeared in his hands. "What's it going to be?"

Segundo could hardly breathe, the air filled with such electricity, such power. The implications of the moment, and of the information he had learned, were packed within the thickness surrounding them. Adrian growled low in his throat and then threw his swords in the air. They disappeared as if gobbled up by the darkness above.

Salvador gave a tiny bow of his head. "And so it is decided. The battle will not be ours on this night."

"Not this one, but soon," Adrian replied.

"I welcome the challenge," Salvador said, and then he was gone.

The two frozen beasts came to life as if they'd lost no time, charging at the empty space that had once held Salvador.

Segundo turned his attention to Adrian, showing no signs of what he'd learned. He needed time to process. To consider what this meant for him. He'd been given the gift of knowledge, delivered by the enemy.

How to use it was the question. One, Segundo would soon figure out.

A second later, a dart of pain flashed in his chest, a fire shot from Adrian's hand. "You are not beast enough to touch me, Segundo. Test me, even in your mind, and next you'll be ash."

Segundo drew a shaky breath, realizing that he was trapped. The truth had been spoken; he wasn't beast enough to defeat Adrian. He repeated that fact over and over, fearful Adrian would hear if he allowed another and do as promised and turn him to ash.

He was now more determined than ever to defeat Jag, to earn back the good graces with his almighty leader…Adrian.

Chapter 13

Jag brought Diablo to a halt in the far north region of the ranch, miles away from the main house.

Reaching forward, he stroked the horse's mane, murmuring his appreciation. He'd ridden him far too hard and long, driven by desperation to put distance between himself and everyone else. Needing space to think and to pull himself together. Karen had been there only a day, yet she'd had a profound impact on him. Something had changed inside of him and he didn't understand what.

The beast within was clawing at him, scratching its way to the surface. No matter how hard he tried to deny its presence, to drive it away, it lived. It breathed.

Though his Knights understood these feelings, they

expected their leader to be the strong one, the one who overcame the beast and showed them how to, as well. Yet each day he battled, it seemed to become harder.

Jag's jaw tightened, one hand holding the reins with a vise grip as he fought the urge to yell. Why he fought it, he didn't know. Something inside silenced his need to let out his rage toward the darkness of his feelings. Something told him to keep his presence here as unobtrusive as he could.

In that moment, if only for that split second, had he possessed the power to summon Salvador, he would have. He needed answers. If his destiny was to be swallowed by darkness, he wanted to know and he wanted to know now.

And that's why he'd come out here, away from everyone. Away from temptation, where he wouldn't do something he might regret. Away from Karen.

He leaned back, resting his gloved hands on the horn of the saddle, and felt a sudden uneasiness beyond his own troubled thoughts. His eyes narrowed, scanning the darkness. He took in his surroundings with newfound interest, and noticed the wind, or rather the lack of wind.

Inhaling through his nose, he used his keen sense of smell to search for the enemy, but found no scent of a beast. Yet…with the wind so tame, how close would the Darklands get before he would know?

Beneath him, Diablo grew restless, letting out two irritable snorts. "Shh," Jag whispered, patting the animal's neck and then rubbing. "You feel it, too, don't ya, boy?"

Still running his hand over Diablo, calming him, Jag scanned the area, and then inhaled again. And he found it—the hint of a scent. A tiny little whiff of Darkland Beast.

Never before had the Ranch been attacked, but tonight that would change. Jag had no doubt.

Grabbing Diablo's reins, Jag nudged the horse with his heels, and reached for the cell phone that doubled as a radio on his belt. "Des." Nothing. "Des," Jag said louder.

A small sound and then, "I'm here, boss. What's up?"

Relief at the contact, at knowing he was getting the warning out to his men, washed over Jag even as the fast pace of Diablo beneath him offered further comfort.

"Sound the alarm," Jag ordered, his tone curt, "and lock down the house. I'll be there in five."

One second. Two. Though brief the silence spoke volumes. Des was as surprised at the attack on the ranch as Jag had been.

"Copy that," Des said.

Jag shoved his phone back on his belt hoop, taking the reins with both hands, and urging Diablo into a faster pace. Any second now, silent blinking red lights would go off inside every structure on the property. Some of his Knights would fight for the first time ever. Many weren't ready for this kind of challenge.

"Damn it," Jag murmured, feeling the wind lift around him. Knowing the beasts knew he'd discovered them and no longer masked their presence.

They were here for Karen and Eva. Every fiber of his being said so. The question was why?

Showered and dressed in a clean pair of light blue Levi's, a red T-shirt with a hotel logo on it she'd gotten from one of her many trips, and a pair of red Keds, Karen felt a bit less exhausted. Of course, the two hours she'd slept in the chair beside Eva's bed had helped, too, as had the sandwich Marisol had forced her to eat after noting her mac and cheese had gone mostly untouched. Not an easy task when her stomach was in knots and not just over worry for Eva. She'd emerged from rest with clarity in her mind over Jag. With a strong sense that her flashback to that day of them together had been just that, a flashback.

She hadn't let herself digest the implications. Somehow it felt too scary and intimidating to delve deeper. She needed a little time to process. To make sure she wasn't losing her mind.

Grabbing her cell phone, Karen plugged it into the charger she'd dug out of her bag. She was about to start for the door when a flashing red light came to life just above the frame.

Stiffening, Karen prepared for the loud noise to follow but it didn't come. But then, it didn't have to. The flashing light said plenty. Either there was a fire, or worse. Either way, trouble had arrived.

"Eva," Karen whispered, and took off for the door.

Flinging it open, Karen stepped into the hallway to find Des in her path. Red lights flashed from the ceiling, casting him in a glow as he peered at her, a strand of dark hair concealing his expression from her view. She did a quick once-over of Des and knew trouble had definitely come calling. A long saber sword hung on each of his hips, and knives were strapped to his sides.

She took in the sight and its meaning with surprising calm. True, her heart beat at triple-time and her blood felt like fire in her veins. Maybe, because she knew the truth already. The silent alarm wasn't about a fire. It was about war.

Expectantly she watched the agile, almost predatory way, Des's big body moved as he flipped open a light switch and hit a previously hidden button. This wasn't the same, playful guy she'd met in the kitchen. He'd been buried and replaced with this one…and instinctively Karen knew that this one was downright lethal.

Her attention went to the picture on the wall as it slid to the side and exposed a cabinet. Des stepped forward and hit another button on the steel surface. A door opened, revealing an arsenal of weapons, mostly swords.

"The beasts are coming," Des said, as if confirming her thoughts, sliding a shoulder holster into place and pulling it tight to his muscular frame. "When you hear the alarm sound you'll know they've crossed the inner parimeters of the ranch." He retrieved a handgun from the cabinet. "Do you know how to fire a gun?"

"I do," Karen said, relieved that her voice came out halfway steady. She closed the distance between herself and Des, more than willing to accept the weapon. Helpless was something she'd didn't ever want to be. Not while traveling. Especially not now. Not with her sister's life on the line.

With a quick slide of his hand, Des loaded an ammo cartridge into the weapon, and then fixed Karen in a stare as hard as the steel in his hand.

He offered her the weapon. "This is a Glock

36/45 mm. You've got a six-round magazine and one bullet in the chamber."

Karen accepted the gun, feeling comfort in its heaviness in her hand. "And enough kick to be considered a handheld cannon," she added as she reached inside the cabinet, grabbed another magazine and shoved it in her waistband.

"Why aren't you carrying a gun?" she asked, noting the absence of one on his person. In fact, there was only one other in the cabinet.

Des cut her a quick glance, ignoring her question as he back stepped and then hit the button to ease the picture back into place.

"Shoot at their heads," he said. "Anywhere else will be wasted ammo."

Her eyes went wide with disbelief. "You're kidding, right? Because this gun is gonna knock me on my ass just getting a shot off." She frowned, realizing he hadn't answered her question about why he didn't pack a gun or two, or maybe even three, himself. "What exactly are we dealing with here?"

"That's what we'd like to know, Karen." The voice came from the stairs as Rock appeared and walked toward them, his short hair making the hard look on his face somehow more intense. "What are we dealing with?" he demanded. "Why do the Darkland Beasts want you and your sister so damn badly?"

Like Des, Karen noted, Rock was armed to the hilt, a walking arsenal of silver. Knives clung to his thick thighs, blades to his waist and body, but he carried not one single gun.

"Not now, Rock," Des said, authority in his words, a reprimand in the harsh look he shot at the other man before refocusing on Karen. "Just do as I said. Fire at their heads."

"Even then they won't die," Rock said, stopping a few steps from her, accusation in his words. "Beasts don't die."

"Not easily," Des corrected.

Rock was fixated on Karen, ignoring Des. "We have new recruits who aren't ready for this. Men who will die this night. Men who will die because of you and your sister."

"Shut up, Rock," Des said, his voice a sharp slice of warning.

Marisol appeared in the bedroom doorway, a gun in her hand. The Healer motioned her forward, the sight of another firearm immensely comforting to Karen for some unknown reason.

"Come, Karen," Marisol urged. "Hurry."

"Oh, no," Rock said, intercepting Marisol with the speed of a panther intercepting its prey, his hand shackling Marisol's arm. "Think again. You're getting the hell away from her and her sister."

Marisol tried to jerk away from him to no avail. "Let go, Rock. I have a job to do and so do you."

Karen felt a rush of nausea at the interaction. She'd already surmised Rock had a thing for Marisol. Now, it was clear he felt protective of her, and saw Karen as the enemy. She didn't want people to die because of her.

"I'll stay with Eva," Karen said. "Marisol, please go. Be safe. Let Rock protect you."

Rock gave an agreeable nod and started walking, Marisol in tow. Marisol's face flashed with anger. Suddenly she shimmered. Lights flashing around her body and she disappeared.

Rock cursed.

Karen blinked. She blinked again. What next? What other powers did these people possess?

Marisol reappeared next to Karen, making her jump. "What…just happened?" Karen asked, trying to understand this new world she had become a part of.

Marisol ignored the question, which seemed to be this group's avoidance method. "We're going to watch over Eva together," she said, and then eyed Rock. "I can take care of myself. Protect the ranch. Protect the cause." She motioned Karen toward the bedroom. "Go now. We don't have much time."

Rock took a step forward as if intending to block their path. Des intervened, cutting off Rock and giving the ladies passage behind him. "Don't do this, man," Des said in a voice laced with warning. "Don't make this a battle between brothers when we have a real war to fight. Jag wants the women protected. They *are* part of the cause."

"We don't know that," Rock ground out, his anger biting through the words.

"We know what Jag wants, and that's enough. When you stop trusting him, you shouldn't be here."

The two men stared at each other, a standoff underway, tension as thick as the danger in the air.

A loud screeching sounded…the alarm. The end of a standoff between friends. The beginning of a battle with enemies.

The beasts had arrived.

Chapter 14

In a scurry of movement, Karen followed Marisol into the bedroom, and Marisol shut the door with a resounding thud. Karen eyed Eva, noting she still rested, unaware of the hell unfolding.

"Help me move this stuff in front of the door," the Healer said, sticking her gun into the waistband of her pants, and then shoving the items on top of the nightstand off to make it mobile.

Karen looked around the room. Until now, she hadn't given the surroundings as much attention to her sister. It was large enough to be two rooms, yet it was near empty but for the bed and a chair.

"There's nothing to move," she said, wishing it weren't the truth. Karen was all for blockading the door.

Marisol shoved her hands on her hips, opening her mouth to respond when the window glass shattered.

A man rolled to the floor, landing on his feet in an agile movement that left him in a squat. No. Not a man, Karen realized, feeling shaken by the evil yellow eyes staring back at her.

If she could have breathed, could have found a voice, Karen might have screamed at the reality of the evil in this world—evil this creature confirmed. The evil she now faced as her own enemy.

But wait…someone *was* screaming. The high-pitched sound permeated the air with pure terror, and for an instant, Karen thought it was her own. She shook herself, forcing reality beyond the shock of seeing this creature, and realizing it was Eva screaming. Eva sitting up in the bed, finally awake.

Problem was, Karen wasn't the only one who'd turned their attention to Eva. The creature, the beast, stared at Eva, a primal look in his yellow eyes, as if he'd found his prey. Karen watched him…expected him to charge Eva, but he didn't.

Why? What was he waiting on?

Screw this. She couldn't just stand here and wait for him to tear Eva to shreds. Karen raised her gun, aware of Marisol's struggle to calm Eva and preparing herself for the kick of firing.

Karen pulled the trigger, feeling her jaws rattle with the explosion, as the bullet sailed toward the creature's forehead. In response, the beast leaned ever-so-slightly outside of the target range, the shiny vinyl of the outfit he wore flexing like second skin across far-too-broad shoulders. His thick, muscular forearm extended between his massive thighs to fist the ground and stay balanced.

She fired again and with a simple, barely there, movement, again, the beast avoided impact. But this time he didn't stay focused on Eva. The ugly-ass creature fixed Karen with an amused stare that said he wasn't afraid of her or her weapon.

God. He was toying with her, Karen realized. Laughter lurked in the depths of those sickly yellow eyes. A yellow that matched the coarseness of his hair, wild around his shoulders, and resembling a lion's mane. His face, half human and half…something else. The thing had fangs. Not teeth. *Fangs.* And both his eyes weren't the same size. One was much larger than the other.

"Marisol?" she asked, still aiming her weapon, seeming to be in some silent standoff with the beast. "What the hell is it doing?"

"What I've been ordered to do," it answered, before Marisol could. "Making sure you stay put."

Eva whimpered as if the words, or maybe the voice, scared her. "Why?" Karen demanded. "What do you want of my sister? Just let her be free."

"She will never be free," it said.

Terror and determination collided inside Karen. This animal wasn't taking her sister. Karen had to shoot it again. Had to. No matter how much her hand and jaw hurt at this point, this was about survival. She fired again, and this time she planned to unload the gun and be done with this beast.

It stood up as she squeezed the trigger, and the first bullet bounced off his thigh. The second off his stomach. The third his chest. The other shots went into the air.

Click. She was out of ammo. Not that she could have fired again. Her head felt like it had been slammed into a door.

The beast snarled, baring his ugly fangs, no longer showing signs of amusement. He was on the move, headed for Karen and the low growl said he was pissed.

Marisol offered support, firing her weapon, giving Karen a chance to retreat. "Reload!" she screamed at Karen.

Karen didn't need to be told twice. Marisol's efforts were slowing the beast but not for long. With shaking hands, Karen used her thumb to discharge the empty magazine, willing herself to find the power to pull the trigger when the time came. But before she could finish her task, a second beast climbed in through the window.

Karen snapped the magazine in place, adrenaline and fear making the pain in her body fade. She aimed at the beast closest to her so Marisol could focus on the newest arrival.

Karen's shot landed in a direct hit between the target's eyes. Bingo. The beast stumbled and hit the floor. Just in time, too, because the second beast was coming for Karen and fast, and Marisol was out of ammunition.

"Holy hell!" Karen yelled, backing up and trying to get a shot off but this new beast was quicker than the other one, and the toll of firing so many times made her slower. She managed to get a shot off but missed the head, the bullet ricocheting off the attacker's chest.

Certain she only had seconds to live, Karen felt her chest tighten with emotion. She couldn't get a shot at his head. The beast was too close and too fast. Plain and simple, she was trapped with nowhere to go. No way to defend herself.

A flash rushed at her. Time seemed to stand still. A memory filled her mind.

She was on a farm, running toward a house, away from a beast. Though she couldn't quite envision herself, she felt it. The rush of adrenaline, the terror of death.

Harder she ran. Harder. Toward that house. Her house, she realized. Her home. "Victor!" *she screamed.* "Victor!"

"Keep running!" *she heard him call after her.* "Faster! Keep running!"

And she tried. She tried so hard. But suddenly, pain shot through her head as her hair was grabbed so hard it felt as if someone had ripped it from her scalp. She was yanked against a hard form, nasty breath flooding her face. As she was rotated around, she found Jag—no, he'd been Victor then—speeding toward her. Hope formed as he charged, but it was quickly lost as a beast seemed to appear from nowhere and yank Victor into his hold.

The beast holding her laughed, deep and ugly. "Now you watch your woman die."

For a moment, just one moment, she saw the torment and pain in the eyes of the man called Victor, the man she now knew as Jag. She saw the tears stream from his eyes. And then, for one long excruciating second she felt

*the sharpness of the beast's teeth on her neck. She heard
her name on the lips of the man who loved her, heard
him scream.*

*"I love you," she tried to whisper, but everything
had just…gone black.*

Karen snapped back to the present as the beast charging at her in present time was yanked away from her, Jag her rescuer. Dampness clung to her cheeks as she realized she was crying. Tears born of that memory.

She swiped at them, refocusing on what was happening here and now, determined not to die again at the hand of one of these beasts. She watched in shock as Jag, who had apparently found his way in the window, shoved the beast across the room and against a wall.

Grateful for what Jag had just delivered, a second chance in more ways than one, Karen shifted her attention to Eva and Marisol, eager to confirm their safety. She found them both on the bed, huddled together, a beast leaning over them. It yanked the gun from Marisol's hand and tossed it across the room. Fortunately Rock appeared in the window, swiftly entering the room and grabbing the beast, only to have it rotate out of his grip.

A moment later, swords were drawn, a full fledged war between him and the beast underway.

Karen backed against the wall, trying to figure out how to help. Scared Marisol or Eva would end up in the way of a blade. She eyed Jag as he matched blades with his opponent. There were too many men. Too many swords. She was afraid to move. Afraid to breathe.

A guttural sound of pain drew her gaze back to Rock,

and Karen gasped, covering her mouth with her hand. A blade had entered Rock's stomach, penetrating deeply. She watched his attacker twist it and then jerk it out of his flesh. Blood gushed from the wound like a waterfall, staining his blue T-shirt a darker color.

"Rock!" Marisol's screamed ripped through the air, a mixture of pain and denial.

At that point, everything seemed to go into slow motion again. Karen turned toward Jag, knowing he was Rock's only hope, probably the only hope any of them possessed.

Jag seemed to know as much himself. He had given his attention to Rock's attacker, turning his back on the beast he'd been battling. With a hard flick of his wrist, Jag's blade sliced through the enemy's neck. Its head hit the ground like a lead weight, a heavy thump sounding with its impact. The body followed, falling on top of Rock, who was forced to push it aside.

Karen swallowed, trying to process what had just happened. This wasn't real. It couldn't be. Beasts. Sword fights. Chopped-off heads…but it was. It was. She'd seen her past in her vision. She'd lived this once before.

She didn't want to lose the same battle again.

Before she could process another thought, the last remaining beast took advantage of Jag's back being turned, his sword slicing deep across his shoulders, just barely missing his neck, and down his side. Karen screamed, covering her mouth with her hand as blood tinged Jag's shirt. Even more so as she thought of how close that blade had come to his neck.

If Jag was fazed by the injury, he didn't show it. With a graceful but deadly move, he rotated around to face his attacker, his sword cutting through the air with the movement, and taking the head of the beast.

Just as Karen started to let out a breath, to allow herself to believe they would survive this, fire erupted on the beastly bodies.

Karen gasped, expecting a blaze of flames to consume the room. Expecting yet another type of battle to fight.

But just like that…the bodies were gone, an ashlike substance in their place. Karen realized then there had been no blood with the beheading. Not a drop. Twenty-four hours ago, she wouldn't have believed any of this was real. Even now, she could almost convince herself all of this was simply a *really long* nightmare.

But it wasn't a nightmare, nor were they out of danger. She knew it. A chill went through her, a warning of more to come. The beasts were gone, but the war had only just begun. And her role here had now become clearer. It went beyond saving Eva.

Karen was here for Jag…for Victor.

Chapter 15

Jag faced the window, sword in hand. For several seconds, he stood there, waiting. Ready for the next Darkland bastard who dared enter that window. No one spoke, as if they knew he needed the silence. Or perhaps they feared what he might do next.

Like hot lava, the heat of battle coursed through his veins, rich with his anger over the attack and the injury to Rock. But even more than anger, he felt fear. Fear over what the beast might have done to Karen had he not arrived when he did.

He drew a deep breath and blew it out, forcing himself to calm. Fighting the adrenaline still so a part of his body. Fighting his own beast, the one who surfaced for battle and cried for blood and revenge. Revenge for so many things. The list was long and continued to grow, sometimes it felt with each breath he drew.

A static sound filled the air. Then, "Jag."

He reached down and hit a button on the side of his phone where it hung on his belt loop. "Yeah, Des. I'm here."

"They've retreated but they hit the bunkhouses hard. We have a shitload of wounded. I need Marisol."

Jag turned to look at Rock, his stomach twisting with the sickly paleness of his face. Already Marisol had slid into a healing trance, absorbed in her task. "We have wounded here, too," Jag told Des, offering no details. "I'll get her to you as soon as I can."

"Tell her to hurry." One second. Two. "Jag, man…we lost three."

He didn't immediately respond, feeling the news with more of a cut than the blade that had sliced through his flesh. "Copy that," Jag said, because it was all he could manage. What else could he say?

He slid his sword into place, self-reprimand burning in his heart. He should have been more prepared. If he'd trained for this, if he'd taught the recruits how to defend against a head-on attack….

"It's not your fault."

Karen's soft words drew his attention. He'd avoided looking at her up to this point, still shaken by what he'd felt while fighting for her life. By how intensely he'd feared her death. It made no sense yet, even now, how close she'd come to it shook him to the core.

A bit more under control, he forced himself to look at her. She sat on the bed beside Eva, who had fallen back into a comalike sleep, looking like an angel who'd just survived the Devil's work.

And she had. Lord help them all, she had.

Her eyes were soft with understanding, her voice a soft caress. His chest tightened with emotion. Damn it, he couldn't deal with this now. Not when he had Knights wounded and maybe even dying. He didn't know how Karen knew what he felt. He didn't know how Karen got into his dreams or evoked such emotions.

It didn't matter, either.

Right now, he felt like shit in every possible way, and besides, she was wrong anyway. He *was* to blame. The Knights were his responsibility. This shouldn't have happened here, at the ranch, the place he swore to them they were protected. He had the placed wired like Fort Knox, but it hadn't been enough. They'd—no, *he'd*—grown comfortable here. Sure this represented a safety zone, the only escape from a war that lived on eternally. A war they could never depart.

Jag turned away from Karen, intentionally shutting her out, refocusing on Marisol. He noted the tears streaming down the Healer's face, despite her departure into a healing trance. Confirmation of what he'd already suspected. Marisol was in love with Rock. She was afraid she couldn't pull him back from the other side, afraid he'd lost too much blood to be healed.

The very things which gave the Knight's life became a weakness in battle. The Knights had blood to drain and souls to darken. The beasts had neither.

"Your wound needs to be looked at," Karen said, once again breaking into his world, refusing to be dismissed.

"I'm fine," he said, cutting her a hard look meant to tell her to back off.

"You're not," Karen insisted, pushing off the bed and she started to walk toward him.

Jag held up a hand, watching her eyes widen as she stopped in her footsteps. "I have to check on my men." He eyed Marisol for a moment and then fixed Karen in a hard stare. His wound did need to be dealt with, but he wasn't about to say that. He'd heal. He was a Knight, which meant he healed quickly from minor wounds. "Make sure Marisol goes to the bunkhouse as soon as possible. Stay with Rock so she won't worry."

"You can't leave," Karen said, disbelief in her voice, as if she couldn't believe he was actually considering it. "You have to stay until she heals you."

He arched a brow, challenging her insistence without a word, the expression on his face one that would make most cower. Taking orders wasn't his style and, certainly not from Karen. Though his senses screamed that he trust her, his desire for her put him on guard, fearful of a trick.

Her cheeks flushed, but she stuck to her guns. "You're hurt, Jag."

While he wasn't about to listen to Karen, let alone do as she wanted, he felt a part of him that was normally detached and cold stir at her concern. It confused him, but then, so did everything about Karen. He shoved aside the feeling, focusing on what was important. The safety of his men. Any one of his could be bleeding to death right now. He wasn't allowing Marisol to waste her limited energy on him. Nor was he going to explain this to Karen.

"Just make sure Marisol does as I say," he told her, his voice cold now, sharp even. He needed out of this room, away from Karen. Away from Rock, lying on the floor half-dead.

He started for the door, walking past Karen. The scent of death and war faded as his nostrils flared with her scent, with her feminine presence. It took him by storm, a primal calling that made him want to yank her into his and carry her from harm's way.

Instead he pushed forward, feeling the urgency of attending his men. But his escaped halted when Karen's warm hand gripped his arm, the touch like an electric shock to his system.

His gaze jerked around, eyeing her over his shoulder, ready to deliver harsh words only be taken aback by what he found, by the concern in Karen's face. The worry for him.

His gut tightened with the impact.

Damn it, he didn't want to react like this to Karen. He needed to deal with his injury and then clear his head and think about how to deal with the beasts.

Drawing a deep breath, he said, "I have to check on my men." His gaze going to her hand before returning to her face. "Lives are on the line."

With scrutinizing attention, she studied his back and shoulders where the blade of the beast had cut to the bone. "It's really bad, Jag. Please stay and let Marisol help you. *Please.*"

For a moment, he wanted to accept her concern. To allow himself to feel comfort in it as he had once with his wife so very long ago. But he hadn't been able to protect his wife, and he'd barely saved Karen from the beasts. No matter what her role in all of this, she was better off at a distance.

"I don't want your help, Karen," he said, his voice as cold as the steel blade that had lanced his skin. "Don't you get that?"

Anger flashed in her eyes. "Damn it, Jag," she bit out through clenched teeth. "Stop with the macho act. You're hurt. You can't go without it being healed." She lowered her voice. "And you do need me."

Her words were mute to his ears as a memory snapped in his mind and pieced his heart. One of Caron standing in front of him, her curls bouncing around her head, reprimanding him for working with an injured hand.

Jag squeezed his eyes shut, shocked at the vividness of the image in his mind. *No!* he screamed in his head, rejecting the memory. He couldn't do this. He couldn't face the ghost of the past while he faced the beasts of the present.

Twisting slightly to reach for Karen's wrist, Jag barely contained a grunt from the pain the movement delivered. He grabbed Karen's hand and removed it from his arm. "I told you to stay away from me, and I meant it."

Karen watched Jag disappear into the hallway, and fought the urge to follow. He needed help. Stubborn man, acted like he needed nothing, no help, no treatment. But it wasn't true. She'd seen the deep wound in his back, and it needed attention. How did he expect to take care of others if he was dead?

He might not like to accept help, but he was going

to have to get used to it. She didn't know what the future held for them together, but she knew the past now. Or parts of it at least. Enough to tell her he'd been her husband, and the love of her life. The more she remembered, the more she felt that love, and the clearer her purpose became. She'd seen the enemy, past and present. Jag needed her help, and he was going to get it.

Sooner or later, he'd accept that. She'd make sure of it.

Casting a quick glance at Marisol, Karen considered her next action, and then sighed heavily. She couldn't leave. She couldn't stay and offer any real help though, and she should be helping.

Yet, Rock still wasn't moving, in fact, he looked... Karen swallowed the bile forming in her throat...he looked dead. The thought made her stomach twist and turn with dread, a feeling that worsened as she surveyed his ghostly white complexion and unmoving body.

"Please let him make it," Karen whispered, watching him, hoping for some sign of life.

Marisol sat on the floor with him, his head in her lap, her hand on his forehead. Karen hoped the Healer could save him, but feared it was already too late. How long would Marisol try to pull Rock back to this world before going to the others who needed her?

How long should Karen wait to interrupt Marisol? Jag hadn't said, and Karen felt the weight of other lives on her shoulders. How many "recruits" were there? Karen wondered. And how many were hurt and waiting on Marisol?

Even as a million questions rang in her mind, another

followed. What must it feel like to be Marisol? To know every day of her life she might be the only hope others had of survival?

Hopelessly in limbo, Karen sat down on the edge of the bed next to Eva, stroking her cheek. Wishing she knew how to make things better. For Eva. For Rock. For the men waiting to have Marisol visit them.

Everything happens for a reason. Her mother's words, spoken often during Karen's youth, replayed in her mind. She had thought of those words during her parents' funeral, wondering what purpose thier death could possibly serve.

Still, those words, *everything happens for a reason,* repeated in Karen's mind. With them, the oddest feeling of belonging, in this room, in this ranch house, in this moment, filled Karen. Even more so, her sense of having purpose grew.

She *belonged* here, a part of this battle being fought. Karen's chest tightened as she glanced down at her sister, wishing she could pull her back into this world. Did Eva belong here or was she simply a victim of association, brought into this because of her relation to Karen?

Fear flooded her mind. Fear of losing Eva. With this fear, Karen thought of Jag. Had he lived with the pain of watching his wife die and not being able to save her? How horrible it must have been, still must be, in fact.

He'd fought for Eva. He had saved them both.

Karen let out a deep breath she didn't even realize she'd been holding. She couldn't dismiss her dream, or the flashbacks, any more than she could pretend the beasts were figments of her imagination. None of this was normal, but it was real.

If everything happened for a reason, then Karen had to believe the dream had been a message. One she had to figure out and fast. Because at this point, for all Karen knew, after what she'd seen this day, that dream held a clue that could save lives. Hers. Eva's…maybe even Jag's.

"Karen."

The sound of Marisol's voice drew Karen out of her reverie. Pushing off the bed, Karen rushed forward, kneeling beside the Healer. Rock stirred, trying to sit up. "How many are hurt?" he asked.

Amazed at Rock's remarkable recovery, Karen struggled to find her voice. "I don't know. Jag…he's hurt but he insists you go to the men. He says there are many hurt. But Jag…his shoulder is ripped open." Picturing the wound, she grimaced. "It's bad. Really bad."

"How am I to leave him injured?" Turmoil flashed in Marisol's face. "Protecting Jag *is* protecting his men. He's their guide. Their strength."

"Do as Jag says," Rock said, his voice weak but authoritative. "I'll go to Jag."

He started to get up and Marisol grabbed his arm at the same moment he grunted in pain. "You're not going anywhere but to bed," Marisol said, her tone firm. "I couldn't risk fully healing you," Marisol said. "I need my energy to help the others. You have to sleep and do the rest on your own." Her gaze went to Karen as she pushed to her feet, and Marisol followed her to a standing position. "Where is Jag now?"

"I think in his room," Karen said, "but I can't be certain."

"I'll be right back." Marisol flashed from the room.

Good gosh. Karen grabbed her chest. This magic stuff was going to take some getting used to. "Can I help you to your room?" she asked Rock, realizing he was now standing, the wound he endured no longer bleeding but still a deep gap in his gut. "That looks painful."

"I'm fine," he said, leaning against the wall. "Our kind heals quickly." Dismissing his injury, he added, "Marisol is going to give you a gel to pack on Jag's wound. No matter how bad the injury looks just remember we aren't like you. Once we start clotting we heal. The biggest issue is stopping the bleeding. The gel will do that better than stitches or any human medicine."

Marisol popped into the room, a jar of blue gel in her hand, which she shoved in Karen's direction. "This—"

"I told her," Rock said. "She knows what to do. Karen has it under control. Go do your thing. Save lives."

Still, Marisol hesitated.

"I'll take care of Jag," Karen assured Marisol, reinforcing Rock's words.

As soon as she knew Karen had a firm hold on the jar, Marisol was gone. Rock gave Karen an expectant look. "What are you waiting on? Go. Find Jag."

Karen didn't have to be told twice. She headed for the door. Rock's words, "our kind," rang in her head, a reminder of the unknowns. Of the need to be cautious.

"Karen." She turned at Rock's call. "He's a stubborn

son of a bitch. He'll bleed to death before he admits
he needs help. His bark is far worse than his bite. Just
be strong."

She accepted his words because they echoed what
she felt in her heart. After a quick nod, she turned away,
already in motion. Jag needed her. And for some reason
she didn't quite understand, that felt more important
than her next breath.

Chapter 16

Stay away from me.

Charging a path down the hallway toward his bedroom, Jag's words to Karen were acid on his tongue. Using the last energy his body possessed, he locked himself inside his bedroom and collapsed against the door. He'd meant what he'd said to her yet, in the same second he'd spoken the words, he'd wanted to pull them back. So much so that he'd turned away without daring to look into those gorgeous blue eyes, fearing the pain he'd intended to cause with his words.

But why would there be pain? Why did she care what he said or did?

Swallowing against the extreme dryness in his throat,

Jag worked his hand to his belt buckle and pushed the speaker on his cell phone.

"Des."

"Yeah, boss."

"Status," he ordered, reaching up to his side where blood seemed to pour in a sudden gush, the sword having dug straight through him. Son of a bitch. That explained why he hadn't started the rapid clotting the Knights were blessed, or perhaps cursed, with. They didn't die easily. Instead they hung out and lived hell on earth.

Sometimes he forgot his greater purpose, the way the men needed him even, and wished for death. Perhaps today he would get that wish.

"We're clear here, but I need Marisol. Where the hell is she?"

Des's words snapped Jag back to the moment. "She'll be there," Jag said. "She's got wounded here, too. Update me in twenty."

"Who?"

"Rock."

Silence. Des and Rock argued like enemies, but there was no mistaking the bond they shared. "How bad?"

Des wouldn't want to be sheltered, not that Jag would have considered doing so. "Bad."

More silence. Then, "Copy that." Static. Des had signed off.

Hearing Des's voice and sensing his struggle to help the other Knights, Jag found new determination to take action. He needed to get himself bandaged up before he keeled over. A little of Marisol's clotting salve, and he should be able to make it to check on his men.

Pushing off the door, Jag headed toward the bathroom. Though only moments before he could easily have wished for death, he knew, as he always did, he couldn't accept it. Not when his men needed him. Not when Karen was here, complicating the world as he knew it, and bringing a mountain of trouble along with her.

Yanking open the medicine cabinet over the sink, he shoved things around, trying to find the blue clotting salve, to no avail. Efforts proving fruitless, Jag cursed and reached for a hand towel resting on the sink's edge.

Pressing the cloth to his side, he contemplated the need to go to Marisol's cathedral where she kept her supplies, knowing he was too weak. The activity would only speed the bleeding. He felt like a damn invalid, not even capable of taking care of his men.

Jag squeezed his eyes shut at the thought of three of his men gone, praying they had, at least, found peace in a better place. Still, he could barely stomach wondering which three he'd lost.

The memory of the beast charging at Karen replaced that of the faces of his men. If he'd gotten to her one second later…just one second…a flash of Caron in his arms crashed into his mind, her body horribly still, limp.

Karen would end up like Caron if he didn't act, and act fast. The realization donned with clarity, and brought to life his worst fears…would the beast within be responsible for Karen's death? His dreams seemed to warn of her destruction at his hand yet, in them, she always welcomed him, encouraging his primal side to take her.

He didn't understand his dreams, but somewhere inside them were answers he needed. Like, how did he protect Karen from the Darklands and still from himself?

The towel held to his side began to drip, and Jag ground his teeth as he tossed it into the tub. "Damn it!" he yelled into the tiny room, frustration as alive as the pain biting at his nerve endings. He should be with his men, fighting, protecting, guiding. Instead he stood here bleeding like a stuck pig. "Where are you, Salvador?" But even as he called to his mentor, he knew it to be a worthless attempt. Salvador would no more answer him now than he ever did.

In light of the day's events, Salvador most likely had nothing to say to Jag. After all, as a leader, the one expected to protect his men, to be prepared for anything, Jag had failed.

Self-doubt beat at him, spurring anger. At himself. At years of Salvador keeping him in the dark. Telling Jag he had to find the answers, the path, on his own.

Why was the Healer able to call Salvador, but Jag, the one supposed to be the leader of the Knights, unable to reach out? He led the Knights in a war against evil, yet he was kept at a distance. Why? The question had come to him over and over, often deep in the sleepless nights of the past century.

He'd become a beast that miserable day two centuries before when his human world, his happy life, had been taken from him. What if Salvador had saved him but not destroyed the evil within? With his restored soul, the beast had not been cast aside. What of the evil of the beast? Perhaps it could only be confined and buried, never destroyed. Fearing his own true nature had become Jag's own personal hell.

Knees beginning to buckle, Jag awkwardly sat down to the side of the tub, weapons still intact. The blood loss was beginning to takes its toll, and Jag blinked away the spots before his eyes. He'd rest a minute and then make his way to the cathedral. Shut his eyes just a minute…

Abruptly Jag jerked to alertness, a sound outside his door drawing his attention. He'd fallen asleep, he realized. For how long? His gaze flashed to his side, taking in the ooze of blood with limited changes, indicating he'd been out no more than a minute or two.

Pain radiated through his body as he pushed to his feet, using energy he'd have sworn he didn't possess, his wound smarting as he reached for the leather-covered handle to the blade sheathed at his waist.

He might die this day but not without taking a few more Darklands with him. A realization came to him, abrupt and fierce, conflicting with that of only moments before. If he, indeed, died, if he met his end, Salvador would come and save his men. And Salvador would save Karen.

Yes. The thought brought peace to Jag.

Maybe, just maybe, death did become him.

Maybe his battle to live was the wrong one. Maybe…he needed to accept defeat. Not from the Darklands. But from himself. A sudden rush of adrenaline coursed through his veins and he charged at the doorway, ready to take his intruder to the darkness with him.

Karen waited outside Jag's door, holding a bottle of salve in her white-knuckled grip. Having knocked twice with no response, she knew she had to act. Simply standing there wasn't an option. For all she knew, Jag could be lying on the ground, half-dead—or worse, *already dead.*

She reached for the knob, and hesitated, her heart kicking into double-time. Intruding on Jag's private space without warning came with more than a bit of risk. With his abrasive insistence she "stay away," he wasn't likely to welcome an intrusion with open arms.

Then again, he hadn't minded intruding on her, she reminded herself. He'd stormed her room when it had served his purpose. She could do the same.

Straightening, decision made, Karen gripped the doorknob, pushed the door open and entering the room. "Jag." His name slid into the air in a gasp, her body pulled backward into a harder one, warm breath blowing along her neck, the chill of a steel blade at her throat.

There was no question her attacker was Jag. She could feel his presence like a second skin, familiar. Safe despite that knife at her neck. "Jag," she whispered, then louder, "Jag. It's me, Karen. I came to help. I brought medicine from Marisol."

For several seconds, he held her close, no words. For a moment, she thought he leaned down and inhaled the scent of her hair, but she couldn't be sure. She didn't dare move, letting him take the time he needed. Hoping a memory of their past might come to him as it had her.

But then she felt the dampness seeping through her clothes, and she knew she had to act. He was bleeding badly. "Oh, God, Jag. Let me help. We have to stop the bleeding."

Abruptly he let go of her, setting her away from him. The sound of him putting away his weapon followed by a grunt filled her ears before she could turn to face him. She had only a moment to take in the bloodstained T-shirt before he snatched the jar from her hand. He moved to the bed and sat down, cursing as his weapons got in his way. Karen stood there watching, not sure what to do next. Without words, he'd rejected her help.

He dropped the jar on the mattress and unhooked the belt around his waist, before dropping it to the ground at his feet. He sank to the bed, his body hitting it with a leaden heaviness.

Next, he needed that shirt off. *Let me help you.* "Do you have scissors?" she asked. "I can cut the shirt off."

Staring straight ahead, giving her his profile, he didn't turn, nor did he speak for what felt a lifetime to Karen. Finally, "Bathroom drawer."

Relief washed over Karen. Success. A little, at least. One step forward. One wall torn down. Fearful he might develop second thoughts, Karen rushed forward, darting to the left to enter the bathroom, and then froze, appalled at the bloodstained floor. Her stomach turned at the sight, her gut twisting into a knot, and spurring her back into action. He'd lost way too much blood.

She rifled through the drawer, finding the scissors, and started for the door, then doubled back, deciding she needed towels—wet and dry—to clean the wound. And bandages. She needed bandages. A few seconds later, armed with supplies, she hurried to aid Jag.

When he came into view, she found him sitting on the edge of the bed, his arms rested on his knees, his head forward between his shoulders, dark hair falling forward, shielding his face.

Drawing a deep breath, she walked toward him, cautious as she approached. His presence screamed with a primal edge, a warrior ready to fight. Almost as if his instincts were there on the surface, holding him when he would fall. An injured wild animal trying to survive.

But she didn't fear him. Not at all.

Stopping at the edge of the bed, she set her supplies on the simple brown comforter now tinged with darker stains. "I'm going to slide behind you and cut away the shirt."

She waited, but he didn't respond. Okay. No objection, at least. Exhaling, she eased to the center of the mattress and grabbed the scissors, raising the material and cringing when she saw him shiver as if in pain, grinding her teeth in sympathy for what he must feel.

Looking beneath the first patch of cloth from his skin, she sucked in a breath at the long, deep cut across his back and down his side. "Oh, God," she whispered. "Jag."

"It'll heal," he managed hoarsely, speaking for the first time in long minutes. "I'm fine."

"You're not fine," she said, refusing his words. She eased the material she'd cut away from his skin, disposing of the soiled cloth on one of the towels she'd obtained. Turning back to survey his wound, finding it worse than expected, she whispered her prior words, "You're not fine."

Though she really wanted to get the rest of the T-shirt off his body, it clung to him, a matted second skin.

The gel being applied came next so it could start working. If it worked. She didn't know what to think. Could some blue gel help a wound this massive?

She reached for the wet towel sitting nearby, deciding again to explain herself. To make sure Jag knew what to expect. "I'm going to clean up this section of your back and then put the gel on before dealing with the rest of the shirt."

"Okay," he said in a low, hoarse voice.

Receiving his approval, Karen dabbed at the blood around the wound. Recoiling, Jag pressed his shoulder blades together and then groaned with the action.

Karen's hand came down on his shoulder, an instinctive act meant to comfort, molding his warm, taut skin. Despite the circumstances, she couldn't help but notice the definition in his arms. The power he must possess. The strength. Yet…

"Easy," she urged. "Easy." His muscles slowly relaxed, his shoulders slumping forward. "That's right." She worked quickly to clean him up a bit and then grabbed the jar, feeling the coolness of the gel through the solid surface. "This is going to be cold."

He nodded and then moved without warning, yanking at the remainder of his shirt and tearing it away, discarding it to the floor. "You need to make sure it's inside the wound," he said, his voice stronger now, as if he'd found a second wind. "Not just on the surface."

"All right," she said, swallowing. It was going to hurt him. "Ready?"

"Just do it," he said firmly.

Figured he'd be a macho man. "All right, then." She

dipped her fingers into cool liquid and lobbed a big bunch of it on the cut.

Amazingly he didn't so much as flinch this time, clearly having braced himself for the impact. Considering the pain he must be enduring, she didn't know how he managed to remain so calm. With as gentle a touch as possible, Karen worked the gel over and into the wound. To her surprise, the blood flow appeared to slow instantly.

Butterflies fluttered in her stomach as she realized she would have to settle down in front of Jag to doctor the rest of his injury. She'd have to face him and look into those dark, mysterious eyes. Part of her wanted to do just that, to search for the familiar presence of the past she knew she'd find there. Another part of her resisted. The part that hadn't quite accepted that she was Jag's wife from the past. The part that hadn't quite connected with the world of "anything is possible" she'd managed to step into.

But it had to be done. The sword had cut right through his body. All the way through. The thought of metal biting through his flesh made her teeth grind together.

Without warning Jag of her intentions, afraid he might object for some reason she didn't quite understand considering she was helping him, she scooted her supplies to the edge of the mattress where she could reach them from the floor. He should welcome anything she was doing. Somehow, with Jag, she doubted it would be that cut and dried.

Easing off the bed, she slid onto the ground at his feet. Before he could object, or she could chicken out for that matter, her hands went to his knees and she settled between them.

The touch of her hand to his leg shot heat up her arms and through her body. Her gaze shot to his, a reaction to the attraction so alive between them.

As she predicted, those dark eyes of his, so intense, so potent, stared into hers, entrancing her with the depth of what they stirred inside her. What *he* stirred inside her. Embracing her with warmth—familiar warmth. She could see he felt it, too. He might not have allowed himself to consider she was his wife, she was *Caron,* but somewhere in the far reaches of his mind, he knew.

In that moment, their gazes locked. There was nothing, no one, but the two of them. Time stood still. She felt Jag on a level beyond the physical. Soul deep. It was the only way to describe the way he reached beyond her surface and touched the very core of her existence.

Emotion stirred, emotion she couldn't touch, couldn't identify, but she damn sure could *feel.* Primal heat coursed through her body, arousal and desire tricking along her nerve endings. But this was more than simple lust. Far more than desire. This was a product of a bond that only two people meant to be together shared.

Unnerved by the clamoring of emotions screaming inside, Karen forced herself back to the urgent matter at hand, appalled at her distraction from Jag's injury. She reached for a towel, determined to get him attended to and resting.

Delicately she cleared her throat, not sure she could

even find her voice. "Can you ease back so I can clean the wound?" she asked hoarsely, her words a barely there whisper.

For several seconds, he simply stared at her, and she thought he might resist. Then he did as she asked, leaning backward to hold his weight up on his arms. The only way she could get to the cut was to push upward, off her heels, leaning across his crotch, her chest pressed against the intimate part of his body.

The sound of his low, guttural moan made her pull back. "Did I hurt you?"

His expression raged with disbelief, which quickly turned to anger. "No," he said as if she should know as much. "You didn't *hurt* me." He dropped to his back and covered his face with his arm.

She'd have spouted back with something about his rude tone, but now wasn't the time. But soon, he'd have to get an attitude adjustment. Karen reached for her supplies and a moment later managed to plop a goodly portion of the remaining gel onto his wound.

"Why are you here?" he asked, not looking at her, his voice weak, as if he was biting back pain as she worked the gel into his wound. "I told you to stay away."

There he went, needing that attitude adjustment again. Perhaps it couldn't wait. Even now, while doctoring his injury, he was digging for reasons to make her the enemy. He was going to have to let go of that need. Otherwise they would never figure out what they faced and defeat it together.

"Leave you alone," she repeated flatly. "Right. And let you bleed to death."

"I won't bleed to death," he bit out through clenched teeth.

Karen would have laughed at the ridiculous, macho statement if she hadn't found the white line above his lip a distraction. In contrast to his warm brown complexion, it warned of weakness in his body. Of the very blood loss he claimed as no concern.

"Right," she said again. "That's why your Healer was so worried."

"I could have waited on Marisol."

His statement, meant to be harsh, came out with a weak delivery, his voice cracking ever so slightly. The fact that he used what little energy he had to push her away upset Karen. A new emotion, one laced with pain, had her lashing out before she could pull back.

"You think I want to be here?" she demanded. "Helping someone who doesn't even appreciate it?" Karen glowered at him for several beats and then went to work. "I don't, you know." She wiped around the wound, cleaning the lost blood from his skin as the gel had already slowed the bleeding. The muscles in his abdominals flexed with the action and she bit her bottom lip. His disposition might be in need of a makeover, but his body rippled with perfection. A body damaged by the bite of a blade. Her voice softened as she realized how much this man had meant to her once and could once again, if she let him. "You saved my life, though. I owed you."

He lifted his arm and stared at her, a hint of shock in his eyes, quickly masked with steely ice. No doubt he intimidated most people with that look. Not her. She'd been to hell and back today. She'd seen far worse than his nasty attitude. Things she wouldn't soon forget.

"You don't owe me anything," he said, finally.

She disposed of the glass jar now empty and her palms settled on his thighs. Strong thighs. He was a powerful man. A force to be feared by many. Just not her. He made her feel a lot of things but not that. Not fear.

It was time he got that through his thick skull. "You don't scare me no matter how much you want to," she proclaimed, and then moved on to business. "I need to wrap the wound. Can you sit up again?"

Without warning, he pushed his body upward, shackling her wrists, his eyes meeting hers. "You need to leave."

He was so close she could see the dark stubble on his jaw. Reach out and touch it even if her hands were free. And she might have, had she been able to. The urge was overwhelming. Like something she'd done in the past. An instinct born of habit.

"I'm not going anywhere until Marisol arrives," she told him. "You might as well let me finish the job I started and bandage you. Then you can lay your stubborn self down and rest."

His expression was hard. His jaw tight. "You have no idea what you are dealing with here."

"Actually," she declared, "I'm pretty darn certain you're the one who doesn't know what you're dealing with." Before he could respond she added, "You've been far from kind to me. You roar big and might even bite." She let out a choked laugh at her choice of words. "Literally, I guess."

"Exactly why you should get out of here. I'm like those beasts that just attacked. You've seen it in your dreams. Don't be a fool. Get away from me while you still can."

"I've seen no beast in you. A cranky man who has locked me up, yelled at me and accused me of nasty things, yes, but no beast."

"The dreams, Karen. Think about what happens in them."

"Oh, I have," she said. "And frankly, I think you are reading them all wrong." She shook her head. "But that's a subject for another time, after you rest. Let me finish bandaging your wounds so you can rest. Then we can talk. After you're healed." He stared at her, unmoving, no response. "Please, Jag."

"I can't let you stay here." His head fell forward, his fingers loosening around her wrists. "I don't want to hurt you, Karen."

"You won't," she whispered, believing it with all her soul. "You won't."

He lifted his eyes to hers, and his look said a million words, exposing deep-felt pain and emotion, even a hint of fear. "How can you be so sure, when I'm not?"

This time Karen gave into instinct, reaching out and pulling a strand of his hair through her fingers. She half expected him to jerk away, but he didn't. It felt right, touching him, talking to him. The warmth and tenderness slowly flooding his eyes told her it did to him, as well.

"I feel no fear of you, Jag. Not in the dreams. Not now."

He took her hand and pressed it to his cheek, his eyes

falling shut for a moment, as if he was absorbing her touch. Sexual friction came with the light scraping of his whiskers against the sensitive skin of her palm.

When he looked at her again, she saw the heat of his gaze. "What do you feel, Karen?"

Chapter 17

When Karen didn't immediately respond to his question, Jag repeated it, burning for her answer more than he did from the wound in his side. "What do you feel, Karen?"

Again, his words hung in the air, taunting him with her possible responses. Being close to her like this, experiencing her tender touch, lavishing in her caring voice and eyes, delivered a jolt. Stirred emotions from times long gone. Of a life he'd lost when he'd lost his wife.

Karen finally opened her mouth to speak, the thoughtful expression in her eyes indicating she'd given great consideration to what she was about to relay. "My mother use to love the saying, 'things happen for a reason.'"

Jag sucked in a breath, barely able to believe what he'd just heard. His wife had used those words, all too often. *Things happen for a reason.* Possibilities rushed at him, along with a wave of emotion. Did he dare let his mind form the thoughts trying to take shape?

"There's a reason why I'm here," Karen continued. "A reason you and I came together." She inhaled and let it out, as if she willed him to do the same. As if she knew he needed to breathe. "I know I'm supposed to be here. It's…destiny. "

Caron had often called their marriage, their love—destiny. She claimed that was why her family had settled on land next to his family ranch. He stared into Karen's eyes, searching the depths of her soul…of his soul. And in that moment, their gazes locked, he felt something deep inside him move, reaching out from her to him, lightening where he'd been dark before. He knew the truth with that feeling. Knew what he hadn't dared think, let alone voice. He knew this Karen was his Caron.

"I need to do this," Karen said, holding up the bandages.

Barely containing the sudden urge to pull her into his arms, to hold her and never let her go, Jag took several seconds to respond. Somehow, he managed a nod. He needed to think. Besides, he didn't want to scare Karen. There was no guarantee she would believe him if he told her his thoughts, though on some level he had to think she knew. He felt it. Still, even if she was his wife from another life, things had changed. *He'd* changed. Seen and done things to harden him.

Why was this happening? Why? He wanted it, yet, he feared it all the same. His chest tightened as a new concern took form. Darklands would destroy him if given an opportunity. What better way than to deliver Caron to him again and then watch as he killed her?

The implications of Karen being here, of him perhaps watching her die again, were like a knife cutting at him. Karen's fingers brushed his skin, goose bumps following in their wake. His fists balled as he fought the desire, the absolute need, to touch her. No matter what might have changed in either of them, she still stirred things emotional and intense inside him.

But what if he hurt her? The dreams said he would. They showed him the horrible truth of his lust turned to damnation.

Karen's hands settled on his shoulders. She was behind him now, on the bed, taping the bandage. As if she'd read his mind, her mouth settled close to his ear, her breath warm on his neck. "I'm not afraid of you, Jag."

"You should be. You had the same dreams I did."

"Perhaps I interpreted it differently than you," Karen suggested, but didn't give him time to respond. Instead she said, "lay back and rest." She scooted to the side so he had room to ease back on the mattress. He didn't argue, avoiding eye contact for fear of what he might find, for fear he'd see his failure in her gaze. Grunting with a sharp pain, he slid backward and rested his head on the pillow.

"Are you okay?" she asked, concern etching her tone, remaining on the bed beside him, seeming in no rush to put distance between them. "Is there anything I can give you for the pain?"

The truth was he suddenly felt pretty damn bad. His vision was spotty, his stomach rolling. He forced himself to look at her, forced his expression to one of a blank mask though his eyelids were heavy. He couldn't manage to get them to above half-veiled.

"I'll be okay when you leave," he said, trying to get her a safe distance from him, so he knew he couldn't hurt her.

"I'm not leaving," she said, no hesitation, voice full of certainty.

He was fading and he knew it. Even his voice came out a whisper. "Leave. I don't…want to hurt you."

"I'll take my chances," she said, rotating to lie down on the mattress beside him.

"You…can't stay," he said, but he wasn't sure she heard the words. Wait. He wasn't sure he really said them. Everything was just so…dark. So black. Then the dream emerged…first sweet, sensual. Karen making love to him. Karen's sweet curves pressed to his. So perfect. But then the beast started scratching at his insides, biting at him, wanting her….

Karen lifted up on her elbow and eyed Jag, feeling a cold vise on her heart at his closed eyes. "Jag?" she whispered, the horrible possibility he might not be sleeping twisting her gut.

Relief washed over her as he murmured something incoherent. She let air trickle from her lungs. Unable to stop herself, she scooted closer to him, inhaling his masculine scent, warmth curling deep in her stomach. Flashes of the past were starting to come at her, revealing how close they'd been. Bringing forward a timeless love she held inside. The kind she'd never felt in this lifetime—until now.

Tentatively she reached out, fingers trailing his jaw. He was a beautiful man, ruggedly handsome, gorgeously sculpted. His cheekbones were high, his lips full. She'd always thought so, she realized. From the moment she'd met him so very long ago. Time stood still as Karen stared at Jag, memories flooding her mind.

Without warning, Marisol appeared in the room, a shimmer of light surrounding her for a moment. Karen jumped, yanking her hand back from Jag's face as if she were a kid caught digging in the cookie jar. She stiffened to a sitting position. "Good gosh, you scared the hell out of me."

"Sorry," Marisol said, her eyes narrowing as she took in Karen's position on the bed next to Jag. "I normally use doors but under the circumstances time seems important." Her gaze went to Jag and she sat down beside him. "How's he doing?"

"Not good. I stopped the bleeding but the wound is deep. He passed out about ten minutes ago." Karen noted the paleness of Marisol's skin. Her brows dipped. "Are you okay?"

Marisol nodded, but she didn't make eye contact with Karen. "I'm fine." She held her palm above Jag's left side. "He will be, too."

Karen watched in amazement as light seemed to beam from her palm. A knock sounded on the door, and Karen scurried toward it, only to have it open before she arrived. Rock and Des entered, their attention on Marisol and Jag. Karen didn't miss how Rock slowly eased in Marisol's direction. The man had it bad for the Healer.

Together, the three of them watched, waiting, tension in the air. Karen pressed her fist beneath her chin, worried beyond words. Suddenly Jag sat straight up, his breath whooshing from his lungs, his features distorted as if in pain. Marisol gasped, pushed from the bed. Rock rushed to help her up. He grabbed her from behind and helped her to her feet.

Jag's eyes traveled the room, wildly hunting, and then fixing on Karen. "Get her out of here. Get her out of here now."

"Jag," Marisol said. "Lie down. *Please.*" She looked at Rock. "I need him down now, before he rips open his wound. I can't do much more. I just can't. I'm too tired."

Rock eyed Des as if waiting for his decision. With a nod, Des moved forward.

"Get back," Jag said, pointing at Rock and then Des. "I swear to God, I'll make you both regret touching me."

The men stopped in their tracks, staring at each other. Jag stared at Karen. "You need to leave."

"I can't do that," she said, her voice low but determined. Clearly he'd been dreaming again. He was so sure he would hurt her. He was wrong.

"Karen, leave," Des said, turning to look at her.

"Ask him why he wants me to leave," Karen said. "Ask him!" This time she screamed it. "He thinks he's going to hurt me. He thinks… He won't." She fixed her gaze on Jag. "I'm supposed to be here, Jag."

Marisol stepped forward, directly beside Jag's head.

"I'm sorry," she said to him, her voice so low it was hard to make out. Then her hand lifted and light sprayed from it, engulfing his forehead. A second later he collapsed. Immediately her palm covered the wounded section of his body.

"*Chingado,*" Des said, moving to stand beside her again. "He's a stubborn Spaniard, that one."

"Spaniard?" Karen asked, brows dipping. Des seemed to be trying to make her feel at ease.

"Yeah," Des said, smiling. "Bossy, arrogant bastards love to tell us Mexicans what to do."

He gave her an inquisitive look and she met it head-on. She wasn't sure what he was seeking as he stared at her, but she was an open book. There was nothing she had to hide. He had the most unique eyes, she realized, with flecks of yellow. An untamed quality lingered in them, wild and potent, hinting at danger.

But she wasn't afraid of him or any of these men any longer. "I can't leave him," she said, unable to take the silence any longer.

His lips thinned, the scar above his upper lip drawing her eyes, making her wonder what this man had endured. Had he lost someone he loved as Jag had. Surely if he had, he'd understand. Maybe she should tell him who she was. *That she was Caron.*

"He wants you to leave," Des said. "If he wakes up and you're here, I'll be in deep shit."

"And you always do what he says," she commented, repeating what he had said in the kitchen, feeling a sudden rush of fear. Leaving Jag felt like the wrong thing to do.

He tilted his chin slightly. "Yes, but maybe not now."

Surprise stiffened her spine, hope filled her heart. "You mean, you're letting me stay?"

"Maybe," he commented. "But like I said. I'll pay for it." He seemed to consider his next move. Then, "I know about the dreams, Karen. Marisol told me." Something flashed in his dark eyes. His gaze went to the bed. "He's been alone a long time."

Something about the way Des said the words told her he was thinking of more than Jag. He understood being alone because he was, too. She was glad Marisol had told him. In fact, she was relieved. If he knew everything, if Des believed what she did, that she was Caron, then maybe he'd understand. Maybe he'd help her.

"What else did Marisol say?" she asked, trying to decide what to say now. How to make sure he really did get how much she needed to stay here with Jag.

"That she believes you have some past connection to Jag." He considered his own words a moment. "There was a time I would have called that bullshit. One thing my very long life has taught me is that anything is possible. I'm living, walking proof of that." He tilted his head to consider her. "The question is—what do you think?"

"I'm supposed to be with Jag," she said, no hesitation. With every passing second, she believed her words all the more. "He thinks he'll hurt me, but I know he won't. He *won't.*"

Before she received Des's decision, Marisol pushed to her feet. "He'll be fine. Just let him—" Her words were lost as her hand went to her head. "Oh."

Rock cursed as he rushed toward her, lifting her in

his arms. Karen started toward them, but Des caught her arm. "She's fine. She's just exhausted. We told her not to come over here but she insisted. She just needs rest. Same with Jag."

Karen crossed her arms in front of her body, confused, cold in an unnatural way. "How many did she heal?"

"Not everyone." He shook his head. "We lost good men today."

"I'm sorry," she said. "I…I wouldn't have come if I thought I'd bring this to you. I swear, I wouldn't have."

"If you're referring to Rock's accusations, ignore him. You didn't bring this on us. My gut says the Dark-lands are using you to get to Jag, and I always trust my gut." His eyes darkened. "I'm counting on you getting through to him before they do." Then he cut his gaze away, motioning Rock forward.

Karen stood there, feeling overwhelmed with emotions. Des's acceptance of her past with Jag somehow delivered validation. Before he could leave, she turned. "Des?"

He rounded to face her as Rock carried Marisol from the room, his brow lifting in silent question. "Take care of my sister," she said, needing the security of hearing him say he would.

"You have my word," he said.

She let out a breath she didn't know she'd even been holding, turning away from Des, and hearing the door shut behind her. With Des's vow, she felt she could focus on Jag. She could know Eva was safe. She'd left her sister once, she wouldn't do it again.

Just like she wouldn't leave Jag again. She stared at

the bed, at the man sleeping peacefully. But there was nothing peaceful about Jag and she knew it. Tears burning in the back of her eyes, emotions surfacing, her chest tightening with crushing force. Without him saying so, Karen knew Jag felt he'd failed her, but she could see it was the opposite. She'd left him alone, an eternal lifetime to feel guilt. If only she'd run faster. Acted somehow differently. If only…wait. She thought of the dreams. Thought of what she felt in them. Jag was the one who'd been afraid. He'd feared himself.

Things happen for a reason. The words popped into her head and with them, a sense of peace began to settle inside. The tightness in her chest eased. It was clear Jag was a leader, that he fought a battle greater than her life or even his own. Things did happen for a reason. And she was back here, for him, for a reason. Jag needed her. He needed to let go of the guilt and the fear. He needed to be loved.

Not willing to waste another minute, she crawled onto the bed, and snuggled up to his side. When he woke, she was going to be close and she planned to stay close. Too close for him to ignore. She smiled as her cheek settled back on his shoulder. Karen felt the most amazing thing in that moment. She felt she'd found what she'd been looking for all these years. She'd found her purpose. She'd found Jag. There was a war raging around them and they were meant to fight it together.

When Jag woke she'd make sure he knew he wasn't alone anymore. She was here to stay.

Jag blinked awake, staring at the ceiling, trying to clear the fog of the heaviness of a healing slumber. The dim lighting spoke of nightfall, which meant he'd been asleep for quite some time. Normally he was a light sleeper, ever aware of possible trouble. The healing needs of his body had overcome all else.

Slowly awareness and warmth crept over him, his nostrils flaring with a soft feminine scent. *Karen.* He tilted his head down, inhaling the scent more fully, her hair brushing his face, a whisper of a touch that assured him the reality of her presence. Pleasure filled him at her nearness before he could think to feel otherwise. In truth, for just a few moments, he didn't want to allow himself to feel anything else. He simply wanted to absorb her presence.

She wasn't supposed to be here. He remembered telling his men to take her away. At that moment, he was thankful they hadn't. And he wasn't willing to think of the consequences of her being here. Of what could go wrong if he allowed himself to forget the warnings in his dreams.

Not an easy task to achieve when he could feel the soft curves of her body melded to his side, the gentle weight of her head resting on his shoulder. Unable to stop himself, he reached down and stroked her hair, the urge to touch her too great to ignore. The silky strands teased his fingers, and his eyes shut as he inhaled the moment, taking it in as he would a breath, letting it stir him deep inside.

He felt her shift a moment before she spoke. "Jag?" Her hand settled on his chest as she rotated to look at him. Their eyes locked, awareness charging the air with electric current. "Hi," she whispered, her lashes fluttering almost shyly.

"Hi," he said, knowing he should say more, knowing he should demand she leave. Somehow, he just couldn't.

"How are you?"

A loaded question for sure. The woman he wanted but couldn't have was in his arms. How was he? He was both in heaven and hell at the moment, thank you very much.

"Better," he finally managed, and then reached deep for discipline, forcing himself to say what he didn't want to. "You shouldn't be here."

"I remember, Jag." Her lashes fluttered a moment before her eyes once again found his. "I remember Victor."

Everything inside him went still. His heart seemed to stop beating, his breath lodged inside his throat. "What?" he asked, sure he'd heard wrong. Certain this couldn't be happening. "What did you say?"

"It's coming back in pieces, but I remember. I… remember how in love we were." She reached out and touched his jaw. "You used to have a goatee. I liked it."

Jag might have questioned her, if she hadn't added that part about the goatee. No one knew that. He'd shaved it, just as he'd shaved away his past. Shaved it because his wife had loved it and it reminded him of her.

In one move, he rotated their bodies and pinned her on the bed, hands over her head, knees trapped between his. Fury and pain burned inside him, a rage of ache, of memories. "Who told you to say that?" he demanded. "Who?"

She stared up at him calmly, unaffected by his anger. "It's not like that and you know it. Look inside your heart and you know it's me. You *know*. You know just like I do."

He shook his head, fighting the rush of emotion overcoming him. Her hair was lighter, her skin paler, but her eyes…they were the same. When he looked into her eyes, he felt the same. "It can't be."

"Yet, it is. I don't know how. I just know that the memories…they are coming to me. I know you. I know *us*."

Slowly he loosened his grip on her hands, burying his face in her neck, and he was trembling, he realized, as shaken as the day she'd been taken from him. She felt so amazing in his arms, so perfect. He pulled her closer, wrapping her with his body, afraid it would be another dream and she'd be gone.

Her hands stroked his back, his shoulders, his neck. She tangled her fingers in his hair, calming him with the caresses, soothing him with her presence. He couldn't look at her. Not knowing he'd failed her that day so long ago. "I'm so sorry," he whispered.

"What are you sorry for?" she asked. "Jag, please. Look at me." Her hand went to his face. "Please."

With a deep breath, he forced himself to lift his gaze to hers. "I didn't get to you in time."

"Have you considered maybe you weren't supposed to? I lay in the bed for a long time while you rested, thinking about this. Asking the same questions I'm sure you've asked for years. Really one question. Why?" Her knuckles grazed his jaw. "And one answer came back to me. Things happen for a reason."

He shook his head. "No. There is no reason a man watches his wife die. Do you know how many times that day has played over in my head?"

"I wish I could take that away. It hurts me knowing

I caused you that much pain but I'm here now. We're together."

If only it were that easy. "We can't go back." He rested his forehead against hers. "I'm not the man you knew. I'm not Victor anymore."

She pressed her palms to his face and then brushed her lips over his, and he felt that touch, that barely there caress in every inch of his body. He was aroused and growing hungry. Not a good thing. He'd already seen how easily he became primal and out of control with her. But even knowing this, a need drove him onward. A need to find out if she still loved him despite all that had happened, despite all he'd become. God, how he needed her, too.

"I've lived a lifetime without you just as you have me," she said, their lips still close. So close he could still taste her. So close he could barely contain his need to feel them touch his again. She continued, and he forcefully reined in his desire. "I'm not the same person I was, either, but the bond we shared then is still alive inside me. We can discover each other all over again. I know we can."

His restraint snapped and he kissed her then, claiming her mouth without the tenderness he would have liked to. But there was no other way he could deal with this now. It was a kiss meant to sate a hundred years of starvation. A kiss meant to give him peace. But as he felt the slide of her tongue against his, tasted the sweetness of her pure passion, he burned inside with the truth. He burned inside with the danger he represented to her. He was a beast, a monster, a man no longer worthy of her.

Tearing his mouth from hers, he rolled off her, his breath coming out in heavy pants, his arm covering his face. "You have no idea what I've become."

"I know what you fear," she said softly. "I felt it in my dreams. You think you're one of them."

He dropped his arm, turning to look at her, shocked to hear the words he thought so many times spoken aloud. "Because it's true."

She didn't move, didn't touch him. She seemed to understand for at least a moment, he needed his space. "I don't believe that," she said.

"They turned me into one of them, Karen. They stole my soul and turned me into one of them."

"Now I know you're crazy."

His eyes narrowed. "Why is that?"

She sat up, determination flaring in her eyes. "Think about it, Jag. Think about what we share. I know you and you're a good man. You help people. You aren't like those things I saw you battling."

If only it were as she said, but she didn't know everything. Jag had to look away from her as he told her the rest of his story, as he tore down her rosy picture. "When you died," he said, his voice a bit hoarse even to his own ears, "the beasts attacked me next. I didn't fight. I wanted to die. As they drank my blood I kept thinking, *just do it.* Just *kill* me. But no. That would have been too simple. Too painless. When I finally thought it might end soon, that I was close to gone, my chest started burning." His hand went to his heart, still feeling that pain like it had just happened. "I felt my soul yanked from my chest as if were my heart. It was unbelievable pain I can't begin to explain. Then, just like that—" he snapped his fingers "—nothing. No pain. My soul was gone and so was every human emotion I'd ever known." He squeezed his eyes shut. "What was so bad about it was that…" He didn't know if he could even say it out loud. "Was that I…"

She reached out and touched his arm. "What?" she prodded gently.

"It felt good," he said, the truth like acid on his tongue yet liberating at the same time. He'd never admitted this to anyone. Jag turned his head and looked at her. "The pain of losing you was gone. Nothing mattered. I hate how good that moment felt. How losing my soul freed me from the loss. It haunts me every second of every day."

She scooted closer to him, her fingers brushing hair from his eyes. "It shouldn't." Her soft voice held a caress. It held comfort. "Who wouldn't have felt the same?"

The understanding in her voice brushed his nerve endings, calming him when he wouldn't have thought it possible, but not near enough. His self-hatred was a vicious thing time had ripened to a nasty wound.

How could she forgive him for what he couldn't forgive himself? But then, she hadn't heard everything. He turned away from her again. "A man appeared then, battling the beasts. I remember the thirst for blood, the desire to take his life before he did mine. I tried to attack him and with a wave of his hand, my limbs were heavy, almost frozen. Then the pain in my chest rocked me, took me down to my knees. And then the sorrow over losing you took hold again. I begged him to take it back. Begged like I've never begged in my life."

A hoarse sound drew his attention. Jag turned to find Karen crying. "I'm so sorry, Jag. I…hate that you went through that. I didn't want to leave you."

She was apologizing to him? He'd never felt anything like what he felt in that moment. Never felt the kind of love. Not even in his past life. Here he was, worried she would think him a monster, and she was apologizing. All she cared about was his pain, not her own.

Jag sat up and pulled her into his arms, using his finger to brush away her tears. "Shh," he said. "Don't cry, *cariño*. Please. I don't want to cause you any more pain."

"I'm not the one who lived all of this, Jag. I basically slept through the pain. You," she said, pausing to draw a shaky breath, "you've been through hell. I'm here now, though. You're not alone anymore."

Her words warmed him, filled him with such joy he wanted to shout out. At the same time, he checked himself, reality a hard sell against such actions. "The dreams—"

Karen's lips brushed his, cutting of his words. "Were about your own fear." Her mouth touched his again. "Kiss me, Jag. Make love to me and show me how much you missed me."

"You don't know what you're asking," he said, but he could barely contain his need to claim her as his own. "I won't see you hurt again."

Her hand went to his cheek. "You won't. I know you won't."

"I wish I could feel so sure."

"Trust in me, in us, and you will be."

"I want to," he whispered.

"No one is stopping you but you," she responded. "Kiss me, Jag."

But she didn't wait on his response. She found his mouth with hers and he was lost. The soft tease of her kiss quickly claimed him with temptation. He'd fought hundreds of battles over the years but this one, he couldn't win. His woman, his life, she had power like no other over him.

He was lost and found all at once.

Chapter 18

Karen tasted like honey and vanilla wrapped in temptation, just as he remembered, so sweet and perfect.

Jag savored that flavor, tenderly brushing her jaw with his fingers, angling so he could deepen the kiss. Without question, she was beautiful. Yet, his attraction to her went so much deeper than the physical. It was the way she touched him inside that made him burn for her. The life she breathed into his existence. Her exterior only housed what was inside. The soul that called to him. The woman he'd loved, and thought lost forever.

His emotions raged with intensity, a mixture of love from the man and the lust of the beast. The primal part of him clawed at his core, begging to take Karen. It wanted to claim her as much as the man did. And Lord help him, he wasn't sure he had the will to tell it no. He needed this too much. He needed Karen like he didn't remember needing anything in his life. Not since the day Caron had died. Not since he'd wanted to turn back time and run faster, fight harder, do anything to bring her back to life.

Karen moaned into his mouth and he swallowed the sound, greedily claiming it as proof of the impossible reality of her presence. Of the impossibility of her being in his arms, in his life. It drove him into a haze of desire with the force of a head-on collision. Logic and caution dissolved in an explosion of pure demand.

Jag tumbled from a sitting position to lie down on the mattress, pulling Karen with him so that they rested side by side. Kissing her. Touching her. With his body and hands, he molded her against him. He wanted all of her, to feel her naked body against his. To kiss her from head to toe. So much so he didn't even know where to start.

Hand on her lower back, Jag pressed her hips to his. Every inch of him burned with the touch, every nerve ending screaming with life. *Yes.* This was what he needed, what he'd been missing.

She was what he needed.

Her arm slid under his shoulder and she snuggled closer, as if she, too, couldn't get enough of him. Their legs entwined, hips parallel. He could feel her heat, his aroused body settling in the V of her legs. *Slow,* he reminded himself. Savor this.

But the beast was clamoring with demand, the man

falling into the shadows of its existence. He was beyond fear for what that might mean, beyond thought. Those things no longer guided him.

He knew only what he felt, what he desired, acting on it without hesitation, acting on pure instinct. "I missed you so much," he whispered, running fingers through her hair, easing his head back enough to look into her eyes. He wanted her to see the fire there, to run if she would before it was too late.

But she didn't run nor did she hesitate. "Prove it," she replied, her voice laden with emotion, her lips hungrily seeking his again.

He needed no further urging. Jag gave her what she sought without words, taking her mouth, and kissing her, hot and hungry, deep and full of demand. His desire to claim her, body and soul, rapidly becoming a driving force, pushing him forward. Taking the man and leaving the beast, just as he wanted to take the woman.

Hands sliding under her shirt, soft skin became his reward. She shifted, sitting up to tug it over her head. Jag could barely breathe as he watched her undress. Hanging by a string, he barely contained his desire to simply rip the barriers away.

He simply watched her. Wanting. Burning.

After the shirt came her shoes, but his eyes lingered on the soft ivory of her skin as she gave him her back. Her long blond hair sprayed across her shoulders, reminding him of dreams where the silky strands teased his chest and face. The room was dark but for a small light by the bedside, casting the room in a sensual spell, his cock hard as he devoured the beauty of her presence.

The anticipation, the waiting, as she undressed, had him mesmerized but, oh, so on edge.

Forcing himself to look away, he went to work, taking off his own clothes, standing up beside the mattress, shoving down his pants and ripping apart the unneeded bandages in the process.

Before he could turn around, before he could find Karen again, he felt the touch of her hand on his back. The soft touch, erotic and gentle, sizzled on his skin, stilling his actions. Jag felt his arousal thickening with the promise of what was to come, his blood pumping with the fire of desire.

Karen's fingers trailed over his skin, over the location of his injury, a delicate caress leaving behind scorching flames. "I can't believe it's healed," she whispered.

His body had, indeed, healed from his injury, but neither magic nor medicine could cure what still needed healing. Only Karen could do that. Only she could take away the emptiness eating at his insides.

He turned to face her, intending to thank her for all she had done for him earlier, but her hands were all over him, taking his words with her actions. Touching him as he rotated, her body pressed to his as soon as he faced her.

"Oh, my God, you feel good," he murmured against her lips, Karen's arms wrapping his neck, pebbled nipples teasing his chest hair.

And then they were kissing, devouring each other with their mouths and hands. He found one of her breasts, molding it with his palm and tweaking the nipple, his other hand skimming her perfect backside and then pulling her tighter against him.

He fit his manhood between her thighs, and together they moaned with the pleasure of the joining. Her head tilted in pleasure, exposing her neck, hands on his biceps. But it was her breasts that drew his attention, rosy-red nipples filling his gaze, begging for his mouth.

When she fixed him in a hot stare, her eyes were dark with passion. "I want you inside me, Jag," she whispered, the words a plea. "I want to feel us like we were."

A low growl escaped his throat at the erotic play of her words on his body. Jag barely remembered acting then. Somehow they were on the mattress, Karen beneath him. Jag used his knees to press her legs farther apart, settled between them with an urgency bred of the beast. An urgency she fed with her touch. Her hands were in his hair, on his face, calves wrapping his as she arched her hips to receive him. She wanted him. And Jag had never, ever denied his wife anything she wanted.

He didn't plan to start now.

Driven to satisfy the yearning between them, he sank deep into Karen's wet heat. But when he thought he'd be driven to press onward, he stilled, his face buried in her neck. The impact of their joining washed over him, overwhelming in its potency.

Jag leaned back, staring into her eyes, confirming she felt what he did. The tender heat of her gaze said she did. With that confirmation, peace came over him, drowning him in the rightness of them being together, in the perfection of the feelings that had crossed over from one lifetime to the next.

For long moments, all he could do was gaze into her

eyes, lost in their joining, feeling their intimacy surrounding him, inside and out. It was Karen who moved first, her hands caressing his skin, her soft voice whispering his name.

With abruptness, his mood shifted, and he could feel the primal side of him taking hold. His jaw clenched, his muscles tensed with the need to move, to take. He stared down at her, reaching for words, but unable. The rage of sudden lust was too fierce. He fought it, feeling the danger of its primal making. Feeling the shift from simply primal need to beastly demand.

He'd only thought he was out of control before, but it had been nothing compared to what flared within him. Karen seemed unaffected, staring up at him, her eyes tender, too tender for what must be blazing in his. Her fingers brushed his jaw, a familiar gesture he'd missed so damn much.

"Take me," she said, as if she responded to what pressed him onward. As if she knew he needed urging. "Take me now."

In his head the monster that was himself, no matter how hard he denied it, screamed to obey. Obey Karen. Obey the beast. Take her…devour her….

Fire coursed through his veins and he pulled back and thrust into her, pumping back and forth, in and out of her, no holding back, no hesitation. Her wet heat stroked him, silently telling him to give her more. Harder, deeper, longer strokes. She met him with each lunge, each stroke, her hips rocking to meet his.

Karen's breasts bounced with the movements, pleasing his visual senses just as her slick, wet heat pleased his physical ones. Every inch of his skin sizzled. Every nerve ending screamed with life. He'd been lit up, set on fire with a rage of passion like none he'd ever known, not even with Caron.

Harder he thrust. Faster. His face nuzzling her neck again, his nostrils flaring with her sweet scent. So synthesized to her presence, so in tune with all that she was, he could hear her heart beating, hear her blood coursing through her veins. Her hand was on the back of his head, her body caressing his hair, whimpers of pleasure teasing him, pleasing him. He was lost to the moment... lost.

And then, another shift in mood, another change he couldn't control Before Jag knew what was happening his cuspids were extending.

"No!" he screamed, but he didn't dare lift his head. He had just enough logic left, just enough conscious thought to not want her to see his teeth. This had never happened to him except in his dreams. "This can't be real."

Karen responded by lifting off the bed, tilting her hips upward, tempting him to move against her. She tore down his mental defenses, physical need taking control as Jag lunged into her. He forgot about his teeth, forgot about the danger. He sunk deep to her core, the beast screaming in his head, in his body.

Karen cried out in pleasure, tensing before she cried out in orgasm. Her spasms overtook him, milking him for his own release and delivering ecstasy beyond anything he'd ever known, ever dreamed of.

Thrusting one last time, Jag shook as he spilled himself inside her. But the release unleashed another need, powerful and beyond his control. His teeth sunk into Karen's shoulder, coppery sweet blood slicing through his taste buds, feeding his hunger.

Karen stiffened, her fingers tightening on his hair, but he barely felt it. The taste of her blood on his tongue spurred a hunger for more. Jag growled low in his throat, a familiar sound more beast than man, born of battle not lovemaking. Yet, at the same time, he felt no desire to destroy. No desire to hurt her. He simply had to taste her, to know her on the most intimate of levels.

Karen's body began to ease, her fingers loosening in his hair. "Jag," she gasped, and then, "I… Jag…I love you."

The words reached inside his head, reached beyond the sensation of the act he committed. This was Karen. *Caron.* He loved her. He shook his head, trying to clear the yearning to steal just one more drink, blinking as he took in the puncture marks on her shoulder. Oh, God. What had he done?

He'd tried to pull back sooner, tried to reel in the beast. What if he had taken too much blood? He had to get Karen to Marisol. Then, he'd get the hell away from her and stay away.

So she'd be safe.

One minute Karen was beneath Jag, the next he had her in his arms, making a quick path toward exiting the room. "What are you doing?" she screamed, panic in her voice. "We're naked! Don't you dare take me out that door."

"You'll bleed to death," he said ignoring her, still reeling from the impact of what he'd done to her. He could have killed her. "I have to get you to Marisol."

Karen shoved at the door, using her foot, her hand, anything she could get placed on the hard surface, making Jag's efforts to reach for the knob impossible.

He grunted. "Damn it, Karen. I'm trying to save your life."

"If you take me out of this room with no clothes on you're the one who'll need saving."

"You're hurt," he insisted.

"I'm *not* hurt! You, on the other hand, are going to be if you don't *put me down!*"

He considered throwing her over his shoulder, desperation taking hold. She'd died once because of him. Jag wouldn't let it happen again. He went for the knob again.

She made a frustrated sound and stiff-legged the door. "Will you *please*—" the words came through clenched teeth, but turned to a shout again "—just listen to me!" She drew a breath, lowering her voice. *"Please."* Her eyes locked with his. "Please, Jag. I swear to you. I'm not hurt."

He shook his head, rejecting that idea. He knew what he'd done to her. "Put me down and see for yourself," she challenged.

"You *think* you're fine but you are *not* fine. You're in shock. For God's sake, I just bit a hole in your shoulder." Shame stung his gut and mingled with his words, uncontainable. Defeated, he slid her to her feet, cutting his gaze, unable to look at her. "I'll be back. I'm going to get Marisol."

She spread her bare body wide in front of the door. "Not naked you won't."

He reached for her as if to move her aside and she was no match for his strength. "*Cariño,* I'm getting help and I'm getting it now, if I have to throw you over my shoulder and carry you to do it."

That seemed to get her attention, her eyes going wide. Still, stubborn as she was, she stayed in front of the door. "I don't even think it's bleeding." Her hand went to the wound and then she held it out for his inspection. "See. No blood."

His brows dipped and he shoved her hair aside, inspecting her shoulder. "Impossible. It's nearly healed."

He touched the wounds, amazed at the reality of what he found. She wasn't bleeding. But…he'd bitten her. She reached for his wrist, her touch calming him. Comforting when she should be running.

"See," she said, her gaze snagging his, "I really *am* fine. Whatever happened between us, it didn't hurt me. And whatever bad you think you did, you didn't do. You aren't bad, Jag." She searched his face as if looking for acceptance. She repeated her words in a whisper. "You aren't bad."

For several seconds, he stared into her beautiful blue eyes, forgetting the urgency of help, replaying that moment when he'd bitten her. The force of need pulsing in his body. But then something had happened. Something had changed. The beast had succumbed to the man when Jag thought only the opposite to be possible.

Was it possible that all this time, the beast had only controlled him because he had allowed it to?

"I don't understand any of this," he said, studying her skin again, seeking confirmation she really wasn't bleeding one last time. It was almost as if he hadn't bitten her at all, the pricks were shrinking so quickly. "I still want Marisol to check you out."

"That's not necessary."

He shot her a look that said he wasn't about to listen.

"Fine then," she said. "Can you at least put some pants on before you go get her?"

He wanted to argue, still fearful he could have caused her serious damage, but he did as she asked. Illogical as it was considering the timing, a part of him even enjoyed her insistence he get dressed. The idea that she claimed him, that she didn't want the rest of the world seeing him as she did, warmed him a bit. Still, he made quick work of shoving his jeans over his legs, not bothering to zip them before he was out the door.

The sooner Marisol checked out Karen, the better he'd feel.

Once he knew Karen was safe, then and only then, would he figure out what all of this meant.

Karen watched Jag depart before rushing toward the closet.

The idea of getting caught with one leg in her pants and one out didn't appeal. As much as she wanted to go to the mirror and look at her shoulder, she had to get decent before she ended up with a room full of arrogant men. Around this place, she never knew what to expect.

She needed to talk to Jag, but he had to calm down a little first. The truth was, she really was fine. More than fine, actually. The first prick of Jag's teeth on her skin had shocked her more than hurt. After that, the intimacy of the act had been amazingly erotic. There had been nothing violent in his action. Like in the dreams, it felt as if it had to be. As if this was part of their destiny.

Greeted with a row of neatly hung shirts, she yanked down a shirt and quickly pulled it over her. It went to her knees, sufficiently covering her, thank goodness. She'd managed to button it almost all the way up when Jag and Marisol appeared in the doorway.

"Are you okay?" Marisol asked rushing forward.

"I told Jag I'm fine," Karen said, eyeing him where he stood by the door, as if he was afraid to come near her. If only he would talk to her. They needed to be alone. He was trying to make himself into a monster again, and she couldn't let that happen.

"Let me be the judge of that," Marisol said, motioning for Karen to sit. "He bit you?"

Karen sighed. "Yes, but it's nothing." She settled on the end of the bed as Marisol stopped in front of her. "A prick. He's freaking out like he nearly killed me or something." Karen eyed the Healer. "What about you? How are you? The last time I saw you, Rock carried you out of here."

Marisol cut her gaze as if she was hiding her expression. "Show me your shoulder."

Karen shrugged the shirt down a bit, not missing how Marisol had avoided her question. "It's not even bleeding."

Marisol eyed her skin and then ran a finger over it. "There's nothing here." She eyed Jag. "Nothing but a tattoo." Her gaze slid between the two of them. "Are you sure you weren't both dreaming again?"

"It wasn't a dream," Karen said, eyeing her shoulder, or trying to without success. "I don't have a tattoo."

"Sure you do," Marisol insisted. "A star."

"No," Karen said, *"I don't."*

Jag appeared and eyed her shoulder before exchanging a look with Marisol, shaking his head as if in disbelief. "I don't know what's going on." He ran a hand through his hair, confusion and concern etching his features as his hands went to his hips. "I bit her and I'm not talking a prick. *I bit her.*" His attention was on Marisol and Karen got the distinct impression he was ashamed to look at her. "I tasted blood. Lots of it."

"It has to have been a dream," Marisol said, rejecting his words.

"It wasn't." Karen and Jag spoke at the same time.

Their gazes caught and held, guilt flashing in his. "But it healed, Jag," Karen said, trying to make him ease up on himself. "You didn't hurt me."

He inhaled and turned his focus back to Marisol. "Something strange is going on. That star on her shoulder. It wasn't there before I bit her. Find out what I did to her before it has some permanent effect."

Karen touched her skin, trying to find some proof of the star they claimed was there, but there was nothing there to feel. Not even a puncture mark. Jag was right. He'd bitten her deeply, but she could see why Marisol thought it had been a dream.

She wanted to see the star for herself. "I need a mirror."

"I'll go check my *Book of Knowledge,*" Marisol said, and flashed from the room.

* * *

Adrian stood beneath a tree, just outside of the ranch boundary lines, and smiled. He knew the minute Jag had mated with Karen, instead of destroying her. Salvador must have helped Karen pull Jag from the beast. He had to have.

Predictable.

He loved being right. The great Salvador had played right into his hands. And he'd underestimated Adrian if he thought this was over. Adrian had learned centuries before that the frontal attack never succeeded like the one that slid beneath the radar, unexpected.

After all this work, all the perfect planning to keep Jag on edge, hungry for the blood, lost between his dark and light side, he planned to have what he'd come for.

He planned to see Jag destroyed.

The second tier of his plan was already underway. It would have been convenient if Jag would have devoured Karen and accepted his beast. And certainly it could have happened. Adrian had made sure Jag questioned Karen enough to suspect she was evil.

But in the end, he hadn't counted on it.

Now that Jag knew of his mate, of his past, he'd do anything to save Karen. To save her where he'd failed her before. And there lay his true plan. The one unfolding even as he stood here.

That thought excited him. He smiled, thinking of how devious and perfect it all was. Salvador and Jag would both think this was over. They'd have their guard down.

Segundo was still lurking the ranch grounds, as was

a small force of his beasts, inside the range of the alarms. If Segundo wasn't called back by a certain time, he'd kidnap Eva and Jag would come after her. After all, Jag wouldn't want his poor darling wifey to be upset.

A low laugh escaped Adrian's lips.

Success with entertainment value. He couldn't wait to get the final confrontation in play.

Chapter 19

Several hours after the attacks, Des walked toward the main house, having just finished a quick check on the trainees. Thanks to Marisol, the men were healing well. He'd reset the alarms and secured the ranch, all without a word from Jag. Hopefully that meant he and his woman were on the way to a happy ending. Des would like to think that really happened in their world, but he was skeptical.

The aches in his body demanded attention over his thoughts. He hadn't slept, hadn't eaten, nor did he have time for either now. Right now, his destination was Eva's room, where he planned to camp out and live up to his promise to Karen. Not that he thought she was in the kind of danger he could defend her from, but he'd do what he could.

A loud shout from the house drew his attention. Des responded instinctively, taking off in a run, scanning as he moved, hand on a weapon. Cursing under his breath, he spotted a figure on the roof. Some of the beasts must have hung back, inside the radar, waiting to attack again. Guilt and self-reprimand bit at him. This was his fault. He was in charge whenever Jag was down. He had let this happen.

Rock came out of the house, just as Des arrived, his lip tinged with blood, blades in his hands. "They took Eva," he said, already moving down the porch stairs to stand in front of Des.

The news came like a blow, but Des didn't show it. There wasn't time to do anything but act. He'd promised Karen he'd protect Eva and he couldn't fail. If Marisol was right, if Karen was Jag's wife, then this was going to have a huge impact on him. On them as a group. The beasts must know that. They must be planning to use Eva against Jag with Karen in some way.

Rinehart shoved through the front door to stand on the porch, his trademark cowboy hat missing, lost somewhere in the war zone. "Where's your damn radio," he shouted at Des.

"I gave it to one of the men. I figured you two could handle things for the three minutes I was out of contact. Apparently I was wrong."

"Don't start with me, man," Rinehart grounded out through clenched teeth. "I'm really not in the mood."

"Yeah, well, that makes two of us. They can't be far ahead. Let's move out and get the girl back before they get off the property."

"What if it's a trap?" Rock asked, shoving his weapons back into their holsters. "For all we know there's another hundred beasts waiting for us."

"Pendejo," Des said, calling him a dumbass in Spanish. "Must you always argue? There is more going on here than you know about. Trap or not, we have to get Eva back."

"No trap," Rinehart said, motioning behind Des with his chin. "We have a dead-on confrontation. Maybe you better fill us in and fast."

Des turned to see ten beasts standing in a line, no more than twelve feet away. The beast in the center held Eva in front of him. Des cursed as he took in the sight, turning back to his fellow Knights, giving them a quick rundown of Marisol's suspicions about Karen.

"Clearly they plan to break Jag through his woman," Rinehart commented.

Des nodded. "Whatever they're here for, you can bet its not going to be good."

"No kidding," Rock said, making a disgusted sound.

Des's lips thinned. "Let's find out what they want before Jag does."

They all shared a look and silent agreement. The Knights had to be there for Jag this time, like he'd always been there for them. Des, Rinehart and Rock lined up and began walking.

If the beasts wanted to play a game with their leader, they'd have to go through his men first.

Standing in the bathroom, Karen shrugged the shirt off her shoulder and inspected it for a tattoo. And there it was. A five-pointed star. She touched it, amazed by its presence. What could it mean?

Hopefully Marisol would find the answer. Karen was eager for her to get back from checking her journal, whatever that meant. She gathered it was some sort of answer book. There was still so much she didn't understand. All she knew for certain was Jag, and this place, held her destiny.

"I'm sorry," Jag said, appearing in the doorway, his broad shoulders consuming the entrance. He'd gotten dressed, even strapped on weapons as if he expected some new battle beyond the one they were fighting emotionally. "I don't even know what to say. One minute I was… I mean, we were—"

He never finished the sentence. Karen made sure of it. She turned to him, forgetting the etched mark on her skin, hand going to his chest as she pressed to her toes and kissed him. "You have nothing to apologize for. You want to know a secret?"

His brows dipped so she wrapped her arms around his waist, pleased when he returned the hug. "I kind of liked it," she admitted.

"What?" His tone was filled with disbelief.

She nodded and smiled. "It was kind of sexy."

"I could have killed you, Karen."

"I don't think so," she said. "It was just like in the dreams. I felt like you were supposed to do it. It felt right somehow."

"What can be right about a man biting the woman he loves?"

"You love me?" she asked, her heart swelling with

the words. He hadn't said it until now, even when she had, and a tiny bit of concern had started to form. Could he love and accept her as she had decided she could him? She had the advantage of feeling the closure of a destiny she'd felt she'd searched for all her life. Somehow, things seemed more complicated for him. He'd been through so much. "Do you think you can love me as you did Caron?"

"I already do," he said, his expression softening instantly. "You know that."

"No. I guess I don't. Not yet. I really need to know you love *me*. As in the person I've become now."

Jag stroked her hair, tenderness shining in his eyes. "If there is anything the past few days has proven, it's my love for you. You are my soul mate, Karen. Nothing will change that. Not in this lifetime or any other one. But, Karen, I…" He looked down and drew a breath before looking at her again. Pain had replaced the tenderness. And torment. "It's because I love you that I'm afraid to be near you. What if I hurt you?"

She dismissed that concern without hesitation. "You won't. You didn't. Think about it, Jag. You already faced temptation and turned away. You could have killed me, but you didn't." Her lips firmed. "And you won't."

He rejected her response, but she saw a flicker of hope in his eyes. "You don't know that."

"I do. I know. Deep down, so do you. If you really believe we're soul mates, then trust in what we share. This thing between us is supposed to happen. We just don't understand why yet."

"She's right." It was Marisol who spoke from behind, in the bedroom.

Karen and Jag followed her voice, to find her sitting on the end of the bed, her journal in hand. "The star is a mating mark."

She flipped a page and began to read.

The man must control the beast, to prove he is the stronger of the two. His reward will be his mate. She will be blessed with the image of a star on her shoulder, a five-pointed pentacle. With this star she will enslave the demon so that it can no longer steal the man, the woman eternally bound to the Knight of White. Darkness will be replaced with light and with this light, great powers will be bestowed upon the Knight.

"Oh, my God," Karen said, turning to Jag, tears gathering in her eyes. She knew what this meant for him. What it meant for them. She understood the whispers in her dreams and the reason he had to bite her.

"Now it all makes sense," she whispered. "You're free."

Jag looked stunned but it didn't keep him from gathering Karen into his arms. His eyes were filled with emotion as they met hers. "Do I dare believe it's true?"

"Believe it," Marisol said. "My *Book of Knowledge* speaks nothing but truth."

But Jag's attention was on Karen, his hands framed her face. "You believed in me when I didn't," he said, his voice low and intense. "I don't know how or why. You'd only just learned of the past."

She understood completely. Smiling, her hands settled on his waist. "I've missed you all this lifetime, Jag. I traveled around the world, searching for something that I found when we came together again. The emptiness I felt inside is gone."

An alarm sounded, a shrill warning destroying the soft moment of happiness.

Marisol slammed the book shut and pushed to her feet. She opened her mouth to speak but Karen's instincts told her exactly what was going on, issuing a warning. "Eva!" Karen shouted. She grabbed Jag's arm. "I have to check on Eva."

"I'll do it," he told her. "You stay here so I know you're safe."

She wanted to argue but she wanted him to go save Eva more. "I will. Okay. Just don't let anything happen to her, Jag. Please."

Jag rushed into Eva's room to find her missing. His heart sunk to his stomach as he turned back to the hallway. How the hell was he going to tell Karen her sister was gone? He'd failed her once before. He couldn't do it again.

His hand went to the radio on his waistband as he headed for the stairs. "Des. Where the hell are you?"

Nothing. "Des!"

The lack of response told him all he needed to know. His men were head-on with trouble. Jag drew two blades as he reached the front door. He made it to the porch and stopped dead in his tracks. Rock, Rinehart and Des stood several feet away in a face-off with a group of Darklands. How the hell the beasts had gotten back on the property without the alarms going off he didn't know. Unless, they never left. Damn it, he should have checked on things himself. This needed to end, and it needed to end now.

Jag started forward, preparing to join his men. As he moved something inside him twisted and turned. It was as if evil crawled beneath his skin and taunted him with its presence.

This is where the shit hit the fan and he knew it. Whatever was going down was about Karen, about him. And in that moment, he knew why. He knew with all of his soul that the Darklands were using Karen against him. Using her as a weakness. He was being tested. A test meant to destroy him and probably Karen along with him.

The Knights parted to allow Jag entry into their line-up, instinctively moving as if they sensed his approach. Instincts born of their unique existence, not quite human. The same instincts even now shouting warnings in Jag's head.

As Jag stepped to the center of his men, one of their enemies met him nearly toe-to-toe. A man in appearance, no beastly side exposed. Ah, but he was beast, and a powerful one for sure. Jag bet he was the one who'd been controlling Eva, as well. His very presence reeked of darkness, of evil. Of power. His long blond hair a contrast to the blackness his presence oozed.

"So good to finally meet the great leader of the Knights of White," the man said. "Never understood that name. 'Knights of White.' Speaks of purity and good." He leaned forward a bit as if sharing a secret. "But we both know you are far from pure, now, don't we, Jag?"

"Who are you?" Jag asked, hand itching to put to use one of his weapons.

"I am Adrian," he said. "Surely you've heard of me. Oh, wait. Salvador likes to keep you in the dark. Maybe you haven't heard of me."

But Salvador *had,* indeed, warned Jag about Adrian, the beast who served directly under Cain, the fallen one. Not that Jag planned to tell Adrian what he knew. Jag let Adrian continue his self-serving dictation. "Let me bring you up to speed. I rule the demon world, and Salvador pretends he can stop me. It was a fun little diversion for a while, but I've grown tired of it. I've decided it has to end."

"Jag!"

Karen's voice ripped through the air, the fear it evoked in Jag as real as the steal knife that had sliced his flesh. He forced himself to stay steady, not to move, knowing his men would do the same until he indicated they do otherwise. If any of them acted rashly, as outnumbered as they were, it could well be a death sentence.

As much as Jag wanted to take Adrian's head right now, he needed to know what he was dealing with. The beast had a plan yet to be revealed. Jag was going to press to find that plan and to do it now.

"You can't fight one-on-one, I see," Jag said instead. "You have to hide behind the women."

"Women make life so much more interesting," Adrian said, snapping his fingers. "Segundo."

The beast Segundo moved forward, Eva wrapped in his arms. She was awake now, clinging to the beast, pawing him as if he was some precious jewel. Smiling as if she'd been brought to life with him as a gift.

"She wants to give herself to me," Segundo said. "Shall I take her?"

"No!"

It was Karen who screamed the word. She was being dragged closer to Jag, and he knew her presence was meant to torment him. Marisol was beside her, a beast holding her, as well, but unlike Karen, she didn't fight. The Knights all knew Marisol could flash herself out of captivity, but she wouldn't. Not without Karen. It was up to the Knights to help her get free long enough to get them both out of there.

Jag didn't dare make eye contact with Karen, fearful of losing his concentration. He focused on Adrian. "Let the women go. Fight like a man."

"But I'm not a man, Jag. I'm a demon and I fight like one. But don't worry. I won't be hurting your darling wife, *Caron,* today." He walked over to Eva and stroked her bare arm. "Eva here is another story."

"You bastard," Karen shouted. "Leave her alone!"

Adrian laughed and kissed Eva. Karen's sobs drew Jag's attention. And though he knew it was a mistake, he looked at her then, tears streaking her cheeks, her pain wrapping around him like a vise, choking the life from him. He couldn't take it. He couldn't stand her pain. Adrian would pay for all he and his kind had done to Karen. Jag raised his weapons and started to charge.

Des and Rinehart reached out and grabbed his arms,

though neither took their eyes from the beasts. "Easy, boss," Rinehart whispered.

"Yes," Adrian said, walking to stand directly in front of Jag. "Take it easy, my dear Jag. Someone might get hurt if you aren't careful."

His gaze locked with Jag's, a dare burning in them. Jag ground his teeth together. "What do you want?" he spat at the beast.

"I want *you*, Jag." He let the words lace the air, lethal in the implications of what was to come. "I'll give you Eva, but I want your soul in exchange."

Sickness rushed over Jag. And so here it was. He could hear Karen crying, hear his men whisper their disapproval, their rejection of this proposition.

But what was he to do?

He'd watched his wife die once. How was he to look her in the eyes every day for eternity having failed her yet again? Having let her sister die?

She'd blame him. Maybe even hate him. He couldn't live with that. "The women go free." It wasn't a question but a confirmation. He was going to accept the terms Adrian had offered.

"No," Des said. "I won't let you do this."

"He's right, Jag," Marisol called out. "Not even Salvador can bring you back this time. Not if you give yourself freely."

Jag looked at Karen, her lips trembling. "No," she whispered.

But even as she said the word, he sensed her terror of losing her sister. Felt her pain. He couldn't choose himself over Eva. He couldn't.

He opened his mouth to say as much when the air kicked up in a sudden rush, dirt lifted. In a flash of light, Salvador appeared to Jag's right. Adrian growled, his face twisted in fury before his beast showed itself. He no longer hid behind the shell of a man.

"Enough is enough, Adrian," Salvador ordered. "This has gone far beyond acceptable."

Adrian turned to him, and the two powerful beings stood toe-to-toe in the center of Knights and beasts. "You're not allowed to interfere, Salvador."

"Nor are you, but still, you are here," Salvador countered. "I'm simply leveling the playing field. This is between your Segundo and Jag."

"I'm here to do what Segundo can't. To take Jag's soul."

"You can't take what he doesn't give freely."

"I know the rules," Adrian said. "I am well within my rights."

"By using manipulation."

"This is nothing new," he said, a snide smile sliding onto his face. "I am evil, Salvador. This decision is Jag's to make, not yours."

"Then you won't mind if I share a few little details with him so he can make an informed choice."

Salvador turned toward Jag, but Adrian wasn't pleased. "Attack!" he yelled. The beasts started forward, and Jag and his Knights prepared to battle. Salvador's eyes lit with white light and he turned to face their attackers. His hand waved over them, a barrier forming, shoving the beasts back. Only a few beasts remained on the Knights' side of the barrier—those holding the women, along with Adrian.

Adrian roared with anger, his fists balled in front of him. "You cannot interfere."

Salvador ignored him, turning his attention back to Jag. "Know this, my friend. Eva will have another life. If you do this, you will not. This will be the end for you. I cannot pull you back."

Jag absorbed the words, trying to figure out what to do. Trying to understand the meaning of all of this. But there was only the pain of what would face him tomorrow. Of knowing he'd failed Karen once again.

Adrian snapped his fingers at Segundo who pushed the hair off Eva's neck. He then showed his extended teeth. Jag looked at Karen, torment in her face, fear in her eyes.

"Make your choice, White Knight," Adrian said. "Will you choose your own life over the woman's?" He narrowed his eyes on Jag. "Better yet, let's allow your wife to decide who dies today. Which will it be, Karen? Eva or Jag? Who lives and who dies?"

Fury ripped through Jag. "Stop it," he yelled, digging his sword into the ground and dropping to his knees. He wouldn't allow Karen to live with the guilt of that choice. He'd felt the stain of guilt far too long himself. It was a poison his wife would never endure.

"Take my soul," Jag said, lowering his head between his shoulders, defeated. "I give it freely."

Adrian walked to stand in front of Jag. "Look me in the eyes and give me your soul, White Knight."

Jag was shaking from head to toe, cold with the moment, with the reality of what he was doing. Still, he forced himself to do as ordered. Forced himself not to look at Karen, not to respond to her cries to him.

"Take my soul," he said, looking into the deep pits of evil that were Adrian's eyes. "I give it freely."

Chapter 20

Seconds that felt like hours ticked by as Salvador watched Adrian hold out his hand, his invisible grip reaching for Jag's soul. Jag clutched his chest, face contorted in pain.

And Salvador knew he had to put a stop to this.

He hesitated, troubled by the price he would pay. Seconds had already passed. Too many. Salvador had to make a choice.

But there was no real debate. He'd pay the price dealt to him, most likely a longer sentence to his duty in this realm of existence. What was another century in his world?

He would live through it so that Jag could live, as well. Jag had unselfishly offered himself in place of another and that deserved a reward. It also proved what Salvador had always known. Jag was a worthy leader. An important part of this war. And Adrian's form of evil couldn't be allowed to survive.

Decision made, Salvador lifted his hand and shot a white light at Adrian, knocking him off his feet. Jag fell to the ground as Salvador looked at the Knights. "Take him to the house and tie him down. And do it well."

He faced the beasts holding Karen and Marisol captive, prepared to turn them to dust, but they'd already flung the women to the ground, making their departures. His attention went to Segundo, who still held Eva.

Adrian pushed to his feet. "Let her go," he said to his second before squaring off with Salvador. Marisol darted for Eva pulling her away from Segundo.

"Take your beasts and leave before I turn them all to ashes," Salvador ordered.

"Surprise, surprise," Adrian said, evil in his voice, in his eyes, even in his smile. "The great Salvador broke the rules. Too bad you hesitated. He's too far gone. He'll be mine in another sunrise anyway."

"We shall see," Salvador said.

"Yes, we shall," Adrian said, and he disappeared.

Segundo ordered the Darklands retreat, but not without a long pause. He stared at Salvador, his eyes narrowed, greed radiating from his core. In that moment, Salvador knew Segundo had taken the bait he'd given him earlier that day. Segundo now knew that Adrian needed him and it was burning a hole in him, making him hungry for power. The kind of power Adrian possessed.

Good news in the midst of a lot of bad. Salvador wanted

nothing more than to see Adrian's army come unglued from the inside out, and Segundo was the key to that.

Salvador turned to find Karen approaching, and he met her halfway.

"Hello, Karen."

Her eyes narrowed. "I know your voice." Her expression registered awareness. "You're the one who whispered to me in my dreams."

"Yes," he said. "And you did well. Jag might not realize it yet, but with your joining, the becoming of mates, he has learned much about himself. He now knows the beast doesn't control him. He controls the beast."

Eva screamed and Karen turned to see Rock carrying her toward the house. "Your sister will live," Salvador said, before she could ask, drawing her attention back to him. "But she will not be as she was. She will be like these men, a Knight in a war against evil. She is special, your sister, strong beyond your understanding of her. Trust me to save her. Right now, you must focus on Jag. He needs you. I've only offered you a chance to save him. He is still in danger."

Her expression flashed with surprised and renewed fear. "I don't understand."

"His soul is stuck between worlds and reclaiming it means reclaiming every emotion, every bit of pain he's ever experienced. He won't want to do that. Love him enough to bring him home to you." He touched her shoulder. "You are his mate for all of eternity, Karen, immortal like your sister soon will be. Like Jag already is. Be the light that will guide him. He is needed in this war. Bring him back, Karen."

"I will," she said, determination in her face.

"It won't be easy. He will…" Salvador hesitated, trying to choose his words with caution, not to scare her. On the other hand, he had to prepare her for what she faced. "He will not be himself. He'll say and do things to hurt you. The dark side can be persuasive. Adrian will fight hard to possess Jag's soul."

Her lips firmed. "He can fight but he won't win. I've waited too long to find Jag again to give him up now."

He studied her a moment. He believed she would, indeed, defeat Adrian. "Go to him and leave Eva to me." He gave her a short nod. "I bid you good luck."

Karen walked to the house, the wind blowing the shirt around her legs. Jag's shirt. The man she loved more in this moment than she'd have ever thought possible. He'd given his life to protect her. Willing to give up his soul to save Karen from a loss. But what he didn't understand was that living without him would have been unbearable. She needed him.

And now he needed her more than ever, and she wouldn't let him down.

Her steps quickened as she made her way to the bedroom, finding Rinehart at the top of the stairs, guarding the door. Des exited the room. "Karen," he said with a nod.

Another time, her skimpy attire would have bothered her. Now, she didn't care. These men were Jag's brothers in battle. They had become that to her, as well. Today, they shared a common cause, and she would be there with them all the way, until this war was no more.

"How is he?" she asked, stopping in front of the two Knights.

Des hesitated. "He's...resting."

She started for the door. Des stepped in front of her. "You can't go in there, Karen. He's not himself. Once Salvador—"

"Salavador sent me to him," Karen said, cutting him off. "I have to see him." She started to pass him.

Des stepped in her way again, shaking his head. "Salvador must not know how bad it is. I can't let you in there."

"Salvador knows. *I know.*" She gave him a direct look, letting him see how firm she was in her decision. "I do appreciate your concern, but I have to do this. He needs me, Des."

"Then I'll go in with you."

"No," Karen said, rejecting that idea. "I have to do this alone."

Des stared at her, his expression concerned. "I'll be right here if you need me. Just yell." He stepped out of her way.

Rinehart spoke up. "*We'll* be right here."

Not a man of many words, when he did choose to be vocal, Karen had already figured out, she should take his words to heart.

Their protectiveness meant a lot to her, as she knew it would to Jag when he was himself again. Karen gave them both a nod and then inhaled. Time to bring Jag home.

Karen stepped into the bedroom, the door shutting behind her, to find Jag was tied down on the bed. Locking Jag in the room was one thing. Tying him up was another. Outraged, she started to turn away, determined to find Des and demand an explanation.

"My woman has come to save me, I see," Jag said, his voice a taunt. "My pure, precious *cariño*." Laughter bubbled from his throat.

Though Salvador had warned her Jag would be different, she hadn't truly believed it. She turned back toward him, suddenly okay with his current state of submission.

"I *am* your woman," Karen said, walking toward him, and stopping at the side of the bed. "The one who loves you."

"If you love me, you'll untie me."

"Because I love you, I can't. Not until you're back to your normal self."

"I am myself."

"Then tell me you love me."

"I'll tell you anything you want me to tell you if you get naked first." His gaze raked her breasts.

She drew a breath, the ache in her heart hard to ignore. Having him treat her in a nasty way hurt, regardless of the reason. "I love you, Jag," she said, willing to say it as many times as it took to get through to him.

"Ahhh. So sweet. Let me taste how sweet. Give me a kiss."

Though she didn't like how he requested the kiss, it seemed a good idea. She had connected with him beyond simple conversation. She leaned over Jag, stopping just before their lips touched. "I won't let you leave me." And then she pressed her mouth to his.

For several seconds, they lingered like that, breathing together. He seemed to absorb her as she did him. He seemed to really feel what she did, the closeness, the perfection of their union.

But it was short-lived success as something changed. Laughter bubbled from his mouth. Evil. Menacing.

She pulled back to look into his eyes, her stomach twisting and turning as she saw the darkness there. She touched his cheek. "Come back to me, Jag," she whispered. "I know you're in there."

"If you want me, *cariño,* come and get me, but take your clothes off first. I want you naked or not at all."

He still called her by an endearment, and she clung to that. The man beneath the monster still knew her as someone special.

She stiffened her spine, reaching for courage. Undressing for the man she loved and undressing for the soulless monster trying to control him were two different things. But *making love* did seem the best way to stir the emotions she needed in him.

Slowly Karen stood before him, undoing the buttons on the front of the shirt. When it fell to the floor, the air-conditioning chilling her skin, the heat of his gaze warmed it back up. He devoured her with his eyes, sweeping them over her with a primal hunger. Ripe. Potent. Charged with lust. It aroused her, which she found a bit frightening. How could his dark side turn her on? But then, she reminded herself, no matter what, this was her man, her mate. The one she was meant to be with.

"That's a good girl," he purred, his voice silky smooth and devious. "Now, untie me so I can touch you."

"No," she said, offering nothing further. Walking to the end of the bed, she tugged his boots. "I'm the only one doing the touching." Karen crawled on the bed and reached for his pants.

"We'd both enjoy this more if you'd rid me of these ropes." His voice softened, taking a gentler tone. "Set me free, *cariño.*"

Her eyes went to his, and for just a second, she saw a flash of Jag, of the man who was her mate. It drew her in, even made her guilty for the ropes. She wished she could say yes to setting him free, but it was too soon. "I can't. Not yet."

And just like that the evil returned. A flash of anger crossed his features before he yanked at the rope on his wrist. "Untie me!" Then he lifted his head and fixed her in angry stare. "I swear, I'll make you sorry for this."

She jumped, surprised by the outburst; more surprised by the sinister crackle in the air. Shivering against the pure darkness closing in around her, Karen knew then that they weren't alone. That man, the beast Adrian, was here. Maybe not in body, but in some other way. And he was feeding Jag's anger. Feeding his desire to drive her away.

Well, Adrian couldn't have Jag. Not now and not ever. Her resolve returned as she worked to finish undressing him. "You can't scare me. You can try but it won't work."

"But you are scared," he said, certainty to his tone. "I can smell it."

She ignored his taunt for the moment, sliding to the end of the bed and working his pants off his legs. Then she crawled back and straddled him. He was aroused and so was she. Her hand closed around his width, guiding him inside her body, just as she hoped she could guide his soul.

Jag moaned as she took him fully, his lids heavy, his lips half parted as he looked at her. Then, knowing she had some semblance of control she addressed his taunt.

"You were right," she said, leaning down to press her hands beside his head. His hot gaze went to her breasts, and she felt it like a touch, her breasts aching, heavy. Her voice was hoarse as she reached for it, trying to sound stronger than she felt. "I am scared."

His gaze lifted to hers as if he hadn't expected such a confession. "I'm scared of losing you," she whispered, staring into his eyes, praying he could see the truth there. Praying that he could feel how much she cared.

But nothing registered in his face, no acknowledgment, no emotion.

Her chest tightened, ripe with the fear she'd just spoken of. "Don't leave me," she pleaded, and then brushed her lips over his. "We belong together."

She kissed him then, her tongue sliding past his lips, drawing a response. He made a sound deep in his throat and then hungrily claimed her mouth, tasting her as if she were an aphrodisiac he couldn't get enough of. And he did want more. She could feel it in each stroke of his tongue, taste it on his lips. She wanted more, too. She wanted so much more. But Karen wanted forever, not just the moment. She had to be strong.

She pulled back, her lips just out of reach. "Stay with me."

He was breathing hard, his intensity still bred of darkness but somehow more sensual. More alluring. A hint of the evil had slid away, replaced by desire. By their connection.

But then he did something that shocked her. He lifted his head and his teeth, sharp now, nipped her lip, drawing a tiny bit of blood. He ran his tongue over his own lip and claimed it. And Lord help her, it was erotic. It turned her on. She should be disgusted but instead she wanted to move against him. To make love to him.

Suddenly with a hard tug, his arms were free and he reached for her, pulling her mouth to his. "I have powers now, little one. Those ropes only hold me if I allow them to."

Before she knew what was coming, he was kissing her, deep and passionate. At the same time, he rolled her onto her back, fully claiming the control she had only moments before possessed.

Karen was lost for a moment, drawn into a spell of desire. She could feel his powerful thighs frame hers, feel the weight of him press against her. And they were moving, bodies sliding together in unison, moving to a sultry tune only they could hear.

But the passion stirred her heart. It reminded her of her cause, of her reason for making love to him. "I need you, Jag," she whispered, desperate to hear him say the words back.

His mouth moved over her jaw, to her ear, even as he rotated his hips against hers. "You're close to coming," he said. "Give me your pleasure, Karen. Give me all of you. I can make sure you never fear anything ever again."

Stiffening with a cold, hard realization, Karen shifted out of her lust-filled haze. She wanted Jag's love and he wanted her soul. Anger overcame her, sudden and painful. Emotions twisted inside, roaring with potency. Her fight instinct kicked in.

"Get off me." Shoving on his chest, on his arms, on his body, she said the words over and over. She pushed and pushed, trying to get him away, trying to stop the hurt of his manipulation, of her loss. Tears burned her eyes, cascading to her cheeks.

Jag was gone. She searched her lifetime for him and he was gone.

And it hurt. It hurt so damn bad.

Jag felt the pain in Karen like a stab of reality. Only moments before, darkness had cluttered his thoughts. He'd hidden from everything but escape. Hidden from anything that might cause pain. He'd felt so much of it in his lifetime, lost so much, he couldn't handle any more.

But he felt it now, because he felt what Karen did. Because she was his mate and he was about to leave her— leave her to suffer the hell he had endured without her.

He stroked her hair, kissed her cheeked, trying to calm her. "*Cariño,* stop. Baby, stop. I'm sorry. Please. It's okay." He couldn't do that to her.

She was shaking, literally shaking from head to toe, and he felt that, too. "I'm not going anywhere and neither are you."

"No," she said. "I don't want tricks. I want up. Let me up." Then louder. "Des!"

He covered her mouth, muffling the scream for Des with a kiss, softly claiming, seducing, soothing. Slowly she eased. Slowly. Slowly. *She* came back to *him.*

When he finally raised his head, releasing her mouth, he spoke before she could, desperate to tell her how he felt. To ensure she knew how much she meant to him. "I love you, Karen," he said. "I love you more than I thought possible. I'm so sorry for what I just put you through. Tonight, and in the past."

She touched his face. "You're back. Really back? Please tell me it's true."

He smiled, his weight on his forearms by her head as he looked down at her. "Yes, *cariño,* and I am not going anywhere without my woman ever again. Not now and not ever again."

Tears filled her eyes again and he wiped at them with his fingers. "That's supposed to make you smile, not cry."

"I just thought…I thought I lost you. I didn't know what to do."

He brushed a lock of hair from her eyes. "You knew exactly what to do. You always do. But I need to know. Will you trust me again? Will you give yourself to me now and always?"

Her hands slid around his neck, a twinkle in her eyes replacing the tears. "I can be persuaded."

His brow lifted in question, his heart filling with warmth as he watched her face light with desire, the pain gone. "You can start by convincing me that you're back by making long, hot passionate love to me."

Jag laughed, deciding the next century would be far more pleasurable than the last without a doubt. "A man must please his mate," he said, claiming her mouth with his kiss, as she had claimed his soul.

Epilogue

Karen and Marisol sat in the corner of one of several training studios inside the ranch, watching Eva and Rock spar. In the three months since making this their home, both Eva and Karen had received training in many skills, mastering weapons, preparing for a destiny certain to pit them against the Darklands. Eva had taken the task on with fierce determination. She, after all, was now a Knight of White and their battle with the Darklands was never-ending.

"I still can't get a hold of the idea of my sister fighting those beasts," Karen said, watching Eva handle a sword like she'd been born with it in her hand. "It scares me."

It was hard to believe her sister had gone from meek

and scared to determined to fight. Karen hoped Eva's obsession with a sword wasn't masking the pain so that she didn't fully heal. Eva's turnaround from a gentle woman to a demanding warrior had been both lightning-fast and extreme.

As if in response, Eva's voice filled the air. "Stop holding back!" she shouted at Rock, blades locked with his.

"I'm not holding back," Rock said, his expression as grumpy as his voice.

"Then you fight like a girl," she countered. "I can't believe you aren't dead yet."

Marisol laughed and turned back to Karen. "I don't think you have to worry. Eva can take care of herself."

Before Karen could answer, Rock let out a loud grunt. "She cut me. Eva cut me."

"That'll teach you to hold back," Eva said, glaring at him. "Marisol is here." She taunted him with a singsong baby voice. "She'll make it all better." Back to her normal tone, she said, "Then we can fight for real."

"As I was saying," Marisol said, pushing to her feet. "Eva can take care of herself."

Karen had to admit that seemed to be the truth. More and more, Karen was seeing her sister in a new light. "Just like you take good care of Rock," she teased, unable to hold back the mischievous comment. Though she couldn't get Marisol to admit there was something between her and Rock, Karen was working on it.

Jag appeared beside her without warning, and Karen jumped, hand going to her chest. His newfound powers were gradually evolving. So far, he could levitate items and even turn a few things to ash. He couldn't go *poof* and make a beast disappear, but the Knights were all encouraged that one day he might be able to.

The newest talent, the ability to pop in and out of the room, had presented itself in the past week. Jag was enjoying it. Karen wasn't so much.

"I hate when you do that," she told him, trying to remain irritated but struggling. His recently grown goatee was so damn sexy, she couldn't stay mad. Every time she saw her man these days, she wanted to drag him off to someplace private and have her way with him.

"I thought you wanted me to practice using my powers," he teased, claiming the chair beside her and leaning over to kiss her cheek, lingering to nip her ear. "Hmm. You smell good."

"Practice so you won't get killed using them. I didn't say scare me to death in the process." He nibbled the sensitive skin on her neck and she swatted at him. "Behave," she said, motioning toward Rock who was staring at Marisol like she was a piece of candy. "What's with Marisol and Rock?"

"I think that's pretty clear. They want each other, but she can't be with him."

Karen frowned, turning to Jag. "What? Why?"

"It's a rule. Healers are forbidden that type of relationship."

"Says who?"

He laughed. "Says those with much more say than you or me. You can't change this even with your stubborn determination."

"But two people who love each other should be together," she argued.

"Everything happens for a reason," he reminded her.

She sighed. "Yes. I know." Still, she hated to see the two of them denied love. "That brings me to another point though. I had this idea."

He lifted his brow, a flirtatious twinkle in his eyes. "I hope it's fun."

Each day Jag smiled more, the darkness sliding into his past. It warmed her to know she'd been a part of that. "Actually," she said, "this idea is full of fun. Until now, all I've been able to do is tell you about my travels. We used to dream of seeing the world together."

"We've talked about this, *cariño*. I can't leave this place. I wish I could."

"But you want to travel," she said, eager to convince him to live a little. If anyone deserved to, it was Jag. For hours they would lie in bed and talk. Karen so desperately wanted to share the places she'd seen with Jag and he was hungry for every detail. She circled his hand in hers, a plea in her voice, in her eyes. "To actually show you the world instead of talking about it would be amazing. We could take a honeymoon after the wedding next month."

"Karen—"

She pressed her fingers to his lips. "Just hear me out."

He gave her a nod, kissing her fingers before taking her hand in his once again.

"Well, now you have this new power. You can just pop right back here if there is trouble."

"I doubt the reason I was granted this power was to take a vacation," he said, taking the cautious approach he was so good at.

"No," she agreed. "But you have to admit, it has possibilities. We *could* travel. You really would love the romance of Venice." Her eyes lit. "Or St. Thomas. You'd love it there. The water is so clear blue, it's like a beautiful painting come to life."

His expression grew wistful. "I'm not even sure how far I can travel. For all I know it's not more than a few miles."

Karen stood up. "What are you waiting for?" she asked. "Let's find out."

"Now?" he asked. "We can't just go now."

Behind them Rock yelled, Eva having cut him once again. Karen rolled her eyes. "Now seems a really good time to leave to me."

Jag laughed and pushed to his feet, holding out his arm to her. "Where to first?" he asked.

She gave him a grin. "I'd be happy to start with our bedroom. From there, the possibilities are endless."

Jag laughed, and pulled her close, kissing her passionately, before flashing them from the room.

* * * * *

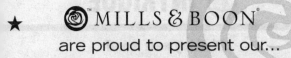

MILLS & BOON

are proud to present our...

Book of the Month

Expecting Miracle Twins
by Barbara Hannay

Mattie Carey has put her dreams of finding
Mr. Right aside to be her best friend's surrogate.
Then the gorgeous Jake Devlin steps into her life…

Enjoy double the Mills & Boon® Romance
in this great value 2-in-1!

Expecting Miracle Twins by Barbara Hannay and
Claimed: Secret Son by Marion Lennox

Available 4th September 2009

Tell us what you think about
Expecting Miracle Twins
at millsandboon.co.uk/community

 INTRIGUE

Coming next month

2-IN-1 ANTHOLOGY

BABY'S WATCH by Justine Davis

Bad boy Ryder is shocked by the connection he feels to the baby he helped deliver, as well as her mysterious mother Ana. But can he put his life on the line for them?

A HERO OF HER OWN by Carla Cassidy

From the moment she arrived in town, Jewel caught Quinn's attention. They're both overcoming tragic pasts, but does Jewel trust Quinn enough to let passion in?

2-IN-1 ANTHOLOGY

BENEATH THE BADGE by Rita Herron

Nothing matters more to Hayes than the police badge he wears. Protecting heiress Taylor is his sworn duty, but could she become the object of his desire too?

MATCH PLAY by Merline Lovelace

Special Agent Dayna jumped at an undercover assignment overseas. However she didn't expect to find former lover air force pilot Luke awaiting her arrival...

SINGLE TITLE

VEILED TRUTH by Vivi Anna

Nocturne

Lyra's skills as a witch can't help her solve a series of gruesome murders. She distrusts brooding Theron, but he could have the answers she seeks. And with the gateway to hell opening, it's imperative the two find common ground...

On sale 18th September 2009

Available at WHSmith, Tesco, ASDA, Eason and all good bookshops.
For full Mills & Boon range including eBooks visit
www.millsandboon.co.uk

From No. 1 *New York Times* bestselling author Nora Roberts

Nightshade available 2nd January 2010

When a teenager gets caught up in making sadistic violent films, Colt Nightshade and Lieutenant Althea Grayson must find her before she winds up dead…

Night Smoke available 5th February 2010

When Natalie Fletcher's office is set ablaze, she must find out who wants her ruined – before someone is killed…

Night Shield available 5th March 2010

When a revengeful robber leaves blood-stained words on Detective Allison Fletcher's walls, she knows her cop's shield won't be enough to protect her…

Passion. Power. Suspense.
It's time to fall under the spell of Nora Roberts.

*The special gift
of love at Christmas*

CHRISTMAS WISHES - CHRISTMAS WEDDINGS!
**BETTY NEELS
DEBBIE MACOMBER
JESSICA HART**

*Sleigh Bells
and
Wedding Rings*

Three classic Christmas romances!

The Silver Thaw by Betty Neels

The Christmas Basket by Debbie Macomber

Mistletoe Marriage by Jessica Hart

Available 2nd October 2009

M&B

millsandboon.co.uk Community

Join Us!

The Community is the perfect place to meet and chat to kindred spirits who love books and reading as much as you do, but it's also the place to:

- **Get the inside scoop from authors about their latest books**
- **Learn how to write a romance book with advice from our editor**
- **Help us to continue publishing the best in women's fiction**
- **Share your thoughts on the books we publish**
- **Befriend other users**

Forums: Interact with each other as well as authors, editors and a whole host of other users worldwide.

Blogs: Every registered community member has their own blog to tell the world what they're up to and what's on their mind.

Book Challenge: We're aiming to read 5,000 books and have joined forces with The Reading Agency in our inaugural Book Challenge.

Profile Page: Showcase yourself and keep a record of your recent community activity.

Social Networking: We've added buttons at the end of every post to share via digg, Facebook, Google, Yahoo, technorati and de.licio.us.

www.millsandboon.co.uk

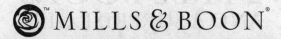

2 FREE BOOKS
AND A SURPRISE GIFT

We would like to take this opportunity to thank you for reading this Mills & Boon® book by offering you the chance to take TWO more specially selected books from the Intrigue series absolutely FREE! We're also making this offer to introduce you to the benefits of the Mills & Boon® Book Club™—

- **FREE home delivery**
- **FREE gifts and competitions**
- **FREE monthly Newsletter**
- **Exclusive Mills & Boon Book Club offers**
- **Books available before they're in the shops**

Accepting these FREE books and gift places you under no obligation to buy, you may cancel at any time, even after receiving your free books. Simply complete your details below and return the entire page to the address below. You don't even need a stamp!

YES Please send me 2 free Intrigue books and a surprise gift. I understand that unless you hear from me, I will receive 5 superb new stories every month, including two 2-in-1 books priced at £4.99 each and a single book priced at £3.19, postage and packing free. I am under no obligation to purchase any books and may cancel my subscription at any time. The free books and gift will be mine to keep in any case.

Ms/Mrs/Miss/Mr _____ Initials _____

_____

Surname _____

Address _____

_____

_____ Postcode _____

Send this whole page to: Mills & Boon Book Club, Free Book Offer, FREEPOST NAT 10298, Richmond, TW9 1BR